Shadows on the Snow

SHADOWS ON THE SNOW

Phyllida Barstow

CENTURY
LONDON SYDNEY AUCKLAND JOHANNESBURG

745048

First published in Great Britain in 1992 by
Random Century Group
20 Vauxhall Bridge Road, London SW1V 2SA

Century Hutchinson South Africa (Pty) Ltd
PO Box 337, Bergvlei 2012, South Africa

Random Century Australia Pty Ltd
20 Alfred Street, Milsons Point, Sydney, NSW 2061
Australia

Random Century New Zealand Ltd
PO Box 40-086, Glenfield, Auckland 10
New Zealand

The catalogue data record for this book is
available from the British Library

Phototypeset by Intype, London

Printed in Great Britain by
Mackays of Chatham Plc, Chatham, Kent

ISBN 0 7126 3572 6

For my brother,
Gerry Barstow

ACKNOWLEDGEMENTS

I would like to thank all the *Daily Telegraph* readers who, on hearing of my interest in the First Afghan War and its aftermath, most generously entrusted me with their family papers, letters, portraits and memorabilia. Particular thanks to Tudor Trevor, for family history and portraits of Akbar Khan's hostages, as well as the jacket lithograph; to K.M. Fox for putting me in touch with Oliver D. Cumming, who lent me the letters of Lieutenant John Haughton; to Alan Philipp for a contemporary map of Kabul; and to Michael Barstow for the letter from Colonel John Anderson Barstow, who was fortunate enough to be invalided out of Kabul before the insurrection.

To these and all the other people who have helped me with information and encouragement, I am deeply grateful.

D.P.B.

GLOSSARY

Ayah children's nurse

Babu-ji respectful form of address; Master or Mr
Badmash rascal, bad man
Bahadur hero or champion
Bhisti water-carrier
Bobaji cook (male)
Bora trader; Bengali cargo boat
Brandy-pawnee brandy and soda
Burra khana big dinner party
Burra peg large drink

Chota hazri breakfast
Chuprassi messenger
Cossid courier

Dashur gratuity; intermediary's percentage of a deal
Dhobi washerman
Dhooli palanquin
Dudwallah milkman
Durbar public audience; levee
Durzee tailor

Feringhi foreigner

Gharri any horse-drawn vehicle
Ghazi Moslem religious fanatic
Ghilzai Tribe controlling the passes between Kabul and
Peshawar

Hakim doctor
Havildar sergeant (infantry)

Jemadar junior Indian officer promoted from the ranks (cavalry or infantry)
Jezail long-barrelled musket

Kajava Afghan camel pannier
Khansamah cook
Khitmutgar waiter at table
Kotwal headman

Lakh ten thousand
Lat-Sahib Governor-General; Bigwig
Lota small brass water-pot

Maidan parade-ground; open space in or near a town
Mali gardener
Mofussil the backwoods; the outskirts of a city
Munshi teacher; writer
Mussalchi servant responsible for lighting the lamps

Nautch dance performed by women
Nuzzur tribute, offering

Ottar coarse flour

Palki palanquin or traveller's litter
Pani water
Puggaree a turban
Punkah swinging overhead fan pulled by a rope
Pushtu language of the Pathans

Rani queen

Sahib-log 'White folk'
Sekunder Alexander
Sepoy infantry soldier
Shaitan devil
Shikar hunting and shooting game
Sirdar Indian officer of high rank; leader
Sowar cavalry trooper

Sowaree mounted parade
Subadar native officer of infantry, equal to rank of captain
Syce groom

Tiffin lunch

Zenana women's quarter

PROLOGUE
1829

'Come here, Ayah! My ribbon's undone. You didn't tie it tight enough.' Dorothea Dundas's round, eight-year-old face was full of naughty glee as she tweaked off the white silk bow securing her thick braid of red-gold hair.

Ayah sighed gustily and waddled across the day nursery yet again. 'Do not touch it, Missee-Baba,' she chided, patiently replaiting. 'Making late for partee.'

She took a fresh ribbon from the press and tied it while Thea squirmed in protest.

'Not pink!'

'Prettee pink, Baba.'

'I'll pull it off again. I want a white one.'

Ayah looked at her in despair, knowing she would not be good until she got her own way. Before the argument could develop, the door opened and Mrs Dundas drifted in, small and delicate and beautiful in her wide-brimmed straw hat trimmed with streamers of the same green silk as her lavishly flounced, tight-bodiced gown. She moved in a rustling cloud of scent and Thea gazed at her adoringly.

'Oh, Mamma! You look lovely.'

'Do I, darling?' Mrs Dundas patted her eldest daughter's cheek. Poor child, it was a pity she took after her father, with her red hair and big bones. It had been a shock to Mrs Dundas to discover recently that her own shoes fitted Thea, but mercifully the twins, Sukie and Louise, were small and dark like herself, with delicate features and big violet eyes. One could only hope that Thea would fine down later.

'You look very nice, too,' she said encouragingly.

Thea glanced down with disfavour at her organdie party

frock. It prickled under the arms and she hated being dressed like her sisters.

'Aren't the twins ready yet, Ayah?' Mrs Dundas clicked her tongue. 'Why are you so slow? It's too bad of you. The guests will be here any minute.'

'Babas ready veree soon, Memsahib.' Ayah's fingers flew, fastening tiny hooks.

'Hurry!' urged Mrs Dundas, but she guessed the cause of the delay. 'Come with me, Thea, while Ayah dresses the twins.'

'She's *my* ayah, not theirs,' said Thea resentfully. 'Why can't Nasi dress them?'

'You know very well that Nasi has gone away.'

'Why doesn't she come back?'

'*Because*.' Her mother gave her a measuring look. 'Now don't make that sulky face, my girl. What if the wind changed? With things as they are, you're very lucky to have a birthday party at all.'

Things as they are always meant they were short of money. Thea hugged her mother and said, 'Oh, I am! I know. Thank you, Mamma!'

For an instant the little crease between Mrs Dundas's high-arched eyebrows smoothed out. Thea was a warm-hearted, affectionate child, for all her faults. 'Here's my workbox,' she said, taking it from the shelf. 'Sit here and tidy it while you wait for your guests. That will keep you out of mischief.'

Thea leaned on the verandah rail, watching the scurrying servants in the garden. They wore spotless white tunics with fringed red sashes and snowy *puggarees*, and were carrying loaded trays from the kitchen, set on its own just behind the long bungalow, to the white-draped table on the lawn. Wafer-thin sandwiches and enticing little iced cakes. Jellies like jewels, gingersnaps and dark, damp fruit cake. The *bobaji* had made Thea's favourite mango ice-cream as a special treat, and her mouth watered at the thought.

Mrs Dundas was frowning again. 'I told them to put the table in the shade! Really, servants are hopeless.'

She hurried away to scold them, and Thea, alone on the verandah, pressed the catch that released the workbox lid. Tidying it was usually considered a privilege, but today she was hot and cross and nothing pleased her. Why couldn't the twins have their own ayah, even if Papa was short of money? It wouldn't cost much.

She began to tidy the box in a desultory manner, but today even the green velvet trays with their neat compartments for silks, pins, needles and buttons failed to charm. There was a gold thimble, an ivory ribbon-threader, and pretty, pointed gold scissors in the shape of a stork.

Thea took these from their velvet nest and tested their sharpness on the organdie frill at her hem. They cut beautifully, but not quite straight, she thought, inspecting the result. She had better trim a bit off the other side to even it up.

Kneeling on the verandah floor, she cut carefully round the dress as far as she could reach, only to discover with dismay that when she stood up the front barely covered her knees, though it still drooped to her ankles at the back. She cast an apprehensive glance across the lawn. Her mother was still ordering the servants about, but when she came back she could hardly fail to notice the abbreviated hem. Desperate measures were needed. Grasping a handful of frill behind her, Thea sawed wildly. Then, since the jaws were too full to cut, she tore the mangled material away in strips.

'My dear child, whatever are you doing?'

Scarlet with effort and guilt, Thea looked up to see her father's assistant sitting his mare by the verandah rail. She scowled. She did not like Dr Black. She thought he looked like a devil, with his peaked black brows and long nose above a wide, straight mouth, which had a little crease at each corner, making it difficult to tell if he was smiling or serious. This combined with a certain teasing look in his bright narrow eyes to make Thea uneasy when she told lies about headaches and tummyaches so that Mamma would fuss over her and forget those silly, babyish twins.

He was tall, with a lean, well-knit body, and sat his

14

dish-faced Arabian pony with the ease of a man who rode rather more than he walked. The intricately folded blue cravat secured with a pearl pin, together with his high-lapelled, full-skirted linen coat and matching narrow-cut Unmentionables instead of breeches and boots gave him a dandyish air, accentuated by the flowing, silky curls which fell nearly to his shoulders in a way that excited her father's particular disapproval. 'More like a damned poet than a sawbones,' Thea had heard him mutter.

Mamma liked Dr Black, but Papa did not. Sometimes it seemed to Thea that he went out of his way to tease Papa, and make her mother laugh.

'What's the matter? Lost your tongue?' His white teeth flashed and she disliked him more than ever. 'Where's your mother?'

'Over there. She's busy. Why do you want her?'

'Curiosity killed the cat. What I have to say to your mother is none of your business.'

'Have you come to say goodbye to her?'

'If you know so much, Miss Nosey, why ask?'

'I wasn't sure.'

'I suppose you are pleased that I'm going?'

'Well . . .'

'You need not spare my feelings.'

She stared at him silently, suspecting he was teasing her. It was true: she was glad he was going away and her parents need not argue about him any more. Sometimes the arguments ended with Mamma in tears and Papa stamping out of the room.

'Where are you going to?'

'The Punjab, for my sins.'

'The Punjab!' That strange, wild land across the Sutlej River, beyond the Governor-General's sway, where the one-eyed Lion of the Punjab, Maharaja Ranjit Singh, ruled the warrior Sikhs. 'Don't you want to go?' she asked curiously.

Dr Black pulled the sort of face Thea was not allowed to, and despite herself she laughed.

'I never like leaving my friends,' he said solemnly.

15

'Mamma doesn't want you to,' she said with a sly glance towards him, and his dark eyebrows drew together.

'We all have to do things we don't want to at times.' He surveyed her dispassionately. 'Shall I help you complete the destruction of that garment?'

'N-no!' She tugged at the skirt, trying to make it longer, and he shrugged.

'Just as you like. Goodbye, then. Enjoy your party.'

He rode across the lawn as her mother left the servants and hurried to meet him. She stood by his mare's shoulder, looking up with a strange expression, almost as if she were going to cry, and with a quick movement he dismounted, standing so close that his wide shoulders screened from Thea's view all but the ribbon of her hat. How easily, she thought, he could lift Mamma on to his horse and carry her off! That was what he wanted to do.

Thea shifted uncomfortably, unable to turn her eyes away, her heart full of conflicting, disturbing emotions. She hated the way he held her mother's hand and gazed at her as if they were alone in a world where she and the scurrying servants, and even Papa did not exist. It frightened her to see him so much in earnest, as if he did not realise this was just a game Mamma played with all the gentlemen who kissed her in the rose garden. Dr Black did not play by the rules. He held Mamma too long and too tight, and instead of telling her she was beautiful in a light, bantering way, he sounded as if the words were being dragged out of the bottom of his heart.

Part of Thea wanted to warn him about Captain Bowman and Mr Jeffreys and the other gentlemen, but another part was scared that one day Mamma would succumb to his demands and go away with him for ever.

She knew that Papa feared him, too. He had been pleased when his assistant had transferred to the Political Service.

'Best thing he could do,' he had grunted. 'Clever fella. Wasted here as a common sawbones. Let him spread his wings! Turn his talents to politics. Better for everyone in the long run – especially his patients!' Papa had snorted.

He and Dr Black seldom agreed on medical practice. Then he had twisted his red moustache sideways in the special way he had, as if there were a bad smell under his nose.

'You shouldn't encourage him, Eleanor. He's not one of your usual lap-dogs, you know. Give him an inch and he'll take an ell.'

Mamma had pouted prettily. 'He's only a boy. Besides, he sings divinely.'

Later, Thea had been playing with her doll in her secret nest among the clumps of lavender while Dr Black walked with Mamma in the rose garden.

'Why must you go?' she had asked. 'What will I do without my *cavaliere servente*?'

'Don't make it harder for me, Eleanor,' he had said in a low, harsh tone. 'You will be better off without me here.'

'How can you say that? What shall I do without my Black Doctor? How shall I bear the boredom, the pettiness, the terrible ennui?'

There had been quite a long silence, but Thea dared not raise her head above the lavender to see what they were doing. Then Dr Black had said urgently, 'Come with me then, my dear love! I will look after you. Only say the word, and I will take you away from him for ever.'

'Ah, don't tempt me! How could I leave my children without a mother's care?' her mother had sighed, and Thea had frowned a little, for she had heard her say very much the same to Captain Bowman behind the bandstand on the racecourse.

'Bring them, too.'

'Now you are being absurd.' Mamma had moved a little away, then come back to tap him on the cheek with her fan. 'Oh, you men! How lucky you are.'

'Lucky?'

'Able to come and go as you please.'

'As my superiors direct me.'

'You know what I mean,' Mamma had said bitterly. 'You will never have to spend years and years stuck in a dreary place like this with a man you – '

Dreary? Thea had been so shocked she had paid no further attention to their talk. She thought Faisalabad the most beautiful place in the world. She knew and loved every corner of the compound: the long white *pukka* bungalow with its flat roof and shady verandah; the cool rooms with their high ceilings and polished wood floors; the dusty lawn set with croquet hoops, just like every other bungalow in the Civil lines; the cannas and marigolds and straggling rose bushes; the shrubs where the weaverbirds nested; and the irrigation channels of smooth, hand-moulded mud that carried water to the flowers and vegetables.

Then there were the other lovely places, where the servants played with her and petted her. The kitchen, where the *bobaji* crouched over his three-brick stove and let her taste mysterious delicacies destined for her parents' table; the servants' quarters where fat brown babies tumbled in the dust; the kennels and stables where the syces rubbed their charges' satiny coats with hard brown palms, and sometimes dyed the tail of the grey stallion bright red, though Papa roared at them and made them wash it all out again.

The servants were her friends and allies, from the dignified white-bearded *khansamah*, Ahmed, who had been with Papa long before he married Mamma, through the *khitmutgar*, who waited at table, the *mussalchi* who washed the dishes and cleaned the silver, the two *malis* who were endlessly hunkered over the flowerbeds, to the *bhisti*, whose patient buffalo carried water to each one of Mamma's cherished roses in turn, and who filled every receptacle he could find with water drawn from the deep dark well.

Then there was Ghulam, the *dudwallah*, who milked his buffalo on the lawn each morning and, if Ayah was not watching, would add just a 'littlee littlee *pani*' from the ditch to bring the milk up to the rim of the biggest *lota*.

Best of all, she loved Ayah, who had been her nurse from the very day she was born, and a fierce, primitive

18

anger burned in her when she saw Ayah – *her* Ayah – attending her small sisters.

'You are a big girl now, and must learn to dress yourself,' Mamma had told her when she protested. 'You don't want the other girls to laugh at you when you go Home to school.'

No, she didn't want to be laughed at, and neither did she want to go Home, as Mamma always called England, although she had lived in India all her life. Hal, three years older than Thea, had been sent Home to school when he was eight. She remembered how white and sick he had looked when he said goodbye, and how he had clung to old Ahmed until his father sharply told him to get in the carriage.

The soft shuffle of feet behind her made her turn guiltily, clutching the mutilated dress about her knees. There was Ayah, holding a twin by either hand.

'Aiee, Missee-Baba! What have you done?' she exclaimed in horror. Six-year-old Sukie tossed her curls and giggled, but Louise, the serious twin, said solemnly, 'Mamma will be cross.'

'No, she won't,' Thea tried to brazen it out. 'It's my birthday.' But even this magic formula seemed to offer little protection when they heard the scrunch of wheels on gravel and Mrs Dundas hurried towards them over the lawn, eyes bright and green silk swishing.

'Here are your first guests, Thea. Are you ready? You must stand here with me on the steps to receive them. What is the matter? Why are you hiding behind Ayah like that? *Oh!*' She broke off, her gaze riveted on Thea's trembling knees. 'You wicked, wicked child! What have you done? Your beautiful dress – *ruined!*' She caught Thea by the arm and shook her violently. 'Just as everyone is arriving! Oh, what am I to do?'

'Changing dress *juldi*, Memsahib,' suggested Ayah, instinctively protecting her nurseling.

Mrs Dundas threw a distracted glance at the two carriages which had just pulled up in a cloud of dust, and said in a low, fierce tone, 'Go to your room at once and stay there! I cannot allow you to be seen in such a state. I shall tell your guests you have a touch of the sun.'

A sob rose in Thea's throat. 'Oh, Mamma! It's my birthday!'

'You should have thought of that before.' She hesitated, realising it was already too late to banish Thea. The four Dowling children were scrambling out of their carriage, and any minute the Lort-Smiths would follow.

With an exasperated sigh, Mrs Dundas bowed to the inevitable. 'Take her and put on the – the green muslin. Be quick!' she snapped. 'You needn't think you'll get off scot-free, my girl,' she added as Thea smiled in relief. 'What are you looking forward to most at the party?'

That was easy. 'Mango ice-cream,' said Thea, and the words seemed to fill her mouth with their indescribable, fruity sweetness.

'Very well, you shall have no mango ice-cream. I forbid it. Do you understand? Not a single mouthful. That shall be your punishment.'

'Yes, Mamma.' Thea hung her head, swallowing tears of disappointment. The mango season was nearly over and *Bobaji* had made the ice for her special treat. Now she would not taste it again until next year – perhaps not even then, for Mamma might decide to send her Home at the end of the Cold Weather. Oh, why had she ever touched those hateful, tempting scissors?

All through the party the vision of the great mound of mango ice glistening on its silver frosted dish tormented her. Twisting the knife in the wound, Mamma insisted she served it to her guests with her own hands, and each child thanked her, and exclaimed how delicious it was, and told her no one made mango ice like the Dundas *bobaji*.

'Tell me his secret, Mrs Dundas,' begged Captain Bowman. 'I swear it will go no further, on my honour!'

And her mother laughed, and fluttered her eyelashes, saying she didn't know the secret and even if she did it would go with her to the grave, which gave Captain Bowman the chance to lean very close to her and call her

'Fair Cruelty' in the silly, mooning tones which Thea had noticed gentlemen often used when speaking to her mother.

But even while she smiled and flirted, Mamma kept a sharp eye open to see that her eldest daughter did not evade her punishment. Twice Ayah tried to slip her a small helping of the delicious ice and each time Mamma intervened, so that Ayah ended up eating the rejected plateful herself. None of the other servants would have eaten from a dish touched by their employers, but Ayah had been brought up at a Christian Mission and had adopted European ways, which made the other servants despise her.

After tea, Captain Bowman organised games and races for the children, while the parents joined Dr Dundas in long rattan chairs on the verandah, where they drank *burra pegs* from tall frosted glasses and mulled over the station's gossip. The heat was too oppressive for much exertion. Even before the carriages assembled on the gravel to take the guests home, Sukie had been sick and hastily removed to bed, and several other children had declined to race any more and gone to sit languidly by their ayahs.

'Overtired. They are not used to so much excitement,' said Mrs Burton diplomatically as she swept up her three pale little boys and looked about for her daughter. 'Thank you for a lovely party, Eleanor dear. You do these things so beautifully. I only wish I had half your energy.'

It must be the brim of Mamma's big hat that cast greenish shadows on her face, thought Thea, as she stood with her parents to bid her guests farewell. Her father kept running his hand round his stiff collar, as if it felt too tight, shifting uneasily as he responded to the smiles and thanks. Now and then he bumped against Thea, which nearly made her laugh because he was always telling her to stand straight without fidgeting. On her other side Mamma was doing just the same.

As the last carriage disappeared between the gateposts, Dr Dundas said urgently, above her head, 'Are you quite well, my dear?' and there was a long pause before Mamma replied in a faint, faraway voice that did not sound at all like her own:

'I feel . . . very strange. Not well. I must go and lie . . . '

'Bearer!' shouted Dr Dundas as his wife swayed on her feet, and two *chuprassies* came running to lift her into one of the long rattan chairs.

Thea touched her hand. It felt clammy.

'Send Ayah to me,' said Mamma in the same faint voice, and closed her eyes. Thea ran into the bungalow.

She looked in the nursery and then the night nursery where Sukie lay tossing on her bed with Louise crouched beside her, holding her hand and grizzling. Ayah was not there.

'Where's Ayah? Mamma wants her.'

The twins didn't answer.

'Oh, you stupid things!' exclaimed Thea and ran out of the room. She tried her own bedroom and the bathroom, and then with increasing alarm she ran through the drawing-room and dining-room, and even into Papa's study, but Ayah was not to be found.

There was one other place she might be, but it was unthinkable that she should go back to her own quarters without tucking Thea, her own Missee-Baba, into bed. Such a thing had never happened in the eight years of Thea's life. Unthinkable – unless something terrible had happened.

She didn't stop to consider what that might be. She ran as fast as her legs would carry her across the compound to the servants' quarters, ignoring the startled looks of the native women and children squatting near their cooking fires. With her heart thumping wildly, she pulled aside the curtain hanging over the entrance to Ayah's own little hut, and slipped inside.

'Ayah? Where are you?'

Silence greeted her. Silence, and a strange, disagreeable smell. As her eyes grew used to the dimness, she took in the hut's few furnishings. A string bed, under which was a rag rug which had once graced the nursery floor, a brass *lota* for water, two small bowls, a wooden chest covered with a fringed shawl, a wooden crucifix, dark against the limewashed wall, and in the corner a heap of bedding. Over everything, choking her breathing, was the vile, overpowering smell.

'Ayah?' She took a step forward, and the heap she had taken for bedding stirred and groaned. For one appalled moment Thea stared at her beloved Ayah doubled up on the floor, her arms hugging her stomach and lips drawn back to show blackened teeth. Then she fled in pure terror, racing across the compound to the safety of the bungalow.

'Ayah! Oh, Ayah!' she sobbed.

The native women at their cooking fires watched with dark, incurious eyes and went on stirring their pots. They knew better than to eat filth defiled by the *Sahib-log*.

'It was my fault,' whispered Thea.

Pale and solemn in one of the ugly black dresses which Mrs Tomlinson, wife of the new doctor, had caused the *durzee* to run up hastily after the disaster and had made the orphan wear ever since, she faced her father's man of business, Mr Bannerji, across the table in what had once been her father's study. With rare tact, Mrs Tomlinson effaced herself in a corner. She was a thin, tense, overconscientious woman, whose sharp, lined face spoke of past hardships. She found it hard to adjust to the expansive ideas of Anglo-India.

'No, no, Missy-Baba. You are quite mistaken. The mango ice was the clear culprit,' said Mr Bannerji emphatically. 'All are agreed on that.'

Thea wanted to believe him, but her eyes filled with tears. She could not stop crying; it seemed she had been crying for the whole of the past year. Not only Ayah, but Papa and Mamma, Sukie and Louise had died within days of her birthday party, and every household in the station whose children had eaten the mango ice had been similarly afflicted. Captain Bowman had died, two of Mrs Burton's three boys, and Sarah Kennedy's parents and two sisters.

Altogether eleven children and nine adults had succumbed to acute food poisoning – a wholesale disaster even by Indian standards – and Dr Tomlinson's first days in his new post had been hectic ones.

'Believe me, Missy-Baba, the fault was with the cook, not with you,' urged Mr Bannerji. 'You must not cry so much or you will make yourself ill.' His kind, heavy-featured face had a strong, hooked nose with grey hairs sprouting from it, and further bushy tufts protruded from his ears below the rakishly perched flat-topped turban. Behind wire-framed half-moon spectacles dark eyes surrounded by purplish wrinkles regarded her anxiously.

'Now we must look to your future, and cease repining about the past.' He pulled a sheaf of papers from his scrip and sorted them with care. 'Here is your father's will, but I fear you will find little comfort in that. Here I have written to Alfred Dundas Esquire of Nether Wayton in the county of Leicestershire, begging to inform him of the sad demise of your esteemed parents and enquiring if he is willing to become your legal guardian until you come of age or marry, whichever should be sooner.'

He beamed at her, inviting her admiration and gratitude, but Thea merely sniffed and gulped, scrubbing her eyes with a damp handkerchief.

'He is my great-uncle,' she said in a wavering voice. 'He was angry when Papa ran away to India.'

'Alas, that is very true.' Mr Bannerji drew out another paper and adjusted his spectacles. 'Here I have the reply of Alfred Dundas Esquire. Ahem! He acknowledges my letter and so on . . . hm, hm . . . where is it? Yes . . . but regrets his health is too poor to undertake responsibility for the child of a nephew who showed himself incapable of gratitude or family feeling . . . hm, hm . . . There is more in the same vein.'

He leaned back, putting the tips of his fingers together, and unconsciously his slippered feet crept up to their accustomed position on the seat of his chair. 'So now we must consider gravely what is to be done for you for the best.'

Thea tried hard to pay attention. This was her future they were talking about, but the mist of grief made it hard to think clearly. She only knew she did not want to leave India. She said pleadingly, 'Can I not stay here? If I'm good – very, very good?' Then a fresh burst of sobs at the thought of being banished from the home she loved choked any further attempt at speech.

'Control yourself, child,' said Mrs Tomlinson sharply, and was rewarded with an angry flash from Thea's hazel eyes.

'Can't you see I'm trying to?' *You stupid woman* trembled unspoken in the air.

Mrs Tomlinson bit her lip: her fingers itched. She had tried – heaven knew she had tried – to do her Christian duty by this shorn lamb. An unrewarding task it had proved. While letters to and from England made their slow way across thousands of miles of ocean, Mrs Tomlinson had laboured to undo Ayah's work of eight years and teach young Dorothea Dundas a proper respect for her elders. She was no longer Missy-Baba, petted by her parents and spoiled rotten by their servants. The fatal birthday party had put an end to all that. Even so, the child hardly seemed to realise that she was now dependent on charity and living on sufferance in her former home. When she was not crying her eyes out, she behaved exactly as if she were still the young mistress. She was naughty and rebellious, what Mrs Tomlinson called in her own mind 'a proper little madam'.

She bullied the Tomlinson children, terrified them with tales of giants and demons, and broke their toys. She contradicted Mrs Tomlinson's orders to the servants and encouraged them to disobey her. Good? She didn't know the meaning of the word.

It was the same with all these Anglo-Indian children, she reflected with the clear sight of one only recently arrived in the subcontinent. From earliest infancy they were given their own way and pampered like miniature rajas by their native servants, who also taught them to lie, cheat and evade parental discipline – if any – and then used pagan threats to terrorise their charges into acceptable behaviour. Why, she had heard her own little Amelia, barely six years old, declare solemnly that inside the big drum on the bandstand were all the naughty boys and girls who would not stand still to have their hair combed. Ayah had told her so! And four-year-old Eddie had run shrieking from the room at the sight of poor Major Dunwoody, calling him the *Bora* with the big stomach who dined off a dozen wicked children each day.

'Can I not stay here with you, Aunt Tomlinson?' Thea pleaded.

The indiscriminate way in which Anglo-Indian children addressed adult Europeans as Aunt and Uncle, instead of using a proper title, also jarred on the doctor's wife. She had five children of her own to feed, clothe and educate, and she considered she had done enough for Thea.

She shook her head slightly at Mr Bannerji, who said at once, 'The Memsahib has been very kind to you, Missy-Baba. You must not ask too much or outstay your welcome.'

'But this is my home!' exclaimed Thea, outraged. 'Why don't you want me here any longer?' she demanded of Mrs Tomlinson, who, flustered at the conflict between Christian duty and protecting her own brood, answered more sharply than she meant to that wanting had nothing to do with the matter. Thea must be educated. Her ignorance was perfectly shocking. It was high time she went to school, but there was no suitable institution in Faisalabad.

Thea thought Mrs Tomlinson's ignorance of how to treat her servants perfectly shocking. She turned with confidence to Mr Bannerji.

'Will you educate me, then, *Babu-ji*? You have all the knowledge in the world.'

Behind the wire-framed spectacles his eyes twinkled, but he said seriously, 'Alas, Missy-Baba, my poor skills are not what the esteemed Memsahib has in mind.' He cleared his throat. 'If I may venture a suggestion? There are those who speak well of the Female Orphanage in Ludhiana. The Principal is a most respected lady, beloved of all who know her. She could, perhaps, advise you.'

'Ludhiana! That is miles away,' objected Thea.

So much the better, thought Mrs Tomlinson. While it would hardly be fair to blame the child for last April's disaster, there was no denying that the very sight of Thea was salt in the wounds of families bereaved at that time. In a small station like this it was impossible to keep her out of their way, and the sight of her romping with the dogs or laughing with the servants grated the nerves of parents whose own children would never laugh or romp again.

'Thank you, Mr Bannerji,' she said with real warmth. 'That is a valuable suggestion.'

'I don't want to be an orphan,' Thea wailed. 'I won't go. I'll be so naughty they'll send me away.'

'Pull yourself together, child.' Mrs Tomlinson rose briskly to indicate that the interview was at an end. As soon as Mr Bannerji had collected his papers, she began to shoo him towards the door.

CHAPTER ONE

It worried Kate Quinn that the girl in the garden was wearing no hat. She sat on a bench in the April sun, a sheet of paper on her lap, and from time to time would spring up and pace rapidly to and fro before returning to her seat. That child, thought Mrs Quinn, watching through the long window of the Orphanage Assembly Hall, will ruin her complexion.

As Major Thayer, the Treasurer, droned out figures, and the *punkah* flapped and insects buzzed in the noon heat, she wondered if Miss Ellis, the Principal, knew the girl was there. She had no wish to get the poor child into trouble, but she really should not sit hatless in the sun. At the very least she would get freckles, which would be a pity for any girl but a tragedy for one so strikingly attractive as this tall, graceful creature with her fair, blooming skin, wilful mouth and abundant Titian hair.

The annual examination of accounts and report on the year's activities of the Ludhiana Military Orphanage for Females was an affair requiring considerable stamina on the part of the Governors. For as long as Kate had served on the Committee the problem had always been money, and this year was no exception. Though nominally funded by the Honourable East India Company, who might, in principle, be accounted responsible for the orphans' plight (since it was in Company service that their fathers had perished) and therefore bound to provide for their support, the gap between income and expenditure grew steadily wider.

Despite valiant efforts by Miss Ellis and her deputy, Miss Oldershaw, their books would never balance. Even with the most stringent economy they were obliged to rely heavily on fund-raising by the charitably minded ladies and gentlemen of the Ludhiana station if the girls were to be adequately fed, clothed, and educated to the point where they might hope to attract a husband. The obligation irked Miss Ellis, who was of an independent nature, and though she accepted their bounty, she sometimes received it less than graciously.

Kate understood her feelings and knew what sacrifices Miss Ellis made personally for her charges, but others – like peppery Major Thayer – resented the Principal's inability to thank them after they had put aside valuable time to bring order into the tangled financial affairs of the Orphanage.

'This sum of two thousand rupees, Miss Ellis, received on the tenth November last. How do you account for that?' he was asking now, in the dry, precise voice that always held a note of reproof.

'Two thousand . . . ?' Miss Ellis searched her memory. She was an angular, raw-boned spinster in her fifties, deaf in one ear since her youth, when the mutineers at Vellore had blown up the magazine only a hundred yards from where she had been hiding. She had a pretty talent for drawing miniatures on ivory in the Persian style, but no head for figures.

'Ah, yes,' she said with relief after a painful pause. 'That was a donation from Mr Josiah Harker on the occasion of his marriage to little Emily Woods.'

'Donation, eh?' Major Thayer was disapproving. 'We must be careful, Miss Ellis, that gentlemen in need of a wife do not get the notion that they may *purchase* them from you.'

'Major Thayer, I resent that imputation!' Miss Ellis flushed to her ears.

'Naturally, I intended no reflection upon you,' went on Major Thayer, smiling thinly. 'Nevertheless, we must be vigilant. May I proceed?'

Meetings were frequently strained occasions, needing, if clashes were to be avoided, a good deal of diplomacy from those who, like Kate, could see both points of view. Today she sighed with relief when Major Thayer's interminable accounts were unanimously approved, and thanked her stars that the most notorious quibbler on the Board, Mrs Pennyfeather, the Adjutant's wife, was laid low with a feminine complaint and unable to attend the meeting.

As voting began for the re-election of various officers, a bell clanged faintly from the dormitory wing and she saw the pupils who had been strolling about the gardens or sitting in the shade in small groups troop indoors to begin their siesta. Kate envied them. Her head was aching and she would have given a good deal to be able to lie down with a cold compress across her eyes.

Ten minutes later only the girl on the marble bench remained in the garden. A native boy was sent out to fetch her, but she waved the messenger away and continued her lonely vigil.

A few minutes passed, and then the bustling, black-clad form of Miss Oldershaw approached the girl, laying an authoritative hand on her shoulder. There was a brief flurry of movement, after which Miss Oldershaw, too, retreated, pausing to deliver a few sharp words over her shoulder from a safe distance. Fascinated, Kate watched her swishing, indignant withdrawal across the dusty grass. The girl bowed her head on her hands in a classic gesture of despair.

'Will you, Mrs Quinn?' Major Thayer spoke with the exaggerated clarity he might have used to a slow-witted subaltern. Kate realised it was not the first time the question had been asked.

Guiltily she switched her attention to the matter in hand. 'Forgive me. My thoughts were elsewhere. Will I do what?'

'I asked you if you would be kind enough to take charge of the Sale of Work. It had such a success last year.'

Oh, no! thought Kate. Not again! Why did she never have an excuse ready? Last year she had found herself committed to an endless round of negotiation and manipulation as she tried to solicit saleable articles and fend off unwanted ones in a small community which knew one another's possessions far too well to want to pay good

30

money for them, and had ended up by feeling she had offended most of the station.

'I thought we agreed that this year there should be no Sale of Work? A dance, perhaps, instead? A fresh approach. I would gladly take charge of arranging a dance.' Her eyes roamed the assembled faces in search of support and found none.

'We always have a Sale of Work, Mrs Quinn,' reproved Major Thayer.

'My girls are already busy with their contributions,' agreed Miss Ellis. 'Pot-holders and samplers from the juniors, embroidered traycloths from the seniors.'

How many traycloths and pot-holders cculd one sell to the ladies of Ludhiana? wondered Kate bleakly.

'The Shale hash become an inshtitution,' declared old Mr Lavelle through ill-fitting teeth. He rarely spoke at meetings, but as Acting Magistrate his word was law and Kate knew she had no choice.

'Very well. If you insist,' she murmured, and there was a general murmur of approval. The meeting drifted on. When it eventually ended, Kate noticed the girl was still sitting in the same place.

As the Governors began to disperse, Miss Ellis drew her aside.

'About your letter, Mrs Quinn. You asked if I could recommend a governess for your daughter.'

'It was unfortunate that Miss Peabody had to leave so suddenly,' said Kate guardedly, and Miss Ellis nodded with understanding.

'I believe I have the very girl to suit you. Her name is Sarah Kennedy, and she has all the accomplishments you mention. A girl of excellent character and, between ourselves, not the type to be for ever falling in love and neglecting her duty!'

'She sounds a paragon,' said Kate, smiling. 'If only Rohais will not drive her demented with her fits and starts! She was so ill as a child. Time and again we thought we had lost her. I fear we have been inclined to spoil her as a result.'

'Well, you shall judge for yourself,' said Miss Ellis briskly, and sent a servant to summon the paragon.

It took Kate a bare ten minutes to decide that Sarah Kennedy would not do for Rohais at all. Certainly there was nothing in the girl's plain, sallow face and lumpy figure to incite young men to lust, and her bookishness was unquestionable, but she was such a dull, self-righteous creature that Kate knew by experience that her wilful daughter would lead her a miserable dance and learn nothing from her. Rohais needed a companion more than a governess. Someone she would admire and, with any luck, imitate. Poor Sarah Kennedy was decidedly not inspirational.

'I am sorry,' said Kate after the girl had been dismissed. 'I fear my daughter needs a stronger hand . . . a more lively nature.' On impulse she added, 'I have no wish to pry, but that girl in the garden, on the bench – has something happened to distress her? It seems curious that she should wish to remain there so long.'

'Distress her?' Miss Ellis followed her glance. 'Ah, yes. Dorothea Dundas. A sad story. You remember the food poisoning at Faisalabad? The mango ice?'

Kate searched her memory and nodded. 'Of course. I knew Major Dundas slightly. He was Medical Officer in Futtehpore when my husband was serving there. He was known as "Waspie", I recall. Do you mean that child is his daughter? I thought the whole family perished.'

'Dorothea is his only surviving daughter. I forget the details, but for some reason she abstained from eating the poisoned ice.'

'Poor girl! A dreadful tragedy!' Kate's eyes went back to the figure on the bench. 'I had no idea she was among your charges. I should like to do something to help her . . . But by now, surely, her spirits must have recovered?'

'Indeed, yes.' Miss Ellis allowed herself a smile. 'In the normal way there is nothing melancholic about Dorothea. On the contrary! When she came to us, she was quite out of hand and inclined to lead the other girls into all kinds of mischief. We have had our difficulties with her, I don't deny, but so often difficult children turn out best in the end. That is one of the compensations of our work here.'

'Then what is troubling her now?' persisted Kate, who liked to get to the bottom of things.

'Oh, that is quite another matter. I had arranged for Dorothea to marry Mr Barnes, clerk to the Acting Magistrate. A respectable widower, with a reasonable competence. Unfortunately, he, too, has been struck down very suddenly, which has reopened old wounds, and she believes her life is blighted. But she is young. She will soon get over it.'

'I wonder . . . ' mused Kate, her eyes returning to the garden.

'If you are wondering whether Dorothea would make a satisfactory governess for your daughter, Mrs Quinn, I advise you to put the idea out of your head,' said Miss Ellis with unusual firmness. She had no intention of wasting a perfectly marriageable girl who would bring a much-needed donation to the Orphanage which had fed and sheltered her for nine long years.

She lowered her voice. 'I may tell you in confidence, Mrs Quinn, that another gentleman has already offered for Miss Dundas . . . In fact, his offer was made even before Mr Barnes expressed his attachment.'

'Indeed?' Kate's eyebrows rose. 'May I ask why you preferred Mr Barnes's suit? There seems, on the face of it, to have been a large disparity in age.'

'To be perfectly frank with you, I was not convinced of Major Le Griffe's financial security,' Miss Ellis said sedately.

'*Major Le Griffe* offered for her?'

'I had difficulty in refusing him. I have no doubt that when he hears of Mr Barnes's unfortunate demise, he will at once renew his suit.'

Kate drew in her breath sharply. Financial security or no, the idea of that pretty girl in Roderick Le Griffe's hairy hands was perfectly sickening. Four times widowed, and with the worst reputation for womanising in his regiment, the Major's catholic taste in bedmates was an open secret. 'Black or white, it's all the same to me,' she had once overheard him declare to a grinning subaltern. 'Beats me how some fellows sleep with the same woman year in year out. I like a bit of variety between the sheets.'

'You must be aware of Major Le Griffe's reputation,' she said, covering her revulsion as best she could.

Miss Ellis flushed unbecomingly, drawing her long upper lip down over her teeth. 'He is not, perhaps, the ideal choice of husband,' she admitted, 'but beggars cannot be choosers. In my situation I take what I can find, and Dorothea will soon be eighteen. I cannot keep her here for ever.'

'Would you not prefer to find her a teaching post?'

'I fear that would not answer.'

'Why not? Has she no accomplishments?'

'On the contrary!' Miss Ellis revealed her rare, charming smile. 'She sings and draws very prettily. Plays the piano, speaks a little French – the usual things, you know.'

'Then, why?'

Miss Ellis sighed. 'You and I, Mrs Quinn, have lived long enough to recognise that there is a certain type of young woman who has – how shall I put it? – a *disturbing* effect upon gentlemen.'

She made it sound as if the girl on the lawn was a very Messalina, but of course a maiden lady like Miss Ellis would have different standards from her own, Kate reflected.

'I know what you mean,' she said, stifling her desire to laugh.

Miss Ellis nodded briskly. 'I believe you have a son?'

'You fear he would fall victim to Miss Dundas's charms?'

'I should not wish you to blame me if he did.'

'Dear Ma'am, you may rest easy on that score. James has recently announced his betrothal to Miss Green, Mr Hathaway's niece.'

'An excellent connection,' approved Miss Ellis.

'So we hope.' Kate's tone was neutral. Many parents would have been overjoyed to see their son marry two thousand pounds a year, but neither she nor General Quinn quite liked the prospect of James living off his wife's income. When she had voiced her reservations, her son had chosen to be offended, declaring haughtily that he was not marrying Charlotte for her money and it wounded him that his mother should suppose him a damned fortune-hunter.

How difficult it was, she thought, not to rush in with warnings and advice when you saw someone you loved heading for a precipice! Even the best-intentioned advice often produced the wrong result, or provoked the very crisis it was designed to avert. Take the case of Rohais. No one could blame the doctor for recommending that she should not be coerced into doing her lessons or, indeed, anything she disliked, since opposition to her wishes provoked terrifying attacks of asthma which frightened them all into fits. From a medical point of view the advice had been sound enough. A less happy result was that Rohais at fifteen, though perfectly healthy, was headstrong, disobedient, and wilful.

Time was pressing. If Miss Ellis could not help her find a governess, what was she to do? She looked again at the girl in the garden. Poor child! Fate had dealt her a cruel hand. She thought of Roderick Le Griffe and shuddered.

'I should like to meet Miss Dundas,' she heard her own voice say, and Miss Ellis looked astonished.

'I have already explained why she would not be suitable,' she protested, seeing Major Le Griffe's donation evaporate. 'I could not recommend her. For a governess, she lacks *gravitas*.'

'So much the better!' Kate smiled. '*Gravitas* is the last quality I am looking for. If Miss Dundas can teach my daughter to draw and sing, she will have done better than her predecessors, and if she can set her an example in manners I shall be everlastingly grateful!'

She saw by the compression of Miss Ellis's mouth where the real trouble lay, and added winningly, 'I know my husband wishes to make a substantial contribution to your fund for the chapel roof. Such a worthy cause, as he observed to me this very morning!'

May I be forgiven the lie, she added silently, watching Miss Ellis weigh this bird in the hand. She frowned, sucked her teeth, glanced at the girl and back at Kate, and finally nodded. Clapping her hands, she told the servant who answered that she wished to see Miss Dundas in her study immediately.

CHAPTER TWO

Rohais's expressive mouth drooped, and her large blue eyes filled with tears.

'You never *told* me you were going to engage a new governess, Mamma! I thought you would let me leave the schoolroom now that I am fifteen.'

Small and fine-boned, with fair hair waving back from her smooth white forehead, a tiny waist set off by a wide sash of pale blue satin, and elegant small hands peeping from ruffled muslin cuffs, Rohais looked as delicately perfect as a doll. Kate hated to make her precious daughter cry, but knew she must be firm this time. It had been a shock to discover upon Miss Peabody's departure that the succession of governesses who had passed through the schoolroom had taught Rohais so little.

'I am sorry, my pet, but fifteen is too young to give up lessons, and I am sure you will like Miss Dundas. She is only a year or so older than you, and such a handsome, well-mannered girl! I took to her at once. Poor soul, she has had a sad life.'

Too late, she saw that praise for the new governess was a mistake, and the attempt to arouse Rohais's pity was merely stiffening her resistance to the newcomer.

'I don't want her. I won't obey her.'

'Then you shall not come with me to Simla this year,' said Kate, steeling herself against the look of reproach. 'If you think you can go through life a barbarous little savage, you are much mistaken.'

'Mamma!' Rohais was outraged by this threat to the year's greatest treat. 'You wouldn't – you *couldn't* – leave me!'

'I would and I could unless you treat Miss Dundas with respect and do your best for her.' With a sinking heart she observed the mutinous jutting of her daughter's chin, and went on. 'Be reasonable, my love. I have gone to the trouble of engaging a teacher who is young and lively because you said you dislike old governesses – not that poor Miss Rose or Miss James or Miss Peabody were anything but kind to you.'

'Horrid old things, ugh!' Rohais saw the struggle on her mother's face and added cajolingly, 'If I'm good, may I go to dances this year? Oh, please!'

'Perhaps. But you must promise to behave civilly and do as Miss Dundas wishes.'

Rohais sighed elaborately. 'Oh, very well! She can hardly be worse than old Pease Porridge. May I put up my hair for the Governor-General's ball?'

'We shall see.'

'Play fair, Mamma! I've promised, so you must too.'

'All right, wretch! But only if Miss Dundas gives you a good report.'

'She will. You'll see.' Rohais hugged her mother and skipped away, determined that Miss Dundas's reign in the schoolroom should be the shortest of all.

Rohais's first view of the newcomer, as she strolled down the shallow flight of marble steps to the shady terrace where General Quinn's family had gathered before *tiffin*, was reassuring. She paused on the last step to survey her, secure in the knowledge that her own appearance was as perfect as starching and bleaching, combing and plaiting, threading of ribbons and goffering of frills, plus the undivided attention of two ayahs, could make it. Miss Dundas was certainly no beauty. Carroty hair and a great wide mouth, and so tall! Why, she is nearly the same height as James, thought Rohais. What a great, hulking, untidy creature! She looks as if she might burst out of that terrible dress at any minute. The straining fabric had certainly been designed for a slighter figure. Not that her brother James seemed to mind. To Rohais's surprise he was talking animatedly to the new governess, though schoolmarms were hardly his style, and as Miss Dundas's wide mouth broke into a smile at something he had said, she suddenly looked – well, not pretty, exactly, but unmistakably attractive.

Jolie laide, thought Rohais. It was one of the few French phrases she knew. It flashed across her mind that gentlemen might take a different view of the carroty hair and straining dress. They were such strange creatures! Frowning, she moved to break up the conversation.

'How-de-do?' she drawled, extending two languid fingers.

But Miss Dundas had just made the fascinating discovery that Captain James Quinn had known her own brother Hal at school in England. The drawled greeting and languid fingers went unremarked. For a mortifying moment Rohais found herself ignored, and her face burned.

'James, you wretch!' she exclaimed, pitching her voice in the little-girl whine that never failed to make people attend to her. 'I declare you have quite forgotten your promise.'

As her fingers pinched his arm, he turned, an athletic, open-faced six-footer with sleek dark hair and a clear-cut profile. He wore the dark green frogged tunic and white breeches of the newly formed Shah's Service.

'What promise, my love?'

'You said you would show me your new mare, and I have been waiting for hours and hours.'

'Oh, so I did.' He patted her shoulder absently, as one might a dog. 'I haven't forgotten, but surely tomorrow will do? That is, if Miss Dundas will let you off your lessons in time?' He cocked a quizzical eye at the governess, saying, 'This, by the way, is your pupil. I warn you, she has a bad reputation with teachers, but you, I am sure, will tame her.'

When Miss Dundas laughed her greeny-hazel eyes lit up and her rippling chuckle was infectious. 'For shame, Captain Quinn! I will not permit you to blacken my pupil's reputation before we are even acquainted. How do you do, Rohais? I hope very much we shall be friends.'

Rohais muttered a less than gracious greeting. Miss

Dundas seemed too much at ease in company for her taste. Instead of looking flustered when a gentleman spoke to her, as Miss Peabody used to, this newcomer appeared to enjoy James's banter. She watched with some irritation as her brother again claimed the governess's attention, even though Charlotte Green, his betrothed, stood alone and neglected, pretending to admire the flowers in a marble urn. Nor was her temper improved when Mrs Quinn, hurrying up, made it clear she must spend the rest of the day showing Miss Dundas around and vetoed any suggestion of an evening ride.

'It would be uncivil to leave her alone on the first day,' she whispered, 'and tomorrow you must start lessons again. You have missed a month's schoolwork since Miss Peabody left, and will have to work hard to catch up.'

Catch up with what? Rohais wondered crossly. It was only a faint consolation to notice that she was not alone in her resentment of the newcomer.

Charlotte Green, whose rapt contemplation of the urn had failed to attract James to her side, had now begun to behave like a hen who has seen the slinking form of a mongoose near her nest, fluffing up her feathers and making a great deal of noise.

She took James's arm in a possessive manner, begged him to see where she had left her shawl, and tapped him archly on the cheek with her fan when, instead of fetching it himself, he sent a servant.

Rohais knew these tactics were ill-judged. Instead of responding to his betrothed's playful scolding, her brother withdrew his arm gently but firmly and refused to engage in a discussion of the hat she would wear for their wedding.

'Wear what you like. It is all the same to me,' he said coolly, and Charlotte bit her lip.

James could be led but never driven. Rohais observed with a sinking heart how his eyes strayed away from the plump prettiness of Charlotte in her billows of figured muslin and blue silk, to the governess whose tight, shabby dress served to emphasise her striking colouring and generously proportioned figure.

Surely he does not admire her? thought Rohais anxiously. No one is better qualified to pronounce on the state of a brother's heart than a jealous younger sister, and Rohais was quite familiar with the pattern of James's infatuations. Had he not stared at Charlotte herself when she first appeared with her uncle at the Regimental Ball with the same expression of a man seeing a strawberry ice on a hot day, and for the rest of the evening quite ignored his own partner?

If it came to a battle for James's heart, Rohais knew whose side she would take. She was to be principal bridesmaid at his wedding, if this tiresome war with Afghanistan did not upset their plans. Charlotte had even hinted that when James got his Home leave, she would take Rohais with them to London and present her to the young Queen. If James succumbed to a stupid infatuation for a governess, all these plans were at risk. Rohais resolved that it would be in everyone's interest if she engineered Miss Dundas's speedy dismissal.

It was strange, thought Thea, how life could jog along for years with no perceptible change, and then in the space of one day turn violently upside down. On her eighth birthday, the wheel of fortune had spun away her happy childhood and propelled her along the bleak road to the Female Orphanage. Now, with the same lack of warning, had come this second revolution.

Long dreary years in the Orphanage had blurred most of her early memories. Mamma, Papa, and even Ayah were no more than dim recollections now. She could hardly remember what the twins looked like, and though Hal's stilted letters from school spoke of passing examinations and playing in teams, she still pictured him as the white, sick-faced eight-year-old who had clung to Ahmed before her father forced him into the carriage.

After her own pretty dresses, the Orphanage uniform had been hard to bear, and still worse were the lack of privacy and the petty rules. From the moment they rose until they went to bed, the girls were never alone, and as they hurried from one task to the next they were pursued by a stream of orders, advice and criticism.

During those years time seemed to stand still, and yet it had passed with frightening speed, each birthday bringing closer the moment when she would go into the world to fend for herself. Marriage was every female orphan's preoccupation. Marriage was both the goal and the duty towards which all their schooling was directed, and any girl who attracted no offer before her eighteenth birthday was regarded as a failure. The men who came in search of brides were generally the dregs of the European community, whom no respectable woman would marry, but neither this nor wide differences of age and interests troubled Miss Ellis, who had long become accustomed to seeing beautiful, innocent eighteen-year-olds walk down the aisle on the arm of desiccated widowers old enough to be their grandsires.

Thea had not much cared for Mr Barnes, with his yellow complexion and tendency to spit when he spoke, but the rapture with which Miss Ellis had greeted his offer of 4,000 rupees for the chapel roof had convinced her there was little point in objecting, particularly when the alternative was marriage to Major Le Griffe, whose hot hands and rank breath filled her with disgust. As the date of the wedding approached, she had begun to look on it as her passport to freedom after all these imprisoned years, and the news of Mr Barnes's death, slamming the door on these hopes, had brought her close to despair.

My Guardian Angel must have been watching, she thought now, arranging the schoolroom to her liking. Governess to the General's daughter! She smoothed her hair and skirt and, glancing in the mirror, assumed the kind of expression a governess should wear, calm yet authoritative, but her pleasure in her new circumstances kept twitching her lips into most ungovernessy smiles.

She laid out paper, pens and schoolbooks, amused to see the well-thumbed primers inscribed *James Alexander*

Quinn in a round, boyish script. How long since he had written that? It was hard to imagine the dashing young officer as an inky little boy.

Her musings were interrupted as Rohais pushed open the door and flounced towards the solid square table without a word of greeting. Her pretty face was tight with resentment as she took her seat on the more comfortable of the chairs.

'Mamma says I must do lessons for two hours,' she announced, planting her elbows on the table in a way that would have drawn a sharp rebuke from Miss Oldershaw. 'I shall not stay after ten. James is taking me to the races.'

The hostility of this delicate, doll-like child shocked Thea like cold water dashed in her face.

'Let us start by making out a timetable,' she said as pleasantly as she could, but Rohais would not respond to her smile.

'*I* will make my timetable. You do not know which subjects I hate.'

'A fine timetable that would be! You mean the subjects you are bad at?'

For answer, Rohais fanned out the textbooks, picked out two, and tossed them aside. 'What do I care about the stupid old Romans? I will learn French, so Mamma can take me to Paris, and I like drawing maps. I hate arithmetic.'

'Then we will do just a little every day.'

'No!'

'Yes.'

'You can't make me.'

'We'll see,' said Thea. 'Now if you will stop behaving like a baby and take your elbows off the table, we can begin. Write "Timetable" at the top of the page.'

With the blackest of looks, Rohais scrawled TIMTABEL in irregular capitals, then glanced up in time to catch Thea's expression of astonishment. 'It's wrong, isn't it?'

'Never mind. Try again.'

'You write it.' Rohais pushed the paper across the table. Thea promptly returned it.

'Is that what Miss Peabody did?' she asked.

'Of course.'

'And your other governesses?'

'They did as I told them.' Rohais giggled, clapping her hand over her mouth in a gesture Miss Ellis would have abhorred. 'Miss Rose used to write my exercises with her left hand.'

Thea said curiously, 'How will you ever learn if you don't even try?'

'I don't need to,' said Rohais loftily. '*I* shall not be a governess! I mean to go Home and marry a rich lord, and never open another book in my life.'

This was hardly encouraging. Thea tried another tack. 'I will tell you the letters and you write them down. T-I-M-E . . . Joined-up writing, please.'

But Rohais, it seemed, had never mastered joined-up writing. 'The letters dance about,' she complained when Thea stood behind her to guide her hand.

Slowly, with much grumbling, she copied out the alphabet with large letters and small, then pushed the exercise across the table and laid down her pen.

'My head aches,' she announced. 'I will go and lie down. If you try to stop me I shall scream.'

She looked very pale, and her screwed-up, rapidly blinking eyes suggested that the headache was real enough. Thea glanced at the schoolroom clock, saw the lesson had only twenty minutes to run, and decided discretion was the better part of valour.

'All right. Put your books away, then you may go.'

'You can put them away.' Rohais jumped up so quickly that her chair tipped over. Pressing her hands to her temples, she ran out of the room.

A fine start! thought Thea, surveying the scattered books and single sheet of paper covered with sprawling letters. Cramming a little learning into the head of this spoiled brat was going to be difficult.

When she had put the room to rights, she walked on to the verandah just in time to see her pupil ride out through the gates on a spirited Arab pony, with her brother beside her on his chestnut countrybred. Rohais was chattering and laughing, all trace of headache vanished.

As they passed the verandah, James looked up and seeing Thea raised a hand in salute. She wondered if his sister was amusing him with the tale of how she had hoodwinked her new governess.

I *will* teach her to read and write properly, she vowed, her resolution returning with a rush. I owe it to kind Mrs Quinn. It would be a weary slog for them both, she knew, unless she could overcome Rohais's resistance. 'Take one step at a time,' Miss Ellis had used to say. 'Don't try to run before you can walk.' What advice would she give about a pupil who determinedly walked backwards?

Lessons followed the same disheartening pattern for several weeks. Rohais would trail into the schoolroom late with a string of excuses on her lips, work reluctantly, and then find some reason to cut the lesson short, leaving Thea uncertain as to whether she really did feel ill, as she claimed, or was simply an accomplished liar. When at last she nerved herself to confess the difficulty to Mrs Quinn, she sensed at once her employer's disappointment.

'You mean *that* is the best my daughter can do?' exclaimed Kate, scrutinising the ill-spelt scrap of dictation Thea had brought to prove her point. 'My dear Miss Dundas, I do not mean to criticise your teaching methods, but you must make her work harder.'

'She does try – at least, I think she does. She says that writing makes her head ache. I wonder if there could be something amiss with her sight?'

'Impossible! She has eyes like a hawk. Oh dear! I must confess I am disappointed. In the last month Miss Peabody was with us, Rohais made excellent progress. Certainly she never showed me work like this.'

'It is Rohais's unaided work,' said Thea, and Mrs Quinn gave her a sharp look.

'Unaided? Are you implying that Miss Peabody *improved* Rohais's writing?'

'I understand she used to copy out the exercises herself.'

'How very deceitful!' Mrs Quinn frowned, then laughed despite herself. 'Poor creature! I expect she feared I would dismiss her. I must admit I did sometimes marvel at the strides Rohais was making. Well, at least you have been honest with me, and if you are prepared to persevere, I will give you all the help I can. One way or another, we shall win through! I believe these headaches are largely imaginary. Rohais has become so accustomed to getting her own way that any attempt to thwart her makes her think she is ill.' She paused, sighed, and then said firmly, 'The next time she complains of a headache, you must insist she continues her work.'

'She will be angry,' said Thea doubtfully.

'Never mind. She has to learn. She was so ill as a child! The doctor warned us not to frustrate her, and this is the result. The plain truth is that she has never acquired a habit of concentration, and once she leaves the school-room, I fear it will be too late.'

Privately Thea thought it was too late already, but to say so would have sounded like croaking, besides endangering her own position. 'I will try,' she said.

'Good! Stick to your guns, and make her obey you. You have my full authority.'

The opportunity for such a trial of strength was not long delayed. Next morning Rohais arrived late as usual. After rattling off the French verbs she had learned and reciting multiplication tables, she demanded rather than asked permission to stop lessons early. Her father expected a visitor. She wished to look her best.

'So that is why you are in such a hurry,' said Thea, smiling. 'Who is coming?'

'No one you would know. May I go now?'

'Finish the page first. There will still be plenty of time to change your dress.'

'My head is aching. I want to lie down.'

'I am sorry, but you use that excuse too often,' said Thea resolutely, though she dreaded her pupil's reaction. 'Today you must stay until I give you leave to go.'

Rohais sat perfectly still for a moment, then quite deliberately upset the inkpot all over her painfully copied sheet of verse. The black stain spread across the table and dripped on to her white skirt.

'There!' she said triumphantly. 'Now I will *have* to go and change.'

'No, you won't. Sit down again at once. You are going to finish your lessons today whether you like it or not.'

'My dress is ruined!' Rohais wailed. 'Mamma will be angry.'

'You should have thought of that before spilling ink on it,' said Thea, trying to speak calmly though her heart was pounding.

'I'll tell her you spilled it. I'll say you're cruel and I hate you, and she will send you away.'

'Sit down and don't talk nonsense.'

For answer, Rohais defiantly pushed over her chair and stalked towards the door, but with swift steps Thea sped across the room and stood with her back against it.

'Get out of my way!' screamed Rohais. She snatched at Thea's shoulder, trying to pull her away from the door, and when she resisted slapped her hard across the face. Thea gasped, but refused to give ground, knowing if she lost this battle she might as well give up all hope of controlling her pupil. She clung to Rohais's arm to prevent her dealing another blow, and Rohais began to scream at the top of her voice.

'Help! Stop it! Get off! You're hurting me!'

Footsteps clattered on the marble floor outside and she redoubled her screams. The door burst open as a booted foot was set against it, and Thea was propelled forward. She struck her head on the corner of the cupboard in which the schoolbooks were stored. She leaned, dazed, against the wall, but Rohais, instead of making her escape, continued to wail and shake her by the arm as the boot's owner followed it into the room.

He halted on the threshold, surveying the disordered furniture, spilt ink and struggling girls. 'What the deuce is going on here?' he demanded, and strode across to pull them apart. 'Ro, my angel, what is the matter?'

47

Rohais stopped wailing. She turned with a little sob and flung herself against his chest. His arms folded around her.

'Save me! Save me! She's so cruel!'

'All right, my love. You're safe now.' He caressed her hair and turned angrily upon Thea. 'Striking your pupil? A fine way for a governess to behave, upon my word! Does Mrs Quinn know of your teaching methods?'

'Of course she does. And I did not strike her.' Thea rubbed her bruised head. 'Who are you, sir? What right have you to come bursting in here without my leave?'

'Without – ?' He laughed shortly. 'That's rich! I am Dr Tobias Black, miss, and I am not in the habit of asking leave to visit my patients.'

'Dr Black? Oh!' She stared at him, astonished. Gone were the dandyish cravat and pearl pin, and the elegant linen Unmentionables had been replaced with boots that had seen hard service. Gone, too, were the flowing romantic curls that had aroused her father's scorn; cropped now and brushed straight back, they gave his head a harder, sharper outline, but the devilish peaked brows and bright, narrow eyes were instantly recognisable, as were the long, sunburned face and determined mouth. Ten years in Political Service had given him authority, an air of impatience tinged with the arrogance of a man used to having his needs attended to and his orders obeyed promptly. Even so, the years rolled back and she was a child again, watching him lean on the piano as her mother played, their voices rising together in *Greensleeves*, and the bitter twist of her father's lip under the red moustache. Memories crowded in: Mamma's melting glance up at him as they stood in the rose-scented dusk, her soft murmur, 'Ah, don't tempt me!'

It was not Mamma but Rohais he held so protectively now, yet Thea's heart filled with the same disturbing mixture of pity and exasperation. Was he blind? Could he not see that she was deceiving him?

'Well?' he said impatiently. 'I am waiting for an explanation.'

'Don't you know me, Dr Black?'

His glance was quick, indifferent. 'Should I?'

'Miss Dundas is cruel to me,' said Rohais plaintively.

'Rohais! That's not true!' said Thea, shocked.

'Miss . . . Dundas? *Thea*?' He stared at her, frowning, then nodded. 'Oh, yes, I remember you all right. Who would have thought of finding you here? Well, my dear, if you mean to make a career in teaching, let me offer a piece of advice. Kindness will produce better results than cruelty. I've seen enough bullying schoolmarms to know what I'm talking about.'

'I don't bully her!' she protested, but he was not listening.

'Come on, Rohais. You've done enough work for today.'

Without waiting for Thea's permission, he swept Rohais out of the schoolroom, leaving her governess with a bruised head and a strong desire to burst into tears.

She summoned servants to clear the mess, but before they had finished putting the room in order, the door opened and Mrs Quinn hurried in. She wore a becoming new hat and her face was flushed and animated.

'Oh, Miss Dundas! Will you excuse Rohais the rest of her lessons today?' she exclaimed, looking about her as if she expected her daughter to pop out of a cupboard. 'Where is she? I thought – '

'Dr Black insisted on cutting short her French lesson,' said Thea, steadying her voice with an effort. Mrs Quinn gave her a glance in which comprehension and annoyance were mixed.

'Very wrong of him. He has no business to interfere, and so I shall tell him. I am sorry, Miss Dundas. He can be very high-handed at times, and Rohais has always been such a pet of his. Never mind! Tomorrow you can see she makes up the work she missed today. Don't look so downcast, my dear,' she went on impulsively, taking Thea's hand and giving it a friendly pressure. 'Together we shall win through, I promise! Dr Black is on his way to Simla, to report on the negotiations between Ranjit

49

Singh and Mr Secretary Macnaghten for the invasion of Afghanistan. I have persuaded him to eat *tiffin* with us, so he can give us all the very latest news.'

At table the subject of Afghanistan dominated the conversation, despite efforts by Rohais and Charlotte to steer it away from politics and into matters of more immediate interest to themselves. Since everyone else was eager to hear what Dr Black had to say, however, they found themselves outnumbered.

Lord Auckland, India's new Governor-General, feared that the Czar of Russia planned to extend his influence towards the subcontinent. Recently there had been clear evidence that the Shah of Persia inclined towards Russia, and it was Lord Auckland's anxiety lest Dost Mahomed, ruler of Afghanistan, should also support the Russian cause that had given him the notion of invading that country before it succumbed to the Czar's blandishments. However, the only loyal ally on whom British India could count was the Maharaja Ranjit Singh, ruler of the Punjab, and even his support had its price.

For a year now, the Government in Calcutta had been hatching plans to oust Dost Mahomed from his throne and replace him with a former Afghan king, Shah Shuja, who had lived peacefully on a British pension in Ludhiana for the past thirty years. Though stout now and elderly, he was eager enough to accept British help to regain his throne, but since Dost Mahomed had been careful to give the British no solid cause for complaint, it was necessary to manufacture an excuse that would justify an invasion of his country.

The best brains in Calcutta had wrestled with this problem for months, but now Mr Macnaghten and his Assistant Secretary, Mr Torrens, had devised a strategy based on the long-standing enmity between the Afghans and their neighbours, the Sikhs. If Ranjit Singh could be persuaded to invade Afghanistan (so their argument ran), would it not be proper for his British allies to give him their support?

'Poor Mr Macnaghten!' said Dr Black, attacking his roast fowl with the zest of a man who has lived on curried goat for many moons. 'You should have seen his face when he learned the price of Ranjit Singh's co-operation! The Maharaja looks like a little old grey mouse, but there's nothing wrong with his wits. When it came to haggling, he ran rings round Secretary Macnaghten!'

'Did he get what he wanted?' asked Mrs Quinn eagerly.

'Everything! Troops, horses, money, jewels, and the title to Peshawar and Kashmir for good measure. You can imagine how pleased the Directors will be! However Lord Auckland chooses to gloss it over, the fact is that we'll be paying twice as much as Ranjit or Shah Shuja for the privilege of putting the old fellow back on the throne he lost thirty years ago.'

'Shah Shuja could hardly support an army on the pension we give him,' said Mrs Quinn, smiling at the doctor. Her cheeks were pink and her eyes shone. In youth she must have been handsome, thought Thea, and wondered at the enlivening effect Dr Black had produced on the ladies of the party. Rohais, too, was transformed. Her mouth had lost its sulky droop and she listened like an eager child. Charlotte's eyelashes fluttered as continually as her fan. She leaned across the table until her bosom nearly touched her plate in her efforts to capture his attention.

Thea's fingers itched for pencil and paper. She would call the sketch 'The Judgement of Paris', and represent Mrs Quinn as Minerva, Charlotte as Athene, and Rohais as Venus . . .

'Tell me, Dr Black,' breathed Charlotte dramatically, 'is there certain to be war?'

'In my opinion, yes. Torrens and Colvin are as set on it as the Secretary himself, and they have the Governor-General's backing. Between them I believe they will carry the day.'

'Then we must advance the date of our wedding,' said Charlotte importantly.

'Or delay it until the campaign is over,' said James.

51

Charlotte tossed her curls and looked offended.

Hastily Mrs Quinn enquired which regiments were to take part in the invasion, and good-naturedly the doctor began to list them. There would be a Bengal contingent and another from the Bombay presidency. Each would include a brigade of artillery and cavalry with one or two infantry divisions. The Company's European Regiment and several others of the Queen's Service would take part, among them the 16th Foot, the 3rd Buffs, and 13th Regiment of Foot.

'My father's regiment!' Thea exclaimed, forgetting that governesses should be seen and not heard.

'And mine.' James turned to her, charmed to discover this link in common. 'Oh, I am only seconded to the Shah's Service,' he added. 'My heart is with the 13th.'

'And your pension,' put in Rohais pertly, to general laughter.

My pension, thought James, cast into sudden gloom. If I marry Charlotte and am killed, *she* will have my pension to spend on her damned shawls and fripperies, little as she needs it. How much I would rather it saved Miss Dundas from a life of drudgery!

James had a susceptible heart and was easily moved by the plight of those who were down on their luck. Ever since hearing Thea's story, he had pitied her sad situation and wished it in his power to make her happy. Quite suddenly he found himself disgusted by Charlotte's plump prettiness, the complacent pout of her rosebud mouth and the fat white fingers on which his ring already looked tight. He could hardly bear to look at her simpering smile when she addressed him. How the devil did I come to ask her to marry me? he wondered. I must have been mad. She doesn't care tuppence for me, and the last thing I want is to be tied to her for life. How can I escape?

With an effort he switched his attention to the discussion of Lord Auckland's Army of the Indus.

'Eighteen battalions of infantry!' marvelled Mrs Quinn. 'Is that not excessive? A hammer to crack a nut?'

General Quinn, who rarely spoke at table, shook his

head and frowned. 'I don't like it,' he muttered in his usual hoarse whisper. 'I've read the Simla *Manifesto* that his lordship has been pleased to publish, and it is nothing but a pack of damned lies. Auckland should be ashamed.'

'You must agree, Father, that it's our duty to teach Dost Mahomed not to sully his hands with Russian gold,' said James doggedly, and the General gave his sardonic cackle of laughter.

'British gold, Russian gold – what's the difference? All food's the same to a starving man! The Dost would have supported us if we had given him the least encouragement, and he's a better man than Shah Shuja any day.'

'A luckier man,' agreed Dr Black, helping himself to a peach.

'Same thing,' grunted General Quinn. 'Once a loser always a loser. The Ghilzais say Shuja was born under an unlucky star.'

'Surely you do not believe in such superstitions, General?' enquired Charlotte archly.

He turned his grim scarred face to her, unsmiling. 'What I believe is neither here nor there, miss. It is what the Afghans believe that matters. If we force a king they do not want on them, how long do you suppose he will last once we leave the country?'

'Perhaps we could leave a regiment to support him?' suggested Charlotte, less certainly.

'Or two, or three, or four! You don't know the Afghans, Miss Charlotte. They won't stand and fight. Pitched battles are not their notion of warfare. But they'll slink back like wolves to harass you no matter how often you chase 'em away. They're good marksmen with those long-barrelled *jezails*. Lie behind rocks and pick off their enemies one at a time. Never waste a bullet.'

It was the longest speech Thea had ever heard from him. The young men exchanged glances. Trust Father to look on the black side, thought James, who was inclined to view the whole Afghan adventure as a lark. A lark – and a chance to get away from Charlotte's niggling and nagging.

Mrs Quinn's bright smile had faded. She imagined those slinking wolves of Afghans sniping at stragglers, ambushing lonely patrols and melting back into their bleak hills.

Dr Black caught her anxious glance and nodded. 'The General is right. It may be easier to get into the country than out of it,' he said soberly.

Mrs Quinn was as good as her word. Barely had Thea retired to the schoolroom with a borrowed novel at the conclusion of the meal, than Dr Black walked in unannounced.

'Sit down, Miss Dundas,' he said as she started up in surprise. He gave a short, exasperated laugh. 'Damn it, I can't call you Miss Dundas! Go on, Thea, sit down. I've come to apologise.'

He waved her back to the long wicker chair from which she had risen, dropping her book on the floor as she groped for the shoes she had just kicked off.

'Mrs Quinn has been hauling me over the coals,' he explained. 'She refuses to let me leave without making amends for my conduct this morning. No, hear me out! She tells me you were acting entirely according to her instructions and I should have taken the trouble to discover the facts before jumping to conclusions. In short, she has administered a thorough dressing-down and sent me here as a penitent to ask forgiveness for my unwarranted interference.'

He was laughing at her, she knew, but nevertheless she felt comforted that Mrs Quinn had vindicated her.

'Well, Thea? What do you say? Am I forgiven?'

'Of course,' she said, trying with one toe to locate its missing slipper. 'Really, there was no need – '

'Is this what you are looking for? Allow me.' He retrieved the scuffed old slipper from under the chair and knelt to slip it on her foot. She stared down at his dark head, embarrassed by his closeness. 'On the contrary,' he said, straightening up, 'even if Mrs Quinn had not sent me to apologise I should have felt compelled to get to the root of this affair. I cannot understand why you – or she – should find it necessary to use methods more suitable to a house of correction than a schoolroom in teaching poor little Rohais.'

She let the description pass, saying only, 'I wish I did not have to, believe me! If you can suggest some better means of teaching her to read and write, I shall be only too pleased to try it.'

'To *read and write?*' He looked astounded. 'My dear girl, Rohais is not simple-minded!'

'That is why it puzzles me that she has not mastered such basic skills.'

'Are you serious?'

'Of course I am!' she said with a flash of anger. 'Oh, she conceals it very cleverly, and her memory is prodigious, but the plain fact is that when confronted with a page of text she does not already know by heart, she can barely decipher it.'

His eyes searched her face, then he said quietly, 'If this is true, it is scandalous. How has she hidden this – this disability so long?'

'By persuading her governesses to conspire with her in concealing it,' said Thea rather bitterly. 'Because I will not do the same, she has taken a dislke to me and does all she can to get me dismissed.' Sensing that he only half believed her, she added, 'If only she would realise I am trying to help her, not to show her up as a fool! Mrs Quinn says she will listen to you. Could you use your influence to persuade her to trust me?'

He looked surprised, but said promptly, 'Of course. I will see what I can do. Have you told Mrs Quinn that Rohais cannot read?'

'Not in so many words. She knows she is backward, of course, and attributes it to laziness.'

'You do not agree?'

'No, for the effort involved in concealing her illiteracy is so much greater than learning to read could ever be.' He smiled at this logic, and she went on. 'Mrs Quinn tells me she must be taught to concentrate, but without co-operation from Rohais, it is like running my head against a wall.'

'So I imagine.' He rose with an air of decision. 'Very well. Leave it to me. Goodbye, Thea. I am glad to have made your acquaintance again, and I will call the next time we ride through Ludhiana. Meantime, I wish you better success.'

Thea never learned all that passed between Dr Black and Rohais that afternoon, but the result was satisfactory. When the girl entered the schoolroom the following day, her manner was subdued, even conciliatory.

'Good morning, Miss Dundas,' she murmured, and took her seat at the table, eyes downcast. It was plain there was something on her mind. After a moment's silent fiddling with paper and pencil, she raised her eyes and said penitently, 'I am sorry I was horrid and hit you. There! I've said it. And I will let you teach me to read, because Toby wishes it and he has promised me a new bonnet if I can read a story to him when next he comes here.'

Evidently bribery had played some part in her conversion, but Thea was too relieved to quibble.

Rohais said conspiratorially, 'He thinks his money is safe, but you will help me, won't you? I do so want a new bonnet.'

'Then we must waste no time.'

'How surprised he will be!' Rohais clasped her hands. 'Will you promise not to laugh when I make mistakes?'

'Why should I laugh? Everyone makes mistakes.'

'Good!' Rohais smiled winningly. 'Shall we be friends, then?'

'Of course,' said Thea.

CHAPTER THREE

Captain James Quinn tapped the red croquet ball smartly through the hoop and it came to rest against Thea's blue one. Cigar in hand, he strolled up to it, and bent towards her as if to examine its lie.

'Beautiful angel, I adore you,' he said in a low, passionate whisper. 'I can't live without you.'

'Hush!' She turned away to hide her confusion. His dark eyes surveyed her boldly while he went on whispering things that made her ears tingle. In all Mr Barnes's courtship, he had never mentioned love, let alone said he adored her. She felt out of her depth, troubled yet intoxicated by James's practised flattery.

'You must not say such things to me!'

'Why not, if they are true? I love and adore you. I am bewitched by you. What is wrong with telling you so?'

'Oh, please be quiet!' she begged, putting her hands to her hot cheeks. 'What if they hear you?'

'Don't worry.' He glanced over to where the other players were gathered about the last hoop. Rohais and Charlotte vied for position while Dr Black leaned on his mallet, talking to Mrs Quinn. James was a better player than any of them. Thea could not doubt that the series of muffed shots which left him behind with her had been intentional.

'Have you any idea how beautiful you are looking?' His eyes caressed her while the mischievous smile played about his mouth. 'Oh, say you'll marry me!'

'You know I cannot.'

'Why not? Don't you want to?'

There was nothing in the world she wanted more. It was cruel of James to tease her. She swung her mallet and hit the blue ball with more strength than judgement. It rose in the air, skimmed the irrigation channel, and landed among the onions.

She hurried to retrieve it, but James was quicker. 'Why can't you?' he persisted, holding it behind his back.

'Because you are engaged to marry Miss Green.'

'Is that all? Engagements can be broken, you know.' He spoke as if a broken engagement was of no more importance than a broken glass. Thea looked at him doubtfully. Surely he was not serious?

'You would not treat her so shabbily.'

'Would it not be far shabbier to marry her when I love you?'

'You are unkind to joke about such things,' said Thea in a low voice, turning away. He caught her hand before she could leave him.

'Joking? I was never more serious in my life. I love you, Thea. Don't you love me? Not even a little?'

She was saved from having to reply by an impatient call from Rohais. 'Hurry up, James! We've finished. We want to start a new round.'

'Miss Dundas has lost her ball.' Quickly he tossed it into a tangle of vines.

'Leave it there, then!' ordered Rohais imperiously. 'Come on, we're all waiting.'

'Shall I help you look for it?'

Hastily James dropped Thea's hand as Dr Black spoke close behind them. Neither of them had heard him approach.

'Strange how often balls go missing at this end of the lawn.' He poked his mallet into the vines. 'Ah, here it is. I am to partner Miss Dundas in the next round,' he went on, ignoring James's look of irritation. 'As you can hear, your sister is anxious to begin. Shall we join them?'

The game proceeded, but for Thea the pleasure had gone. How much had Toby Black heard? she wondered; and then, what am I to do about James? It was clear from Charlotte's angry glances that she suspected Thea of poaching on her preserves, and even Mrs Quinn addressed her with unusual sharpness, begging her to make more effort to keep up with the other players.

Having no wish to endure a lecture from Dr Black, she did her best, but her lack of skill soon told and inexorably the other couples drew ahead.

'I fear I am a sad handicap as a partner,' she said as yet again her ball stopped short of a hoop.

'Oh, croquet is merely a matter of practice. I don't suppose you played much at the Orphanage?'

'Hardly at all.'

'Then you will forgive me a word of advice?'

'Of course.' She could guess its drift, and was not surprised when he went on:

'It is this. Never permit young officers to make love to you during a game of croquet. It annoys other players, particularly ladies with a better claim to their affections.'

'I didn't,' Thea protested. 'I couldn't stop him.'

'Did you even try?'

'Of course I did!'

'Then you had better try harder or you will cause mischief you cannot undo,' he warned. 'My turn, I think?' He hit the ball and walked on.

She stared after him with a swelling, indignant heart. How dare he accuse her of mischief-making? She swung her mallet hard and the ball cannoned straight into Dr Black's, knocking it off course.

'Now look what you've made me do!'

'Good shot,' he said ironically.

The flash of her eyes reminded him piercingly of her mother. Toby bit his lip. It was quite illogical to blame Thea for that long-ago disaster, or dislike her because she reminded him of her father, but logic and love seldom run in double harness. He had adored Eleanor Dundas with the idealistic, uncritical passion of first love. She had befriended him, given him love and warmth and laughter, and shown him an aspect of womanhood very different from that of the grim spinster aunts who had reared him. All the pain of losing her had been revived by the sight of this daughter – this great lump, as Eleanor used to call her despairingly.

He stared critically at Thea's bent head, overloaded by its heavy coil of red-gold hair, at her opulent figure and the faint suggestion of overhasty dressing which put sensual thoughts into a man's mind. No beauty, yet she radiated the animal attraction of health and youth and vitality which was hard to resist. Before transferring to the Political Service his early experience doctoring malingering memsahibs and languorous *zenana* beauties had left Toby with few illusions. This girl was a natural troublemaker. Already she had set James at odds with his bride-to-be. Should he warn Mrs Quinn? Did she need any warning?

'Go on, hurry,' said Thea. 'We'll be left behind.'

'We'll never catch them now.' He forced a more agreeable note into his voice. 'I know your position is a difficult one, Thea, but I do urge you not to place any reliance on the things Captain Quinn whispers in your ears.'

'You think he did not mean them?'

'As to that, I have no means of knowing,' he said slowly, 'but you would do Miss Green a great wrong if you allowed yourself to take him seriously. I am sure you have too much sense to be deceived by mere flattery. Can you really suppose that Captain Quinn would give up Miss Green, with her fortune and her great connections, to marry a pretty face?'

Seeing her silent and crestfallen, he went on more kindly, 'I must congratulate you on Rohais's progress! She has won her new bonnet fair and square, thanks to you. I fear she found it too easy to hoodwink poor Miss Peabody.'

'Poor Miss Peabody!' she echoed with feeling.

'She was a shocking teacher,' he agreed. 'I suppose it was the only career open to her. I doubt if a man made her an offer in her life.' He smiled. 'You, on the other hand, will be besieged with proposals and will have to fight hard to preserve your independence.'

'I have little enough of that!' she exclaimed. 'If you had

spent even a day in my shoes, you would know that a governess is the most dependent of creatures.'

'Yet at least she does not pass her whole life under male domination. In that sense she is better off than most females.' When she did not reply, he added, 'This may be the last chance I have to speak with you for some months.'

'Why? Where are you going?'

Much as she resented the way he treated her as a child still, she had begun to look forward to his visits, which brought a whiff of the glamour of high places into their up-country lives, and kept them informed of the political manoeuvrings which would shape their futures. He was, besides, her own private link with her old happy world before the mango ice disaster. The news that he would be away for so long left her feeling vulnerable and rudderless.

He said in a low voice, glancing round to make sure no one was listening, 'Ranjit Singh is dying. God knows how he has lasted so long, ill-treating his body as he does, but this time it looks like the end of the road, and when he goes, all hell will break out in the Punjab. Sons, half-sons, grandsons – the classic recipe for trouble. Before his kingdom disintegrates, I must ensure that every one of his provincial governors on the road to Afghanistan is prepared to honour his pledge to let our troops pass safely through his domain. Without that, our campaign is doomed before it begins. Do you understand?'

She nodded, and he took her hand, saying, 'Promise me you will do nothing rash before I return?'

'Rash?'

'You know what I mean.' He would have said more, but a chorus of impatient shouts reached them.

'We must go,' she said. 'The others have finished.'

As they joined the rest of the party, James moved close to Thea. 'Why were you so long, my angel?' he murmured. 'Will you partner me again?'

Charlotte gave him an angry look. 'Miss Dundas seems in the habit of losing her ball when she plays with gentlemen,' she said in a tight, high voice. 'Perhaps if she

61

partnered *me* she might be able to keep up with the rest of us.'

But at that suggestion James refused another round. He had work to finish, he said, and begged them to excuse him.

At once Charlotte laid her hand on his arm and pressed him to dine at her uncle's house, but he refused with bare civility and departed abruptly, leaving his sister puzzled, Charlotte affronted, and his mother uneasily aware that all was not well between the engaged couple.

One sultry morning as the grip of the Hot Weather tightened on the great mass of tents and baggage, men and animals assembling in the dusty plains around Ludhiana, Rohais ran sobbing into the schoolroom. Her face was very pale, but when Thea took her hand to comfort her, it burned as if with a fever.

'James is a cruel beast and I hate him,' she wept.

'What has happened?' asked Thea, much surprised. James was a most forbearing brother and generally allowed his younger sister to order him about to her heart's content.

Nearly every day for the past month, after drilling his recruits he had made some excuse to visit the schoolroom during their last lesson of the morning, though lately these excuses had become so flimsy that Thea feared Rohais must guess at an ulterior motive. She knew she ought to forbid these interruptions, or banish him as soon as he had delivered his message, but the truth was that she had grown to look forward to them as much as Rohais did, and when brother and sister combined to cajole her, she was no match for them.

'Oh, let him stay,' Rohais would plead. 'The lesson is nearly finished.'

'But he distracts you.'

'I won't say a word, on my honour. I'll sit here quiet as a mouse until you set her free,' James would promise.

Of course he did not, and of course the lesson would end prematurely, with a good deal of chaffing and laughter. Then Rohais would skip away to change her clothes, and James would seize the chance to invite Thea to stroll with him in the shady garden.

Sometimes in the cool evening he would drive them farther afield – to the cantonments, perhaps, or the bandstand on the *maidan*, where they would listen to the native bandsmen playing English country airs in their own inimitable fashion. While Charlotte was in Simla, visiting her aunt, there was little fear of her displeasure at these harmless pastimes, and Thea was careful to ensure that Rohais was included in the party. Nevertheless, she was aware of playing with fire, not only on James's account, but also her own. It was so easy for him to distract Rohais's attention just long enough to slip his arm round Thea's waist, or plant a lightning kiss on her cheek, and no matter how often she told herself he was only amusing himself in Charlotte's absence, for her own part the affair was becoming serious.

His face came between her and sleep. Alone in her bedroom, tossing and turning through the breathless nights, she thought of him constantly. His smile, his bold dark eyes haunted her dreams. In the mornings when she rose, pale and headachy after long sleepless hours, she would resolve that *today* she would tell him this could not go on. Either he stopped his attentions to her, or she would go to his mother and say she had decided to resign her position. It was not fair on Charlotte or on herself to continue in this way.

Then, as the day wore on, her resolution would begin to waver. One more day, she would think. Just one more precious day of letting herself believe he loved her. All too soon Charlotte would return and their idyll would end. Thea was enough of a realist to know the power of money in adding to a woman's attractions. Two thousand pounds a year was a sum not lightly thrown aside, and however much James might sigh and murmur endearments to his sister's governess, he was not likely to jeopardise a match that would bring such solid advantage.

And yet . . . And yet . . . ! However rational she might

be by day, at night Thea could not help dreaming that he was telling the truth when he said he loved her and cared not a fig for Charlotte or her money.

Now she put a comforting arm round Rohais's shaking shoulders. 'Tell me what the trouble is, my love. What has James done to make you cry?'

'He has quarrelled with Charlotte,' said Rohais in tragic accents, and Thea's heart gave a sudden lurch, as if she had placed her weight on a missing step.

'I daresay that does not mean much,' she said as calmly as she could. 'Lovers often disagree, you know, and make it up later.'

'Not this time,' said Rohais with a small sob. 'I heard them. It was all James's doing. She – she asked if he had missed her, and why he did not answer her letters, and he said he had been too busy. Then she asked him to fetch her fan and – and he told her quite rudely that he was tired of running errands for her. He said she must find some other l-lapdog to fetch and carry. Then she took off her ring and threw it at him, and said she had been a fool to think of wasting herself on an ill-mannered wretch like him; and *he* said if there was one thing he could not stand it was a nagging shrew, and he must think himself lucky in his escape. Then Charlotte began to cry, and James said he was d-damned if he would stay there to be screamed at, and now the engagement is broken, and I shall not go to England to see the Queen, and my life is ruined!'

'Come, cheer up,' said Thea bracingly. 'You will have plenty of other chances to see England.'

'I shan't! I shan't!' Rohais worked herself into a fury. 'What do you know about such things? You are only a governess.'

'Only a governess,' repeated Thea slowly, and deep within her a tiny bubble of hope began to rise.

'Have I got ink on my face?' asked Rohais suspiciously.

'No.'

'Then why are you smiling?'

'I suppose because I feel happy,' said Thea, and closed her book with a snap. 'I mean to give you a holiday.'

'A holiday? Why? What will Mamma say?'

'I shall tell her you deserve one,' said Thea gaily. Rohais pushed back her chair, staring at her as if she suspected some trick.

'Why didn't you tell me you were going to give me a holiday?'

Thea laughed. 'Because I didn't know myself! Off you go! Make the most of it.'

Rohais took a couple of irresolute steps towards the door, which opened suddenly. On the threshold stood James, face flushed and dark eyes glowing. In his high-collared green tunic, frogged and sashed with gold, he looked excited and very handsome.

'Miss Dundas! I must talk to you.' He strode forward to grasp her hands, quite ignoring Rohais, whose eyes darted from one to the other with dawning comprehension.

'What are you doing here? Why did you say such terrible things to Charlotte? I shall never forgive you. James, answer me!' She caught his arm and shook it.

'Go away, Rohais,' he said absently, without even looking at her. 'I want to talk to Miss Dundas. Alone.'

'But – but you can't – '

'I said, go away. Now!' he snapped in a tone Thea had never heard him use to his sister, and taken by surprise, Rohais obeyed. As the door slammed behind her, James pulled Thea towards him, gripping her fingers so tightly she feared he would crush the bones.

'I've done it! Done it!' he said exultantly. 'You didn't think I meant it, did you? I've sent Charlotte packing. We can get married as soon as we please.'

'M-married?' The room seemed to whirl about her. 'What will your parents say?' she gasped, clinging to reality though her breath came fast and her heart had begun to hammer joyously.

'Leave that to me. All you've got to do is say Yes, and make me the happiest man on earth,' he said in a low, vibrant voice that set her pulse racing. 'Dearest Thea, don't keep me in suspense. Will you marry me?'

If Mrs Quinn was chagrined to lose her daughter's new governess so soon, she concealed her feelings bravely. Privately she might regret the manner in which James had broken his engagement – it was bound to offend Charlotte's influential uncle and might damage James's career – but above all she wished to see her only son happy in his marriage, and she had often doubted whether a girl of Charlotte's domineering nature would make him a suitable wife.

General Quinn agreed. 'Never does a man any good to live off his wife,' he grunted. 'Miss Know-all had you heel-roped, but you've cut loose just in time. Wish you joy, my boy.'

With the invasion of Afghanistan looming ever closer, the wedding was a hasty affair, but what it lacked in ceremony it made up for in gaiety, and for several days Mrs Quinn kept open house for crowds of well-wishers who gathered to drink the health of the bride and groom.

Ludhiana was crowded, pulsating with men and beasts assembling there to await their marching orders. The narrow twisting streets were thronged with every type of feature and shade of skin, and every garb, from the flamboyant uniforms of the Irregular Regiments of Horse to the Political Officers' sober morning dress.

James and Thea were not the only couple to hasten their wedding before the threat of war. A score of other brides did the same, and that last tumultuous month before the Army marched was filled with festivities and celebrations.

For Thea, trying to cram the joys of ever-after into a few short weeks, every minute had to be treasured, distilled into a precious essence that could be added drop by drop to the dreary oceans of loneliness ahead.

'If Miss Ellis and Miss Oldershaw knew how delightful love is, they would certainly forbid it,' she observed one drowsy afternoon, her cheek pillowed on James's chest, and he laughed so that the rumbling vibration throbbed through her ear.

'We must take care they never find out, though to be honest, my love, I think there is little fear of that.'

Thea smiled, remembering how they had looked, sitting in the front pew of the English Church, *in loco parentis* to the bride. From the corner of her eye she had observed their smirks and bows, and knew they regarded her marriage as a very fine feather in their overloaded hats. Magistrates' clerks and corporals of Horse were the sort of husbands they expected for their charges. A general's son was a dazzling catch.

Charlotte, too, had attended the wedding, head high, smile defiantly brilliant, daring anyone to whisper that James had jilted her – as they certainly would have had she stayed away. Instead, she had let it be known through the usual channels of ayahs to memsahibs, barbers to sahibs, that she herself had broken off the engagement, since when she had been besieged by hopeful suitors anxious to take James's place in her affections.

'Penny for your thoughts?' James propped himself on an elbow to lean over her.

'I love you. What shall I do when you are gone?'

'Wait for me to come back.' He yawned and stretched, and the echo in her ear was like a great cat purring. 'This war won't take many months. I'll be home before you can say Jack Robinson. God, look at the time! I'll be late on parade.'

She lay and watched him pull on clothes. There were so many things she wanted to ask, but he was always busy training his levies, playing polo, buying baggage camels and all the necessities that would be unobtainable in Afghanistan.

Too soon the honeymoon was over, and she was watching again as he packed his trunks, or, rather, interfered as Ahmed, slim, brown, and silent, padded to and fro packing them.

James stamped about the marble floors, opening shutters and closing them, picking books from the shelves and dropping them, unable to decide what he might need. He pulled folded garments from the tin trunks, examined them, flung them aside for patient Ahmed to smooth, refold, and replace.

Unperturbed, Ahmed checked the contents of boxes containing linen, china, silver and glass, and called the coolies to carry them away. Five camels, three horses and six bullock-*gharries* loaded with camp equipment were to accompany James to war, plus an elephant to carry his tents.

Thea watched him ride away at the head of his levies in their fine green tunics with white crossbelts, tall shakos and loose white trousers. He blew her a kiss as he passed the balcony where she stood with his parents and Rohais.

Mrs Quinn dabbed her eyes, Rohais waved and threw flowers, and the General snorted with contempt for the sleek young officers with their prancing chargers and burdened baggage animals.

'Damned fools of transport officers should be shot,' he muttered. 'Camels can't climb. They'll never get the poor brutes over the passes.'

'The 13th have two camels just to carry their cigars,' said Rohais mischievously.

'Damned disgrace. Call themselves soldiers!'

'James says any fool can be uncomfortable,' said Rohais, ignoring her father's frown.

Thea stood silently watching the waves of men and animals pass the length of the *maidan* and out through the city gates. Drums thudded and fifes squealed. Hoof, boots and bare brown feet scuffled in the dust until horses and marching men could only be seen through a reddish haze.

Next came the artillery, bullocks straining and bellowing as the guns rolled slowly forward, and then, at last, the vast sprawling assembly of pack animals, camp-followers and baggage waggons, jostled by women and children running alongside, cramming last-minute comforts into knapsacks, calling and sobbing as husbands, fathers, lovers and sons marched away. Only when the last of the straggling multitude was swallowed by the haze did Mrs Quinn lay her hand on Thea's arm.

'Come, my dear. You have been standing in the sun too long. We will go home now.'

Thea would have preferred to keep her secret to herself a little longer. Nine months is a long time to be under constant scrutiny, but if she had not conceived on her wedding night it must have been soon after, and in India there is no chance of hiding any change in the female condition. Servants' eyes note every detail and busy tongues pass on the information. Before she had been pregnant two months, everyone in the station knew of it.

Recurrent bouts of morning sickness did not improve her spirits. She moped, feeling sorry for herself all alone in the bed she had so briefly shared with James.

'I don't want you, baby,' she muttered, resenting the intrusion of the little stranger.

In April, when the thermometer soared, Mrs Quinn removed to Simla, as was her custom, taking with her both daughter and daughter-in-law. They left the General to sweat out the Hot Weather in the Plains.

'I like it,' he said obstinately when Kate begged him to accompany them. 'No damned dinners or parades. The Hot Weather is a perfect oasis of peace here, my love, and I wouldn't exchange it for the Simla Season for a raja's ransom.'

Twenty-six years of marriage had taught Kate the futility of trying to change his mind. 'You'd enjoy it when you were there,' she said, nevertheless.

'I should not. I should simply spoil your fun,' he said decidedly, and with a sigh she abandoned the argument.

The neat hill station amid its encircling snowy peaks was already bursting with visitors and throbbing with gossip when Mrs Quinn's party was carried up in the coffin-shaped litters known as *dhoolies*, in which it was impossible to find a comfortable position. Still, the change from the oven-blast of the Plains to cool, pine-scented breezes made these sufferings well worth while.

Every Hot Weather for the past decade Mrs Quinn had rented Ferndale, a sturdy, gabled house perched on a crag to the east of the town, with fine views to the distant snows. It was an uncompromisingly British haven of chintzy armchairs and polished wood floors, with bright log fires to ward off the evening chill, and Kate loved it.

The surrounding hillsides were thickly wooded, green with fern in many hidden dells, and beside the winding goat tracks grew tiny irises and mountain geraniums. Rohais was in her element. She had been coming here since she was a child, and knew all the best rides and picnic sites. Eagerly she renewed her acquaintance with dashing young aides on Lord Auckland's staff, as well as the many fashionable young ladies who had travelled up from their stations in the hope of snaring an eligible bachelor during the many open-air fêtes, balls, cosy dinners, concerts and all-day picnics for which Simla was renowned.

Time hung heavy on Thea's hands. Young women who joined too enthusiastically in the Simla gaiety while their husbands were away at the war were frowned on by Lord Auckland's sisters, the Misses Eden.

'Too absurd,' said Mrs Quinn. 'Why shouldn't you enjoy yourself a little?'

Thea felt too unwell to care that other matrons did not share her mother-in-law's liberal views. During the first months of her pregnancy, she felt quite incapable of making merry. Born and bred in the Plains, she soon found that Simla's altitude did not suit her. Between breathlessness and morning sickness, she had energy for nothing more strenuous than reading or sketching in Ferndale's pretty, tranquil garden planted with roses, delphiniums and sweet-scented mignonette, and dreaming about James.

He had warned her he was no great hand at letter-writing, but he did his best. Rambling screeds declaring his love arrived by nearly every courier during the campaign's early stages, and with them came scraps of military news as the Army marched down the line of the Indus and entered Scinde.

It was another month before the cumbersome force reached Afghanistan itself, and already the deficiencies of the commissariat had led to the troops being put on quarter rations. When Shah Shuja's contingent caught up with General Sir Willoughby Cotton's force, it found them in dire want of food.

His Majesty the Shah would prefer to live off the land and leave its inhabitants to starve, wrote James, *but Mr Macnaghten will not permit it. His Majesty grumbles, and complains he never had so much trouble and bother in his lifetime, which is saying a good deal since all his campaigns up till now have ended in disaster. He frequently refers to his subjects as a pack of dogs, but on the occasion of his entry into Kandahar, the dogs barked a hearty enough welcome to please him.*

Once the Army reached Kabul, whence Dost Mahomed had already fled to rally support in the hills, James's letters became more scrappy.

Compared to life on the march, our existence in Kabul verges on the humdrum, he wrote. *Buying a house, engaging servants, and arranging for supplies of the many commodities unobtainable locally are now our principal concerns, and to read of such dull matters would entertain you no more than it does me to write of them.*

All I need tell you is that I have a roof over my head, which I share with Mr Sturt, the officer in charge of engineering works, who is now engaged in building cantonments for the occupying force, since His Majesty the Shah resolutely refused to allow us – his deliverers! – to supplant him in the Bala Hissar, which is this city's only defensible fortress.

We have servants enough to attend to our needs, but since the Afghan merchant's notion of business is to cheat his customer for all his worth, I mean to learn enough Persian to 'frustrate his knavish tricks'! To this end, I have acquired a

slave boy, formerly the property of a band of ruffianly Ghil-
zais, who stole him from his family to sell in the Great Bazaar.
His name is Hinghan Khan and he cost me (after haggling)
the equivalent of six shillings. He is wretchedly dirty, but
Sturt assures me a good scrubbing will work wonders, and Sir
Alexander Burnes, the Resident, who is well acquainted with
these Afghan gentry, says he comes of a good family . . .

Thea smiled when she read this. It was typical of James
to find another lame dog to help over a stile. Evidently
the scrubbing had the desired effect, for a few weeks later,
he wrote:

Did I tell you I bought a boy for six shillings? He has proved
a sound investment and takes his duties as seriously as any
munshi. He allows no fault of grammar or pronunciation to go
unrebuked, and thanks to him my studies in Persian progress
well . . .

What a dear, kind fellow he was, she thought, and how
he would enjoy having a child of his own! The baby was
due in September, but there was no hope that James
would return in time for his birth. Already the military
expedition that the Army of the Indus had embarked on
so gaily had taken twice as long as forecast, and the end
was not yet in sight.

Daniel Alexander Quinn chose 15 September to make his
appearance in the world. As if to compensate his mother
for an uncomfortable pregnancy, his arrival caused the
minimum of fuss or difficulty. So trouble-free, indeed,
was the Happy Event that his aunt Rohais, who had spent
all day assisting with preparations for Miss Eden's Grand
Fancy Fair, was miffed to discover on her return to Ferndale that the drama was already over.
   'I thought only native women gave birth easily,' she
remarked, and then, peering into the crib, 'Oh, what a
fright he is!'

'Darling little hideosity!' said his doting grandmother. 'Look at those tiny hands.'

'Just like a horrid little old man,' said Rohais, and Mrs Quinn laughed.

'At that age *you* used to remind me so much of my father in one of his rages! He would throw his wig on the floor and stamp on it, and when you cried, you looked just the same.'

'What are you going to call him?' Rohais asked, displeased by this reminiscence. 'Daniel Alexander is such a mouthful.'

'Danny?' suggested Mrs Quinn.

'Sandy?' offered Thea.

'Dandy,' said Rohais. They all laughed, but Dandy he remained.

Mother and baby throve in the crisp air of the hill station, but when October brought frosts and a sprinkling of snow, Simla society began to disperse. The Governor-General departed with his entourage for Calcutta, and Mrs Quinn decided it was time to return to Ludhiana.

A steady trickle of Army wives had begun to pass through the station en route to join their husbands in the Afghan capital. When Thea broached the idea of attaching herself to one of these convoys, Mrs Quinn begged her to wait.

'James will send for you when he wants you,' she said. 'Wait until Dandy is a little bigger.'

'If I do not go before the first snow falls, I will have to wait until spring.'

'Would that be so terrible? Oh, I know it must seem a long separation to you, but be patient, my love. Next spring will be time enough to embark on such a journey.'

James's letters echoed his mother's view. The Afghan passes in winter were no place for a baby. She must not worry about him. His health was excellent and the city was quiet, though the Kabulis complained that bread prices had trebled. Sturt and he were well provided for. They could even look forward to hunting with the foxhounds which the 16th Lancers had been generous enough to leave behind them. Every week there were horse-races on the *maidan*, which the Afghans enjoyed mightily. There were also cock-fighting and wrestling matches to entertain the men.

It was likely that in the spring the Army would be ordered to withdraw, its mission accomplished. Meantime, she must give his love to little Dandy and be patient.

Thea reread the letters with a growing sense of unease. Where were the lover-like yearnings of his earlier correspondence? Clear through the careful circumlocutions and dutiful enquiries came the message: *Stay away.*

Had he tired of her? She remembered how rapidly he had transferred his affections from Charlotte to herself, and felt a chill of fear. Could he have fallen in love with an Afghan woman? Half-heard, half-remembered scraps of conversation came back to her: returning officers discussing the charms of the ladies of Kabul – and their availability. Sir Alexander Burnes, the Resident, was notorious for his liaisons with Afghan beauties. What if one of these haughty, slant-eyed charmers had captured James's all-too-susceptible heart?

Once this fear had taken hold, it was impossible to dislodge, but it was not one she could confide to her mother-in-law, still less to Rohais. Thea began to dream of black eyes beckoning from behind gauzy veils, of supple golden limbs and long dark hair. Who was she, this unknown rival? How could she unmask her?

From letters alone it was impossible to gauge the extent of the threat, but all Thea's feminine instincts warned that it was real. Yet what could she do? James disliked criticism as much as the next man, and she knew that accusations or reproaches would alienate him – that had been Charlotte Green's downfall. Nor could she learn anything from the returning officers who passed through Ludhiana. Their code of honour forbade any mention of a brother officer's indiscretions while on active service. If only I was there, I could do something about it, thought Thea, tormented by her own helplessness.

It was while she was in this unhappy frame of mind

that she heard that Mrs Quinn's old friend Florentia Sale, godmother to James, was travelling to join her husband in Kabul, and would be staying a week in Ludhiana on the way.

CHAPTER FOUR

'Florentia!'

'Dearest Kate!'

Skilfully avoiding a clash of hat brims, the ladies exchanged affectionate pecks. Mrs Quinn had not seen her old friend since General Sale had been rewarded with a knighthood for his gallantry during the invasion of Afghanistan.

'My warmest congratulations!' she exclaimed. 'Never was honour more deserved.'

The new Lady smiled deprecatingly. She was tall and though already past fifty and the mother of a dozen children, retained her rosy complexion, dark hair barely tinged with grey, and shrewd, snapping black eyes.

'Oh, you know Sale! Never happier than when he is in the thick of the fight. I tell him it won't do for a General, but do you suppose he listens? Quite incorrigible. They tell me he would have been killed for sure at Ghazni if young Captain Kershaw had not passed his sabre through Sale's assailant in the nick of time.'

'So you go to Kabul to keep him out of trouble?'

'My dear, I do not delude myself!' Lady Sale shrugged. 'If Sale chooses to fight like a private, there is nothing *I* can do to stop him. Still, I have a fancy to see Kabul, and by all accounts the Lughman Valley is a very Eden. Alexandrina and I are resolved on visiting it, come what may.'

She drew forward the pale, slightly built young woman with a cloud of fine, dark hair who had been supervising the disposal of various boxes and trunks. 'Do you remember my daughter, Mrs Sturt?'

'I am so glad to see you again!' Kate in turn drew Thea into the group. 'My daughter-in-law, Dorothea. Lady Sale. Mrs Sturt.'

The four exchanged smiles and bows. Thea looked with special interest at Alexandrina Sturt, with whose husband James shared lodgings. What might Captain Sturt have written to his wife? She found a pair of lively brown eyes regarding her just as closely.

'I feel I know you already,' said Alexandrina with a smile. 'Sturt often speaks of Captain Quinn in his letters. If you have anything you wish conveyed to him, I would be happy to take charge of it.'

Thea warmed to her friendliness. 'I wish I could come with you myself,' she said wistfully. 'Perhaps later, when Dandy is bigger . . .'

'Your baby? May I see him?'

In the shaded day nursery, Alexandrina bent briefly over the cradle where Dandy was sleeping, cheeks flushed and both small arms flung up behind his head.

'Forgive me,' she said, brushing away a tear. 'I lost my daughter last year when she was just that age.'

Despite her slender build, it was plain that before long the empty cradle would be filled again, and Thea marvelled at her determination to travel in such a condition. The thought must have shown on her face, for Alexandrina said a little defensively, 'Mamma did not wish me to come, but I told her I would certainly miscarry through fretting if she did not allow it! I am stronger than I look, you know.'

Indeed, there was something of tempered steel about her fragility, a touch of daredevilry in the jaunty set of her narrow shoulders. She put her arm about Thea's waist and together they descended the shallow flight of steps to the rose garden, where the older ladies were in animated discussion.

'Where memsahibs meet, the talk is always of black-spot!' murmured Alexandrina. 'Will you and I ever become so obsessed?' Impulsively she added, 'Change your mind and come with us to Kabul! Mamma and I will take good care of you.'

'My husband does not wish it,' said Thea unhappily.

'Not wish it?' The slim eyebrows rose.

77

'He thinks the baby too young for such a journey.'

'What nonsense! It makes no difference to an infant whether he is travelling or not, since he cannot stir from his cradle!' cried Alexandrina. There was a look of speculation in her eyes, and Thea's heart sank, believing she guessed the true reason.

The week-long visit stretched to two and then three as Lady Sale sought to replace her baggage camels with mules and 'tats' – the tough little native ponies which General Quinn advised her were better suited to Afghan terrain. Thea enjoyed Alexandrina's company, though she was a little in awe of Lady Sale, whose tongue was as sharp as her eyes. All the same, she was sorry when at last their transport arrangements were complete and they had no further reason to linger in Ludhiana.

Though it was more than a quarter of a century since she had first arrived in India, Mrs Quinn still regarded it as a treat to eat out of doors most days of the year, and in her household family tea beneath the spreading jacaranda was something of a ritual. For Thea, the mere sight of a white-draped table under a tree was enough to wake unhappy memories, and she usually contrived to miss this meal.

On the eve of Lady Sale's departure, however, this would have seemed churlish, so after playing with Dandy and watching his bath, she made her way across the shady lawn to where the ladies were grouped around the table, with General Quinn at its head.

A short while ago, a *cossid* had arrived with despatches, and it struck Thea even before she could distinguish words that the voices on the lawn were agitated, with the gruff staccato of the General's speech punctuating the ebb and flow of feminine chatter. As she approached, she saw a sheaf of papers lying beside his plate.

'I am sorry to be late,' she murmured, slipping into the place beside Alexandrina. All eyes turned towards her, and the expression in them frightened her. Anxious eyes, pitying and uncertain. The way people had looked at her after her family died.

'What is the matter?' she asked, dreading the answer.

Alexandrina had appeared to shrink away when first Thea sat down, but now she leaned towards her and silently placed an arm about her shoulders.

'My dear child, you must be brave,' said Lady Sale gravely.

'Why? What is it? Mrs Quinn – ?' With a shock of dismay she saw that her mother-in-law held a handkerchief tightly pressed against her lips, stifling sobs. The dreadful, half-guessed possibility grew into certainty.

'Has something happened – to James?' She appealed directly to her father-in-law, and after a momentary hesitation he nodded.

'Is he wounded? *Dead*?'

'Wounded.'

A sigh of relief escaped her, and as if to dash any false hopes he went on in his jerky fashion, 'Badly wounded. Set on by a party of Afghan ruffians, not five miles from Kabul. One of our patrols found him unconscious and brought him in.'

'Unconscious?'

Into the silence that followed, Lady Sale said briskly, 'Never mind what the doctors say, child. I've seen men right as rain after lying senseless for a week. Captain Quinn may well have recovered by now. That despatch has taken ten days to reach us.'

Considering the difficult terrain he had crossed, with the ever-present danger of attack, the *cossid* had made good time. Thea shivered. James might have died on any one of those ten days.

General Quinn was nodding. 'Doctors always look on the black side. It would take more than a crack on the head to kill James.'

'How badly is he hurt?'

'We can't tell exactly, my dear.' The General looked at Thea with approval. Thank God she wasn't going to faint or throw a fit of hysterics. 'Fellows attacked from behind. Good job his boy was with him. Raised the alarm.'

'I must go to him at once.' The words were out before

Thea even knew what she meant to say. To her surprise there was no chorus of dissent, rather the opposite. Alexandrina's arm tightened round her shoulders and Lady Sale nodded briskly.

'That's the spirit. See for yourself.'

'I only wish I could go with you,' said Mrs Quinn, putting aside her handkerchief and straightening her shoulders as if ashamed of her weakness. 'You'll leave the baby here, of course?'

Should she? After a short hesitation, Thea shook her head. 'I will take him with me.'

'Oh, but my dear, consider! He is too young!'

'Nonsense, Kate, the chit's right,' said Lady Sale in her downright fashion. 'Never does to separate mother and child. The sight of his son may be just what your boy needs. Don't you fret, child,' she went on, turning to Thea. 'You shall travel with us. We will delay our departure while you make preparations.'

Winter was closing in and a light sprinkling of snow lay on the great rampart of Afghan hills above the city of Peshawar when Lady Sale's party reached it after six weeks of struggling over the vile tracks that served for roads in the Punjab.

Peshawar was the most westerly of Ranjit Singh's conquests, and though the old Sikh Maharaja had died the year before, leaving his domains in turmoil, the city remained in Sikh hands, thanks to the determination of the Governor, General Avitabile, an Italian by birth and the most ferocious and ruthless of all Ranjit Singh's foreign mercenaries. Extorting taxes, imposing fines, hanging offenders and dealing out rough justice to Sikh and Afghan alike, he kept the turbulent border tribesmen in a state of submission and, through his system of watchtowers and patrols, continued to ensure the safe passage of British convoys from Hindustan to Kabul, just as Ranjit Singh had promised.

General Avitabile rode out to greet his visitors with Latin gallantry, begging them to stay in Peshawar as long as they wished. Tall and burly, running somewhat to fat, with a booming voice, strong, heavy features and deeply pitted olive complexion, he was treated by his retinue with terrified deference and, despite his jovial manner, Thea had no doubt his reputation had been well earned.

'A jolly ogre, but an ogre for all that,' murmured Alexandrina at her side. 'Did you ever see such a uniform?'

A gold-laced forage cap perched rakishly on Avitabile's thick greying locks, and his fiercely curling mustachios were stiffened and twisted like skewers. His barrel chest was tightly encased in a much-laced and befrogged Horse Artillery tunic, below which loose Turkish trousers of crimson silk drawn in at the ankle and a sabre slung from a wide golden sash completed his attire. Extraordinary though he looked, even Lady Sale – whose sense of the ridiculous was keen – felt no inclination to mock, and she allowed him to kiss her hand with becoming dignity.

'Thank you, Your Excellency. You are most kind. *Molto gentile*,' she said, bowing.

As they rode towards the city walls, the General surveyed their small escort with surprised disapproval. He urged them to remain with him until another convoy arrived to protect them on the last lap of their journey.

'Is no good in *montagna quand les grandes neiges tombent*,' he declared in the curious mixture of tongues that reflected his early career in Napoleon's army. '*Molto pericoloso. Mechant* mens in hills.'

Thea waited anxiously for Lady Sale's response. She hoped they would not delay, even though their men and beasts were tired after the wearisome march from Ferozepore, where loose sand had bogged the waggons to their axles and done nothing to improve the temper of the riding horses. Once again, Sarah Kennedy, nominally her companion and maid, was suffering from a low fever and unable to carry out her duties.

It had been only reluctantly, at her mother-in-law's insistence, that Thea had agreed to take Sarah. She would have preferred to rely on the services of her little ayah, fifteen-year-old Laila, and Alyosha, the baby's nurse. But

81

when Mrs Quinn developed a fixed idea she was difficult to resist, and she had been determined that Thea should not prove a nuisance to Lady Sale.

'Sarah will dress your hair nicely and look after your clothes. You will find her useful in all those small duties which native servants neglect,' she insisted. 'Believe me, my dear, it is absolutely necessary on an expedition of this kind to be able to call on the services of a woman you trust – if only for the well-being of your child.'

Thea did not trust Sarah. Even at the Orphanage they had avoided one another, too close in age and background to be anything but rivals. Thea's abrupt transformation from charity child to General's daughter-in-law had filled Sarah with bitter, corrosive jealousy. Despite her meek appearance, she was clever, ambitious and sly. It had been a blow to her when Mrs Quinn chose Thea as governess rather than herself. That post should have been hers, she thought, and it was easy to convince herself that had things fallen out differently, James would have been hers as well.

Nevertheless, Thea had eventually allowed herself to be persuaded. Sarah had joined the expedition, and a thoroughgoing nuisance she had proved.

'That gal of yours is no good,' Lady Sale told Thea after Sarah's complaints, petty indispositions and quarrels with the servants had plagued them all the way from Ludhiana to Amritsar. 'Ideas above her station. I know the kind. You had better send her back with the next military convoy. She'll never be anything but trouble.'

The threat of dismissal had reduced Sarah to such snivelling, grovelling wretchedness that Thea had relented.

'You'll regret it,' warned Lady Sale. 'You won't find it so easy to send her back from Kabul.'

'I know, but she has promised she will not trouble us any more,' Thea assured her; and indeed thereafter Sarah was careful to give no cause for complaint, but it did not make her like Thea any better, and she kept her eyes open for any chance to make mischief for her.

To Thea's relief, Lady Sale shared her impatience to

finish the journey, and declined the Governor's offer of a winter in Peshawar.

'You are very kind, Your Excellency, but we cannot put you to so much trouble. If we press on, we should reach Kabul before the winter snows.'

Avitabile frowned, shaking his heavy head. He eyed their small escort with contempt and muttered about '*Voleurs*' and '*Badmashs*'. Plainly he was equally reluctant either to send them into danger without proper protection or part with any of his own hard-pressed troops.

'Is better you wait. Convoys coming one, two weeks. Conduct you *sauf et sain*.'

'I fear we cannot delay that long,' said Lady Sale, polite but inflexible. 'Cannot Captain Macgregor, the Political Officer, provide an escort?'

Again the heavy headshake. Captain Macgregor was out leading a patrol against some rebellious tribesmen. Then General Avitabile's mood lightened magically. '*Bene!*' he exclaimed, striking himself on the brow so violently that his forage cap was knocked askew. '*Il Dottore* take you, *pas de problème*.'

'A doctor, Your Excellency, or a Political?'

'*Si, si!*' He nodded vigorously. '*E politico*.' With a strange sense of inevitability, Thea heard him add, 'Is name Blek. *Il Dottore Blek*.'

As Toby Black swung down from his tough hill pony two days later he was enveloped in a bear hug by the Governor, whose swarthy face wreathed in smiles hardly seemed to belong to the tyrant whom they had just seen ordering a dozen unhappy tax-evaders to be locked in a windowless dungeon. It was impossible to ride about the city without encountering bodies swinging from gibbets or grinning skulls stuck on pikes.

'*Pour encourager les autres*,' commented Lady Sale grimly when confronted with this evidence of the Governor's handiwork. 'One cannot approve such barbarity, but where would we be without him?'

Now, however, the General was in high good humour,

slapping Black's shoulder and calling him, '*Mon ami*'. He presented him to Lady Sale with all the satisfaction of a conjurer pulling a rabbit from his hat.

'Take you to Kabul, milady,' he said, beaming.

'We are very much obliged to you, Dr Black,' said Alexandrina in her gentle way, shaking his hand warmly. 'If you had not come to our rescue, I believe General Avitabile would have kept us here until spring.'

'He would have been wise to do so, Mrs Sturt,' Toby assured her. 'Summer or winter, the eastern passes are no place for women and children.'

Alexandrina raised her eyebrows. 'I thought the country was supposed to be settled.'

'*Supposed to be* is a long way from *is*,' said Toby, unsmiling. 'Let us say, Sir William Macnaghten would like to believe the country is quiet and the tribesmen satisfied with their new ruler.'

'You mean he is deceiving himself?'

'Oh, not himself alone. Sir Alexander Burnes is just the same.' He appealed to Avitabile. 'Generalissimo! How many rebels have you hanged today?'

The Governor shrugged and spread his hands. '*Vingt-cinq*? *Trente*? Who knows? I do not count.'

'And if you did not hang so many, what would happen?'

'*Mon ami*, you know as well as I!'

Toby nodded. 'Our supply lines would be cut and every convoy coming up from Hindustan would be plundered. And yet Sir William can persuade himself that General Avitabile is too severe, and a softer approach would make the Ghilzais our loyal supporters.'

'Macnaghten is three parts a fool,' observed Lady Sale dispassionately. 'I have often remarked that the *cleverest* men are the worst judges of character, particularly native character.'

'*D'accord!*' boomed Avitabile. 'You are quite right, milady.' They looked at one another with approval.

Toby turned to Thea, taking her left hand and examining it with a familiarity that made the colour rise in her cheeks. 'I see I might have saved my breath. You wasted no time in putting on the golden shackle! So now you are coming to Kabul to compound our problems, eh?'

'I am coming to look after James,' she said, snatching her hand away. 'Why should that trouble you?'

An interesting question, he thought, and I'm damned if I know the answer. Why should I trouble myself about this tiresome chit, who makes it all too clear she is determined to go her own way whatever I may say? I have only to make a suggestion for her to do the opposite. I should wash my hands and let her go to the devil as she pleases.

Aloud he said, 'Non-combatants always add to the problems of fighting men. So you have come to tend your wounded hero? Odd that he said nothing of it to me.'

'Oh, when did you speak to him? How is he?' she asked eagerly.

'He'll live, I don't doubt.' He gave her a measuring look. '*Does* he know you are on your way?'

She was obliged to admit he did not. 'I want to surprise him,' she explained.

'Is that wise? Surprises often rebound on their makers,' he warned, but she shook her head vehemently.

'He will be so glad to see us! As soon as I heard he was wounded, I could not bear to stay in India a moment longer. I made up my mind to leave at once, and Lady Sale was kind enough to let me join her.'

'But my dear Thea, you must give him some warning at least,' said Toby, who was very far from certain that James – or, indeed, any man – would welcome the sudden appearance of a wife he supposed to be hundreds of miles away. 'He will want to make arrangements for you. I will send a *cossid* ahead of us to announce your coming.'

'Oh, pray do not! That would spoil it all,' she exclaimed. 'Please, Toby! What do I care for arrangements? They can be made later. Lady Sale!' she appealed. 'Persuade Dr Black not to send word to James. I do so wish to surprise him!'

'Are you lost to all notions of chivalry, Dr Black?' Lady Sale's smile held a hint of roguery. 'How can you resist such a plea?'

General Avitabile, too, took Thea's part, declaring her secret arrival 'Molto romantico', and even gentle Alexandrina begged Toby not to be a spoilsport. Assailed by their scolding and beseeching, Toby eventually consented – albeit reluctantly – to respect Thea's wishes.

'On your own head be it, then, but I think you are making a mistake. In Captain Quinn's place, I would certainly wish to know you were coming.'

However, neither the ladies nor the Governor agreed with this prosaic view, and when the small company set off at last on the final leg of their journey, James was still unaware that the rest of his family was on its way to join him in Kabul.

Glad though she was to be on the move once more, Thea felt a strange oppression settle on her as their small convoy wound slowly up the rough road of rock and shale towards the dark mouth of the Khyber Pass that marked the beginning of Afghan territory. Behind them in the plain, Peshawar's gilded domes glittered in the sunlit distance, but as the mighty cliffs closed over their heads, making noon dark as midnight, her spirits were clouded by a sense of fear and foreboding.

In this she was not alone. The towering rockfaces that loomed on either side, with rivulets streaming down their greenish-black flanks, were in places no more than fifty yards apart. The gloomy chill of the place oppressed man and beast alike, and the column marched in near silence, broken only by a camel's groan, a neigh from the tough native ponies known as *yabus*, or Dandy's fretful whimpering.

'Teething, I expect, poor mite,' said Lady Sale, taking a thoughtful look into the cradle. 'I think it is so hard that the moment a baby conquers the colic, he becomes a martyr to his teeth.' She rummaged in her reticule and produced a small lump of red, doughy substance, no bigger than a nut. 'Opium,' she said, giving it to Thea. 'I keep it by me to ward off aches and pains. Tell your ayah to rub it on his gums, and it will soothe them.'

The treatment took rapid effect. Dandy's whimpers ceased and he fell heavily asleep.

The following night they camped on a dry flat ledge above a stream, having sent a strong party of Afridis ahead as an advance guard, and doubled the pickets about the tents. Thea slept badly, troubled by a persistent headache behind her eyes and a feeling of dread she could neither rationalise nor dismiss. Was it the dismal and sinister gorge, where only a thin sliver of starlit sky could be seen between the sheer black cliffs whose impenetrable shadow formed so perfect a cover for an ambuscade? Or had her uneasiness another cause which instinct recognised before reason?

Several times in the night she rose and lit a candle, holding it close to the face of her sleeping son, but although his cheeks were flushed he breathed softly and steadily, and she could find no good cause to rouse him or the snoring ayah who lay with head muffled and legs bare, Indian-fashion, across the threshold of the baby's tent.

At length, as a reluctant grey light began to filter into the gorge, Thea fell asleep, only to be roused by a nervous plucking at her bedclothes and Alyosha's frightened whisper.

'Memsahib, come quick, quick! Baba not waking.'

'Not – not waking?' she repeated fuzzily. As the words sank in, she started up in alarm from under the heavy sheepskin *poshteen* which she had bought in Peshawar at the Governor's insistence. Though crudely cured and smelling strongly of its original owners, it provided better insulation than half a dozen blankets, and served equally well as cloak or bedcover.

Now she pulled it round her shoulders and asked: 'Did you give him more opium?'

'No, Memsahib,' said Alyosha dolefully, following her mistress through the dividing curtain. Dandy still slept in his cradle, but since Thea had last looked at him the rosiness of his skin had become a hectic flush. When she touched his brow it was damp and radiating heat. Breath

87

wheezed and rattled in his small chest; it needed no medical training to see he was seriously ill.

'Run and ask the Doctor-Sahib to come quickly! Hurry!'

Alyosha moaned and pattered away. Thea picked up the sleeping baby and cuddled him against her shoulder, but his eyes remained shut. Increasingly agitated, she paced up and down, frightened by her own ignorance. What did she know of babies? Scraps of ill-digested information teased at her brain. Scarlet fever, blackwater fever, measles, cholera, typhoid, malaria . . . The list of India's killer diseases would fill a book, and any one of them might snatch her precious baby away. With shame she remembered how she had not wanted him. Now he was her most precious possession.

Restlessly she tapped her foot. Why didn't Toby come? It must have been ten minutes since Alyosha had gone to find him.

'Wh-what's the matter?' Shivering and yawning, her sallow face puffy with sleep, Sarah pushed through the curtain.

'Find Dr Black!' said Thea breathlessly. 'Dandy is ill – look at him! I don't know what's wrong. It came on him so suddenly.'

Sarah bent over the cradle, then laid her hand briefly against the baby's flushed brow. 'Burning!' she exclaimed, and turned worried eyes on Thea. 'What can we do?'

'Find Dr Black!' It was all she could do not to stamp with impatience.

'But he's not here. Don't you remember? He left before dawn to go up to Ali Masjid's fort. He is going to ask the provincial governor for a bigger escort.'

She was right. Thea felt as if a chasm had opened at her feet. Ali Masjid's fort crowned the steep hill on the far side of the gorge, its squat towers just visible across the intervening jumble of broken cliffs. To reach it was a three-hour climb at least, and if Toby had left before dawn . . .

'We must stop him! Send someone after him!'

'Who would go?'

They stared at one another in perplexity. No Afridi would undertake such an errand, and none of their own people knew the path.

'Alidad Khan, the *jemadar*, is still here,' said Sarah doubtfully. 'Dr Black said he was too old for the climb.'

'Send him to me.'

For once Sarah did not argue, but hurried to find the dignified old Pathan. Alidad Khan eyed the baby's hectic colour, stroked his hennaed beard, and agreed there was no time to lose. He knew another path that led to the fortress. Though steep and dangerous, it was shorter than the one the Hakim-Sahib had taken. He would go at once.

He salaamed gravely, hitched up his robe to leave his sinewy legs bare, and set off uphill with the long, tireless stride of a mountaineer.

Thea watched him out of sight, then returned to hang over the cradle where Dandy's laborious breathing seemed to grow louder every moment.

'Sponge him with vinegar and water,' advised Lady Sale, arriving in haste with her clothes half buttoned. 'Courage, my dear. Babies often recover as quickly as they fall ill. If we can reduce the fever he will be easier.'

They tried all the standard remedies, waving smelling salts and burning feathers under his nose, patting his back, even trickling a teaspoon of brandy into the corner of his mouth, but he remained comatose.

'Stop! You will choke him,' said Thea, in agony to see her baby manhandled. The flame was burning low. Presently it would flicker and go out . . .

An hour dragged by and then another. Unable to bear the sight of Dandy fighting for life, Thea told Sarah to call her if his condition changed, and went to sit on a rock from which she could see the track towards the fort. After a time, Lady Sale joined her and they sat in silence.

'If any man can scale those heights in time it is Alidad Khan,' said Lady Sale at last. 'I heard he once outran a mountain goat for a wager, and caught it by the horns.'

But would he return in time to save Dandy? The

unspoken question hung between them, and behind it loomed one even more difficult to confront. Even if Alidad Khan delivered his message in time, would Dr Black turn back? Would he put the safety of the convoy at risk for the sake of an ailing baby?

Mahomed Abdullah, the Mir of Dusht, was an irascible old brigand, hand in glove with all the cutthroats in the area and inclined to stand on his dignity with the British who passed through his territory. By now he must have seen Toby's approach and prepared his welcome. He would certainly take offence if his visitors withdrew, and would probably refuse to supply the armed escort they needed.

'Do not blame him too much if he does not come back,' said Lady Sale quietly, but with another worried glance at her watch.

Thea nodded, knowing in her heart that she would never forgive him. She raised her eyes again to scan the path, but nothing moved on the thin line of lighter grey against the black rocks.

'Mrs Quinn! I think you should come.' Sarah stood in the tent's entrance, a look of anguish on her plain, pale face. Silently Thea rose and hurried to look in the cradle.

Dandy's mouth gaped open as he struggled to draw air into his lungs. The hectic flush had gone and now his skin had a waxen look, with blue-tinged lips. Holding the candle close, Thea saw that the back of his throat was clogged with a greyish mass that looked like sodden parchment. She recognised it; in the Orphanage, more babies died from diphtheria than any other cause.

'I feared as much.' Lady Sale was beside her, looking sombrely at the gasping baby.

'He's dying,' said Thea in agony. 'What can we *do*?'

'Nothing.'

A death sentence. Thea's sight blurred. With no clear idea of what she meant to do, she picked up Dandy and carried him outside the fuggy tent into the bitter, clear air.

'Please, God, don't let him die!'

90

She hugged him tightly, willing him not to leave her, and the baby moaned faintly.

A rough hand grasped her shoulder, spinning her round. 'Where are you going? Give him to me.'

Toby's face was streaked with sweat and dust, his chest still heaving from the downhill dash. She looked up at the wall of rock and saw the rest of his party, tiny as ants above them.

'You came,' she said on a sigh, and surrendered the small, limp body.

'In here.'

Dandy breathed in shallow gasps, lying on the bare table of the dining tent with Sarah, shaking but resolute, holding his shoulders and Lady Sale his feet.

'Take Mrs Quinn away,' said Toby, choosing a small, bright knife from his instrument case. He made a swift incision at the base of the baby's throat and Thea gave a muffled scream.

'Mrs Sturt,' grated Toby, without glancing up from his task, 'be so good as to take Mrs Quinn outside. At once!'

'Come, my dear.' Alexandrina pulled her firmly out of the dining tent. Outside in the grey, cold morning, Thea burst into tears.

'I thought he would never come. I thought Dandy would die.'

'Trust Dr Black,' said Alexandrina softly.

'I must go back!'

'Wait here a while. They will call us.'

Gradually Thea's sobs died away. She stared blindly before her, exhausted by emotion, as the other members of Toby's party descended the final slope and came towards them. Two carried a crude stretcher made of poles and a blanket on which lay a long, covered bundle.

'Alidad Khan, God rest his brave soul,' said Alexandrina quietly as they passed, and Thea turned to her in horror.

'*Alidad Khan?*'

'I fear so. The climb broke his heart. They are taking

his body to Peshawar.' Seeing Thea's stricken look, she added quickly, 'You must not blame yourself.'

'But I do. I must,' said Thea in a low voice. 'I sent him to his death.'

'He would have said it was the will of Allah.'

But what would Toby Black say? Thea remembered his affectionate teasing of the stately old man who had shared a dozen tight corners with him.

'Memsahib! Come quickly.'

She started up at the call, and found both Alyosha and Sarah bending over Dandy's cradle. Though dreadfully pale, he was alive. Even with a hollow reed still protruding from the base of his throat, she knew the immediate crisis was over.

'A miracle!' she said softly.

Overwhelmed with relief, she knelt beside the cradle and offered up the most heartfelt prayer she had ever addressed to God.

She opened her eyes to find Sarah watching her intently, her expression a curious mixture of envy and disapproval.

'Where is Toby?' she asked, rising.

'Dr Black has gone to his tent.'

'I must speak to him. Stay here with Dandy until I come back and call me if you are worried.'

'You can't go like that!' exclaimed Sarah, scandalised not merely by the impropriety of seeking out a man in his tent, but doing so in a stained dress that had seen better days and hair still in its night-time braid.

'Why ever not?'

'Your hair!'

'He's a doctor. I expect he has seen worse,' said Thea with a glimmer of a smile. 'I won't be long.'

Sarah watched her walk quickly across the encampment to Dr Black's tent, which was pitched a little apart from the rest. She would not have dreamed of speaking to any man looking such a scarecrow, particularly not Dr Black, around whose handsome person Sarah's love-starved heart had begun to weave romantic fantasies. Had he not complimented her on her assistance just now, and said he wished all nurses were as brave and as dextrous? She treasured the words, and thought it too bad of Thea to thrust herself on him at such a moment. She hoped he would send her away with one of his sharp rebukes.

Karim, his bearer, came to the tent flap, and a moment later Dr Black also appeared, wearing loose native robes, evidently interrupted at his toilet. His expression was forbidding, and Sarah waited with pleasurable anticipation for Thea to be repulsed.

But greatly to her disappointment, on seeing his visitor Dr Black's grim face relaxed. Without a word, he put an arm round her shoulders and, as she leaned against him, sobbing, he pulled out a large handkerchief and gently wiped away the tears.

CHAPTER FIVE

James trotted his sweating chestnut mare through the archway and old Mustafa, his syce, ran out to catch the reins.

'What of the game, Sahib?' he asked with the freedom of one who had saddled ponies ever since his master had worn short coats and ridden in a basket-chair.

James grinned through the dust coating his face. 'Would we let those dogs of Dragoons beat us?'

'God is great!' exclaimed Mustafa, whose arrears of pay had ridden on the result. James slid to the ground and stayed for a moment leaning against the pony, his hand straying to the broad shaven stripe across the back of his head.

'The Sahib is weary.' Mustafa eyed him anxiously, and James dredged up another grin.

'Just a trifle. Rub her down well, my son, for she gave us the winning goal.'

He strolled off stiff-legged across the courtyard. Mustafa was right. He was tired. That damned sabre-cut had taken its toll. Sometimes his head ached so much he thought it would split apart, but he couldn't have allowed that conceited young whippersnapper Gregory to take his place in the team.

Mellow evening sunlight slanted across the tiled roofs surrounding the courtyard. The house he and Sturt had rented from a Kabuli nobleman was a handsome two-storied building constructed as a hollow square round several courtyards. It presented a blank, unwelcoming wall to the street, reserving all its charm of tinkling fountain and intricately carved wooden shutters for the interior.

Two sides of the principal courtyard were given over to stables, domestic offices and servants' quarters; a third formed the *zenana*, with fretted marble screens through which ladies could peep at the bustling world outside; and the fourth was composed of a series of large, high-ceilinged, well-proportioned apartments where the men of the household took their ease.

James's eye roved over the heaps of boxes and trunks in the outer court, and appraised the tired baggage animals feeding and sleeping through the arch. So the old dragon's arrived at last, he thought with an inward laugh. I was beginning to think the snow would beat her, but nothing much ever beats Lady Sale! I must mind my P's and Q's tonight, or my mother will be the first to hear of it. Well, that's the last of Sturt's time at Liberty Hall. Can't pretend I'm altogether sorry. These bachelor messes are always the same. Begin as the best of friends: 'Do just as you please, old chap! Treat the place as your own.' Then, after a month or so, you begin to wonder if he's pulling his weight and paying his fair whack, and before half a year has gone, you can hardly bear the sight of the fellow. Even his voice sets your nerves on edge.

He and Sturt hadn't reached that stage yet, but they were headed that way. Not a bad fellow, but Lord! how he did prose on about those damned cantonments he was building! To hear him, you'd think no one had ever constructed a barracks before. First he didn't like the site, said it was overlooked by other forts and impossible for cavalry on account of all the gardens and irrigation channels in the orchards; then he tried to have Shah Shuja turned out of his own fortress, the Bala Hissar, but the old fellow had dug his toes in and refused to budge.

Next Sturt had discovered there wasn't room for the commissariat stores within the walls he was building, and there was hell to pay over that. From the way he carried on, you'd think the Afghans were going to rise up tomorrow and murder their English friends in their beds!

Well, now Sturt could take his wife and his mother-in-law to the new quarters he had rented near Mahmood Shah's fort, where he would be better placed to supervise all his precious building works; and I, thought James with

95

a grin, will continue to enjoy myself in my own fashion without his disapproving eye on everything I do.

His spirits rose at the prospect. He ran up the few steps from the courtyard to the hall humming a Pathan love-song, and collided with a small tornado running full tilt in the opposite direction.

'Sahib!' cried the boy, picking himself up and making his salaam in a graceful, fluid movement. 'Did we win? Why were you so long?'

James half-closed his eyes and assumed a teasing expression. 'Ho, Worthless One! What if I said we were beaten?'

The boy drew himself straight and his eyes flashed. He was a slender, handsome youngster with the high cheekbones and aquiline features of the mountain tribes-men. He had a haughty expression, long, heavy-lidded eyes, and skin of a remarkable ivory pallor.

'Beaten by those jackals? Truly, you would deserve to die!'

'Spoken like a true savage,' said James, his smile broadening as the boy's hand moved to the jewelled dagger in his sash. 'Calm yourself, my lad, I was only teasing. We won, all right. Beat them hollow.'

If he expected congratulations, he was disappointed. Hinghan Khan nodded as if he had known all along, and gave his master a sly, sideways glance. 'If you had lost I would have been angry,' he said softly in Persian. 'I would have punished you.'

'Would you, indeed?' said James thoughtfully. 'And how would you have done that, my little man?'

'Some way. Many ways.' Again the sly look. 'The Mem-sahib has come,' he said, elaborately casual.

'So I see. You had better be on your best behaviour while she is here, or you will find yourself back in the slave market before you can say knife,' said James warn-ingly. 'The Burra-Mem can be a tartar at times.'

'She is very ugly,' said Hinghan Khan with sudden venom. 'She looks like a devil.'

96

'Oh, I say, that's a bit hard. She's not a bad old sort. Always used to tip me when I went back to school.'

'I do not speak of the old one,' said the boy scornfully. 'It is the young one who has hair like a devil.'

'Has she?' James frowned, trying to recall Alexandrina's colouring. It was years since he had seen her, but he thought her hair was dark. He could hear the murmur of female voices in the salon and the chink of china.

'Cut along now,' he said to Hinghan Khan. 'Time I made my salaams.'

Instead of obeying, the boy fell at his feet, clasping James's knees so that he could not move and gazing up at him with urgent supplication. 'Promise me you will send her away soon, Sahib! I beg you, do not let her stay here.'

'She won't stay long, Foolish One,' scolded James, half irritated and half amused. 'She and her mother and Sturt-Sahib are moving to that house by Shah Mahmood's fort – I told you so.'

'But the other one, Sahib? What of her?'

'She'll go with them, of course,' said James impatiently. 'Let me go, or it will be the worse for you.' He aimed a blow at the head of the boy, who grinned and ducked. James shoved him aside and strolled forward to stand in the door of the salon.

'Ah, there you are, Quinn,' said Sturt genially, and three bonnets turned simultaneously in his direction.

Lady Sale, bronzed as a gipsy, her dark eyes shrewdly observant.

Alexandrina Sturt, tiny, radiant with smiles, scarcely able to tear her gaze from her husband's face, and –

'Thea!' exclaimed James. 'What – what the *devil* are you doing here?'

'James!'

She jumped up to run to him, but instead of hurrying to clasp her in his arms, he moved a pace backwards, hands hanging by his sides, blood draining from his face.

'A chair!' ordered Lady Sale quickly. 'Hurry. He's going to faint!'

Sturt and his bearer were across the room in a flash, steadying the swaying James, guiding him to a chair and forcing his head between his knees.

Lady Sale rose majestically and subjected her godson to a brisk scrutiny. 'My dear boy, you should know better than to play polo with a cracked skull! A child would have more sense. Off to bed with you at once! You can hear all our adventures after you've had a good sleep.'

Sturt gave orders, and James was borne away with Thea following behind, horrified by the effect of her surprise. She wished now she had listened to Toby's advice and sent word of her coming, but it was too late now: the damage was done.

As they entered the large, light bedchamber, a boy glided quickly from behind the mosquito-netting that shrouded the bed, like a cat surprised in the master's armchair.

'Who are you? What are you doing?'

She put out a hand to detain him as he sidled away.

'Well? Answer me!'

'Captain-Sahib telling to wait,' he said softly, eyes on the floor.

'On his *bed*?'

With the dent in the cover clear proof of recent occupancy, he could hardly deny it. He shrugged gracefully. 'Waiting very long, Memsahib.'

'Who *are* you?' she insisted, and then, as the explanation suddenly came to her, 'Oh, I know. You must be Hinghan Khan.'

He tilted his chin, looking her in the face with veiled insolence. 'The Memsahib knows of Hinghan Khan?'

She did not care for his manner. Clearly James had indulged him more than was good for him.

'You can go now, Hinghan Khan,' she said firmly. 'Your master will give you orders in the morning.'

He hesitated, and just then James opened his eyes. Seeing her by his bed, he smiled uncertainly.

'Sorry, my dear. Not much of a way to greet you, eh? I'm still as weak as a kitten. Didn't want to miss the

98

match. Should have told me you were coming. I'd have come to meet you . . . '

'It's all right, my love.' She took his hand, thankful that he had not questioned her decision to come. 'Now I am here to look after you, you'll soon be strong again.'

He held her hand for a while, then released it, saying, 'Is Hinghan Khan there? I'd like him to read to me.'

The boy came forward eagerly, drawing a book from his robe of richly embroidered brocade sashed with a wide gold cummerbund. She guessed his age at eleven or twelve, the soft contours of childhood fining into young manhood, and already a faint shadow of down on his jaw and upper lip.

Thea put out a hand. Reluctantly he surrendered the slim volume bound in tan leather.

'I will read to you.'

'You must ask Hinghan Khan for Persian lessons first, my dear.'

Was he laughing at her? She glanced down, saw the flowing, indecipherable script, and returned the book to Hinghan Khan with a sigh. At once the boy squatted on his heels close to James's pillow, and began to read in a low, soothing monotone.

Thea felt excluded.

'I'll come back later,' she said, but neither of them responded. Quietly she left the room.

For James's sake, Thea tried to establish good relations with Hinghan Khan in the weeks that followed, but the boy remained aloof, faintly hostile and, when he dared to be, insolent. She felt that he resented her presence, and was all the more conscious of this when Lady Sale left to join her husband the General in his quarters near the Shahbagh, just across the road from the Mission compound. A week later, Captain Sturt and Alexandrina removed to their new house near the fort of Shah Mahmood.

As soon as they were alone, James began to criticise her decision to join him in Kabul.

'Why could you not wait until I sent for you?' he demanded.

'Would you have sent for us?'

'Of course, when I considered it safe.'

'Other officers think it safe enough for their wives and children, and so do the men,' she said, fighting her disappointment at finding herself unwelcome. 'I wanted to be with you. Is that so strange?'

'If you wish to live in your husband's pocket, you should have married a clerk, not a soldier,' he said shortly. 'Oh, spare me, I beg!' as her eyes filled with tears. 'You are here now, and I hope you are satisfied.'

It was a shock to find him so changed from the warm, loving bridegroom she remembered, but she could not doubt that both his moodiness and the violent headaches he suffered stemmed from the sabre-cut that had so nearly ended his career. There were times when he seemed his old happy-go-lucky self, but at others he was cold and distant, or flared into sudden rages which reminded her all too vividly of Rohais.

'You must not expect miracles,' Toby Black told her bluntly, calling on her after riding up from Peshawar with reports from General Sale. 'Given the severity of the injury, I think he has recovered well, but you should face the possibility that he will never again be quite as you remember him. Head wounds have strange effects.'

'*Never?*'

Seeing her look of dismay, he said quickly, 'I've come to ask if you'd like me to take your letters when I return to Peshawar. They will be safer with me than with a convoy, since the Ghilzais have taken to plundering our columns.'

'But we pay them to give our goods free passage!' she exclaimed.

His smile twisted. 'It would take more than a few lakhs of British gold to stop the tribesmen pursuing their age-old custom! Imagine how they must feel, seeing mule-loads of treasure carried through their barren hills. It's like dangling bones in front of starving dogs.'

100

'What was that fellow doing here?' demanded James, on his return. 'You want to watch your step with the Black Doctor. He's too thick with those light-fingered Ghilzai gentry for my taste.'

'What do you mean?'

'To put it bluntly, he tips them off when there's a convoy of gold coming up to Kabul, and they help themselves.'

'Why should he do anything so terrible?'

'To guarantee his own safety, of course.' He eyed her speculatively. 'Why do you think Toby Black is the only Political who can ride to Peshawar and back without being attacked?'

She hated his suspicions; hated, also, the tiny seed of doubt he planted in her own mind. It *was* strange that Toby was never harassed in his comings and goings, and his remark about dangling bones before starving dogs had implied a degree of sympathy with the Ghilzais.

'I don't believe it,' she said. 'He is a doctor. That's why the tribesmen let him pass. They know they may need him some day. You told me yourself that Dr Hopkirk and Dr Brydon have never been molested by Afghans.'

'Brydon and Hopkirk don't have Black's opportunities for intrigue. They're regimental doctors; he's a Political,' he said truculently. 'I warn you, Thea, keep that fellow at arm's length. No smoke without fire, you know.'

He put a hand to his head, a sure sign that one of his migraines threatened, and she let the matter drop. Why should they quarrel about Toby Black?

Lady Sale, too, had noticed how cool a reception her godson had given his wife, and feeling herself in some sense responsible for Thea's presence in Kabul, she invited her to a picnic at the tomb of the Mogul emperor Baber, on the side of the Khoja Sufur hill overlooking the Four Villages and the Kabul River, a site the emperor had selected as the most beautiful spot in all his dominions.

'Do come,' she urged. 'We can sketch the marble

mosque built there by Shah Jehan. I know you will admire its elegance.'

Already she was an expert on the archaeological curiosities of Kabul, but even while absorbed in sightseeing and other excursions, she kept her ears open for gossip, particularly gossip affecting Sale's young officers, and disturbing accounts of friction between Captain and Mrs Quinn had reached her and been duly noted. Florentia never shirked her responsibilities.

As she and Thea settled at their easels, with the tomb's fine walls in the foreground and a background composed of the soaring snow-capped peaks of Taghau Sufi, she set herself to uncover the trouble.

'Migraine? Moodiness? Very trying for you, my dear, but you must be thankful he is no worse. Sale tells me they feared at first that he would never speak again. You must count your blessings.'

'Oh, I do – at least, I try to. But he seems so unhappy. Almost as if he wishes I had not come here. I don't know what to do.'

'Try to see his point of view, my dear. It is natural that he should not like you to see his weakness. Men are so proud – the absurd creatures!' She regarded Thea thoughtfully, and said with tact, 'It is always bad for a young man to be underemployed, and James is such a good officer. Sale thinks very highly of him. I understand he means to put him in charge of supplying the commissariat – he says that Afghan boy will be useful to him as interpreter. Such a little peacock he looks in his silks and jewels! You must not let James spoil him.'

'He owes his life to Hinghan Khan,' said Thea with some constraint.

'And the boy exploits his gratitude, no doubt.'

Thea sighed assent and Lady Sale said vigorously, 'Moral blackmail! You must not stand for it. These Afghans are as acquisitive as jackdaws. I suppose young Hinghan Khan takes his tithe from all the merchants who supply your household?'

'Does he? I don't know.'

'You watch him,' Lady Sale advised. 'You will soon see the measure of his private transactions. I know his kind! He is probably richer than James.'

She had put her finger on a sore point. Money was a perpetual cause of friction between them. James complained that his household expenses had trebled since Thea arrived, and she could hardly persuade him to give her enough money to pay the servants.

'He finds it difficult to live on his pay,' she admitted.

'He would live on it more easily if he was not buying jewels for that boy,' said Lady Sale caustically. 'Don't let him slide into debt, my dear. It is the ruin of so many young officers. Shall I ask Sale to speak to him? No one has a better understanding of money problems. He was in and out of debt a dozen times before I took him in hand!'

'Oh, no!' said Thea hastily. 'There is not the least need to worry Sir Robert.' How well she could imagine James's fury if he traced a dressing-down by the General to her interference! She had said too much as it was. He would accuse her of 'blabbing to the old dragon', as he disrespectfully referred to his godmother, and withdraw still further into his shell.

Not even to kind Lady Sale could she bring herself to confide her deep, chilling fear that James's love had been no more than infatuation, dazzling her with the sudden brilliance of a shooting star, and as quickly turning to ashes. His moodiness and headaches were the symptoms, not the cause, of a deep unhappiness. He felt guilty because he no longer loved her, and reacted by snapping and snubbing her, just as he had done to Charlotte when her attraction for him waned. The more she had cajoled and clung, the further he had withdrawn.

It will be the same with me, thought Thea wretchedly. What a fool I was to believe I could hold him when she could not! It is not in his nature to love one woman for long. A new star will beckon, and the old one grow dim in comparison. Toby tried to warn me. He knew what

James was like, but I would not listen, and now I must live with my mistake.

Was it too late to blow life into the embers of his love? Should she cling on here where she was not welcome, trying to rekindle his passion, or was it better to acknowledge defeat and go back to India, as he so clearly wished she would, leaving him free to enjoy his military adventure without the shackles of domesticity?

Either way, she risked losing him – if she had not lost him already. She picked up her pencil and began to draw with rapid, agitated strokes, though the graceful lines of Shah Jehan's white marble mosque were half obscured by tears.

It required only the minimum of detective work to convince Thea that Lady Sale was right: Hinghan Khan was using his favoured position to ensure that a proportion of the money involved in every household transaction stuck to his slim fingers.

If another servant wished to speak to James, he must first approach Hinghan Khan, who would decide, according to the bribe offered, whether or not to promote his cause. Merchants, too, paid Hinghan Khan when the Captain-Sahib purchased their goods, for they well knew that if they withheld his tribute he would find fault with the merchandise and the Captain would take his custom elsewhere.

It was easy enough for Thea to find this out, but far more difficult to persuade James there was anything wrong in it.

'Of course he takes his cut,' he agreed. 'Time-honoured custom, you know that as well as I do. I assure you he earns it. If I had to deal with every merchant who comes here trying to sell corn to the commissariat, my life wouldn't be worth living. I can trust Hinghan Khan to sort the sheep from the goats.'

'The sheep being those who pay him most?'

James's thick brows drew together. 'Do you really begrudge a trifle of *dashur* to the boy who saved my life?'

'The servants complain that he makes them pay before he will allow them to speak to you. If they refuse, he says you are too busy to see them.'

'Really, Thea! I wish you would not listen to servants' gossip! Can't you see they are jealous?'

'I can see they have good cause to be.'

'You should not interfere in matters that are none of your business,' said James, and rose abruptly. 'I'm off to poor Captain Morrison's auction. I wanted to bid for his wine, but now it looks as if a few cigars will be all I can afford, now I have so many mouths to feed.'

'Why are we always short of money?' she risked asking. 'Is it only servants' gossip that you spend half your pay on jewels for Hinghan Khan?'

James flushed darkly. 'Who told you that? It's a damned lie.'

'Those pearls he wears. Mrs Anderson said you outbid the Shah's agent for them.'

'That woman is a mischief-maker. I wish you would choose your friends more carefully.'

'Is it true?'

'I see you have been making a study of my extravagances,' he said petulantly. 'What else have you found to reproach me with? Since you are evidently determined to quarrel, let us have everything in the open at once.'

'I *don't* wish to quarrel with you,' she cried. 'Oh, James, what has gone wrong? We can scarcely exchange a word without some disagreement.'

'That is hardly surprising, since you have changed so much. I never thought I'd find myself married to a scold.'

'A – a *scold*?' she said, shocked.

'At times you sound worse than Charlotte.'

As he spoke, she saw herself through his eyes, and realised with dismay that he was right. She *had* changed, and not in a way he liked. No longer was she the vulnerable governess who blushed at his compliments. He had never asked her to come here and ask awkward questions, offer unwelcome opinions, criticise his behaviour. No wonder he resented it.

105

'I am sorry,' she said with an effort. 'I don't mean to interfere or – or scold. Truly. Of course you are right to reward Hinghan Khan for saving your life. All I ask is that he should treat *me* with a little more respect. It is not only servants who gossip, you know.'

Something moved behind his eyes. For a moment he was silent, and she dreaded an outburst of wrath. Instead, he surprised her by placing his hand on her shoulder and saying quietly, 'Why, Thea, you should have told me this before. Has he shown you any disrespect? It is too bad! Leave it to me, my dear. I'll teach the young monkey to mind his manners.'

'Oh, do not be too hard on him,' she said, fearing to make matters worse.

'Tell me exactly what he has done, and I'll see it does not happen again.'

Thus challenged, she found it difficult to cite any particular instance. 'It is his manner,' she said lamely. 'He behaves as if I have no right to be here.'

'Does he, by Jove,' said James thoughtfully. 'I'll soon make him change his tune.'

He left the room before she could reply.

Sir Alexander Burnes, the British Resident in Kabul, had chosen, like James, to live in the throbbing, bustling heart of the city near the Chandon Chowk, or Great Bazaar, rather than join his fellow-countrymen in the Mission compound two miles outside the city gates on the road to Jellalabad.

The former palace he had dignified with the title of Residency was large and handsome enough to satisfy the newly knighted Burnes's idea of his own importance and to entertain his many friends, both British and Afghan.

It was hardly surprising that Sir Alexander had a high opinion of himself, for although he was only twenty-six years old, his career had been meteoric. Since arriving in India in his late teens, he had travelled widely in Persia, Bokhara, and Afghanistan. He spoke and wrote Persian fluently, and knew far more about the wild regions of

Central Asia and their inhabitants than his superior, the Envoy, could ever hope to. Sir William Macnaghten's working life had been spent among Government offices in Calcutta, and he was no linguist.

The talk of the Residency, and indeed of all Kabul, one morning in the spring of 1841, concerned the appointment of a new Commander-in-Chief to replace fat, genial Sir Willoughby Cotton, who had been recalled to India. Would it be a Company man this time, or would Lord Auckland follow his usual practice of handing the command to some long-in-the-tooth Queen's officer with more breeding than ability?

'General Nott would be my choice,' declared Captain Sturt, whose frustrating experiences as Engineering Officer in charge of building the new cantonments had soured his opinion of the present High Command. 'He's a crusty old stick, I grant you, but his heart's in the right place.'

'Not a hope, old fellow. Not a hope,' groaned Captain Colin Mackenzie from the other side of the long table. As one of the Envoy's ADCs, Mackenzie was always first with the news. 'Have you ever listened to Nott on the subject of Politicals? Hates the lot. Macnaghten would never work with him, though I agree he'd be the best man for the job. Ten to one, he'll be passed over in favour of some Queen's officer with political connections. Care to bet on it?'

James looked up from his devilled kidneys. 'Don't touch it, Sturt. He knows already!' he said with a grin. 'Come on, Colin, out with it. Who are they sending us?'

Thus challenged, Mackenzie grimaced. 'Damn you, James, for spoiling my game. I was going to propose long odds against Sir William Elphinstone – '

'*Elphy Bey*? You can't be serious!'

'I only wish I wasn't.'

All along the table eyes turned towards him in stunned disbelief.

'Why, he can't have seen active service since Waterloo!' said Sturt disgustedly. 'Must be sixty if he's a day, and a martyr to gout. No, Mackenzie, you must be mistaken.

Even Lord Auckland would draw the line at sending old Elphy Bey to command here.'

'There's no mistake,' Mackenzie assured him. 'I heard it at Headquarters. If His Lordship had been through the Army List with a fine-tooth comb he could not have chosen a worse man for the job. He is the most incompetent soldier to be found among general officers of the required rank. I knew him in Calcutta, and such a ditherer you never did see. He could change his mind fifty times between *chota hazri* and *tiffin*. Order, counter-order, disorder.'

'My brigadier won't like that,' observed James, adding scrambled egg to the mound on his plate and moving up the table to sit beside Mackenzie. 'Shelton likes everything cut and dried, and he has the devil's own temper when he's crossed. If you are right about Elphy Bey, we must look out for fireworks.'

Just then their host, Sir Alexander Burnes, came in, plump cheeks aglow after an early ride. His lively dark eyes lit up with pleasure to find his friends at breakfast. 'My dear fellows! Good of you to drop in. Have you heard the news?'

'Tell us it ain't true!' begged Sturt.

'It's true enough.' The Highland lilt in Burnes's voice grew more pronounced. 'He'll take over the command next month. Brigadier Shelton's gnashing his teeth, and Nott is sulking in his tent like the Achilles of Kandahar. His Majesty the Shah is graciously pleased to approve the appointment – that's to say, he knows he has no choice in the matter – and the Envoy is busy writing memoranda to prove that whatever happens, he is the only person not to blame.'

'And you?' asked James curiously, and Burnes grinned.

'Oh, you know me! I don't give a fig for the Envoy. If he would go quietly back to the fleshpots of Hindustan and leave me in charge here, all would go well, Elphy Bey or no.' He helped himself largely from the dish of grilled chops the servant was offering and twinkled across the table at James.

108

'Good to see you here again! How does the lovely Mrs Quinn take to Kabul life?'

'Well enough,' said James curtly, and mischief danced in Burnes's eyes.

'Lets you off the lead now and then, does she? Will she allow you to attend my *nautch* in honour of Aminullah Khan tonight?'

'I'd like to see her stop me,' growled James.

'That's the spirit! Keep her breeding, my dear fellow, and she won't have time to meddle in your pleasures.'

'Why do you keep the Memsahib here? You told me you would send her away soon,' said Hinghan Khan peevishly as they rode away from the Residency. 'We were happy before she came.'

'Patience, my lad. We'll be happy again, never fear. Next week I go on patrol, and you shall come with me.'

'Patteroll is men's work,' said Hinghan Khan, his face clearing magically. James felt his own spirits lift. A few weeks in the hills would do them all a power of good. There was nothing like a forced march and a skirmish to make men forget the shackles of domesticity.

Suddenly light-hearted, he urged his horse to a canter and lifted him neatly over a trestle piled high with sacks of pulses and dried fruit.

Hinghan Khan whooped with delight and tried to follow, scattering the stall's contents.

'Infidel dogs!' The furious trader bared yellow pointed teeth in a snarl. He flung wide his arms, appealing to his comrades. 'How long must we suffer them? Is Dost Mahomed dead, that there is no justice?'

A low growl greeted the words. The Dost might be languishing in exile now, but before his surrender he had trounced the British cavalry at Purwandurra, and what he had done once his favourite son, Mahomed Akbar Khan, might do again, when he had gathered his strength in the western hills.

When the British Mission first marched into Kabul, the Afghans had been overawed by reports of their military might, and believed that if they submitted quietly the conquering *feringhis* would soon tire of occupying their bleak, poverty-stricken land and return to Hindustan.

Eighteen months later, to their dismay, the occupying force had been increased fourfold as women and children poured up from India in a never-ending stream. Taxes were high, the price of bread had rocketed, and still the sahibs showed no inclination to leave. From the highest to the lowest Afghan, resentment was growing, and familiarity with their conquerors was rapidly breeding contempt.

Thea was aware of surly looks and muttered insults as she ventured into the lofty splendour of the Great Bazaar one sunny morning in April, but she was too happy to care. The months of jarring discord between her and James were over. Hinghan Khan now did her bidding without complaint, the trees were bursting into blossom all round the city, and best of all, she was going to have another baby.

Her object in visiting the bazaar, with Sarah in reluctant attendance, was to find a christening present for young Thomas, son to her friend Mrs Anderson and her husband the dashing Major who commanded the Shah's Irregular Horse. As godmother elect Thea wanted a special gift, and she roamed ever deeper into the maze of alleys behind the wide central passage where Indian silks, cashmere shawls, furs of every description, Chinese porcelain, weapons, jewels, and even articles of European manufacture were displayed in tempting abundance.

Sarah was nervous, constantly glancing over her shoulder to make sure of the way out.

'Do let's go back,' she urged. 'I don't like the way they stare at us. I am sure they mean mischief.'

'Let them stare.' Thea pushed forward. Wherever they moved, they were ringed by a mass of bodies packed so tight it was hard for their bearer to clear them a passage.

Sarah shivered. The dark, flashing eyes and fierce hawkish faces of these Afghans were so different from any

110

native of Hindustan. These were bold, insolent ruffians who swaggered and postured and made chopping, stabbing gestures. Their hostile meaning was easy to interpret without knowing the language.

'They are telling one another that we are shameless hussies to show our faces here,' said Thea with a half-laugh.

Sarah moaned. 'Oh, I knew we should not have come. I told you we should have waited for Captain Quinn to escort us.'

'We might have waited a month. You know how busy he is.' Thea gazed about, and her eye lighted on a small silver drinking-horn set with garnets and turquoises. 'The very thing! Wait here while I strike a bargain.'

Sarah sighed and tapped her foot. When Thea returned in triumph with her prize, her companion was too anxious to be gone to make even a pretence of admiring it.

Sarah led the way back, retracing their route down the Street of the Harness-makers, past the silversmiths, whose tinkling hammers fell silent at their approach, and round the corner to the alley where spice merchants sat cross-legged in tiny cubby-holes, surrounded by great heaps of red powdered chillies, yellow turmeric and virulent green henna powder, all ready for weighing out in shiny brass scales and highly polished measures.

She hurried past the long row of barbers, who suspended their shaving, haircutting, tooth-pulling and whisker-trimming operations to stare and whisper rude jokes in their customers' ears as the memsahibs hurried by.

'We turned right at the basket-makers, and right again before that lane with those horrid butchers' shops . . . ' Sarah muttered, peering to right and left like a ferret in a rabbit warren.

'Look, there's the legless beggar. Over there! Don't you remember? We passed him on our way in.' Thea tossed a coin into the outstretched palm and took Sarah's arm, pushing on with renewed confidence. The crowd parted to let them through, and suddenly the sky was blue overhead and they emerged blinking into the sunshine.

After the noise and bustle of the bazaar, with its strong smells of spices, ordure, roasting meat and vegetable putrefaction, the crisp air blowing down from the mountains tasted as cleanly invigorating as champagne. Snow had vanished from the Kabul valley, though it still glittered in a dazzling rim round the bowl of hills surrounding the city. In its place, great drifts of fruit blossom – peach, plum, cherry, almond, apple and pear – covered the adjoining orchards like a pastel quilt. Knobby vines had begun to sprout fresh greenery in every trellised courtyard, and snow-water rushing along the open drains hid, under a sparkling surface, the nameless horrors washing to their last resting-place in the Kabul River.

'Come on, we must hurry,' said Thea, as the wail of the muezzin floated across the city. 'The christening is at four, and I must not be late.'

The present was wrapped, the litter-bearers waiting and Thea ready dressed when James rode into the courtyard and handed his reins to the waiting syce. She flew down the steps to meet him.

'Where have you been? We'll be late!'

'Late for what?'

'Little Tom Anderson's christening.'

'Oh, Lord! I'd clean forgotten.' He put his hand to his head, thinking, then said apologetically, 'Make my excuses, will you?'

'I can wait while you change.'

'I haven't time. We've been ordered out on patrol.'

Thea tried to hide her fear. 'How long will you be away?'

'Oh, just a week or so, I expect. There is trouble in the Lughman Valley. Those damned Afridis feeling their oats. The Envoy wants a full report.'

She could see he was pleased at the prospect of action. 'Promise me you'll take care?' she begged, and he laughed, quite in his old open-hearted way.

'I wouldn't be much of a soldier if I did!' He came closer, putting his hands on her shoulders. 'Don't worry, my dear! Lightning never strikes in the same place twice. Now off you go, and tell Mrs Anderson I am sorry I can't be with you. She'll understand.'

It was only two miles to the cantonments. Her litter-bearers jogged over the main bridge that spanned the Kabul River, and ran through the city gate, then down the long straight road flanked by gardens and orchards to the junction opposite the Shahbagh, or King's Garden.

Here the right-hand branch of the road led back north-west to the great stronghold of the Bala Hissar, where Shah Shuja kept his state. Straight ahead lay a group of three small forts, separated by a line of trees from Sturt's still unfinished barracks, which were set on a low-lying piece of flat ground between the road and the river.

The Mission compound was home to most of the married officers and their families, but here a disappointment awaited Thea, for young Tom was unwell, and Mrs Anderson had decided to postpone his christening.

She met Thea at the gate, her plump, pretty milkmaid's face drawn with worry, and Mary, her small daughter, clinging to her skirt.

'I am sorry! I would have sent a chit to stop you, but this morning he seemed better,' she explained. 'I consulted Dr Hopkins, and he advised me to put off the christening, to be on the safe side.'

'Never mind,' said Thea. 'I am glad to come, christening or no. May I see my godson? Is he asleep?'

Together they gazed into the basket where little Tom lay well swaddled, with just one tiny fist escaping from the shawl. Gently Thea replaced it. 'How small he is!' she said, smiling. 'It's hard to remember that Dandy was once that size. Is he good? Does he sleep well?'

As the bearer brought tea and small sweet cakes, they embarked on a long, satisfying conversation revolving entirely round their offspring which would, Thea knew, have bored James and Major Anderson to tears.

'I must go,' she said at last, with a guilty glance at the clock. 'James has to leave on patrol at dawn.'

113

'Come again soon!' said Mrs Anderson, embracing her warmly, and stood waving until the litter was out of sight.

Leaning back on the cushions as the homeward-bound *dhooli*-men jogged along the road, Thea wished her imagination did not conjure up such vivid pictures of the kind of trouble there might be in the Lughman Valley. Did James know she spent sleepless nights whenever he went out on patrol, visualising the dark, unfriendly hills with their human wolves waiting to ambush *feringhi* stragglers, every rock concealing a sharpshooter, every smiling, bearded face masking blackest treachery . . . ?

All was quiet in the house as she hurried down the cloister that led to James's study. She expected to hear him stamping about, shouting at Ahmed and tossing garments out of bags, but instead there was utter silence.

The study door was ajar, but on the threshold she hesitated. He did not encourage intrusion into this private sanctum. As she stood irresolute, she became aware of a curious quality in the stillness, a tense expectancy that told her the room was not empty. Somewhere close at hand, perhaps behind this very door, someone was standing with wide eyes and straining ears, just as she was, waiting for a footfall, a rustle of cloth. Waiting to pounce.

Her nostrils caught a familiar whiff of cigar mingled with the faint muskiness of pomade. Why should James be hiding behind the door of his own study? Was he trying to catch a pilfering servant red-handed?

Stealthily she began to retreat, but before she had gone two yards a sudden scuffle on the other side of the door confirmed her guess. There was a gasp, a grunted curse, and the quick pad of bare feet.

'Got you!' exclaimed James triumphantly. Then she heard the unmistakable high-pitched giggle of Hinghan Khan.

Mystified, she peeped round the door. James must have been roused from his bed, for his legs and feet were bare and a loose white shirt seemed to be his only garment. Even so, he was more conventionally dressed than Hinghan Khan, who wore half a dozen pearl necklaces and nothing else at all. His slender body glistened with oil, and his dark, unbound hair streamed down his back as he twisted and turned in James's grip.

'Now I've caught you and I'm going to punish you.'

Again Hinghan Khan giggled. It did not seem to Thea that he was trying very hard to escape; he sounded more excited than frightened.

Perhaps, she thought confusedly, James is only pretending to be angry. Perhaps it is just a game.

The intertwined bodies swayed briefly apart, then locked together again. James bent his head, pulling the boy's mouth against his own, and suddenly Thea saw, with a feeling of sick horror, just what kind of a game it was.

Respectable Englishwomen pretended ignorance of such matters, though the rows of long-eyed, painted boys plying for custom under the arches of the Great Bazaar made it difficult to feign total ignorance of love, Afghan-style. Like every Army wife, Thea had heard of officers who had succumbed to their blandishments and had to resign their commissions, or men who had been caught and flogged for consorting with Afghan boys. Now the shock of discovering her own husband in the same situation gave her the sensation of stepping on a rock tilted over an abyss.

Small things that had puzzled her dropped suddenly into place. How could I have been so blind? she thought, and then, with a stab of fear, does anyone else guess – or know? James had hardly bothered to hide his infatuation. She felt appalled by his recklessness. Discovery would mean the ruin of his reputation and career.

Shock numbed her emotions. Only later would pain follow as the extent of his betrayal sank in. Fear of a rival for his love had brought her to Kabul, but the truth was worse than anything she had imagined.

Sick at heart, she saw James lift the boy and carry him to the bank of cushions outside the circle of lamplight. Now he had only to glance sideways to see her.

Hastily she stepped back. Her heel caught in her hem

115

and she put a hand against the door to save herself. It swung inward, and the movement drew James's attention.

For a long moment they stared at one another. The greedy, furtive excitement faded from his face, leaving it frozen in a mask of guilt. He stretched out a hand in a gesture that begged for . . . what? Understanding? Forgiveness?

With a choking cry, she whirled round and fled to her own room.

'It will never happen again. I swear it.' He stood before her, stiff-legged and white to the lips. Thea could hardly bear to look at him. She would have given anything to blot out the memory of what she had seen, but the image of entwined bodies was imprinted on her brain. Even when she closed her eyes it remained.

'Has it happened before?'

He bowed his head in silence.

'You will have to send him away,' said Thea, and he glanced up quickly, a stricken look in his eyes.

'I can't. It would be signing his death-warrant. His people would kill him for consorting with us. Oh, Thea, please try to understand! I didn't mean to love him. Truly! Sometimes I think I even hate him.'

'Then for God's sake – *why*?' she said in anguish.

He put his face in his hands. 'He has stolen my heart,' he said in a muffled voice. 'I can't help myself. Even that first day in the slave-market, wearing filthy rags and crawling with lice, he bewitched me. I wanted him. Can't you understand?'

'No,' she said bleakly.

He hardly heard. The fever of confession was upon him. He sat down, resting his elbows on the table and pressing his fingertips against his temples.

He said jerkily, 'It was just a game at first.'

'*A game?*'

'That's how it began. When he did something he knew was wrong, I'd threaten to thrash him, and he would cry and kiss my hand until I gave him a hug to make him smile again. And then he would call me his great lord, and one thing would lead to another . . . '

She could imagine the rest unaided. James's rough kindness; the boy's fawning gratitude; the presents, the caresses. She swallowed hard and said, 'Don't tell me. I don't want to hear.'

'But I want you to understand. I fought against it, you know. For weeks – oh, months! – I resisted him. I thought I would go mad, unable to tell anyone of the hell I was going through, and scared stiff I would give myself away. When you arrived it made matters worse, for I feared you must guess. These past months have been a torment for me.'

He looked so wretched that her first impulse was to comfort him, but she hardened her heart. *She* had been unhappy, too, but he chose to ignore that. It was almost as if he took a perverse pleasure in dramatising his sufferings and exaggerating his self-abasement.

'What are we going to do?' she asked, and saw by the quick shift of his glance that he would do nothing unless she insisted. Despite the alleged torments he had gone through, he was the same old James, and would try to persuade her to let him have his cake and eat it.

In the past, she might have allowed herself to be persuaded, but this was different. It was not her happiness alone that he was putting at risk, but his whole career. She had been too naïve to read the signs; others might well interpret them correctly.

'It's no good, James. You will have to send him away. I cannot keep him here, knowing what I do. If you think it would be dangerous to send him back to his own people, it must surely be possible to find another situation here in Kabul. Some other officer would find use for him as an interpreter, or in charge of his stables. While you are out on patrol, I will make enquiries.'

'No, Thea! I beg you! That would be punishing him for no fault of his own.'

'But can't you see the danger you are in? What if someone should guess, and tell the General?'

117

'Oh, Sale wouldn't listen to that kind of talk,' he said with a complacency that shocked her. 'Besides, the old dragon's my godmamma. So long as you don't blab, I am safe enough.'

She said fiercely, 'Anyone can see there is something unnatural in the way you – you *pamper* that boy! Why should I shield you?'

'Because you are my wife,' he said with a half-smile, 'and if I fall, you will be dragged down with me. Do you wish for that?'

She was silent, and he went on quickly, 'Look, my dear. Do nothing for the moment, until I can make other arrangements for Hinghan Khan. I regret what happened – I regret it very much. I give you my solemn promise it will not happen again. On my honour!'

She wanted to believe him, and tried to ignore the cool, detached echo of her father's voice, dredged up from some dark corner of her memory. 'An honourable man, my dear, need not invoke his honour. Those who do so generally intend to deceive.'

Did James intend to deceive her? Was he really promising that he would take good care *she never saw* such a thing again?

She looked at him with new eyes. He had begun to recover from the shock of discovery, and his busy brain was evolving schemes that would save his face while allowing him to do as he pleased. Beneath the apologies, the self-castigation, she was aware of a small, disquieting element of calculation. If she gave in now, she would find it more difficult to protest later, yet she longed to trust him. Without trust, their marriage was dead.

He said coaxingly, 'Be fair, my dear. Don't spoil everything just because of a moment's madness. A temporary lapse that means nothing.'

'Yet you admit this has gone on for months.'

'That means nothing. *Nothing!*'

'Are you sure?'

'Of course.' He smiled at her, strong and confident

118

again. 'Dear Thea. I knew you wouldn't let me down. Try to forget all about this unfortunate business.'

'Very well,' she said, 'but on one condition. Don't take Hinghan Khan on patrol with you.'

'I must!' His head jerked up. 'I – I need him.'

'No, James,' she said regretfully. 'It would be tempting fate. Leave him behind, or I will go to Lady Sale myself and tell her what I know. That is the price of my silence.'

It was a bluff, of course, but he could not be certain of it. He darted her a glance in which she read anger, but also an unwilling respect.

'All right,' he said reluctantly. 'It's a bargain.' He shook his head. 'I never thought I'd have you dictating terms to me.'

She wanted to cry out that she wished she didn't have to, but that would undo everything she had just achieved. She said, forcing a smile, 'It's late. You must go and get some sleep. Let's try to put all this behind us! When you come back, we'll make a fresh start. For the children's sake, as well as our own.'

'Of course.' His smile didn't quite reach his eyes. He said, 'We're leaving very early – before dawn. Don't bother to see me off – there's no need.'

'Oh, I must!'

'Dear Thea. Ever the perfect wife!' He placed his hands on her shoulders, fingers pressing lightly yet with a hint of steel. 'Forget what you saw tonight, or it will be the worse for you,' he said, and she found his calm, dispassionate tone more menacing than any of his sudden rages.

'I'll try.'

'That's the spirit. Forgive and forget. That way we'll all be happy.' And he turned and left the room.

119

CHAPTER SIX

The tight-fisted ways of Lady Macnaghten had long been a standing joke among members of the British Mission to Afghanistan. Though she had been left a handsome fortune by her first husband, she was notorious for her parsimony – it was said that she fed the Envoy on scraps left over from the dishes of her beloved cats, and made her servants wear the same liveries for three years at a stretch.

Great was the general astonishment, therefore, when it was announced that she meant to give a ball to celebrate Sir William Macnaghten's new appointment as Governor of Bombay. Nothing could have indicated more clearly her delight at the prospect of leaving Afghanistan for the ease and comfort of Bombay.

For the occasion a great gold and white marquee borrowed from Shah Shuja's extensive equipment had its pillars twined with bunches of luscious green and black grapes from Kardunah and the Kohistan. Banks of flowers filled the air with their exotic scents, and the tables were piled high with peaches as fine as any to be found in an English glasshouse, Orléans plums, greengages, and a great variety of melons.

On a dais at one end, the band of the 13th Light Infantry, who were soon to return to Hindustan with the rest of General Sale's brigade, played tirelessly, and after midnight the band of the 27th Bengal Native Infantry would take their place. In a riot of gold-and-scarlet, gold-and-green, gold-and-blue, the officers outshone the ladies in their pastel silks and chiffons, but even the most dashing mess kit could not compete in splendour with the Kabuli noblemen's gold-encrusted ceremonial robes, brocade sashes and splendid striped *puggarees* surmounted with jewels.

Lady Macnaghten would have preferred not to invite

120

the Afghan noblemen, but the Envoy insisted, and even she had to admit that their flashing eyes, hawk faces and exuberant beards lent a certain barbaric glamour to the ball.

Sir Alexander Burnes, too, had come in native dress. Now that his hour had arrived to step into the Envoy's shoes, he was all smiles and bows, and turned a look of cold contempt on anyone who doubted the wisdom of sending away Sale's brigade just when the turbulent tribesmen through whose territory supplies from India had to pass were protesting at the summary halving of their revenues.

Had it, indeed, been sensible to cut their revenues in the first place?

'Oh, those fellows were bound to kick up a fuss,' drawled Burnes when Lady Sale put this question to him directly. 'We'll soon bring 'em to heel again. The Government insists we must cut our costs here. A saving of forty thousand rupees per annum is a very considerable economy.'

'Since it has already cost us the lives of three fine young officers as well as two convoys beaten and plundered, I would call it a false one,' responded her ladyship tartly.

He smiled. 'Were it possible to make an omelette without breaking eggs, I would be the happiest man in the world. Three officers killed – of course, it is a matter for regret, but the trouble is only temporary, I assure you. No doubt you heard that Captain Macgregor's latest despatch reports that the country round Tezeen is as peaceful as it has ever been?'

'Sir William may interpret that as he pleases,' countered Lady Sale. 'You and I, Sir Alexander, know that Captain Macgregor means us to understand that the area is very far from tranquil. When has it *ever* been at peace? I am surprised you have not tried to acquaint the Envoy with Macgregor's true meaning, but doubtless you know your own business best.'

He bowed, tight-lipped. The old witch is too damned sharp by half, he thought, and took the first opportunity

121

to escape her probing. He knew – who better? – that affairs in Afghanistan were by no means as peaceful as Sir William liked to make out, but if Lady Sale expected him to upset the apple-cart by speaking out of turn, or delay the Envoy's departure by a single day, she was very much mistaken. Sir William wanted to leave a country at peace, so at peace it should remain – officially – until he had left it. Then, thought Burnes with satisfaction, I will run things *my* way, and no one – least of all that old sheep Elphy Bey – shall tell me how to do it.

Lady Sale watched with a sardonic eye as he sauntered across the pavilion, bowing to right and left, until he reached the little group of his Afghan cronies who were impassively watching the dancing. That young man has grown a size too big for his boots, she reflected, and was glad she would not be in Kabul to suffer his airs and graces when he assumed the Envoy's mantle.

If, indeed, he did assume it. That was by no means as certain as Burnes seemed to think. Some people she had spoken to, young Captain Mackenzie among them, thought it was nip and tuck between Burnes and Dr Tobias Black for the Envoy's post. Macnaghten disliked Black for personal reasons, but Burnes's appointment was not yet a foregone conclusion and for her part, Lady Sale would have preferred the doctor. Whatever his youthful indiscretions, she thought him a steadier character than the volatile Sir Alexander, whose cavalier attitude towards honest fighting men like her son-in-law Sturt was hard to forgive. One way and another, she would be glad to leave this whole mis-managed affair and follow Sale's brigade home.

Her quick brown glance surveyed the revellers and came to rest on Thea Quinn and Georgiana Mainwaring, a tall, merry-eyed young woman now, like Thea, in the final month of her pregnancy and condemned to watch the revels rather than take part in them. A restlessly tapping foot just visible beneath a voluminous cloak of sea-green silk indicated that this state of affairs was by no means to Mrs Mainwaring's liking.

Poor girls! thought Lady Sale, and made her way towards them, pausing to congratulate her hostess, resplendent in purple satin, on a delightful squeeze, and listen to Lady Macnaghten's anxieties regarding the transportation of Simkin, her favourite cat, whom she was determined to carry back to India.

'He will so dislike the journey, poor fellow, but what am I to do? If only I could explain to him how much more agreeable his life will be in Bombay!' exclaimed the harassed cat-lover.

When Florentia resumed her progress across the tent, she was glad to see that Captain Godolphin Mainwaring – Dolly to his friends – had belatedly remembered his obligations towards his pregnant wife and come in search of her. Dolly was a tall, fair, square-jawed young officer so upright in bearing that no one would have been surprised to learn that he had inadvertently swallowed a poker. He adored his lively Georgy and presently bore her away in search of an ice, leaving her abandoned chair to be promptly commandeered by Dr Black.

'On these occasions I find it hard to remember how far we are from home,' he observed to Thea with a smile. 'Don't you think it strange how we British cling so tenaciously to our amusements, no matter what our hosts may think of them?'

'On the contrary, I find it surprising how much they share our tastes in sport,' she countered. 'Wrestling, horse-racing, cock-fighting – though I grant you they show little enthusiasm for cricket.'

As always, she welcomed his jack-in-the-box appearances when she least expected him. James might say what he liked about Toby's friendly relations with the tribal chiefs. The fact remained that it was vital to keep the road to India open and the tribesmen well disposed towards the vulnerable convoys marching through those dark, forbidding passes. If it meant paying Danegeld, she considered it money well spent.

'True, but *dancing*, as we know it, fills every Mussulman heart with horror. Lady Macnaghten would have been better advised to celebrate her departure with a mere assembly, instead of flouting their sensitivities in this way. I told Sir William so, but I might have saved my breath.'

'Never mind!' said Lady Sale, joining them. 'Soon we shall be back in dear old Hindustan, and our sojourn here will seem a dream. All I shall be sorry to leave is my garden. Such peaches we have had this year! It goes against the grain to leave Brigadier Shelton the fruits of my hard work. He will let it go to rack and ruin, I know.'

Toby grinned and deflected a diatribe against her *bête noire*, the one-armed Brigadier, by passing on the news that General Elphinstone had asked to be relieved of his command. At once her interest sharpened.

'High time, too!' she exclaimed. 'I never thought he would last more than six months here. Of course, he should not have come in the first place. A sick man is quite unfitted for this command. I suppose Nott will take his place?'

'There has been no announcement yet.' His dark eyes teased her.

'That is not to say you don't know!' She tapped him playfully with her fan. 'Come, Dr Black, you can trust my discretion. I may have the reputation of a busybody, but I flatter myself I can keep a secret. So can Mrs Quinn.'

'Secrets?' James had come up behind them. The sight of his wife's bright head bent close to Lady Sale and that fellow Black made him uneasy.

His hand pressed warningly on her shoulder, and she smiled to reassure him. He had kept his side of their bargain. He need not fear she would let slip any uncomfortable disclosures regarding Hinghan Khan. What it had cost James to deprive himself of the boy's company she could only guess, but he had done it. Sometimes she detected a strained expression on his face when he gave orders to Hinghan Khan, but since that night he had stopped taking the boy about with him.

'My Persian is good enough now to manage without you,' he had told him curtly in Thea's presence, then

124

turned away as if he could not bear the boy's look of hurt surprise.

If Hingham Khan resented his loss of status, he gave no sign of it. He busied himself with the horses and dogs with apparent equanimity, even, she thought, with a hint of relief at shedding the burden of adult emotions and being allowed to revert to childhood.

I am glad I spoke out when I did, thought Thea, and I believe in his heart of hearts, James is too. It was absurd to feel a twinge of disappointment that he was far from being the tower of strength she had naïvely supposed him, but she blamed this on herself. Real men had faults and weaknesses. During their long separation she had idolised an impossible paragon of her own invention.

'You are looking tired, my love,' he now said solicitously. 'Fetch your cloak, and I will escort you home.'

She rose obediently, and he took her chair, saying, 'What secrets are you hatching, Godmamma?'

'Military ones!' Lady Sale's glance was mischievous. She had always been fond of James, and hoped matters would soon improve between him and his wife. She said with a hint of challenge, 'Now, do not, I pray, start to lecture me on *military security*, or any nonsense of that kind, for I will not stand for it. I find it perfectly disgusting the way we are now kept in the dark about matters that affect us all. When Sir Willoughby Cotton commanded here, every despatch he received was promulgated in Orders and we knew where we stood. Today if you wish to find out what is happening, you must ask half a dozen people and guess whose opinion you can believe.'

'Oh, I am entirely in agreement, Godmamma,' said James. 'Elphy Bey plays his cards close to his chest! Since no information is given us, we have to make do with rumours. Have you heard the latest?'

'Tell me.'

'I am informed that the 35th BNI is under orders to march for Bootkhak to suppress the Ghilzai rebels, and we are to follow just as soon as our guns return from Zoormut.' He looked at Toby with barely concealed hostility. 'Am I right? You, of course, will be better informed than a mere military man.'

Toby shook his head, vouchsafing nothing.

'Well, James, I hope you are right,' said Lady Sale briskly, sensing tension. 'We have hung about here too long, and the sooner Sale's brigade goes down to the provinces the better pleased I shall be. I suppose Thea will remain in Kabul until after the Happy Event?'

He nodded, and she bustled away to spread her news.

Toby frowned. 'I don't mean to speak out of turn, Quinn,' he said abruptly, 'but if you are leaving the city, I would advise you to move your wife and child to the cantonments rather than leave them isolated.'

'Hardly isolated, with Captain Johnson's house next door and the Resident just across the street,' James drawled. 'I believe I am capable of arranging for my family's safety without your assistance.'

'All the same, if there was trouble in the city, it would take an hour or more to reach them,' said Toby evenly.

'Are you anticipating trouble?'

'Who can tell?'

'You, I should have thought. People tell me you have a remarkable knack of reading the Afghan mind.'

'Oh, I make no such claim! All the same, I think it would be wise to move your family into the Mission compound while you are gone – just to be on the safe side.'

James shook his head obstinately. 'Sir Alexander Burnes sees no danger in remaining in the city. Why should I?'

'Sir Alexander,' said Toby gently, 'is not a married man.'

'What difference does that make? In my view, to cut and run for cantonments now would show a lamentable lack of confidence in our military power, and would certainly be construed as such by malcontents in Kabul.'

Have it your own way, thought Toby grimly as he watched James stroll away to where Thea was waiting. He wondered if he had made matters worse. James was an obstinate young devil. It was perfectly possible that he

126

would of his own accord have sent Thea and little Dandy to stay with the other ladies during his absence from Kabul, but now he had declared his intention of leaving them in the city, pride would prevent him from changing his mind.

Cursing himself for a meddling fool, Toby watched James and his wife take their leave of Lady Macnaghten, and tried to calculate whether her baby would be born before or after the simmering discontent in the city – to which the British so determinedly closed their minds – broke into open revolt.

On All Saints' Day, the Envoy attended a farewell dinner at the Residency as the guest of Sir Alexander Burnes, and did full justice to the turtle soup, Scotch haddock kedgeree, roast bustard and anchovy toast set before him by the Resident's Goanese cook, before disposing of a large plateful of the jam-filled nursery favourite known to generations of Anglo-Indian children as *Ispunj Rolli*.

Replete at last, he complimented his host. 'When we are roughing it in the Khyber Pass, we will be glad to recall such civilised delights,' he declared, squaring his narrow shoulders in manful anticipation of hardship.

Sir Alexander, who knew very well that Lady Macnaghten, at least, had no more intention of roughing it than he had of converting to Islam, nobly refrained from winking at his young brother Charley and William Broadfoot, who had come out to the courtyard to wish the Envoy Godspeed.

'I trust you will have a safe and pleasant journey,' he said courteously, though he itched to slap the horse's rump and send him away at full gallop. Would the prosy old fool never leave? He added a compliment of his own, albeit with a hidden barb.

'I must congratulate you, Sir William, on leaving at a period of such profound tranquillity. I hope that when my own turn comes to depart, I shall bequeath my successor the same peaceful inheritance.'

The Envoy gave him a sharp look and William Broadfoot fidgeted uneasily. Though he came of a famous fighting family himself, he could not help feeling that in his determination to show a cool front, the Resident had become reckless.

During the past forty-eight hours a disturbing number of well-muffled Afghan gentlemen had called at the Residency with urgent messages for Sir Alexander. Private messages, with a common purport: Danger. The Kabul chiefs were about to rise and throw off the hated *feringhi* yoke. Plans for an insurrection were complete. It needed no more than a spark to light the tinder. The Envoy's departure would provide that spark, for rumours spread by grim old Aminullah Khan, now Sir Alexander's sworn enemy, warned his countrymen that when the Envoy left he would take with him a dozen chiefs and carry them as prisoners to England, never to return to their native land.

Time and again Sir Alexander had listened to the same story from these furtive messengers of doom, thanked them politely, and sent them away. And done nothing. Why? Because Lord Auckland's letter confirming his appointment as Sir William Macnaghten's successor had not yet arrived, and he meant to be at his post in the Residency when it did come.

Surely he cannot pass me over again? thought Burnes in the wakeful, doubtful, still watches. If he does, I cannot stay here. I have gambled too much on this throw. If I am superseded, I shall leave and go to Europe. The humiliation of seeing another man in my rightful place would be too much to bear.

Even young Charley, who hero-worshipped his brilliant brother, had asked shyly if he should not heed these warnings.

'Ain't you going down to cantonments, then, Sandy?' he asked in his soft Highland lilt. 'Mohun Lal swears it is serious this time. He thinks you should leave the Residency.'

'Don't listen to him, young 'un!' Burnes gave him a friendly punch. 'Intrigue is meat and drink to my secretary – he has been saying the same to me for weeks.

How would it look to the Afghans if I showed the white feather now? I have never done them harm. Why should they wish to injure me?'

At last Macnaghten mounted his horse, saying he would see them all in Hindustan, and the party clattered away. Broadfoot and the Burnes brothers returned to the handsome, high-ceilinged salon, where a bright fire was blazing, and the younger men settled to play bezique while Sir Alexander retired to his desk to write his journal. For a long time he sat alone in his study, flipping the pages, rereading earlier entries made with such high hopes. Were they to be dashed? For months he had done nothing but draw his pay and give advice that was never heeded. Yesterday, when the Envoy announced his departure, he had felt that his hour had arrived, but another day had come and gone with no decision on his future.

With a chilling sense of hopelessness he looked at his last entry: *I grow very tired of praise, and suppose I shall get tired of censure in time.* He dipped his pen again, but before it could touch the page there was a hurried step outside the study door and Charley entered, still fully dressed, anxious-eyed and pale beneath his tan.

'What's up?' drawled his brother. 'I thought you were abed long since.'

'S-sorry to interrupt and all that,' said Charley jerkily. 'The Shah's Wazir has come here. Osman Khan. He insists on seeing you.'

'Tell him I'm asleep.'

Charley gulped, and said in a voice he tried hard to control, 'He – he's come to warn you there's treachery afoot. That old brute Aminullah and his crony Abdullah Khan are stirring up trouble in the bazaar. He has come to escort us to the Bala Hissar. He says we – we should leave the house at once.'

'So that his pals can sack it at their leisure? Not I!' said Burnes promptly. He saw his brother's trembling lips and rose to put a reassuring arm round his shoulders.

'Brace up, Charley! We're safe enough here – trust me for that. I have a messenger standing by in case the worst comes to the worst and they try to rush the house. Remember, we've six thousand fighting men within two miles of us! The Afghans aren't fools. They may shout and jaw a bit, but they know better than to attack us. So long as we show a bold front, they'll leave us alone.'

Long years of childhood obedience had their effect. Charley's lips stopped trembling and he stood straighter. 'Of course,' he said more cheerfully. 'What shall I tell the Wazir?'

'Thank him for his warning, but say we mean to stick it out. When he has gone, come and join me in the courtyard. I'm going down to check on the guard.'

'Right!' Charley went to the door, but when he reached it he turned. 'Sandy?' he said uncertainly.

'What is it?'

'I – I wasn't in a funk, you know. Not really.'

Burnes smiled. 'Of course you weren't, old chap. I knew that. Now cut along.'

As they walked on to the balcony overlooking the courtyard in the pearly predawn greyness, the muffled roar which had sounded like pounding surf through the heavy shutters swelled in a wild crescendo. Individual voices rose above the tumult, their message all too plain.

'Death to the unbelievers! Death to Sekunder Burnes! Infidel dogs, come out and die!'

'Keep calm,' muttered Broadfoot as Charley shrank back involuntarily. 'Don't let 'em think we're afraid. Shall I give the order to fire?'

'Wait a bit.' Burnes gave him an approving glance. A cool customer, young William Broadfoot, steady as a rock, just like his brothers. No one could ask for better men in a tight corner. 'I'll talk to 'em first. Ask 'em what they want and why they're kicking up such a deuce of a row. They'll listen to me.'

Dimly they could see the street packed with men, their jostling bodies pressed tight against the tall iron gates of the Residency as they shouted and waved their fists towards the balcony.

'Take a look round the back, Broadfoot,' added Burnes quietly. 'If the wicket gate is clear, send my messenger off to the cantonments. Tell 'em we need reinforcements, quick as they like.'

How quick would that be? wondered Charley, clenching his teeth to stop them chattering. How long would the gates hold back the mob?

The second question was soon answered. The black mass of bodies swaying back and forth suddenly spilled forward into the courtyard as the locks burst and the gates sagged on their hinges. Like a wave breaking on the seashore, the mob surged against the Residency walls, reaching up towards the balcony where the three Englishmen stood.

'Tell the guards to hold their fire!' said Burnes sharply, seeing them raise their muskets. He held out his right hand in a gesture that compelled silence. For a moment the shouting died away.

'Friends! Hear me speak!' he shouted in the fluent Persian that was his especial pride. 'What brings you here to disturb my rest? I am your friend. I have never done you harm. Tell me your grievances and I will see them redressed. Do not believe stories put about by wicked men, inciting you to rebellion. They are your enemies, as well as mine. Trust me – '

A shot struck the wall not a foot from his head, and a great roar drowned his voice. For the first time his composure faltered. He turned haunted eyes on Broadfoot, who had hurried back after despatching the messenger. 'They won't listen!' he said incredulously. 'They're shouting me down.'

Another shot cracked into the plaster between them.

'Shall I give the order?'

Burnes's shoulders sagged. He nodded.

'*Open fire!*'

As the words left Broadfoot's mouth the sepoys' muskets spat flame into the tight-packed crowd which swayed backward, unable to escape even if it wanted to.

Calmly Broadfoot scanned the turreted walls surrounding the courtyard. His quick eye picked out the dark shape of a sniper edging along the parapet towards the balcony, and as coolly as if he were shooting rabbits, he sighted along his own barrel and squeezed the trigger. The sniper cartwheeled into the crowd.

'Good shot!' cried Charley, forgetting to be afraid.

The light was growing stronger as the winter sun rose red behind the Seeah Sung Hills. Without wasting a bullet, Broadfoot picked off five more enemy marksmen, then, uttering a choking cry, he staggered back against the wall, a musket ball through his heart.

The mob roared its delight and surged forward again. Burnes, who had bent to feel for a pulse, shook his head and signalled to Charley, who was firing and reloading as fast as he could, steadying his aim against the corner of the balustrade. Blood was pouring from his cheek, but in the heat of battle he had not noticed it.

'Come away, Charley,' shouted Burnes and dragged him inside. Flinging open a cedarwood chest, he hauled out an armful of native robes. 'Put these on, quick! We'll go out through the servants' quarters and across to Trevor's *bourge*. Hurry!'

With frenzied haste, he swathed a turban about his brother's head, leaving the end free to muffle his face, and then wound a sash about his waist. Charley was a foot taller than most Afghans. Beneath the rich brocade robe his military boots stuck out incongruously, but there was no time to change them. Already the roar of the crowd was mingled with the sound of splintering wood as the lower-floor shutters resisted the intruders' attacks. They would not keep them out for long.

'Follow me!' hissed Burnes, and was off at a crouching run down the narrow back stairway used by the servants and into the maze of small hutches and cubby-holes at the rear of the house. All was dark and quiet there. Every servant who had not fled must have joined the insurgents in the courtyard.

The brothers jinked through passages and down shallow

flights of steps, coming to a sudden halt before a low door barred on the inside.

'Find . . . horses,' puffed Burnes, struggling with the bolts. Good living and lack of exercise had made him fat and the breath roared in his throat, but his quick brown eyes were alight with excitement. Cautiously he peered round the door and beckoned Charley to follow.

'All clear. We'll throw 'em off yet. Over here . . . '

He vaulted a low wall and dived down the evil-smelling alley that led to the stables, but before he had gone a dozen strides he halted again so suddenly that Charley ran into him.

'Damn their black hearts!' he muttered. 'Look at that.'

From the stable rose crackling orange flames and the screams of terrified horses mingled with the crash of falling beams. As the roof caved in Charley stood mesmerised, sick at heart to think of his beautiful mare roasted in the inferno. His brother jerked his sleeve.

'This way!'

As they turned back towards the street, they found the way barred by a thickset, pockmarked man in the dress of a Kashmiri Mussulman. From the flash of recognition in his eyes they knew they were discovered.

Burnes's hand flew to his pistol, determined to sell his life dearly, but the stranger put out a hand and spoke in a soft, ingratiating tone.

'Follow me, Sekunder-Sahib. I swear by the holy Koran neither you nor your brother will come to harm.'

'Don't trust him,' muttered Charley, but Burnes lowered his pistol.

'Come, Sahibs. The Wazir has sent me to guide you to the Bala Hissar,' urged the Kashmiri. Burnes knew they had no choice. The attacking mob had spread through the house and garden in search of plunder. One shout from the Kashmiri would bring a dozen bloodthirsty rebels to his assistance. They would have to trust that he thought them more valuable alive than dead.

'A lakh of rupees when we get there,' he promised, thinking their lives cheap at the price.

'Two lakhs,' countered their guide. 'Cover your faces, Sahibs. Follow me, and do not speak.'

He led them swiftly through the trampled rose garden and back into the courtyard, slipping through a narrow gap in the wall in so familiar a manner that Burnes wondered how he came to know his way about the Residency so well. Few insurgents remained in the courtyard, since most were now engaged in sacking the home of Captain Johnson, Paymaster to the Shah's troops, on the other side of the road.

Johnson was spending the night in cantonments, but lately he had taken to using his own house as the Treasury for the sake of convenience, and Burnes ground his teeth as he saw money chests being hauled on to carts along with all Johnson's stock of wine. To his certain knowledge, there was £17,000 worth of Government gold in those chests, ready to pay the troops tomorrow. The chance of laying their hands on such rich plunder would fan the flames of rebellion faster than any real or imagined political grievance.

Trust Johnson to scuttle away to safety, leaving only the sepoy guard to defend the treasure, thought Burnes bitterly, but their own situation was too precarious for him to cast more than a passing glance at the gleeful looters.

'What! Leaving empty-handed?' exclaimed a big, burly fellow whose blood-spattered robes were tucked into his sash for freer movement. He clutched an armful of silver ornaments and trinkets, and as he passed he thrust a candlestick into Burnes's hands, saying, 'Go on, take it. There's plenty for all.'

Burnes drew back instinctively, and the candlestick fell to the ground.

'Go on, take it, it's yours! A gift from the *feringhis!*' roared the big man, then, moved by sudden suspicion, peered closely at Burnes as he tried to edge past. His gaze travelled over the rich robe, and stopped at the give-away boots.

'Not so fast, my friend!'

With a lightning grab, he stripped off Burnes's turban, and gave a yell of triumph.

'See, friends, see! Here is Sekunder Burnes!'

At the first sign of trouble Charley had moved quietly into the dark mouth of an alley. It was narrow and empty, leading towards the network of small lanes and huts fringing the Great Bazaar, where a fugitive could go to ground like a rabbit in its warren.

Heart thudding, he pressed against the wall and saw the mob close round his brother. Faintly he heard his urgent cry of, 'Run, Charley! Run for your life!'

Instinct battled with duty, the will to survive against brotherly love. The way of escape lay clear before him. For a moment he hesitated, fighting temptation, then drew his sword and plunged into the mob surrounding Burnes. Bearded faces turned in astonishment as he hacked and stabbed in a fury of despair, and the crowd parted to let him through.

Burnes was dying, stabbed in a dozen places, one arm severed at the wrist and the other hacked off at the shoulder, but recognition flickered in his eyes as Charley knelt to raise his head from the cobbles.

'Why didn't you run?' he whispered.

'I wanted to, Sandy, but I couldn't. I couldn't let you die alone.'

Burnes's head sagged back. 'Too late,' he murmured.

Charley looked up at the circle of fierce, unforgiving faces and knew they would show him no mercy.

'Kill the infidel dogs! Kill! Kill!' howled a one-eyed camel-driver.

The crowd surged forward. Five minutes later Charley and his brother had both been hacked to pieces.

CHAPTER SEVEN

Thea woke to a fine, frosty November morning, and lay listening to the familiar sounds of the city while the terror of her last dream ebbed slowly away.

Cocks crowed from dunghills, crows squawked and clamoured, squabbling over the kitchen refuse, the long-drawn howl of the muezzin was punctuated by a dog's bark and the mournful bray of a donkey. In her dream she had heard hoarse voices crying 'Death to the infidel!', the crackle of musket fire and crash of heavy artillery. She had tried to run, and could not . . .

In daylight such terrors seemed foolish. She was restless and hungry. While one part of her mind planned what she would do that day, another listened for the tinkle of cup against plate that would announce the arrival of *chota hazri*.

Hardly had James returned from patrol than he had departed again with the rest of Sale's brigade to quell the rebellious tribesmen of the eastern passes, who threatened to cut British supply lines between Peshawar and Kabul. Since then she had taken her morning meal alone, preferring solitude to Sarah's daily litany of complaints against the ayah, the cook, the weather, the wretched goods brought to the door and, most of all, against Hinghan Khan.

It had been a bitter blow to the boy when he was left behind with the women, and the sulks and insolence by which he expressed his disappointment grated on Sarah's nerves. Strangely, the more she criticised Hinghan Khan, the more sympathy Thea felt for him. After all, he was just a boy, stolen from his family and apprenticed to vice and deceit. You could no more blame him than a cat who killed birds. It was not surprising he used any weapon he could to improve his position.

136

In James's absence, she found it easier to tolerate Hinghan Khan. It was, however, like having a tiger cub in the house. By nature fierce and wild, essentially untameable, he was as liable to respond to friendly overtures with a snarl as to rub against you and purr. All the same, he had his virtues. He adored Dandy, and could be trusted to keep the Chota-Sahib, as he called him, amused for hours.

'I do not like having him hang about the nursery,' said Sarah, but Thea told her not to drive Hinghan Khan away.

'The poor boy is lonely,' she said. 'I will take him to play with the Trevor children when I visit their mother.'

Her friend Mrs Trevor's large brood, whose ages ranged from a few months old to ten years, yearned to wear pearl necklaces and daggers as the Afghan boy did, and gave him the leading role in all their games.

Today Thea planned to call on the Trevors at their *bourge*, or tower, a mile away on the Kohistan road. Mary Trevor knew all there was to know about babies, and she was such a lively, good-hearted, practical woman that she was a general favourite.

For a while, Thea rehearsed her visit, what she would wear, how long it would take to get there, what she would do and say, but all the time the listening part of her mind transmitted disturbing messages, chief among them the fact that while the house was unusually quiet for the time of day, there was a lot of noise and activity in the street. Had her bad dream spilled over into reality?

She sat up and strained her ears, alarmed to hear shots and the confused roar of voices. A riot in the bazaar? The popular uprising Lady Sale feared? For the first time, the isolation of her position here in the city seemed perilous. She resolved to send a *chuprassi* round to the Residency at once to find out what was going on.

Picking up the handbell beside her bed, she shook it vigorously, but no one came running to find what she wanted.

'*Koi hai?*' she called. 'Is anyone there?'

Silence shrouded the big house, a waiting, listening silence that contrasted strangely with the hubbub in the street. There was nothing for it: she would have to go and see for herself what was happening.

Carefully she swung her feet to the floor and rose, easing her back with one hand to balance her burdened stomach as she made her ponderous way to the door. Before she reached it, however, it opened and Sarah burst in, wild-eyed, pale and dishevelled. Her frowsy brown hair still hung in its night-time plait, and in her haste to dress she had left half her buttons undone.

'The servants have run away!' she cried. 'They've left us to be murdered in our beds!'

'All of them?' Thea bit her lip at this news. 'Are you sure?'

'Of course I am! I've looked everywhere. There's not a servant in the place.'

'Not even Ayah?' Anxiety sharpened Thea's voice. Other servants might flee, but not a child's nurse.

'I tell you, they're all gone.' Sarah's tone shrilled into hysteria. 'We'll be murdered, I know it! It's your fault. I told you we should have moved to the Mission compound when Captain Quinn left.'

'Don't be absurd. Why should anyone harm us? Do you mean you have left Dandy all alone in the nursery? Go and fetch him here at once.'

Sarah shook her head obstinately. 'I am not going over there. Not alone. He's your baby. Fetch him yourself.'

There was no point in arguing. As Thea hurried across the innèr courtyard, cursing the bulk that made her heavy and slow, she saw at once why Sarah had not wanted to leave the shelter of the main house.

The outer court, where the horses and baggage animals were stabled, was alive with looters who had evidently managed to force open the gate leading on to the street. They had broken into the provisions store to which only James had the key and were piling carts with sacks of forage and crates full of the tinned delicacies which he had been at such pains to import from India. Dozens of bottles of champagne, burgundy and claret; boxes of cigars; curaçao, maraschino and other liqueurs; hermetically sealed salmon and hotchpotch all the way from Aberdeen.

With helpless rage, Thea saw a string of camels being driven out of the yard, and her own mare, Fatima, tied behind a loaded cart. For the moment the looters were too busy to bother with the house itself, but it would not be long before they turned their attention to the inner gate, and once that was breached there was nothing to stop them from sacking the entire house.

The nursery lay on the far side of the inner court, between the servants' quarters and the apartments James kept for his work. Rather than show herself by crossing the open space, Thea crept round the walls, keeping to the shadowed side of the rectangle, and slipped through the door without attracting attention.

There stood Dandy in his cot, clinging to the bars and crowing with delight at the unexpected sight of his mother. The nursery was clean and tidy, with toys neatly stacked and Dandy's fresh clothes lying folded on the chair, but of Ayah there was no sign and Thea's heart sank, knowing something must be very wrong for a nurse to abandon her charge.

'Come to Mamma, darling.' She held out her arms and Dandy stamped laboriously round the cot from one bar to the next, but when she bent to pick him up, his face crumpled suddenly. Like all males, he was a creature of habit and resented any variation in his daily routine.

Where was Ayah, with his bottle of warm sweetened milk? Where was the honeyed rusk, the snowy napkins? What was Mamma – that remote being whom he visited only for an hour before bedtime – doing in his nursery, and couldn't she see that he needed changing?

Unable to frame these questions or express his displeasure in any other way, he threw back his head and bawled.

'Hush, darling. Hush!'

Dandy refused to hush. She snatched him hastily out

of the cot, almost smothering him against her shoulder in her anxiety to suppress the noise.

This was not the kind of treatment the Chota-Sahib was used to. He arched his back and became rigid in her arms, bawling his head off, while she looked frantically round for something to distract him. This red-faced, angry, smelly little creature was a stranger, and she did not know how to placate him. Any moment his roars would reach the ears of the men in the courtyard.

'Hush, Dandy. Mamma's here,' she soothed, and carried him through the day nursery, past Ayah's empty cubby-hole, and into James's study.

Most mornings Hinghan Khan could be found here, studying the English lessons James had set for him, but a glance round the room told Thea that he, too, had absconded, taking with him everything small and valuable he could lay his hands on. Silver trinkets, curios, sporting trophies, ivory miniatures and chessmen were missing from the tables and shelves, while in the next room the leather box in which James kept his collection of uncut gems lay on its side, empty.

I might have expected it, she thought, sickened by such greed and ingratitude. Dandy had stopped his roaring, intrigued by the unfamiliar surroundings, but as soon as she put him down to rest her arms, he began grizzling, 'Ayah, Ayah!' until she lifted him again.

She was surprised to find how heavy he was. Though he could toddle a few steps, she could hardly expect him to cross the courtyard on foot, so braced herself for the effort of carrying him all the way.

'How long you've been!' exclaimed Sarah as Thea struggled up the steps and into the safety of her own room. 'He's wet, poor lamb,' she went on, taking the baby. 'I suppose you didn't think to change him?'

Too late, Thea remembered the pile of clean napkins at the foot of the cot. Was it worth the risk of going back for them?

'He'll be all right,' she said. She was reluctant to admit

to Sarah how little she knew of her son's daily routine. 'Go and find him some food.'

For a moment she thought Sarah would refuse to do that, too, but with a shrug and a sigh she obeyed and went cautiously down the steps and through the vine-draped archway that led to the kitchen. Minutes dragged by and she did not reappear. Gorging herself before she brings anything for us, thought Thea indignantly. She herself was ravenous.

She gave Dandy her jewel-box to play with, pressing the hidden catch that made the lid fly up to astonish him. He gurgled charmingly, making her repeat the trick until she had long tired of it, though he had not.

'Mamma do!' he urged.

She tried to ignore the smell emanating from his napkin, and wished with all her might that Ayah was there.

The noise from the street had diminished, though she still caught an occasional glimpse of a furtive figure hurrying across the outer court, bent double under his burden of loot. Whatever the origins of the riot, it seemed to be quietening down. She decided that as soon as Sarah reappeared she would send her over to Captain Johnson's house opposite the Residency to find out what was happening.

Where *was* Sarah? It must be half an hour since she vanished through the kitchen arch. She has had time to fill her greedy self twice over, thought Thea, hunger sharpening her annoyance.

She lifted Dandy on to her lap once more as he tired of crawling about the floor and began to whine for attention. Never had she been obliged to entertain him for so long at a stretch. She began to play the counting game beloved of Anglo-Indian children: '*Peely-weely*', pitching her voice as high as she could and pinching his little finger; '*Pally-looly*', down a tone to pinch the ring finger; '*Laidy-wissell*', long finger; '*Lody-Wassell*', index finger; and 'Great *Ona-monadod!*' in her deepest, gruffest voice for the small pink thumb.

Dandy spread his fat starfish hands and laughed delightedly. ' 'Gain! Mamma do 'gain!'

She played all the games she could think of, but when her invention failed he grew fretful.

'All right, my precious *eshweet*,' she said, imitating Ayah's honeyed, crooning singsong, 'be a good *Baba-Sunny* and go sleepybyes.'

She rocked him with the nonsense lullabye her own Ayah had sung:

Little, little fish
In bitter, bitter oil,
I will not part with one of them
For three *pice* and a half.

At long last his head sagged on her shoulder. Gently she placed him on her own bed with pillows on either side to stop him rolling off. Then, furious with Sarah for her delay, she hurried from the room.

With an anxious eye on the courtyard gate, she eased as inconspicuously as she could through the kitchen entrance, and stopped to catch her breath. The combination of worry, hunger and irritation was making her heart pound erratically.

The small quadrangle was quiet. Crows rose in a flapping cloud as she moved cautiously towards the kitchen, a sure sign that the place was deserted, since Camilo the cook and his small scullion Hari Singh waged ceaseless war on these black scroungers, who dared congregate only when their persecutors were at the markets.

There would be no markets today. The bazaar was the barometer of political temperature, sensitive to any disturbance. When rioters thronged the streets prudent merchants kept their shutters up, and the food supply did not flow freely until tranquillity was restored. Against such emergencies, James's stock of imported delicacies had proved a useful buffer in the past; now that it was gone, she must make haste to order more tinned foodstuffs

142

sent up from India – always providing General Sale succeeded in clearing the eastern passes for convoys.

It was the first time Thea had visited the kitchen. Once her eyes became accustomed to the gloom inside the long, low-raftered chamber, with its four simple hearths, each formed by a triangle of stones filled with blackened charcoal, she was overcome by a sense of nostalgia, for it had been to just such a place that she had run for comfort as a small child, knowing that her mother would never seek her there.

Clay bowls, copper pots and blackened cauldron were just as she remembered. There were two misshapen tin spoons and a ladle made from half a coconut shell attached to a stick. A slab of smooth stone with a roller on it and a grimy, scarred wooden table, stained with the preparation of many meals, completed Camilo's *batterie de cuisine*. Her mother's cook, Pedro, used to sleep on a table just like this; no doubt Camilo did the same. The smells, too, reminded her piercingly of childhood. Onions, woodsmoke, spices and the faintly mousy fragrance of rice and lentils assailed her nostrils, together with an underlying pungency of rotting vegetables and far from fresh meat. She lifted lids, peered into bowls and the dark depths of the cauldron, discovering a pitcher full of *ghee*, soaked pulses ready for pounding into *dal*, and a stack of chupatties, dry and stale, but at least they would appease immediate hunger.

What Dandy needed most, however, was milk. Somewhere there had to be a covered jug. Conscious that he would soon wake and would certainly howl if he found himself alone in strange surroundings, she pushed open the fly-screened larder door, and tripped over something large and soft lying across the threshold. As she realised what the obstruction was, a scream rose in her throat.

Sarah lay face down, the fuzzy plait tumbled forward over one shoulder, hands outstretched in a pleading gesture. Her skirt was rucked up, exposing layers of petticoat, and her feet were twisted in a pose that was somehow

143

pathetic, showing her last effort to scramble up before she died.

The cause of death was clear enough. Between her shoulder-blades projected the ivory handle of a dagger that belonged among James's curios, one of a pair. It was not likely to have been removed from the study by anyone but Hinghan Khan.

That strange, wild, tigerish boy . . . Thea's knees felt weak. She stumbled to the kitchen door and, in the weak winter sunlight, vomited helplessly on to the cobbles. Sinking down, she waited for the dizziness to pass. Sarah was dead, and she was alone in a city torn by riots, all alone with a child she hardly knew.

As if to remind her this was not the full sum of her worries, a sudden fierce twinge made her gasp. A pain forgotten since she had last felt it, but one there was no mistaking.

'Oh, no!' she said aloud. 'Not *now!*'

Cautiously, moving like an old woman, she heaved herself upright and shuffled through the archway towards her own room, dreading the second twinge that would confirm her fears.

Dandy was still asleep as she sank down in a chair with a sigh of relief and sat breathing shallowly while her heart slowed to its usual pace. The clock ticked, time passed, and Dandy slept on.

I must have been mistaken, she thought at last. It was the shock of finding Sarah. Poor Sarah! I ought to have covered her face, at least, but I can't go back now. Better stay here. It can't be long before someone remembers where we are and sends an escort to fetch us.

Outside, all was quiet and still. Temporarily satisfied, the looters had gone, taking the livestock and leaving debris scattered about the outer courtyard, broken crates and boxes, papers blowing in the breeze. Faintly in the distance she could hear shots, but that had to be troops sent to quell the disturbances and rescue those other British wives who were, like herself and Mrs Trevor, stranded in the city.

Dandy stirred and opened his eyes. She rose to go to him and stopped halfway across the room, bent double, pressing her hands against her abdomen as the pain came again, fiercely.

The first rumours of the Resident's murder reached the British cantonments at eight that morning and were summarily dismissed. Burnes in trouble? Impossible! Why, he and the Afghan chiefs were as thick as thieves. Who would believe such a cock-and-bull tale?

Nobody wanted to believe it, least of all General Elphinstone, who yearned with every fibre of his pain-racked frame to lay down the burden of this command he had never wanted and had been persuaded into accepting against his better judgement. All he wished for was to take his gout quietly home to India and nurse it back to health.

Nor did the Envoy want to hear about a catastrophe that threatened to unravel his carefully woven web of self-deception and spoil his triumphant departure for his new governorship. He wanted to leave the country quiet, and quiet it should damned well remain until he was well clear of it. He was quite as anxious as Elphy Bey to leave Afghanistan, and tetchily dismissed the first reports of trouble in the city.

'Sir Alexander is too cool a hand to let matters get beyond his control,' he assured the Commander-in-Chief. 'Depend on it, this is nothing to signify or alarm us.'

The second report stated unequivocally that the Resident, his young brother and Captain William Broadfoot were dead, the Residency and Captain Johnson's Treasury plundered, and the sepoy guards shot dead to the last man.

This was more difficult, indeed impossible, to ignore, coming as it did from the mouth of Dr Tobias Black, whose testimony was borne out by columns of black smoke hanging over the bazaar, and the sound of musket-fire. Reluctantly the Envoy and the General faced the fact that something would have to be done.

145

'Though for the life of me I cannot think what,' said Elphy Bey distractedly, running his hands through his thin grey hair. It stood up in a crest above his beaky, fine-boned face, giving him the look of a crowned crane. 'It is all very well for Dr Black to advise me to act at once, but what can we do? We are outnumbered. How tiresome that Sale should have taken his brigade away just now!'

He glanced round the little circle of staff officers and appealed to one of the Envoy's aides, Captain George Lawrence, who had just arrived with a report confirming that the city's shops were shut and the street full of excited and armed men. 'What is your opinion, Captain Lawrence?'

'I believe you should send a regiment to the Residency at once, sir,' replied Lawrence without hesitation. 'We know who is at the bottom of all this. Old Aminullah and Abdullah Khan. If we act swiftly to arrest the ringleaders, the insurrection will collapse at once.'

'Insanity!' exclaimed Captain Grant, Elphinstone's own senior ADC, annoyed that young Lawrence's opinion had been sought before his and contradicting it on principle.

'Out of the question,' agreed the Envoy. 'To reply in kind is the very worst course of action in these circumstances. It would bring all the malcontents in Kabul buzzing about our ears like hornets. In my view, the best we can do is wait quietly until the situation becomes clearer.'

'What! Keep our men standing idle when, as seems all too likely, Sir Alexander and his companions have been foully done to death?' asked Lawrence heatedly, and the Envoy frowned.

'You will permit me to know my own business best, Captain Lawrence. As yet we cannot be certain what has happened, or if Sir Alexander would even welcome an armed intervention.'

'He sent a message! You cannot ignore his appeal for help!'

'*If* Dr Black's report is correct – and you must remember it is still unconfirmed – any help we send now will be

146

too late,' said Macnaghten obstinately. 'Where is Black? Why did he not report to me in person?'

The staff officers looked at one another. At last Captain Bellew cleared his throat and vouchsafed the information that he had last seen Dr Black in native dress, riding off towards the city.

'By whose orders?' demanded Macnaghten, very put out. 'Upon my word, that young man is a law unto himself. He pops up here and there like a jack-in-the-box, exceeding his authority and meddling in matters that are not his concern. What good are his reports if I never have the chance to question him?'

' "The Invisible Man",' sneered Captain Grant. 'That's our name for Black. He comes and goes like a will-o'-the-wisp.'

'The Invisible Man! Ha! That hits him off perfectly.'

'But he is right, sir,' said Lawrence, despairing of getting any clear directive from General Elphinstone, who seemed to be sinking into a torpor, gazing out at the parade-ground with half-closed eyes and his mouth puckered with pain. 'We must crush the rebels before they gather more support.'

Elphinstone shook his head. 'No. I incline to Sir William's view. In General Sale's absence we must take no precipitate action that would leave our military weakness exposed. I understand your feelings, Captain Lawrence,' he added with his customary courtesy. 'I know Sir Alexander is a particular friend of yours. But I beg that in this instance you will allow wiser heads to prevail.'

Wiser! Lawrence cast an agonised glance at his ally Sturt who, as the garrison's only engineer officer, was present at the conference. He responded with the faintest of shrugs. His own long-running battle to be allowed to build the sort of cantonments he considered defensible had taught him that once the Envoy decided that black was white, no power on earth would make him change his mind.

Elphinstone's problem was different, but equally intractable. His mind leaped uneasily between half a dozen

147

possibilities without reaching any firm conclusion as to which he preferred. His usual habit was to follow the advice of the last person who had spoken to him, regardless of age, rank or experience. There were times when both Lawrence and Sturt wondered if the General's long and debilitating illness had actually addled his wits.

'I suppose I will have to recall General Sale,' he said wearily, closing his eyes as he lay back in the wicker *chaise longue* with his bandaged feet propped up before him. A more unmartial figure would be hard to imagine, thought Lawrence, yet you couldn't help liking the old fellow. It was just a pity that Fate – or, more accurately, Lord Auckland – had decreed that he should command the Army of the Indus.

Elphy Bey sighed and spoke faintly, as if each word cost him an effort.

'Captain Lawrence! You will oblige me by riding at once to the Bala Hissar to acquaint His Majesty the Shah with today's events and the measures I have taken to contain the trouble.'

What measures? thought Lawrence, but he knew better than to invite a long, rambling dissertation. Instead, he saluted smartly and withdrew, hearing as he left the room the Envoy recommending that in this emergency it would be proper to withdraw Brigadier Shelton's force into the cantonments, and Elphy Bey's plaintive reply:

'Oh, can't we leave him where he is? You know I can't stand the fellow!'

Heaven help us, thought Lawrence as he and a small escort of sowars spurred down the long straight road to the citadel. It was now ten o'clock, and the bright morning sky had clouded to a uniform leaden grey with a hint of snow in it. The rebels had known when to strike, thought Lawrence bitterly. If they had waited another week, both Macnaghten and Elphy Bey would have been replaced. With Burnes as Envoy and the dour old warhorse General Nott as Commander-in-Chief, things would have been very different.

Deep in thought, he was taken by surprise when his

horse shied violently. He snatched at the mane and saw a burly Afghan in a dirty *poshteen*, his features contorted in hate, leap up from the ditch in which he had been crouching. Steel flashed viciously as he lunged with his thick-bladed, two-handed sword.

Instinct and the agility of his horse saved Lawrence. As the animal curvetted, the sword's blade became entangled in the folds of his rider's cloak. Before his attacker could disengage the weapon, Lawrence drew his own sword and hacked through the would-be assassin's arm.

At once a fusillade of shots rained about him as a dozen more desperadoes sprang from concealment to surround the escort, but the sowars forced their way through. Bending low over their horses' necks, they stretched out at full gallop, never drawing rein until they were clattering under the arch into the heart of the Bala Hissar.

Shah Shuja received Lawrence with none of the usual delays. As the young captain straightened from his bow, he saw that despite His Majesty's age and girth, he was in combative mood, waddling back and forth across the audience chamber like an angry gander, neck out-thrust, and hissing. Fear and outrage were battling for the upper hand.

With his first words, he set the blame squarely where it belonged. 'Terrible! Terrible! Is it not what I always told Macloten-Sahib would happen? Those blackguards Aminullah and Abdullah Khan are at the bottom of this. I would have hanged those dogs, but Macloten-Sahib would not permit it. Now we shall reap a bitter harvest. Which regiment has been sent to crush the revolt?'

'None, Your Majesty.'

'*None?* Is it possible?' Shah Shuja stopped his pacing, his long, heavy-lidded eyes stared at Lawrence as if trying to see into his mind.

Lawrence said carefully, 'When I left to come here, the Envoy was in conference with General Elphinstone. They had agreed to wait for Brigadier Shelton's return to the cantonments before taking any action.'

149

'But is not Shelton-Sahib still encamped in the Seeah Sung Hills? It will take him all day to march back here!'

'Exactly.'

There was a short silence. Then the Shah said excitedly, 'I shall send Campbell's regiment into the city at once, under the personal command of my Wazir. They shall have orders to relieve the Residency, at all costs. I cannot wait for Macloten-Sahib's consent.' He paused, then added darkly, 'We can only pray that it is not already too late.'

Mrs Trevor was very frightened, but for the sake of the children she did her best to remain calm. She gathered them all into the big chamber above the tower's guard-room and set the four elder children to reading and sewing whilst she played with the three youngest. Blood-curdling yells from the crowd outside the gate penetrated only faintly into this sanctum, though as the hours passed they increased rather than diminished in volume. So far the Afghan bodyguards who were their sole protection against the mob had remained faithful, but she feared that at any moment they might respond to the taunts of their fellow-countrymen by throwing down their weapons and joining the rebels in slaughtering this little nest of *feringhis*.

'When will Papa come?' asked ten-year-old Edward for the umpteenth time, and for the umpteenth time Mrs Trevor replied with brisk cheerfulness that their father was very busy but as soon as his duty permitted, he would come to them.

In the event, however, it was not Captain Trevor who appeared but Dr Black, pulling off his turban the moment he realised from Mrs Trevor's stifled scream that she took him for an Afghan.

'Forgive me, ma'am!' he said, taking her hand in a reassuring clasp. 'I did not mean to frighten you. I have come to tell you that your husband is on his way with an escort to bring you and the children and Mrs Quinn's family into the cantonments for safety.'

'Oh, Dr Black, I am so very glad to see you!' said Mrs

Trevor, only a slight tremor in her voice betraying the strain she had suffered in the past hours. 'You say Trevor is coming? I will have the children ready in no time. Now, boys! Run and ask Ayah to put on your warmest coats and pack extra boots for all of you. I suppose we may have to stay there some time?' she added as the children scampered gladly from the room.

'I think you should prepare for it. The city is in a disturbed state and we have reports that some officers' houses have been plundered.' He glanced towards the spiral stairway leading to the upper rooms. 'Where is Mrs Quinn? Lady Sale told me – '

'*Oh!*' exclaimed Mrs Trevor. 'How terrible! I forgot she was coming to visit me today.'

'You mean she is not here?'

'No. You are right – she should be . . . What with the tumult outside and fearing the guards would not prove true to their salt, I had quite forgotten her. I expect she heard the guns and decided to stay at home. Her house is so near the bazaar . . . ' Her voice trailed away. She looked at him with dark-shadowed eyes and said sombrely, 'Oh, Dr Black! What can we do?'

He was already rewinding his turban, his face grim. 'I shall go at once and find out.'

CHAPTER EIGHT

"Fly, brothers, fly!' yelled the wild-eyed ruffian galloping through the bazaar. His dirty sheepskin *poshteen* hung almost to the knees of his sweating, shaggy pony, a long-barrelled musket was slung on his back, and both sword and dagger clanked against his mount's heaving flanks as it slipped and slithered on the cobbles of the narrow alleys between the shuttered booths. The long end of his turban whipped across his face. 'The *feringhis* are coming! Fly for your lives!'

Huddled groups of Afghans broke apart from their anxious conferences to stare at him. Fear and guilt lay heavy on them. After the night of burning and looting, retribution must swiftly follow, and the shouts of this fleeing horseman triggered the alarm in their hearts.

'They follow close behind. Fly, brothers, fly! The Red Regiment – the terrible Lal Paltan – is on the march!'

Like lumps of sugar in water, the groups melted away. Toby rode on towards the Residency, over which smoke hung in a dense grimy pall. Shattered furniture, torn books and smashed cases littered the courtyard. A few furtive looters lingered but they, too, fled at his warning shouts. The bodies of the sepoy guard, slaughtered to a man, sprawled at their posts, but of Burnes and his brother there was no sign.

Captain Johnson's house just across the wide street had the same lingering fumes and scattered papers, and deep wheel tracks in the churned-up slush marked where loaded carts had been driven away full of plunder. The guards had died defending the treasure chests of Army pay, and an eerie silence hung over the scene of recent violence. There was little chance that Captain Quinn's house could have escaped the looters, since it backed directly on to the Treasury garden, with only a low mud wall and strip of orchard between.

Dreading what he would find there, he rode down the narrow alley behind Captain Johnson's house and jumped the mud wall. After tying his pony to the branch of an apple tree he went cautiously forward on foot.

The outer courtyard where the animals were kept had evidently been the looters' prime target. Though the flat-roofed hollow square of buildings had escaped fire damage, not so much as a chicken remained in them. Moving cautiously along the row of deserted byres, Toby reached the arch that led to the kitchen, and the sight of the door hanging open dashed his hope that the house had remained inviolate.

He slipped inside and stood, listening. Anger rose in him – anger at all those whose fear or foolishness had led to this state of affairs. Elphy Bey's dithering and Burnes's recklessness. The Envoy, who would not listen to advice. Above all his anger was directed at those soldiers who brought women and children into an unsettled country.

Soft-footed in his felt boots, he moved through the dim maze of domestic offices and cubby-holes where food was prepared or stored, nerves tightly strung and hand on pistol. Death seemed to hang in the air. Time and again he glanced over his shoulder, believing he heard footsteps, but nothing moved, nothing stirred the cold, still air but his own quick breathing.

He crossed to the gauze-screened larder and stumbled over the body of a woman lying in deep shadow on the threshold. Swiftly he knelt to feel for a heartbeat, then straightened more slowly, ashamed of his relief. Poor Miss Kennedy. It seemed doubly hard that because she possessed neither beauty nor charm he should be glad that she had died rather than Thea.

Where was she – dead or fled? Methodically he searched from room to room, opening doors and pulling aside curtains, not daring to call in case other ears were listening.

This must be her boudoir: a pretty, airy room furnished with armchairs covered in striped Afghan cotton and

screens showing Mogul hunting scenes. On a sunny win-
dowsill a slinky black cat with a white waistcoat stared at
him. As he approached, it jumped lightly down and slipped through the dividing curtain. Cautiously he followed.

'Thea?'

It was as well for him that he was standing to one side
of the entrance, for the response was instantaneous and
deadly. There was a flash, followed by an explosion that
blinded and temporarily deafened him. The ball whistled
by so close that he felt the hot wind of its passage.

As the smoke cleared and his senses returned, he saw
Thea, white and set of face, putting aside the gun she had
just discharged and picking up another. Her red hair
streamed over her shoulders, her skirt hung in sodden
folds, and her eyes stared at him with no flicker of recognition.

'Thea! *Stop*!'

For a dreadful moment he thought she had not understood and watched helplessly as she raised the second
musket. Then, slowly, she lowered it and began to sob.

'I thought – no one – would ever come. I thought we
were going to die.'

His horrified gaze took in the disordered room, its
bloodstained blankets, overturned bowls of water and
shredded sheets. Dandy was cowering against the pillows,
shocked into silence by the gunfire, but beside the bed
lay a small bundle from which came a steady, mewing
cry.

'My dear girl!' He spoke slowly and soothingly, for she
had the wild uncertain look of an animal at bay. 'Where
is your ayah? Who is looking after you?'

'She ran away. All the servants ran away. Sarah went
to find some food . . . Poor Sarah . . . '

She swayed, and hastily he supported her to the bed.
When he tried to make her lie down, she resisted, pushing
him away.

'My baby!'

'It's all right. I'll look after you both. You're safe now.
Lie still and rest.'

154

Gradually the wild look left her eyes. She lay back with a sigh, overwhelmed by deadly weariness. He examined her quickly and turned his attention to the baby, reflecting not for the first time that Nature left alone often did a better job than doctors. A fine, healthy girl, about seven pounds, he judged, with a wise, wizened face and a thatch of dark hair.

By the time he had cleaned and swaddled her and attended to the grizzling Dandy, Thea had fallen asleep – or so he thought until he tried to leave the room, when she started up with a cry of alarm.

'Where are you going?' she said in a confused way, catching at his hand. 'Please don't leave me alone.'

'I must find somewhere for you to rest until the city is quiet again. I will not be gone long, never fear. I have friends in the city – good friends. I will ask them to hide you.'

'Afghan friends?'

He nodded. 'They will take care of you until it is safe to venture out.'

In the absence of reliable information, speculation rampaged through the Mission compound. Anxiety was tinged with impatience, even anger. Why had nothing been done to quell the disturbances in the city? Why didn't the General order out the troops?

From the Bala Hissar came the thunder of the Shah's cannon, but inexplicably the British guns were silent. Four thousand fighting men stood ready and eager to storm the city, but no one gave them orders.

'What is General Elphinstone *doing*?' demanded Lady Sale, muffled to the eyes against the frosty air and pouncing on Captain Mackenzie the moment he emerged from the conference room.

He gave her a look which said more than words. 'He is . . . *deliberating*, my lady.'

'Dithering. I knew it. It is iniquitous,' declared Lady Sale roundly, 'to keep us all in the dark. If only *I* was in command here!'

He had to smile. 'If only you were! I should be happy to serve under you. What a general officer you would make!'

'I could hardly make a worse one than we are cursed with here,' she responded tartly. 'Well? What can you tell me? – Without, of course, betraying *military secrets*.'

'Little enough, I fear.'

'No news of Sir Alexander Burnes?'

He shrugged. 'Several reports, all contradictory. Personally, I am inclined to discount the latest, by which His Majesty claims that Burnes is safe with his Wazir, Osman Khan. If that were true, he would hardly have left us in this uncertainty. The Treasury has been plundered and Captain Broadfoot killed. I find it hard to believe Sir Alexander and his brother did not share his fate.'

'And the ladies? Mrs Trevor? Mrs Quinn?'

He looked graver still. 'No word yet, I fear. Dr Black has gone into the city in native dress to discover what he can.'

'Alone?'

He nodded, and she said quietly, 'He is a brave man. Let us pray he comes to no harm.'

The short November day passed in disconnected flurries of activity which seemed to achieve nothing. Messengers galloped between the Bala Hissar and Brigadier Shelton's camp, ten miles away in the hills. An urgent summons was sent to General Sale, calling for the immediate return of the 37th Native Infantry. Notes were exchanged between the Envoy and the Commander-in-Chief from their respective dwellings which were all of two hundred yards apart. Still the troops stood idle, waiting for orders.

Among the ladies, nothing excited more anxiety than the fate of the Trevor family and young Mrs Quinn. The wildest rumours ran rife. Some said that Captain Trevor and his wife had escaped with one child, but that the rest had been murdered in their beds. This report was soon contradicted by other voices, who had it for a fact that though Trevor himself had escaped with a bullet through the leg, the rest of the family had perished.

156

Great, then, was the joy and relief when soon after nightfall word spread through the cantonments that all the Trevors had ridden in safe and sound, escorted by a detachment of the Shah's bodyguards, who had valiantly defended their commanding officer and his family against the attacking mob.

'Noble fellows, one and all!' exclaimed Mrs Trevor, her pale, strained face dissolving into tears of relief as she hugged her youngest child to her bosom. 'We owe them our lives. They never faltered. As we rode through the streets a fanatic ran at me and tried to strike me down, but the trooper at my side took the blow. His hand was severed, but he walked beside me holding the stump all the way here.'

A hero, everyone agreed, and the Chaplain at once arranged a service of thanksgiving for the Trevors' deliverance, though many of his congregation felt that his optimism was premature. When he added a plea for the Lord to look mercifully on His lost sheep and bring them safe to the fold; no one could doubt that Mrs Quinn and Dandy were foremost in his thoughts.

The four young wives of Jan Fishan Khan, Dr Black's most trusted friend among the Afghan noblemen, accepted their unexpected guests with perfect placidity if no great enthusiasm. They fed and bathed Dandy, threw away his soiled clothes and dressed him in a suit of quilted cotton with a hole in the seat before setting him down in the midst of their own romping offspring.

Nasi Begum, the principal wife, gave Thea infusions of herbs to dry up her milk, and produced a wet-nurse from among the serving-women. Before a week had passed, Thea was strong enough to rise from her pallet, and her children had been so well absorbed into the large household that it was hard to identify Dandy among the children rolling and squabbling like puppies on the floor.

'Where is Dr Black?' she asked the placid, indifferent women, but they neither knew nor cared. After several anxious days slipped past with no word from him, she put the question to her host, Jan Fishan Khan, who gave her a sly, sidelong look.

'The Hakim-Sahib is the Sirdar's guest of peace.'

'Guest of peace?'

Another meaningful look, and she understood. Toby had been taken hostage. Her heart bumped with alarm. Without his protection she felt lost and rudderless. No one else knew her whereabouts; her safety and that of her children depended entirely on Toby's good relations with the chiefs. Had they turned against him for some reason? They were suspicious and mercurial by temperament, quick to suspect treachery. James had accused Toby of having a foot in both camps. Was he right? If the chiefs suspected him of double-dealing, they would kill him without compunction.

'Who is this Sirdar?' she asked, trembling. 'Why should he detain the Hakim-Sahib?'

Jan Fishan Khan half closed his eyes, his long, narrow, ivory face with its blade-thin nose and bearded mouth impossible to read. 'The chiefs have chosen Mahomed Akbar Khan, son of Dost Mahomed, to lead them against the invaders.'

Thea's anxiety sharpened at the name. Akbar Khan was said to be handsome, recklessly brave, unpredictable and devious.

'Why does he need hostages? The Hakim-Sahib has done him no harm. He is your friend.'

'Sekunder Burnes called himself our friend, yet he betrayed us and brought the *feringhis* to steal our land,' said Jan Fishan Khan coldly.

'But Dr Black tried to stop them! Your Sirdar must know that. Why has he turned against him now?'

'The Sirdar has his reasons.'

'What reasons?' she demanded, anger banishing her fear. 'Has the Hakim-Sahib not healed your sick and saved your children?'

For a moment Jan Fishan Khan stroked his beard in silence. Then he said gently, 'When the hawks are hooded, the pigeons are easily scared away. Winter is

coming, Memsahib. It is time the pigeons flew back to
their own land and left us to rule as we please. Once they
have gone, we will set free the hawks to follow them
home.'

He was right, of course. With Sir Alexander Burnes
dead and Toby a hostage, who would stiffen General
Elphinstone's will to fight? Not the Envoy, who longed
for the luxuries of Bombay. Not that cold fish Captain
Grant, or his fellow aide Captain Bellew. General Sale and
his brigade had already gone down to the provinces, and
most of the officers remaining were counting the days
until they could leave Afghanistan. They would persuade
old Elphy Bey into some face-saving formula and march
down through the passes before the snow blocked them,
and what would become of her then? She didn't want to
be left behind.

She said, 'My lord, you have treated us kindly and I
am very grateful. God will reward you, for how can I
repay what I owe you?'

'The Memsahib's presence sheds light on my poor
dwelling,' he said politely.

'But now I must return to my people, and burden you
with my presence no longer.'

He did not reply at once, and she feared he meant to
detain her, too. But at last he made an acquiescing gesture
and said quietly, 'As the Memsahib wishes, so be it!
Tonight, when it is dark, I will arrange your departure.
Cover your face if any should stop you on the way and
say you have the protection of Jan Fishan Khan.'

'My lord, I am for ever in your debt. If there is anything
I can do in return . . . ?'

'Tell your people that Jan Fishan Khan treated you
well,' he said indifferently. 'Be ready with your children
when darkness falls.'

With grave dignity he made his salaam and withdrew,
leaving her astonished that he had placed no obstacles in
her way and demanded no ransom.

When night fell, she was pacing the floor nervously, the
baby clutched in her arms. Dandy watched silently from

a corner, sensing her anxiety, her overpowering desire to be gone from this dingy, cheerless chamber with its clinging aroma of woodsmoke, mutton fat, and unwashed female bodies. The minutes crawled by and she had begun to suspect a cruel trick when at last there was a tap on the door and a muffled messenger beckoned her forward.

She followed him down a labyrinth of small passages until he halted in a room softly lit by candles and smelling of sandalwood.

'Wait here, Memsahib.'

She supposed Jan Fishan Khan wished to bid them farewell, but when the door opened she was astonished to recognise Hinghan Khan, splendidly dressed in a robe stiff with gold embroidery, a low-necked vest, purple sash, and green and gold striped turban.

'What are you doing here?' She was astounded at his audacity. How dare he show his face to me? she thought, as her eyes fastened on an ivory-handled dagger at his waist, pair to the one that had struck down Sarah.

'I have paid the ransom demanded by Jan Fishan Khan to allow you to return to your people,' he said in his soft, insolent voice. 'Thus I repay all I owe to the Captain-Sahib.'

She was outraged to find herself in his debt. 'Oh, I have no doubt he will reward you handsomely,' she snapped.

He shook his head.

'I ask no money, Memsahib. I ask only that the Chota-Sahib stays with me, for his safety.'

Leave Dandy with this treacherous tiger cub? 'Certainly not!'

He said earnestly, 'The Sirdar has sworn to kill all the British. Leave the Chota-Sahib with me, and I will keep him safe. The chiefs have taken an oath that not one man, woman or child of the *feringhis* shall pass through the Khyber alive.'

A chill ran down her spine, but she tried to ignore it. Afghans loved making that kind of grandiloquent threat. She said nothing.

'You must believe me! Do you wish your son to die? Let me hide him until the danger is past.'

Little as she liked him, she knew his anxiety to protect Dandy was real enough. He was tugging at her hand, trying to run to Hinghan Khan, but she held him firmly.

'You killed Miss Kennedy, and left me alone,' she accused. 'Would I leave my son with a murderer of women?'

He did not deny the charge.

'Why did you do it? Was it because she caught you stealing?'

His long eyes flashed as he drew himself up. 'I stole nothing! All will be returned to the Captain-Sahib. I swear it. I, Hinghan Khan.'

'The *palki* is waiting. Let me pass,' she said. 'I have nothing more to say to you.'

'Give me the Chota-Sahib!'

'No.'

He read finality in her face and stood aside.

'When the Ghilzai knives are at your throat, you will be sorry you did not listen to me, Memsahib,' he said, and the cold conviction in his voice again sent a shiver down her spine.

161

CHAPTER NINE

Day and night, the bellowing of hungry camels reverberated through the cantonments. Since the loss of the commissariat fort five weeks earlier, and Akbar Khan's interdiction on selling forage to the Army, the animals had eaten nothing but the branches of trees, one another's tails, and their own dung. Every morning at daybreak, the carcases of those that had died were hauled outside the walls. Horses and mules, though equally emaciated, found a ready market as meat.

Worse even than the stench from the rotting carcases piled by the gates, however, was the smell of defeat within the walls. A strange paralysis had gripped the beleaguered garrison. From the highest to the lowest, no one seemed capable of initiating action, merely responding belatedly and ineffectively to each new Afghan threat.

General Elphinstone, propped in his chair, sought advice from all his officers in turn, thanked each one civilly, and ignored what he had said in favour of the next opinion. So low had morale sunk that a mood of utter pessimism pervaded the cantonments. No one could doubt that the Mission to Afghanistan had failed most dismally, and the best to hope for now was a safe and speedy return to Hindustan. 'When we go' had replaced 'If we go', but even the matter of negotiating a withdrawal was fraught with peril, for any agreement made with one Afghan chief might well be ignored by his rivals.

'The Envoy is far too trusting,' complained Lady Sale. 'He says that Akbar Khan is a *gentleman*, but he judges him by the standards of an English gentleman, which manifestly he is not. No Afghan – gentleman or otherwise – considers breaking his word a dishonour. If only Sir William would leave the negotiations to someone who understands the Afghan nature!'

'I know, Mamma,' said Alexandrina, who had heard this argument before.

'But who does understand it?' asked Thea diffidently.

'That is the question,' Lady Sale sighed impatiently. 'Sir Alexander dead, Major Eldred Pottinger wounded, Captain Skinner taken hostage . . . '

'Like Dr Black.'

'Exactly, my dears. We are faced with Hobson's choice.'

Thea and her children had arrived safely in the Mission compound after their sojourn with Jan Fishan Khan, but it had taken her some days to understand quite how serious the situation had become. Since Burnes's murder, disaster had piled on disaster. The loss of the commissariat fort had been a heavy blow, swiftly followed by Akbar Khan's decree that any Afghan caught supplying the British would be punished by death.

Georgiana Mainwaring had greeted Thea as one risen from the dead, and had begged her to share her quarters, cramped though they already were. She had even pressed her to accept the services of her baby son's wet-nurse. 'The poor mite is quite swamped with her milk,' she said. 'He does not take after me in appetite – at least, not yet.'

Georgy herself was always hungry. She was inclined to speak disparagingly of her baby, who weighed only five and a half pounds at birth. 'Your Vicky is a far finer specimen. Perhaps the competition will encourage my little fellow. Since I make such efforts to obtain special rations for Ayah, it goes against the grain to see him turn up his nose at the result.'

Thea had been shocked, at first, to see how Georgy's dresses hung in folds on her tall frame, and her eyes looked too large in her gaunt face. Yet she was as merry and generous as ever, and wasted no time in putting the *durzee* to work when she realised that neither Thea nor Dandy had more than the clothes they stood up in. Soon she was pressing the best of her own wardrobe on them.

'You can wear green, so fortunate! Dolly was kind enough to tell me it makes me look perfectly bilious,' she said, adding her emerald silk cloak to the pile of offerings.

'Oh, no, Georgy! That's too much. Do you remember wearing that at Lady Macnaghten's Ball?'

'And looking a fright in it! No, I insist. I have far too many clothes – I cannot imagine how I will take them back to India, since we have only one camel left and that will have to carry us all.'

Already, by the third week in December, it was clear there could be no question of taking back more than a fraction of the household goods that the Army of the Indus had brought to Kabul with such labour. Pianos, dining-tables and bookcases were chopped into firewood. Cases of wine were broken open; and carefully hoarded tinned food consumed with no thought of the morrow. The shortage of pack-animals was acute, and the surviving saddle-horses looked like animated toast racks. Although General Sale's brigade had fought through to Jellalabad without great loss, he was now pinned there and heavily outnumbered by tribesmen from the Eastern Ghilzais, fierce fighters all – no help could be expected from that quarter.

'Just think,' said Georgy wistfully, 'how safe and snug we should be in the Bala Hissar, with nice thick walls all round and plenty of food for a year! I would so much rather stay there than march all the way to Jellalabad.'

'To Jellalabad?' exclaimed Thea. 'Surely they cannot mean it? We would freeze before we got halfway.' She had vivid recollections of those narrow, forbidding passes – Khoord-Kabul, Gandamak and Jugdulluk – each of which must be negotiated before they reached the terrible Khyber Pass. How could anyone even contemplate taking fighting men through them in winter, let alone women and children?

'George Mein tells me Brigadier Shelton is determined to return to India, whatever the cost,' said Georgy, shaking her head. 'He refuses to agree even to *try* fighting our way to the Bala Hissar, though it is less than two miles distant.'

'*He* refuses?' Thea raised her eyebrows. She did not like the aggressive, one-armed Brigadier any more than

Lady Sale did, and thought he resembled the bad-tempered, pugnacious terrier on which Miss Oldershaw had lavished her affections. 'How can he dictate to the General?'

'He cannot, of course – yet he does!' Georgy pushed back her hair with a weary gesture. 'Oh, it is all so confusing. If only they could make up their minds to do *something*, rather than keeping us in suspense. Captain Mackenzie told me that the General and the Brigadier do nothing but argue and then write separate letters to the Envoy, and when Brigadier Shelton is called to a conference, he makes his bearer spread his quilt on the floor, then lies on it with his eyes shut so he can pretend not to hear anything he dislikes. Captain Grant took him to task for it, saying it was uncivil to the General, and what do you think Shelton replied?'

'Tell me.'

'He said, "I *will* be uncivil. Dammit, I *like* being uncivil to him." Poor Elphy Bey! What he has to endure from that man! And he is so patient and uncomplaining, like a sick child. I cannot help feeling sorry for him. After all, it is not *his* fault that we are in this scrape, though from some people's behaviour you would think it was.'

Privately Thea thought this was carrying charity too far. Patience and forbearance were not qualities she admired in a commanding officer, and she felt a kind of helpless rage against woolly-minded old Elphy Bey and the self-deluding Envoy alike. Two Sir Williams, and not a penny to choose between them. If they had not landed the whole Mission in this 'scrape', as Georgy chose to call it, she would like to know who had.

'Cousin George tells me – ' began Georgy, then stopped, looking guilty. 'Oh dear! I forgot it was supposed to be a secret.'

'Come on! Tell me – ' Thea encouraged. If there was any fresh news, she wanted to be the first to hear it. Lieutenant George Mein – popularly known as Mein of Information – had a wonderful knack of finding out what was going on. He had been wounded in the head during

the October fighting in the Khoord-Kabul pass, but
claimed that this proved his skull was harder than a bullet,
for the missile had split in two, one part running under
the skin of his scalp to the back of his head, while the
other made a hole in his brain. Despite this gruesome
injury, he had made a good recovery and attached himself
to Lady Sale's entourage, to which his lively spirits and
nose for gossip made him a very welcome addition. Being
distantly related to Georgiana, he took good care to keep
her abreast of every scrap of information he acquired.

Everyone liked George Mein, and nearly everyone confided their secrets to him.

'Don't know why people tell me things they don't want
known,' he had once told Thea with a kind of melancholy
pride. 'They know very well I shan't be able to keep them
to myself, and so do I. If anyone tells me I have abused
his confidence, I plead in mitigation that I've lost part of
my brain, and can't be held responsible. It always works!'

His round, boyish face and awed whisper – '*You don't
say!*' – tempted even those who should have known better
into parting with their secrets, which Mein then spread
gleefully.

'Come on,' Thea cajoled. 'Do tell me what he said.'

'It may be nothing much,' said Georgy with a worried
look. 'You know how dear George exaggerates. But he
told me he had heard that Captain Skinner is to dine with
the Envoy tonight.'

'Gentleman Jim?' Thea was startled. 'But Akbar is holding him hostage with Dr Black. Does that mean they are
to be set free?'

'Cousin George did not say so, precisely.' Georgiana
hesitated, then went on with a rush: 'I think – that's to
say, I understood him to mean – that Akbar Khan wants
Captain Skinner to be his intermediary. His messenger.
He has some private communication to make to the
Envoy, but does not want the other chiefs to hear of it.
You know how – how *political* the Afghans are! They hate
to let their right hand know what their left is doing.'

She paused, still looking troubled, and added, 'I do so

166

dislike all this uncertainty! Cousin George had heard that
Dr Black was offered the commission but turned it down
which was when Captain Skinner volunteered his services.
That is what bothers me. I should like to know why Dr
Black would have nothing to do with this plan, whatever
it is. Some people say Captain Skinner has a foot in both
camps.'

'They say the same about Dr Black,' Thea pointed out.

'I know. If only one could be sure whom to trust!' She
was silent a moment, then rose, giving her skirt a vigorous
shake as if to rid herself of these unquiet thoughts. 'Then
there's another curious thing. You know I took tea with
Lady Macnaghten yesterday? Sir William came in and sat
by me, and his manner was so strange I hardly know what
to think.'

'Strange? In what way?'

Georgy shook her head, trying to pinpoint her anxiety.
'He was smiling a great deal and patting my hand (which
is something I detest), and seemed quite cock-a-hoop. He
told me he had a Christmas surprise for us all, and when
I asked if I should like it, he laughed and said in that
queer, emphatic way of his, "Oh, I would say so, by Jove.
I should be astonished if you did not".

'Then he began telling me what a fine fellow Akbar
Khan is. Worth two of any other Afghan chief, so he said.
It seemed to me,' said Georgiana, choosing her words with
care, 'as if he was hinting at a private understanding
between them. Something General Elphinstone did not
know about. But, oh, Thea! The Envoy is a babe in arms
when it comes to politicking. Even I can see that. I fear –
I fear very much – that he and Akbar Khan are conspiring
together to double-cross the other chiefs, and if they are
caught out, the consequences will be too terrible to contemplate.'

Sir William Macnaghten was in high spirits as he mounted
his horse on the morning of 23 December. Last night's
mule steak lay easy on his stomach, and the feverish cold

that had made breathing a burden these past four days seemed miraculously to have cleared.

Best of all was his conviction that the discomforts and anxieties of the past six weeks were about to be relieved. At last he could see his way clear. This morning's meeting with Akbar would set the seal on his plan to save the whole Mission from failure, and preserve the reputation he had worked so hard to achieve.

The message which Gentleman Jim Skinner and his two Afghan escorts had brought to him at dinner last night was a glorious vindication of his own faith in the young Sirdar. Of course, Akbar himself was doing very well out of the deal. He would have no cause for complaint. The secret treaty they would sign this morning promised him a guaranteed British withdrawal within two years, and in the meantime the lucrative post of Wazir to Shah Shuja. Also a lump sum now, and a pension for life. Even then he had not been satisfied and had demanded more gifts: a pair of pistols, and an Arab mare belonging to that cold fish Captain Grant.

The last demand had given the Envoy no end of trouble to secure. Grant had not wanted to part with his mare, and all Macnaghten's arguments about making sacrifices for the common weal had failed to persuade him to bring his price lower than three thousand rupees – a ridiculous sum. In the end it had been necessary to pull rank and order him to sell, which he had done with a very bad grace. His language had been intemperate and disrespectful enough to verge on insubordination. He had said he was damned if he saw why his animal should be sold into slavery to please a young brute like Akbar Khan, and if the Envoy insisted on doing so, he would damned well have to pay for the privilege.

No sense of public duty, thought Sir William disapprovingly. He resolved to make sure that in the fullness of time, word of Captain Grant's intransigence should reach Lord Auckland's ears.

Time to go: it would be bad policy to keep the Sirdar waiting. The Envoy settled his top hat more firmly on his head and glanced at the small party which was to accompany him. There were Captains Lawrence, Mackenzie and Trevor, his aides; Ram Singh, the Rajput *jemadar* with his men; and there was Captain Grant's mare skittishly tossing her head as she was led from the lines, all tacked up in the kind of fancy trappings that would please her new owner.

But where was Lieutenant Le Geyt with the bodyguard of Bombay Cavalry which had been ordered to escort the Envoy to his meeting? Late, of course! So much for military efficiency, thought Macnaghten angrily. Really, it was intolerable that his careful strategy should be put in jeopardy as a result of an idle young officer's incompetence.

Well, he would not wait. If Le Geyt chose to arrive late, that was his own affair. Black against the freshly fallen snow, no more than a quarter of a mile from the cantonments, Akbar's small group of horsemen moved restlessly, and already curious townspeople were streaming out from the city to join them. Any delay now might easily destroy the young Sirdar's fragile trust in the Envoy himself. He was like a wild hawk, fierce, bold, and wary. Macnaghten nodded to Captain Lawrence, who in turn signalled to Ram Singh's bugler.

'We'll go now.'

As the plangent notes cut through the still, frosty air, the small cavalcade trotted through the gates and headed out across the plain without a backward glance at the many anxious faces staring after them from cantonments.

Lady Sale had brought refreshments and a telescope on to the flat roof of her son-in-law's house, and there Thea and Georgiana soon joined them.

'Sit down, my dears. There will be nothing to see for a time, I daresay,' she said, and hospitably began to share out the remains of the unidentified leathery meat her household had dined on yesterday, together with somewhat gritty chupatties made of coarse *ottar*, with a very tolerable claret to wash down the food.

'Sale would tell me it is a crime to drink this with such

fare,' she said cheerfully, 'but I say it would be a far worse crime to let it fall into the hands of some undiscriminating Son of the Prophet. Tell me, Thea, how is young Dandy? I saw him from the window in his little turban and dagger. He looked quite the Sirdar! Is it true he refuses to wear his English clothes?'

'I am afraid Ayah is inclined to spoil him,' Thea admitted, and Lady Sale smiled.

'You are, you mean! Never mind, it would be sad if we females could not indulge our sons in the few years they belong to us. Before you know it, you will be sending him Home to school, and your influence will be at an end.'

This was a tactful way to put it, Thea knew. The truth – which Lady Sale probably knew as well as she did herself – was that Dandy flew into such terrible tantrums if dressed in the little frilled shirts and nankeen drawers kindly provided by Mrs Trevor that she could not stand the noise, and had weakly given instructions that he could wear what he pleased. This was the Afghan tunic and turban given him by Nasi Begum, complete with sash and miniature dagger. These had been far from new when he acquired them and were now very shabby, but everyone's sartorial standards had declined in the past month.

All four ladies had been muffled in sheepskin *poshteens* when they climbed to the roof, but as the winter sun gained in strength they laid them aside, and she could see what a scarecrow, tatterdemalion crew she and her friends had become. Though carefully mended, their gowns looked and smelt in need of better cleaning than the unfortunate *dhobis* could achieve with their meagre allowances of soap and water. It was even hard to be sure one did not smell oneself. Standing downwind of certain ladies was scarcely agreeable these days.

Still, thanks to the sun and the claret, quite a holiday atmosphere prevailed as they watched the Envoy ride out across the plain. While Alexandrina kept her eye to the telescope and called out details of whatever she could discern through it, Lady Sale and her guests embarked on an enjoyable discussion of baby care and the impossibility of convincing any native ayah that discipline was just as important to the nurture of children as unlimited love.

'They have halted. They are saluting one another. Sir William seems to be making a pretty speech,' Alexandrina reported, easing the sections of telescope in and out to bring the scene into sharper focus. 'Oh, this wretched thing! A moment ago I had it . . . There! That's better. They have all dismounted. I can see a carpet spread on the snow and they are inviting Sir William to sit on it. Now I can only see the top of his hat. One of the ADCs is kneeling just behind him. It looks like Captain Lawrence. The Afghans are crowding round.'

'Oh, look! There goes Mr Le Geyt with the Escort,' said Georgiana, who was watching the scene closer at hand. 'Don't they look splendid! I wonder why the Envoy went off without them? It would have made a better show if they had all ridden up together.'

'Have another chupatty,' Lady Sale urged Thea. 'I am afraid I cannot offer anything more appetising, much as I would wish to.'

'You have eaten nothing yourself, ma'am.'

'Go on, take it.'

'No, really, I have eaten enough,' said Thea, though her growling stomach gave the lie to her words. 'Keep it for Alex – Hello, what's up?'

Even with the naked eye it was possible to see some sort of turmoil among the crowd gathered on the plain. Like a cluster of swarming bees, the black mass seemed to spread out then fold back on itself, and as it did so the red uniforms positioned about the top-hatted form of the Envoy suddenly vanished into the crowd.

Halfway between cantonments and the rendezvous, Le Geyt and the Escort jingled to an abrupt halt.

'What is happening?' said Lady Sale sharply. 'Alex?'

'It's all blurred.' Whipping out her handkerchief, Alexandrina wiped frantically at the lens. Around them a buzz of alarmed speculation broke out among the other watchers on neighbouring roofs. 'I can't – see – the – Envoy,'

she said tautly, her straining eyes searching to pick out
the distinctive top hat among the turbans. 'There's Akbar
Khan – yes, and that might be Sir William . . . No, I
cannot be sure. But look! There's one of the aides. They're
putting him up on a pony. He's hurt! The Afghans are
putting them all up on their horses. One has fallen off.'

'*Let me look!*' Lady Sale almost snatched the telescope
away and focused it. Two red dots clinging pillion behind
galloping Afghan horsemen flashed across her vision, and
behind them ran men brandishing weapons, hacking and
stabbing at them. A third red dot rolled on the ground
and vanished under a black tide.

Just a glimpse, then it was gone and the lens was filled
with a nearer jumble of horses and men, scarlet and gold,
as the Escort broke ranks and galloped back to cantonments, with the young subaltern standing in his stir-
rups, mouth open, shouting at them to return.

'Oh, Mamma!' breathed Alexandrina.

The four women looked at one another in horror. It
had happened so quickly – but what exactly had happened
none of them could be sure. Only that the Envoy and his
suite had vanished as suddenly as if the earth had swallowed them, and whatever Sir William had expected of
this meeting, it had certainly not been what had occurred.

'I shall go at once to the General's quarters,' said Lady
Sale decidedly. 'Possibly Captain Grant will be able to
shed some light on this affair.'

In silence, the three girls watched her descend to the
courtyard and cross with her characteristic long-legged
stride to the verandah where General Elphinstone and
his staff were gathered. Moustaches moved, heads were
gravely shaken.

'Either they know nothing or they will tell her nothing,'
reported Alexandrina, unashamedly staring through the
telescope.

Half an hour dragged past before Lady Sale's face once
more popped up over the parapet, and the girls crowded
round, anxious for news. Florentia's breath whistled in

her throat with the exertion, but her expression was more cheerful.

'The General knows nothing, as one would expect,' she reported, rubbing her hands before the little brazier which Naik Kumar Singh had lit for them on the roof. 'But Mr Waller has received a message to say that the Envoy is safe in the city, and all his aides are with him. There was too great a crowd on the plain for the private discussion he wished for, so the Sirdar has taken him to his own house where they may speak quietly. So all's well that ends well, my dears, and perhaps we may look forward to good news before Christmas after all. What is it, Alex, my love?'

Alexandrina had opened her mouth to say that this version of events hardly tallied with what she had glimpsed through the telescope. There had been a violence about the mêlée which could not be attributed to an agreed decision to change the conference site. She had seen bearded faces contorted with hate, and the flash of steel. Though she could not swear to have actually witnessed it, she had had the distinct impression that the Envoy had been seized and propelled away by force.

Her mother was watching her closely. 'What is it?' she asked again.

Alexandrina shook her head. She could not be sure what she had seen and what imagined. There was no advantage in alarming her companions. If news was bad, it would reach them soon enough. With an effort, she forced a smile. 'Nothing, Mamma,' she said. 'I am sure you are right.'

Back and forth, back and forth, Toby paced his narrow room, three steps one way and three the other. Worry and frustration drew his mouth into a tight line and his movements were tense with bottled-up energy.

For the first six weeks of detention, Captain Skinner had shared his captivity and they had lived in some comfort, with several rooms to move about in and servants to wait on them. But since the Sirdar's visit ten days earlier,

173

Toby had been alone, and conditions had deteriorated sharply. He had been transferred to this miserable chicken coop of a cell, where a small barred window provided the only light. His food consisted of rotting scraps, which had brought on a bout of dysentery, and instead of servants two surly and ill-disposed guards were posted outside his door. From their looks and attitude, at once boastful and bullying, he deduced that respect for the British had vanished.

'I'll do what I can for you, old man,' Gentleman Jim had murmured just before he left in the Sirdar's wake. 'I'll see if I can't agree an exchange of prisoners. Pity you've no wife to offer in your place. Comes cheaper than shelling out a ransom!'

He had clapped Toby on the shoulder and swung away with the stiff-legged stride of a cavalry officer too long out of the saddle, and Sultan Jan, their gaoler, had courteously saluted his remaining prisoner before slamming home the bolts.

Since then he had had only his thoughts for company. Christmas had come and gone, and by his reckoning today must be the Feast of the Epiphany, though days tended to blur when there was nothing to fill the long hours between Sultan Jan's visits but worry and endless sifting of the scraps of information vouchsafed by the guards.

Most Afghans loved fantasy and it was hard to know how much to believe. He discounted the lurid stories of raped memsahibs and butchered babies, but there was a worrying consistency about their claims that Macloten-Sahib was dead and his dismembered body hanging in the bazaar.

The Envoy – dead?

'Impossible!' he said sharply.

The guards grinned and drew imaginary knives across their throats. Macloten-Sahib had tried to break faith with the chiefs, they said. His punishment was death.

'Lying sons of dogs!' said Toby, and they laughed again.

As he lay on his string bed that afternoon, watching a

174

wintry sunbeam's progress across the wall of his prison, the hubbub of voices in the street outside attracted his attention. Moments later, a curled and blackened object like the claw of a large bird was raised by means of a long pole to the level of his window, and waved to and fro in macabre salute. For a moment he stared and then, clambering up to stand on the bed, he caught hold of the bars and pulled himself level with it.

From below, the crowd saw him and howled insults. The man holding the pole manoeuvred his grisly trophy until it was no more than a foot from the window, twisting it this way and that to afford Toby a better view. His breath caught in his throat.

Shrivelled now, and caked with black dried blood at the wrist, it was still unmistakably a European hand, with neatly trimmed nails and, on the little finger, an engraved signet ring. He knew that ring, and felt a flicker of surprise that no one had hacked off the finger to claim it, but then the ownership – late ownership – of the hand might have been open to question. As it was, there could be no possible doubt that the gruesome object now being waved beneath his nose had once belonged to none other than Her Majesty's Envoy to Afghanistan, Sir William Macnaghten.

CHAPTER TEN

'Hide yourself and the Burra-Memsahib among the horse-men. Do not stay near the other ladies, for they will be attacked,' her old acquaintance Taj Mahomed had murmured to Alexandrina when he arrived in cantonments with a message for the General. The red-bearded, foxy-faced horse-dealer had often supplied Captain Sturt with reliable animals at reasonable prices and Alex trusted him.

'Cover your faces, and ride mixed in with the Sowars.' he urged, and in a trembling voice she thanked him for the warning.

Orders for the march to Jellalabad, ninety miles to the east, had been given and countermanded twice already, and everyone's nerves were on edge as they waited for General Elphinstone to make his final decision to abandon what poor shelter the Mission compound could afford and throw his entire force on the doubtful mercy of the Sirdar, Akbar Khan.

'He is probably right. We would be foolish not to heed his advice,' agreed Lady Sale. 'No doubt Akbar Khan would like to have us ladies in his power, for then he could dictate his own terms to the General. Of course, he has obtained quite absurdly generous ones already, but Afghans are never satisfied. It makes me boil with rage to think of all the treasure we must leave him, and as for allowing us to carry away only six light guns . . . ! It is humiliating.'

'Sturt thinks we shall have difficulty taking even those through the passes,' said Alexandrina. 'The poor bullocks have hardly strength to pull them, and now the General has ordered Sturt to build a bridge across the Kabul River for the troops to cross.'

'A bridge!' cried her mother. 'Why can they not ford it in the usual way?'

176

'Exactly what Sturt asked Captain Bellew, and he replied quite rudely that those were the General's orders, and he could make of them what he wished. Nor is that the end of it, for once the troops are over the Kabul bridge, Sturt is to take it up again and carry the planks in case the Loghur bridge has been destroyed.'

'What folly!' said Lady Sale angrily. 'It will cause no end of delay, and I am convinced it is not necessary in the least.'

She bit her lip, for she knew as well as her daughter the impossibility of dislodging any idea that had taken firm root in Elphy Bey's sick mind. '*We* will not bother with any bridge,' she said grimly.

'I wish Thea could ride with us,' murmured Alexandrina.

'Nonsense. She will do very well with Mrs Mainwaring,' snapped Lady Sale, who knew it would be every man for himself in this retreat. She went off to ask permission from Captain Hay to ride with his men next morning.

At daybreak they were ready, muffled to the eyes in sheepskin cloaks, with the leather masks known as *nemkeens* protecting their faces from hostile eyes as well as the bitter wind. As the Advance guard assembled by the gate, they stuck close to Captain Hay, fearful of losing their position in the surrounding chaos.

Two regiments of Horse, Her Majesty's 44th, two heavy artillery guns, Major George Broadfoot's Sappers and Mines, the Mountain Train, and the late Envoy's Escort formed the Advance. Captain Hay placed Lady Sale and Mrs Sturt between two grizzled troopers, and charged them with the ladies' safety, whilst their ayah was seated on a pile of bedding which all but obscured her pony. The rest of their servants were to accompany the baggage train.

the For two hours they waited, growing very cold despite signal layers of clothing, until at nine o'clock the bugle Alexled the Advance, and the gates swung open.

mond-candrina caught her breath, dazzled by the dia-
right glitter of the pure white blanket which

177

stretched away as far as eye could see. Her heart quailed. How could their weak and reduced force, burdened with baggage and hampered with so many women and children, ever hope to reach Jellalabad, five days' march away at the best of times?

No use asking such questions; they were committed now and must do the best they could.

The bugle shrilled and the column moved forward. A crowd of ruffianly Ghazis who had gathered to watch the Unbelievers depart pressed forward, jostling and shouting threats so that the horsemen on either side of Lady Sale had to protect her with their own bodies. Of Akbar Khan's promised guard, which was supposed to escort the retreating British columns through the passes, there was no sign at all. Slowly the Advance guard pushed forward, horses stumbling as snow balled in their hoofs, and turned towards the Kabul River.

Lady Sale's thoughts were bleak. She tried unavailingly to shake off her presentiment of disaster. Last night, while watching her son-in-law choose books from his precious library to leave in Taj Mahomed's care, she had picked a volume at random from the pile he had discarded, and idly riffled the pages. It was a collection of Thomas Campbell's poems, and had fallen open at 'Hohenlinden'.

Few, few shall part where many meet
The snow shall be their winding-sheet,
And every turf beneath their feet
Shall be a soldier's sepulchre!

The verse haunted her, running continually through her mind. *Few, few shall part* . . . How many of these poor, half-starved, half-frozen souls would ever see their sunny homeland again? Her eye rested on a beautiful child, a little girl no more than four or five years old, with wide, wondering eyes and glossy black hair, staggering along clutching a bundle nearly as big as herself in trouble wake of the shawled figure of her mother, bent and babe beneath her burden of cooking pots, bedding, a in arms. The child's ears glinted with gold. Soon, when she could go no farther, she would sink down beside the track and some Afghan boy would test the sharpness of his dagger by pulling back her head and cutting her soft brown throat.

Thea and her children shared the pannier on the left side of the Mainwarings' sole surviving camel, while Georgiana doubled up her long legs and clutched her small son in the other. Baby Vicky should have been carried by the ayah, but it had proved difficult to balance the *kajavas*, and only when Vicky was added to the left-hand side did the load stay level.

The ayah was pleased. She did not like Vicky and resented having a second nurseling foisted upon her. The Jung-i-Bahadur, as she called Georgiana's baby, was her *'eshweet'*, the 'lub of her heart', her own dear 'Baba-Sahib'. She put Vicky to the breast only when the Jung-i-Bahadur had sucked his fill, then rubbed opium on the hungry baby's tongue to stop her crying.

It worried Thea that the bonny, plump baby she had brought from Jan Fishan Khan's house had grown so thin and listless. She and Georgy watched the ayah carefully, but the woman was too cunning to let her partiality show.

'She is sly,' said Georgy. 'I wish I had never engaged her, but Mrs Trevor recommended her so particularly. I am sure she is starving your poor baby. I will give her a good scolding, and tell her I will turn her off unless she feeds Vicky properly.'

But the scolding did more harm than good. The ayah turned sullen, and Vicky grew thinner daily. In any case it was difficult to wheedle extra rations for a wet-nurse from the commissariat when even fighting men had to make do on half a seer – about one pound – of wheat and a little melted butter or lentils per day. Camp followers were issued with just half a pound of wheat or barley.

The ayah grumbled that no one could feed two babies on such fare, but she was a sturdy country girl and did not look ill-nourished herself, and there could be no doubt that the Jung-i-Bahadur was thriving.

179

'If only Dr Black were here!' exclaimed Georgiana, as the difference in the babies' conditions grew daily more marked. 'He would have the truth out of her in a trice. Wretched creature! I feel certain she is to blame, but we have no proof. It is no use asking Dr Harcourt, poor man. He is at his wits' end without dressings or medicines for the wounded men, and would only tell me not to fuss. Oh dear, how worrying babies are! Do you think she is old enough to take pap?'

But Vicky turned her head listlessly from the spoon and vomited back the little soaked rusk they forced down her throat. She struggled weakly, arching her back, and wailed so piteously that they feared she would have a seizure.

The ayah, who had watched the proceedings with disapproval, bore her charge away, muttering darkly, and Thea and Georgy were left with the uneasy feeling that despite the best intentions, they had only made matters worse.

Now, as she huddled in the *kajava* with Vicky's frail body cradled in her arms, looking down at her parchment skin and the deep violet smudges under her eyes, Thea was shocked to realise that not only had she accepted that her baby was going to die, but she even looked forward to release from the slow agony of watching her fade away.

Toiling up to his waist in icy water, shouting orders at his chilled and sluggish men until his throat was sore, Captain Sturt had carried out his orders and achieved a bridge of sorts by laying heavy planks across gun carriages and lashing them in place. It was all labour lost, as he knew perfectly well. The water was easily fordable, being no more than a foot or two deep, and with ninety snow-covered miles ahead of them, the men could not expect to keep their feet dry.

His own saturated uniform froze stiff as boards the moment he emerged from the river, and he knew with gloomy certainty that without fuel or shelter there was little chance of drying it during the entire march, but so fiercely did the flame of anger burn in him that he barely noticed the cold. No one had listened to his protests that this bridge was perfectly useless and would serve only to create a bottleneck and cause delay when every moment was precious. As the sole engineer officer in the entire force, it had been his responsibility to find men and materials to build it – just as he had been expected single-handedly to breach the cantonment wall and throw down the rampart in order to span the ditch beside the rear gate and allow the retreating force to emerge. The wounds he had suffered on the first day of the insurrection had barely healed. They ached fiercely, and the pain of his damaged jaw made shouting a penance, yet shout he must if the river was to be bridged before the Advance guard appeared.

Where were they? He had been expecting to see them this past hour. Already half the morning was gone, and the short winter day made it unlikely they could reach the Khoord-Kabul Pass before dark. All his Afghan friends had insisted that the retreating army's only hope of survival lay in clearing that grim defile before the tribesmen had time to mount an ambush.

He fretted, gnawing his lip. If Elphy Bey had changed his mind yet again and cancelled his marching orders, surely someone would have had the sense to let him know? The bridge was a wretched, ramshackle affair, yet it could not be left unguarded for a moment or the Afghans would swoop down and carry off all its component parts.

Impatiently he checked his watch – eleven o'clock – and wrote down the time in the small notebook he carried in his breast pocket. Urged by his mother-in-law, he was keeping a diary, scrappy and disjointed though it inevitably was, and preserving every scrap of paper that would provide evidence of the gross mismanagement of affairs by the Mission's High Command. Blame for this humiliating retreat should be set firmly where it belonged. If I live to see that brute Shelton court-martialled, thought Sturt grimly, all this will seem worth while.

Twice the order to halt was passed down the line and twice countermanded before Brigadier Antequil, who was commanding the Advance guard, put a term to the day's miseries by bringing the straggling column to a standstill on the frozen marsh near the village of Begramee as the winter dusk began to close in. No more than six miles had been covered at a snail's pace, with frequent blockages and unscheduled stops, hampered by the disorderly mass of camp-followers, and the bellowing, half-starved bullocks that were barely strong enough to drag the two six-pounder guns which were all that remained of their artillery.

As Sturt had predicted, chaos had attended the crossing of the bridge, and though most of the horsemen preferred to wade through the shallows, the foot-followers fought their way on to the rickety planks in a struggling mass that took so long to cross that it effectively banished any possibility of reaching Khoord-Kabul before nightfall.

More serious still, as the ladies discovered to their dismay after waiting an hour in the freezing wind for their baggage to come up, had been the loss of their servants, together with clothes, tents and personal belongings.

'The Ghazis began harassing the poor wretches before they were well clear of cantonments,' reported George Mein, dismounting stiffly and stamping in a fruitless endeavour to restore circulation to his frozen feet. 'I saw them fling away their burdens and run for dear life. Or death,' he added sombrely, for he had ridden past an almost unbroken succession of dead and dying men, women and children since leaving the bridge.

'What shall we do for shelter? We cannot sleep in the snow!' Alex blew into her hands, trying to warm them, as she gazed round at the dreary scene.

An indescribable confusion of men, beasts and equipment sprawled over the darkening landscape, while in the distance whence they had come, a fiery glow lit the sky in a mocking illusion of warmth. The Afghans were celebrating their departure by setting fire to cantonments.

'I believe we shall have to, for all that. Thank God we

182

have some bedding.' Briskly Lady Sale evicted the ayah, who was squatting on the heap of quilts which had formed her saddle, rocking to and fro and moaning, and set her to scraping the ground clear of snow.

'I can do better than that. Trust me!' exclaimed Mein, glimpsing in the dusk the square, harassed face of Captain Johnson, the Shah's Paymaster, supervising the unloading of a camel.

He ran off, and returned in triumph with one of the small tents known as palls, which he and Sturt quickly assembled and into which they all crowded. A few hand-fuls of chopped straw were all they could obtain for their animals, and that at an outrageous price, but no one felt inclined to cavil since on the beasts' well-being depended their one slim chance of reaching safety.

Six bodies huddled beneath the inadequate shelter left no room for movement and they dozed fitfully, with the wind knifing under the sides of the tent, for there were too few pegs to secure them satisfactorily. At two in the morning there was a general alarm and they all started up, but it was only the Rearguard riding in, deadbeat after hours of stumbling through the snow in the dark and shouting in vain to discover where their units were bivouacked.

It was the end of any chance of sleep for Lady Sale, and finding herself almost too stiff to move, she dragged herself out of the jumbled heap of bodies and curled up in a wicker chair also provided by Captain Johnson, spreading her sheepskin cloak to cover herself from head to foot and huffing her breath into this improvised shelter until feeling crept back into her numbed hands and feet. Groans and snores, bellows and sudden wild cries burst from the miserable mass of humanity slowly freezing around her. When in the grey light of dawn she at last rose and looked about, she saw at once that many who had lain down to rest would never move again.

Vicky was one of the many babies who froze that night in their mothers' arms. It was only when she was roused

183

by Dandy's persistent whimpering that Thea realised the small bundle she had pressed to her breast throughout the hours of darkness had become absolutely rigid, a shawl-swaddled block of ice.

Her own hands were bonded to the shawl, completely numb. She could not free them.

'What's the matter?' mumbled Georgiana, hearing her cry out as they huddled together against the rumbling belly of the recumbent camel that was protecting them from the wind. Even with Thea's cloak beneath them and the ayah's and Georgy's spread on top, the bodies of three women and three children had not generated enough heat to save the weakest.

'Oh, my poor baby!' Frantically she shook the icy bundle. 'Wake up! Wake up!'

'What's happened?' Georgy struggled up in alarm.

'I think – I'm so afraid – she's dead . . . ' said Thea in a shaking voice.

'Are you sure? Let me look.' Together they gazed in grief and horror at the waxy, immobile face. Vicky's large black eyes stared sightlessly up at them.

'My hands. I can't feel them.' Thea was shuddering with shock and making ineffectual attempts to straighten her clenched fists.

'Wait. Let me help.' Painfully, Georgiana uncurled the bloodless fingers one by one until she was able to take the dead baby from Thea. With the help of Conductor Riley, who had bivouacked next to them, they scooped a shallow grave beneath an overhanging boulder and laid Vicky in it, still swathed in her shawl.

'Oh, my poor darling! My little Vicky!' sobbed Thea, overcome by her sudden loss. 'Oh, Georgy, how can God be so cruel – to snatch her away after so short a life!'

'Poor mite.' Georgiana looked down at the grave with sombre eyes. 'Her sufferings are over. Ours, I fear, may be just beginning.'

They huddled together in grief-stricken silence, which was only briefly dispelled by the appearance of George Mein.

184

'Cousin Georgy!' he exclaimed, hurrying up as they tried to encourage the reluctant camel to rise. 'I have been looking for you all up and down the line. Thank God you are safe.'

He produced a flask of brandy from under his cloak and pressed it on them, saying with a grin, 'With the compliments of the 54th Mess Stores, my ladies! A trifle more *inspiriting* than snow-water, don't you think?'

In the bitter air Mein's nose was red and his chapped ears stuck out like jug handles beneath his cap, but he was so full of life and energy that even the ayah smiled wanly at him, and his cheerful presence warmed them more than the brandy. After giving them all the news he had been able to gather, he hurried on his way and they were left feeling as if the sun had briefly shone and then hidden behind a cloud.

Although no order to move had been given, so great was the fever to leave that at first light a mass of camp-followers had begun to stream away from their night's bivouac. Many sepoys had thrown away their muskets and broken ranks to join them. Leaving the flat, frozen marsh, they began to wind through the Loghur Gorge, crossing and recrossing the tumbling stream whose banks rose steeply while the path became ever more slippery and precipitous. Great boulders shouldered through the trampled carpet of snow, often reducing the passage to single file.

At seven-thirty the previous day's Rearguard, which was to form today's Advance, although their tired beasts had been allowed no more than four hours' rest, moved off in pursuit of the camp-followers, and once again Lady Sale and Alexandrina rode with them, while at the back of the line, Thea and Georgiana wearily loaded their children into the camel's panniers and scrambled in beside them as the animal lurched to its feet.

Knots of Afghan horsemen had begun to cluster on the slopes overlooking Begramee. Among them Akbar Khan was plainly visible, mounted on a handsome Arab stallion that had been a gift from Sir Alexander Burnes.

185

'Our gallant protector!' muttered Lady Sale bitterly, as she hauled herself, wincing, into the saddle. Every bone and muscle ached, and the cakes and sherry which Captain Johnson had kindly provided for their breakfast hardly made an adequate substitute for a good strong cup of coffee. Clothes, boots and bedding were all soaked through, and they had had no opportunity to change their garments, even if they had felt equal to struggling with hooks and buttons when their fingers were clumsy with cold. She and Alex had taken turns to protect one another's privacy as they relieved themselves, but apart from scrubbing their faces with handfuls of snow, they had agreed to let washing wait for more propitious circumstances.

'Or meet our Maker unwashed,' said Alexandrina with the ghost of a smile. Today, at least, she had the comfort of her husband's company and felt better able to face the hardships of the march without the worry of leaving him behind.

George Mein had also attached himself to their little group and tried to lift their spirits with jokes and anecdotes, but as they rode deeper into the hills, passing ever-increasing numbers of poor wretches who had given up the struggle and were sitting passively in the snow to await their fate, his voice faltered into silence.

The bright clear sky soon clouded into a sullen, bronze-tinted grey, and as they climbed with slipping and stumbling horses, a blizzard began to howl through the funnel-shaped gorge, driving sharp, stinging needles of ice into their eyes.

Yet we are the lucky ones, reflected Lady Sale. We have warm clothes and beasts to carry us. The poor Hindustanis struggling knee-deep through snow and slush have neither. How long can they endure this merciless march? How long can our horses continue without water or food?

Few, few will part where many meet, responded the maddening refrain that had haunted her since leaving Kabul. Little as she believed in premonitions, she could not shake off the conviction that they were all going to die.

186

'Doctor-Sahib! Wake up. Wake up and come with me!'

The soft but insistent voice penetrated Toby's uneasy dreams and he sat up slowly, head swimming, before his eyes could focus on the slim figure crouched at the end of his string cot.

Dysentery had left him as weak as a kitten. For the past two days he had been feverish, unable to distinguish between reality and fantasy. This visitor was real enough, though. He could even – after a momentary effort of memory – put a name to him: Hinghan Khan, the handsome Tajik boy whom that young ass Quinn had lost his head over. What the devil was he doing here?

'Come with me, Sahib,' the boy repeated. 'I have horses waiting. See, the door is open.'

It was true, Toby saw as his eyes probed the shadows of the cell. He swung his legs off the cot and stood up, swaying. Hinghan Khan reached out to steady him.

'Come, we must hurry. There is no time to lose.'

'Where are you taking me?' Toby's voice was hoarse with disuse. He felt too weak to go anywhere, and doubted if he could sit on a horse for more than a mile.

'The army has marched for Jellalabad. Two days since they left Kabul, but the snow is deep and if we hurry we can catch them.'

'For . . . *Jellalabad*?' Toby put a hand to his head, wondering if he had heard right. 'In this weather?'

The boy nodded. 'Very many have died. The Sirdar sends me to fetch you. He wishes you to speak with the General-Sahib so that the rest may be saved.'

'What kind of trick is this? Why cannot the Sirdar speak for himself?'

'Sahib, it is no trick.' Highan Khan struck one fist into the other palm for emphasis. 'The General-Sahib will listen to you. The Sirdar demands that an order be sent to Sale-Sahib, telling him to leave the city of Jellalabad and return to Hindustan. If this is not done, not a man from the Kabul force will live to tell what happened.'

Toby's brain felt thick and fogged. He wished Hinghan Khan would leave him alone. It was only five marches to

187

Jellalabad; even old Elphy Bey could surely get his men down there in less than a week. If they had marched two days ago, they would be almost halfway there by now, and once the Kabul force was reunited with Sale's brigade, the Afghans would find them hard to dislodge. Hence this demand for him to play the Sirdar's game and keep the two forces apart. Well, he would not do it.

'Why should the General listen to me, if he will not heed Captain Skinner?' he asked curtly.

'Because you would not wish all the memsahibs to die,' said Hingham Khan with simple logic. Catlike, he prowled about the cell, looking with distaste at the soiled, flea-ridden heaps of clothes and bedding, the barred window and the bowls encrusted with dried lentils.

'This is a very bad place. Sultan Jan should not keep you in this small room. It is not fitting.'

'Perhaps you would speak to him about it.'

Hinghan Khan flashed him a bright, challenging glance, suspecting mockery. My mistake, thought Toby. An Afghan could endure anything but affronts to his dignity. This boy was no fool – it would be just as easy to make an enemy of him as an ally, and God knew, he needed allies.

'Come!' The tone was peremptory. 'The Sirdar waits.'

He padded away down the passage, leaving Toby to follow or not as he chose. After only a moment's hesitation, Toby tottered after him. The courtyard was filled with a milling mass of men and beasts, among which a number of camels marked with regimental brands caught Toby's eye. His uneasiness grew. If the insurgents could steal army camels they must be in a stronger position than he realised.

The morning mists had cleared, but last night's sharp frost had petrified the churned-up snow of the courtyard into ruts and ridges which by midday would melt into ammoniac sludge. After weeks in the foetid atmosphere of his cell, the first intake of outside air knifed into Toby's lungs, bringing on so violent an attack of coughing that he thought his throat would tear apart. Gasping, his eyes streaming, he leaned against the wall until the spasm subsided, then walked unsteadily forward to join Hinghan Khan, who was waiting impatiently for him to mount a horse which a servant held ready.

Toby raised a foot to the stirrup, then lowered it and stepped back to survey the animal. Surely this was Capain Trevor's mare – the one who left her opponents standing at the races on the *maidan*? White socks, a star, lop-ears – impossible to mistake her. He had heard Trevor declare he would never sell her, so what was she doing here?

More disturbing still, she wore an English saddle. While it was not unknown for a man to change his mind about selling a horse – particularly if he had as many children to feed and clothe as Captain Trevor – it was unthinkable that he would part with a proper Melton-made hunting saddle, which he could not hope to replace before taking Home leave.

'This is Captain Trevor's horse,' he said. 'How did you come by her?'

Hinghan Khan giggled and gave him a sly, sideways glance. Instead of answering, he sprang on to his own mount and spurred towards the gate. 'Follow me!' he called, setting off at a gallop across the snowfield, Toby clinging to his mare's mane as she rocketed in pursuit.

Trevor's mare had a mouth of iron, but many times that morning he blessed her sure-footedness and speed. Hinghan Khan rode like a demon, galloping where a prudent man would walk, plunging in and out of streams, slithering recklessly down slopes where anyone in his senses would have dismounted, and where he led, the mare followed.

Instead of crossing the Kabul River and swinging west towards Begramee as the retreating army had done, they climbed a twisting goat-track above the north bank of the river, crossing its tributaries in wild leaps and splashes and clambering over great slabs of frozen rock where the horses' hoofs skidded sickeningly on the ice. At the junction with the Khoord-Kabul road, they forded the main stream and rode south towards Bootkhak, where the army

189

had bivouacked after its second march. Far to the east the mighty peak of Seh Baba shone dazzlingly white above the nearer scree-speckled ridges of Tunghee and Huft Kotul, but Toby had neither time nor inclination to admire the wild scenery.

'Faster!' shouted Hinghan Khan, leaning back like a steeplechase jockey as his horse slid downhill in a small avalanche of snow and boulders.'We must catch them before the gorge . . . '

The rest of his sentence was lost, but the urgency of his mood infected Toby so that he, too, spurred his mount to a breakneck descent. At noon, they reached Bootkhak, the horses' necks black with sweat and their legs trembling, having accomplished in less than three hours a distance it had taken the retreating army two days to cover. As they slithered down to join the track over which the columns had passed, the full horror of what had befallen General Elphinstone's force became apparent.

Mile upon mile of continuous bloodstains marked the snow. Where an army passes, the quality and quantity of debris left behind is a sure indication of morale, and judged by this criterion, fighting spirit in the Kabul force was so low as to be almost extinct. Household and personal baggage, uniforms and muskets, rifled chests and stores littered the snow to the right and left of the deeply churned, rust-red track.

Dead and dying camels, oxen, horses and mules lay where they had dropped from hunger and exhaustion. Many still wore their harnesses – clear proof that the pursuing tribesmen were glutted with plunder. The mangled bodies of sepoys and their families, many savagely mutilated, lay in heaps where they had succumbed.

A few miles beyond Bootkhak they came on two heavy-artillery guns, spiked and abandoned; a hundred yards farther on the stiff body of old Dr Cardew, lashed to a gun-carriage, showed how valiantly his men had tried to save him.

'Hakim-Sahib, we die! Help us, Hakim-Sahib!'

The cry came from beneath a slab-like rock overhanging

the track, under which crouched a group of wretched Hindustanis, their hands and legs blackened with frost-bite. They were endeavouring to thaw themselves at a tiny fire amid the snow-covered desolation. They would die as soon as the fuel provided by discarded uniforms and bedding was consumed, for there were no trees or plants – not even the artemisia which was the most common Afghan firewood – to feed the spluttering flame.

As Toby rode past, the cry was echoed by other voices on either side: sepoys with missing limbs and gaping wounds, camp-followers who had simply collapsed, numbed with hunger and exhaustion, and would freeze to death as soon as the sun set.

'Help us, Sahib! Save us!'

There was nothing he could do. Nothing but ride on with his chin sunk on his chest, trying to avoid those pleading, accusing eyes. He was powerless to help them and knew that the memory of their groans would haunt him for the rest of his life.

CHAPTER ELEVEN

When the camel crumpled into the snow, shot through the chest, Thea and Dandy were pitched headlong from the *kajava*. Clutching one another, they slid helplessly down the ice-covered bank towards the stream until a rock arrested their progress and they came to a stop, dazed and shaken, some twenty feet below the path.

Above them the vicious crackle of musket-fire was deafeningly magnified, rolling in thunderous echoes from cliff to towering cliff of the Khoord-Kabul Pass, five miles long and for much of that distance barely wide enough for two loaded beasts to pass abreast. Through this choked and treacherous gorge the whole mass of the army was streaming in the utmost confusion. Advance guard and baggage train were hopelessly entangled with the panicking tide of camp-followers, who as soon as it was light, had set off without waiting for orders, only to be mown down in great swathes by the Afghan *jezailchis* hidden behind rocks above the path.

Shouts and groans, screams and curses filled the air. Even as Thea cowered under the rock that had saved them, a bullet whined past to strike the bank with a soft *phut!* She started up the slope on hands and knees, dragging Dandy with her, tearing her skin on the frozen ground without feeling it in her frenzied scramble to regain the path.

A dozen men with ropes were struggling to pull the camel's body out of the way, while more laden beasts piled up behind, unable to pass. The sepoy who had been leading them lay lifeless where he had fallen, but of Georgy and her child there was no sign.

Crack-crack-crack!

Another volley from above felled several mules carrying chests of treasure, and the men dragging at the camel's

192

carcase scattered, leaving those behind to pass the obstacle as best they could. Women screamed, beasts roared – the noise was unbearable.

Dear God! thought Thea. There is no escape. We cannot go forward or back. They are going to kill us all. I must run . . . run . . .

'Mamma!' wailed Dandy, as she dragged him over the frozen rocks, slipping and falling, gasping for breath, desperate to catch up with someone, anyone, who would carry them out of this horrible trap. Her heavy, wet skirt hampered her movements. The sheepskin *poshteen* which had been her only cover during the past two freezing nights was sodden and stiff, but she fought the temptation to throw it away.

' 'Ere, missus! 'Op up behind!' The bearded face of a trooper leaned down to her, hand extended, an answer to prayer.

'My child – '

'Ahmed will take 'im. 'Ere, Ahmed! Take the nipper. *Juldi jao!*' Thankfully she saw Dandy hoisted on to the pommel of a sowar's saddle, and was herself boosted by willing hands on to her rescuer's crupper.

'Mamma! Don't leave Dandee!' His arms reached out to her.

'It's all right, darling. I'm coming.'

' 'Ang on, missus!'

The horse lurched forward, hoofs scrabbling. The trooper rode like a man possessed, ruthlessly trampling those in his path, forcing the horse over rocks and piles of baggage while Thea clung to his broad back with all her strength, determined not to fall off.

Spent bullets struck her, bruising her back and arms without penetrating the sheepskin cloak, but as they rode deeper into the gorge, flurries of snow made the marksmen's task less easy and by degrees the confusion cleared, revealing sudden glimpses of faces she knew, alive and dead. Handsome Lieutenant St George of the 37th BNI, and Captain Paton, the Assistant Quartermaster General, who had lost an arm only a month earlier, lay

193

hacked and mutilated beside the stream. A horse she recognised as Major Thain's was still struggling, shot through the loins, as they floundered past.

The sowar carrying Dandy had ridden ahead, but she could feel their own mount tiring under the double burden despite the trooper's frantic use of whip and spurs. Would its strength endure to the end of this terrible pass?

Hardly was the question framed before it was answered. She felt a sudden violent shock pass through the broad back she clasped, and then the ground rose up to meet her. Her head struck a rock and a black wave engulfed her.

When consciousness filtered back, her clothes had frozen to the ground from collar to hem, and the weight of the trooper across her legs made movement impossible. She tried to wriggle from beneath the inert body, and feebly struggled into a sitting position, waving her arms to attract attention, and calling for help, but the human tide flowing sluggishly past looked down at her with incurious eyes and did not stop. One woman more or less, what did it matter? Thousands had died in this day's march, and many more would succumb before morning. The only hope of survival lay in keeping moving, jealously hoarding the last reserves of strength and warmth. Anyone who strayed from the path or halted, for whatever reason, was lost.

Already the winter daylight was fading. As she finally realised that no one would help her, Thea began to despair. Her struggles to rise grew weaker, her mind more blurred. The thought of giving up and letting herself drift into unconsciousness grew ever more enticing. From time to time the memory of Dandy jerked her awake and she called for help, but by degrees her arms grew numb and her eyelids heavy. The shouts faded to whispers, and finally she fell silent, unaware of hoofs and wheels and feet passing by, or the occasional soft thump as yet another body collapsed in the snow.

When musket-balls began to hum about their heads like

angry hornets, Alexandrina Sturt and her mother, who were riding with the Vanguard, clapped their spurs into their ponies' flanks and galloped at such reckless speed through the pass that it was not until they burst into dazzling sunlight at the farther end that Lady Sale realised she had been hit.

'Safe!' Alexandrina slid off her pony and buried her face in its thick mane. 'Well done, old fellow! Oh, Mamma, my heart was going so fast I thought it would burst. Galloping over those rocks! Every moment I feared we were done for.' She looked up, saw her mother's face twisted with pain, and with one swift stride was beside her. 'Mamma! You're hurt!'

'Just a spent ball,' said Lady Sale through clenched teeth. 'All the others were stopped by my *poshteen*. I shall be black and blue . . . '

Gently Alexandrina examined the wounded wrist. The ball had lodged between two bones and was clearly visible, but her tentative attempt to remove it made Lady Sale gasp and turn very white.

'Leave it, my love. I'll ask the doctor to dig it out. Where is Sturt? Was he not with us?'

'He went to help Major Thain.' The glow in her daughter's face faded as anxiety returned. 'I begged him not to, but he *would* turn back. He said he would join us directly . . . '

Other horsemen began to emerge from the narrow cleft between the cliffs, dismounting to rest their horses, who stood with heads hanging low and legs trembling. The men talked excitedly, comparing narrow escapes and the fate of friends. With growing anxiety, Alexandrina questioned each one, but learned only that Sturt had been seen riding towards the place where Major Thain's horse had been shot. Some thought George Mein was with him, but others said he was alone.

Time passed. The group of survivors grew larger, but there was no sign of either Sturt or Mein.

As it was growing dark, Georgiana Mainwaring stumbled wearily towards them, her baby clasped in her arms.

She was utterly exhausted, having trudged through the snow and turmoil nearly the whole length of the pass. She sank down wearily and bowed her head to her knees, speechless with fatigue. Anxious friends crowded round, for Georgy was a general favourite. Alexandrina took the baby from her, and Lieutenant Eyre offered what remained in his flask. A little colour crept into her cheeks as she sipped, and she whispered her thanks as he draped a saddle-blanket around her shoulders. Her clothes were soaked through and now the need for exertion was over, she had begun to shiver violently.

'Where's Mrs Quinn?' she murmured, but no one could tell her. Then a cry which was half a moan burst from Alexandrina, still anxiously watching the entrance to the gorge. Two men had appeared out of the dark shadow of cliff: George Mein and the black-bearded giant, Sergeant Deane of the Sappers, walking one each side of an artillery horse stripped of most of its harness, on whose back they were supporting a wounded man. His head lolled with each stride of the horse, and his dirty sheepskin cloak was stained rusty red.

'It's my husband!' exclaimed Alexandrina, and turned blindly towards her mother, whose own face looked stricken. Sturt meant more to her than just a daughter's husband: in her heart she looked on him as her own son.

'Find a doctor!' she snapped, and hurried forward to supervise the care of the wounded man.

'Oh, Alex! I am so sorry. So very, very sorry,' said Georgiana, but Alexandrina stood as if turned to stone, murmuring over and over again:

'*If only! If only* he had not gone back!'

A white devil with frosted eyebrows and rough, relentless hands was slapping Thea's face, shaking her back and forth, ordering her to wake from the deep sleep that would end in death.

'Get up! Move! Stamp! Again! Faster! Now walk. Go on, walk!'

She cowered away, trying to escape his shouting, his

ruthless commands. 'Lemme 'lone,' she mumbled through frozen lips. 'Wan' sleep. Go 'way.'

She hated him for dragging her back to the cruel, pain-filled world from which she had just escaped. When she fell, he dragged her upright. When she closed her eyes, he shook her until she opened them, all the time shouting at her and forcing her heavy, stiff, reluctant limbs into movement. Every part of her hurt. She looked at him helplessly, tears freezing on her cheeks, begging him to leave her in peace, but instead he scrubbed handfuls of snow on her face and hands until she screamed at him to stop.

Why was he so cruel? All she wanted was to sink back into the soft nest of snow and sleep for eternity, but he made her stand upright in the freezing wind, and shuffle forward on feet whose first stirrings of circulation made them throb agonisingly.

'Hurting. Leave me 'lone,' she begged, but she had no strength to resist him.

When it grew dark and she could go no further, he bundled her into the lee of a rock that gave some shelter from the wind, and spread on the frozen ground the *poshteen* he had taken from the dead trooper. His own he flung over her, then crawled into the improvised lair and took her in his arms, holding the length of her body against his own warmth.

Why do I bother? he thought. Why couldn't I let her slip into oblivion, instead of making her face whatever horrors tomorrow will bring? Dispassionately Hinghan Khan had watched Toby's attempts to revive her. Now that the army was trapped between Khoord-Kabul and the even narrower pass at Tunghi Tareki, his haste to catch up with the Sirdar had been replaced by the simple pleasure of looting the dead. There was no need to hurry. One more freezing night without food or shelter would further undermine General Sale's resistance to giving up British women and children as hostages, and make the Hakim's mission all the easier.

'Before morning she will die,' he said, laughing, and

rode away. Toby thought he was probably right. But as the hours crawled past, the rigid body in his arms became more pliant. She whimpered a little, like a puppy, then eased into a more comfortable position, with her face pushed against his chest and the top of her head in the angle between his neck and chin.

Strange that he should be holding Eleanor's daughter as he had so often longed to hold Eleanor herself during that long-ago summer! How different all their lives would have been if he had prevailed upon her to run away with him . . .

She had pretended to consider his plan. 'They would call me a cradle-snatcher,' she had said, her long, dark eyes crinkled with laughter. 'Oh, no, my dear boy. I don't think my pride could stand that, not even for you.'

Eleanor had been amusing herself; he recognised that, now. How many young officers had she bewitched and discarded? How many moonstruck, callow youths like him had imagined themselves in love with her? He, not she, had agonised over the likelihood of her husband discovering their rendezvous in the rose arbour; he had longed to protect her from old Waspy Dundas's bitter tongue. He could have saved himself the trouble, but perhaps it was all part of growing up . . .

He dozed fitfully, and woke in another icy, grey dawn, with the first rays of the sun rose-tinting the tremendous peaks rising in jumbled layers above them.

Thea was asleep, her face framed in the sheepskin which sparkled with icicles formed by her frozen breath. He lay still, reluctant to break it to her that the day's troubles had begun.

Where were her children? How had she become separated from them? Objectively he admired the feathered line of eyebrows and sweep of burnished lashes, the wide, generous mouth and delicate complexion chapped rough by the wind. A fine face, if one admired that robust style of beauty. Strong, determined, wilful . . . His own taste was for something more delicate and ethereal, though in these conditions, he thought ruefully, only a woman of exceptional physical strength and stamina stood the least chance of survival. Besides the all-important will to live, there was much to be said for a respectable layer of blubber.

She stirred, and he said softly, 'Well, my dear? How do you feel?'

'Warm,' she murmured sleepily, snuggling nearer. 'Warm and safe. Oh, darling, I have had the most terrible dream.'

He couldn't bring himself to tell her it was no dream, and lay silent until she opened her eyes. With regret he saw yesterday's horrors crowd in on her consciousness. She blushed, and pulled away.

'Where – where am I?' she exclaimed. '*Toby*! What are you doing? How did I come – ?'

'I found you lying half-frozen and wrapped you up for the night,' he said in a calm, matter-of-fact tone. He turned away, giving her time to collect herself before saying casually, 'Did you leave the children with Mrs Sturt, or Mrs Mainwaring?'

'My children!' A sob caught in her throat, and then a look of terror crossed her face. She started up, saying, 'Dandy! Oh, where is he? He will be so frightened, wondering where I am.'

Toby's heart sank. He had hoped Dandy was with the other ladies. The chance of a small child surviving yesterday's chaos and carnage was very slim.

'Where did you see him last?'

'He was with me in the *kajava* until the camel fell, then we walked – oh, for miles! A sowar of Anderson's Horse took him up, and went ahead, but then our poor beast was shot and I could not get up.'

Hurriedly she threw off the sheepskin covering and stood up in the damp, crumpled habit and boots she had worn ever since leaving Kabul. She staggered a little as stiff muscles protested, and after a horrified look at the bloodstained snow all around them, said, 'Oh, let us go on and leave this terrible place. They cannot be far ahead. If we hurry we shall soon catch up with them.'

'Eat this first,' he said, and gave her one of the dry cakes he had taken from a dead cavalryman's knapsack. She ate it ravenously and he wished he had more to offer, but the light was growing stronger every minute and soon the Afghans would arrive to plunder the fallen. It was no more than half a mile to the far end of the pass; he prayed they would not find their way blocked when they got there.

'Come on,' he said, stifling his anxiety to know what had become of her baby daughter. He took her hand to help her over the icy rocks to the stream, and found it warm and firm. Could her strength sustain her through three more marches as bad or worse then yesterday's? Most of the ladies had only the haziest idea of the country between here and their goal of Jellalabad, but he knew it well. Khoord-Kabul was the longest pass, but by no means the most dangerous. Tunghi-Tareki was less than four yards wide at its narrowest point, and the column would be forced to run the gauntlet of Afghan bullets in single file. Another twenty-odd miles would bring them to the grim two-mile pass of Jugdulluk, in territory dominated by the most embittered and ferocious of all the Eastern Ghilzai tribes, whose excesses even Akbar Khan was powerless to control, and from there on, through Sourkab, Gandamak and Futtehabad, every man's hand would be against them.

So long as hope sustained them, Thea and her like might force themselves to keep going, but once the true hopelessness of their situation was borne in on them, morale would collapse and they would undoubtedly perish. As far as he could see, their one faint chance of survival lay in persuading old Elphy Bey to place all the ladies and their children in Akbar Khan's care. A capricious young devil the Sirdar might be, but he was enough of an Afghan to be well aware of the advantages to be gained by protecting them, not to mention the bargaining power such hostages, freely given, would bestow on him. But would Elphy Bey agree?

Selecting and rejecting arguments, Toby slithered over

the frozen ground, with Thea dragging him forward in her impatience to catch up with the column.

A mile beyond the gorge's mouth they came on the spot where the army's survivors had spent the night: a wilderness of trampled snow and scattered debris among which frozen bodies, both human and animal, had been abandoned with no attempt at burial. There they found an emaciated artillery horse still picketed, trailing his harness as he munched at the tail of his dead team-mate.

Toby cut him free and boosted Thea to his back. With her mounted they made faster progress, for though she had begun the march in her stoutest boots, these were already falling apart and added greatly to the hardship of forcing her sore, blistered feet over the rocks and snow.

Discipline, it was plain, had effectively broken down. The troops had moved off in no kind of order, with units intermingled and stragglers stripped of any equipment that might benefit a comrade. The retreat had become a rout, and Toby was astonished to find the remains of the army halted in a bleak open space less than a mile from their previous night's bivouac.

Why had they stopped, when every moment's delay made destruction more certain?

Heads bowed before the icy wind, pale, haggard officers sat their mounts in grim silence while their men slumped in the snow, nursing frost-bitten feet, the picture of despair.

'What's up? Why the halt?' asked Toby.

Haunted eyes stared at him from blackened, peeling faces. Hopeless shrugs greeted the question.

'God knows! Ask Elphy Bey!'

'I will,' he said grimly, pushing on.

Near the head of the line, a group of women and children huddled round a tiny fire. Toby recognised Mrs Mainwaring among them, and waited only for Thea to be drawn into their company before hurrying on to where General Elphinstone sat in his battered straw chair, his feet as usual propped on a stool, his staff standing or kneeling round him.

201

Compared to the remnants of his tattered and demoralised army, Elphy Bey still looked remarkably spruce, his long face a little gaunter, perhaps, his gout-knotted hands more helpless, but when he saw Toby approach he beckoned him forward with his usual affability.

'My dear fellow! I am so glad to see you. The very man whose advice I need. Captain Grant, be so good as to find a seat for Dr Black.'

With a bad grace, Grant surrendered his own camp stool. 'So you decided to join us at last! What will your Afghan friends say to that?' he enquired in a disagreeable undertone.

'I was – unavoidably delayed,' said Toby, restraining the impulse to plant a facer on Grant's coldly sneering mouth.

'Indeed?' He had no further opportunity for baiting, however, for the General's pained and puzzled eye was on them and the one desire that united Elphy Bey's warring staff was to protect their chief from life's unpleasantnesses.

'I am so glad you have come, Dr Black, for I confess I am puzzled to know what to do for the best,' the General said in his gentle, complaining tone, twitching at the horse-blanket which covered his knees. 'Had I been aware that the Sirdar would fail to honour his promises to provide us with food and fuel, I should never have consented to leave Kabul. As you can see, our situation is now extremely difficult. Time and again I have asked the Sirdar to supply us as he agreed to, but all I receive is excuses. I am beginning to wonder if I was wise to place any reliance on his word.'

Wise – dear Heaven! thought Toby. 'I do not suppose you had much choice, sir,' he said tactfully, then caught Captain Bellew's sardonic eye and cursed himself for a mealy-mouthed fool. This was no shorn lamb. Why did everyone feel compelled to temper the wind to Elphy Bey?

'I know! I know!' said the General testily. 'I had no choice *then*, but I am asking you what I should do *now*. The Sirdar proposes that I should place all the ladies and their children under his protection, and promises to bring them down a day's march behind the army. He swears on his father's head they will come to no harm, but as I have just pointed out to you, he has broken solemn promises before. I am beginning to question his good faith.'

Ye Gods, thought Toby savagely, what would it take to convince Elphy Bey that the Sirdar was unlikely to lose any sleep over breaking faith with an infidel? But if he said as much, the old fool would probably decide to refuse this proposal, in which lay the poor ladies' sole hope.

'Well, Dr Black? I am waiting to know your opinion.' The General's guileless blue eyes showed a trace of impatience. 'Captain Grant advises against accepting the Sirdar's offer, while Captain Skinner, who brought the proposal, recommends me to agree to it. What do you say?'

'I think you should accept, sir.'

'Despite his earlier behaviour? You believe he would keep his word?'

'Sir, I am convinced of it.'

The mild gaze studied him in some perplexity. Conviction was foreign to Elphy Bey's nature. For an uncomfortable moment Toby feared that by making his advice too uncompromisingly plain he had undermined his own credibility in the General's eyes – perhaps even raised the suspicion that he was an Afghan-lover, not to be trusted.

At last, to his relief, the long, heron-like head nodded sagely, and the mild eyes surveyed the group of officers.

'Well, gentlemen, you have heard Dr Black's opinion, and we can be in no doubt that both he and Captain Skinner are more familiar with the workings of the Afghan mind than the rest of us can claim to be. Though I cannot deny it makes me uneasy, since you recommend it, Dr Black, I will give orders that the ladies and their children be placed in the Sirdar's care at once, along with any wounded officers who wish to accompany them. We will continue our march without them.' He smiled in dismissal. 'I am obliged to you, sir. Good day.'

While the army waited the outcome of the General's deliberations, Captain Sturt breathed his last. One look at the gaping wound in his stomach had been enough to tell Dr Bryce that the injury was mortal, yet Sturt survived the bitter night and the next morning's progress in a jolting camel's *kajava* before dying at last in his wife's arms.

Alexandrina was distraught, and though Lady Sale was practised at controlling her emotions, she, too, let tears slide unchecked down her cheeks to freeze on her chin as Sturt's own Sappers, led by black-bearded Sergeant Deane, lowered the body, shrouded in his military cloak, into the grave they had scraped among the rocks.

Captain Lawrence read the Burial Service, keeping one eye cocked towards the group of Afghan chiefs surrounding Akbar Khan, for the Sirdar had been careful to insist that the three experienced Political Officers who might have given General Elphinstone sensible advice – Major Pottinger, Captain Colin Mackenzie, and Lawrence himself – should accompany the ladies into captivity. His mission completed to Akbar Khan's satisfaction, Dr Black was to return to Kabul with the wounded officers and join those left there in Dr Primrose's charge. Like Jan Fishan Khan, the Sirdar believed in hooding hawks before scaring away the pigeons.

As soon as the service ended, General Elphinstone's decision to commit them to the Sirdar's care was made known to the ladies, most of whom were too numbed by hardship and exhaustion to make much protest.

'It is difficult to imagine any situation worse than this,' said Mrs Trevor frankly. 'In the past three days, I would have looked on death as a blessing were it not for my little ones.'

Her seven children crowded round her skirts like chicks seeking shelter beneath a hen, looking up at her with anxious eyes, ready to detect the least hint of failing resolution. She was careful to maintain a calm and cheerful expression, scolding them when they complained, and urging them into any sort of activity that would distract their minds from the present peril.

204

Only she and Lady Macnaghten had managed to save a proportion of their baggage during the march, thanks to the valiant efforts of their servants, who had fought off Afghan attempts to plunder it. One of Lady Macnaghten's cats, the nervous Simkin, had succumbed to the cold, and grief-stricken though she was at Sturt's death, Lady Sale could not repress a spasm of disgust as she listened to the shrill voice of the Envoy's widow upbraiding the servant who had looked after her pet.

'That woman cares twice as much for her wretched cat as she did for the poor Envoy,' she murmured to Alexandrina. Lady Macnaghten's lack of feeling on hearing of her husband's murder had been the subject of much scandalised comment among the ladies. She had enquired of the Political Officers if they would uphold her claim for the pension of a Governor's widow, even though her husband had died before taking up his appointment.

'She started counting her shekels while poor Sir William was still hanging in the *Chandra Chowk*,' said Captain Mackenzie with revulsion. 'It beats me how he ever came to marry such a woman.'

Lady Sale agreed wholeheartedly. Whatever his faults, the Envoy had been a brave and gallant gentleman. She watched sardonically as Lady Macnaghten unlatched the travelling cage and allowed her surviving cat to jump into her arms, while the children clamoured to stroke him.

Now Mrs Trevor gave orders to her ayah that the trunk containing their clothes should be opened and the children dressed in as many garments as they could heap on top of those they were already wearing. Knowing the Afghan appetite for plunder, she was determined to preserve as much as she could of her children's wardrobe, with the result that when the little procession of hostages set off across the dazzling snowfield towards the fort in which Akbar Khan had established his headquarters, the young Trevors resembled nothing so much as a row of pegtops, as they rolled stiff-legged over the snow, arms stuck well out from their sides by many thicknesses of wool and cloth.

Thea refused to go. 'You cannot make me. I am going back to look for Dandy,' she said, and would have struck off alone across the white waste if Toby had not caught her arm.

'Don't be a fool,' he said urgently. 'What chance would you have on your own?'

She flung back her head, her eyes wild. 'What chance has he? Let me go. If I cannot find him, I do not wish to live.'

She tried to pull free, but he held her firm. However much he pitied her distress, he could not let her go blindly to certain death. Literally blindly – tears and the fierce light off the snow had inflamed her eyes so that only a slit of iris showed between the puffed lids.

'Listen,' he said firmly, 'the Sirdar wishes me to return to Kabul to help Dr Primrose look after our wounded left there.'

'Let me come with you! Please, Toby. Only let me come back and search for Dandy.'

'I'm sorry,' he said with regret. 'The Sirdar would never allow it. You must go with the ladies.'

'Then why does he let *you* go free?' She stared at him with terrible intensity. 'Is what they say about you true?'

'What do they say?'

'That you have a foot in both camps.'

Toby's mouth tightened. He took her by the shoulders, asking quietly, 'Do you believe that?'

'I don't know! Why else would the Afghans let you come and go as you please? Why do they treat you as a friend?'

'More can be achieved through friendship than enmity, you know that. Try to trust me,' he said, seeing her uncertainty. 'I will do the best I can for you – for all the ladies – but I have to do it my own way.'

'But, *Dandy*!' she wailed.

'I will look for him as I ride back to Kabul.' He paused, then added deliberately, 'If I find his body, I will see him properly buried.'

'He's alive! He must be!' Her voice held a note of

206

hysteria. 'I told him I was coming. He will be so frightened, wondering why I do not come.'

Her voice choked, remembering yesterday's freezing
turmoil, the screams as each deadly fusillade cut down
rows of men and beasts. Clear in her mind rose the picture
of Dandy's outstretched arms, his pitiful wail, 'Don't
leave me, Mamma!' rang in her ears.

'Let me go!' she raged, but instead of obeying, Toby
tightened his grip. He exchanged a worried look with
Georgiana, who said soothingly:

'Be reasonable, my love. Look at your boots – you
cannot walk in those. Dr Black is right. If Dandy is alive,
he has a better chance of finding him without you to
hamper him.'

Her matter-of-fact tone had its effect. Thea said hopelessly, 'He will not know where to look.'

'No more will you. Now come along and help me calm
poor Mrs Anderson. Her little Mary has vanished, too,
and so have Hugh Boyd and young Seymour Stoker. But
Captain Skinner tells me that several of our children have
been brought in to Akbar Khan, and there may be more
to follow.'

'Oh!' Hope blazed in Thea's eyes. 'Why did you not
say so before?'

'Because I did not wish to raise your hopes too high,'
said Georgy soberly, but Thea was hardly listening.

'Let us go over to the fort at once. Dandy must be
there. He must!'

'Did I do wrong to tell her?' asked Georgy, watching
her hurry away.

Toby shook his head. 'Time will show. Well, Mrs Mainwaring, I wish you a safe journey and happy reunion with
your husband before too long.'

'Thank you,' she said, but added in a low voice, 'Do
you truly believe the Sirdar means well by us?'

'I wish I knew! All I can say is that Akbar Khan is no
fool, and it is in his best interest to bring you down safely.'

'Even if the rest of the army perishes? Oh, I have heard
the stories!' She hesitated a little, then said resolutely, 'Dr

207

Black, I do not like to bother you, but if – if anything happens to me and you should succeed in reaching Jellalabad, may I ask you to give my husband a token?'

He assured her he would be honoured to undertake the commission and she took a small gold locket from round her neck and pressed it into his hand.

'Goodbye, then,' she said, blinking back tears. 'I will take good care of Thea for you, never fear.'

Now why the deuce did she say that? he wondered, watching her hurry over to join the little group of hostages waiting to be conducted to Akbar Khan's headquarters. He counted seven officers, walking wounded, among them Vincent Eyre and George Mein; nine ladies, some dazed, some weeping; and about a dozen children. He wondered bleakly what their chances were and if he would see any of them alive again. It was true it would best serve Akbar's interests to treat them well, but his moods could change with lightning speed: charming, courteous, civilised one moment, a cruel barbarian devil the next. No one could predict how long he would be able to control his fanatical followers. While Ghilzais and Ghazis snapped at their heels, the hostages would never be safe.

CHAPTER TWELVE

The fortress of Budeeabad was the largest and newest of
the long chain of fortifications which stretched from the
Panjshir River at the lower end of the Lughman Valley
to the snow-capped mountain ranges of Kaffiristan. So
new, indeed, that although the apartments in the innermost courtyard, destined to be a summer retreat for the
fierce old zealot, Mahomed Shah Khan, and his favourite
wife, had been finished, those of the outer court where
his three other wives would live still lacked roofs, and
some of the mud walls were roughly shored up with
planking.

Mahomed Shah Khan was Akbar's father-in-law and
evil genius, instigator – along with Aminullah and Abdullah Khan – of the murders of both Sir Alexander Burnes
and the Envoy, and implacable enemy of the British. The
news that his fortress was to be their prison was hardly
comforting to the hostages, but when they arrived there
on 17 January, the towering mud walls with their flanking
towers and defensive ditch seemed a haven of security
compared to the wretched, smoke-filled hovels they had
endured since parting company with the rest of the army
some ten days earlier.

The lofty apartments were divided by sliding wooden
partitions which had been designed to withstand summer
heat better than winter cold, but after sleeping in the open
for several nights, heads pillowed on their saddles, the
ladies were glad of any improvement in their accommo-
dation and tried hard not to complain even when they
discovered that only six rooms had been allocated for the
use of the officers' families and the servants who had
faithfully followed them into captivity.

'It will be a squeeze,' admitted Georgy. 'Perhaps it is
as well that we have lost all our possessions.' She surveyed

the room which she and her baby were to share with Lady Macnaghten, the Anderson, Boyd, and Eyre families, as well as Thea and the teenage Hester Macdonald, sole survivor of Sergeant Macdonald of the 44th's large brood. The married ladies had agreed to share Hester's services and keep her close to them, thus preserving her from exposure to the vices and temptations of life in the *tykhana*, or cellar, of the outer court, where the other ranks and their women were lodged. Hester would have much preferred the free and easy life in the *tykhana*, but her wishes were not consulted and she dared not protest.

Though the room was large, sixteen mattresses occupied the whole floor space, and in order to reach their own beds most of these enforced room-mates were obliged to step over other mattresses, a proceeding which the children found so entertaining that, led by young Edward Trevor, the ringleader in any mischief, they embarked on a game of Musical Mattresses, capering over the beds and plumping down at Edward's signal until Lady Macnaghten was moved to protest strongly and call for Edward's banishment to the room shared by the bachelor officers.

Thea could hardly bear to watch the laughing children. It was just the sort of romp Dandy would have loved. She could imagine so clearly his peals of merriment as he hopped and skipped after the others . . .

'Don't cry,' whispered Georgy, putting an arm round her, but it was no use. The pain of losing Dandy seemed to get worse rather than better as time passed and hope faded. She could not now imagine how confidently she had looked for him at Akbar Khan's headquarters, where other distraught mothers had been reunited with their missing children.

Hugh Boyd had been found there, sleeping in Captain Lawrence's arms, and little Seymour Stoker, playing with the dagger of an Afghan noble. Only she and Mrs Anderson had looked in vain but whereas the Andersons had two other children to distract them from their grief for four-year-old Mary she was alone for the second time in her life.

Love was dangerous. It made you vulnerable, putting you at the mercy of forces you could not control. She would never, she vowed, give her heart to anyone again. She had loved James and found he had feet of clay. She had loved the children who were flesh of her flesh, and all the time God's eye had been watching her. *I, the Lord thy God, am a jealous God* . . . Like Mamma with the mango ice and Miss Oldershaw with hoarded sweetmeats, He had seen what she loved best and waited His chance to snatch them away.

She had endured the hardships of the journey here in a kind of frozen trance, oblivious to the discomforts of wet, evil-smelling clothes, cramped quarters and food she could barely swallow. Day after day she had followed blindly, riding up steep, rough tracks where the slightest stumble might have pitched her into an abyss, and far from fearing danger she had welcomed it, welcomed even the lice that infested her hair, the chilblains and cracked, blackened lips, anything that seemed likely to shorten the life she no longer valued.

But Akbar Khan had no intention of letting these valuable hostages die. The route he took across the mountains avoided those villages most hostile to the British, where fanatics might attack the infidels. It was one thing to let Afghan women insult and threaten them, quite another to let anyone hurt them. A strong body of cavalry, deserters from the British Irregular Horse among them, travelled with the Sirdar's party, ready to intervene to protect the hostages if the Ghilzais became too threatening, and the British officers were warned to keep their swords and pistols ready for use.

At the Panjshir River crossing, where the water was too deep and swift for their ponies, the ladies were taken up on the saddles of Afghan chargers, while others led their mounts splashing and floundering through the dangerous rapids. Five horses and several men perished, but all the hostages landed safely on the farther bank.

Afghan ideas of comfort being rather different from British ones, the captives soon learned to do without such refinements as linen or cutlery. Although the ladies found it hard to suppress their screams when they encountered a real live louse in their clothes, and everyone was soon crawling with vermin, they ate with their fingers from a communal pot without a word of protest.

Very soon after reaching Budeeabad, however, it was unanimously agreed that Afghan cooking was no longer to be endured.

' "God sends the meat but the Devil sends cooks," ' quoted Lady Sale, looking with disgust at the rags of greasy mutton-skin perched on a half-charred, half-raw chupatty made from coarse, unsifted flour which served as both plate and bread. Such fare had been their sole sustenance every day of their captivity and they were heartily sick of it.

'Our Hindustanis would certainly make a better hand of it,' agreed Lady Macnaghten, whose *embonpoint* had been much reduced by three weeks' Spartan diet. 'Sometimes I dream of the soufflés which Buonaventura used to make me! Light as thistledown. I vow they melted in the mouth. But we have so few servants. Who could spare one to cook for us?'

She certainly did not intend to offer the services of her own four, but Lady Sale said at once, 'Of course! Why did I not think of it? I have no objection to washing my own linen or cleaning my quarters if by doing so I may release one of my people. Captain Mackenzie! You know how to extract favours from our gaoler. Tell him we propose to cook the food ourselves if they will supply us with provisions.'

This was voted a capital idea, and that very evening Captain Mackenzie was able to announce that the Mirza Bowaddin Khan had graciously sanctioned this arrangement. There was a particular skill to extracting concessions from the heavy-featured, hook-nosed Mirza, who had been put in day-to-day charge of the hostages, and Captain Mackenzie had refined it to an art.

'Two parts of flattery to one of bribery, sprinkle well with compliments and allow to simmer for several hours before demanding an answer,' he said, grinning, when asked the secret of his success. 'The poor chap is so torn between feathering his own nest, running with the hare and hunting with the hounds, that he hardly knows which way he is facing. Even the Afghans think him a rogue, and that is saying a good deal!'

'Oh, he is not all bad, you know,' said Lady Macnaghten in the affected, simpering tone she used to cover her uneasy vowels and the occasional missing aspirate. Her little beringed hands caressed the ginger cat who stretched out on her lap, the picture of indolence. 'At least he found Caesar and brought him back to me after he was lost, the naughty pussy.'

'For which he was handsomely rewarded, no doubt?' suggested Mackenzie, with a suspicion of a wink at Captain Lawrence.

Lady Macnaghten looked a trifle flustered. 'Well, naturally! I was so relieved to see the dear fellow alive. I could hardly refuse the Mirza his reward, though to be truthful I did think twenty rupees a trifle excessive.'

Mackenzie's eyebrows climbed steeply. 'Twenty rupees! My dear Lady Macnaghten, at that rate I fear you will find Caesar vanishing pretty regularly.'

'Are you implying, Captain Mackenzie, that my cat was deliberately abducted?' said Lady Macnaghten, her pink cheeks quivering with indignation.

'I have not the smallest doubt he was.'

Captain Lawrence nodded. 'Danegeld. Once you start to pay for hostages, you encourage the abductors. Stands to reason.'

'I hope the Governor-General does not share your view, Captain Lawrence,' said Lady Macnaghten, quite put out to discover she had been hoodwinked.

'I don't suppose he does,' said Lawrence amiably. 'No doubt we shall all be ransomed in time, and pay for our liberty just as we are now paying for goods the Afghans stole from us on the march.'

Lady Macnaghten looked at him sharply, suspecting criticism. She alone of all the captives was still well pro-

213

vided with clothes and money, and her reluctance to share the former with less fortunate ladies was causing a good deal of ill feeling. Though well aware of this, Lady Macnaghten obstinately refused to make any distribution of her surplus gowns, on the grounds that if she gave to one, she would feel obliged to give to all. It would make her quite ill, she thought privately, to see that odious Mrs Riley preening in one of her own beautiful dresses, and it was not the slightest use Florentia Sale telling her that Mrs Riley was a very superior woman, for nothing could alter the fact that she was only a common soldier's wife. Lady Macnaghten's own origins were far from aristocratic and she was sensitive about matters of rank.

Before they had been long at Budeeabad, however, the ladies' dress problems were partially solved by a gift from the Sirdar of a bale of chintz and eight pieces of longcloth, which had almost certainly been the property of some unfortunate who had perished in the Khoord-Kabul Pass. They were received with general gratitude, nevertheless.

The news he brought of the army was far less welcome, and struck them silent with horror. Of the sixteen thousand who left Kabul on 6 January, Dr William Brydon alone had succeeded in reaching Jellalabad.

'All killed but one? Just as Taj Mahomed foretold?' whispered Alexandrina, white to the lips. 'Can it be true?'

Lady Sale nodded gravely. 'I incline to believe it for that very reason. From the moment our army left the cantonments it was doomed, driven like a flock of sheep to slaughter, with one man left to tell the tale.'

Letters from Jellalabad confirmed the disaster. It was tantalising for the captives to know that General Sale was only thirty miles away, yet powerless to help them. He had troubles of his own.

We can hold out here until Spring, he wrote to his wife, *though the enemy is active in harassing our patrols. Last week we made a sally and chupaoed a party of Sultan Jan's horse, taking a good few prisoners. Thanks to Major Broadfoot's*

214

heroic efforts our walls have risen from the dust to present the enemy with an obstacle, at least. I send you herewith some boxes and your chest of drawers, in the care of Abdul Ghofar Khan. I have ordered two pairs of shoes made for you, and will despatch them when I can . . .

The safe arrival of the chest of drawers and its contents occasioned great joy, as did the boxes despatched by Captain Mainwaring to his wife. He had excelled himself in guessing what was most needed. Shoes, shifts, stockings, hair and clothes brushes, needles, silks, scissors, shawls, and many other useful articles.

These Georgy distributed with a liberal hand.

'Dolly meant them for all of us,' she insisted when her fellow-captives protested she was keeping nothing for herself. 'The dear fellow! I own I am greatly astonished that he should show such an intimate knowledge of the female toilet! There must be corners of his past he has concealed from me.'

The very idea that the upright Captain Mainwaring could be suspected of a murky past made them all smile, and soon the courtyard was full of ladies and ayahs stitching and snipping and gossiping cheerfully. Lady Macnaghten sniffed when she saw that Georgy had given Mrs Riley a handsome length of material, but beyond remarking rather sourly that she hoped young Mrs Mainwaring knew what she was doing, she made no comment.

So great is the human power to adapt to circumstances, no matter how strange, that before the captives had spent a week in Budeeabad, they felt as settled as if they had lived there all their lives. Though they pined for the sight of a blade of grass, and dreaded the nightly clang of the gate confining them to the inner court, by day they were relatively free to roam within the perimeter walls or climb to the flat roof above their quarters, which provided the best drying ground for their linen.

Mrs Trevor prevailed on several ladies to assist her in teaching the older children, while Alexandrina and Georgiana took turns in keeping the younger ones amused.

Hester Macdonald was still child enough herself to enjoy romping games of Tag, and Blind Man's Buff; she had, besides, a pretty gift for music, and having bartered her shawl for a little three-stringed viol, she played and sang for the children to dance off the surplus energy which would otherwise have made their confinement still more oppressive.

Up to the end of the first week in February, relations with their captors remained good, with the Sirdar even permitting correspondence between Budeeabad and General Sale's garrison at Jellalabad, providing it passed through his own hands. But, on 9 February, he rode up to the fortress with a face black as thunder, and the next morning his wrath broke over the heads of the Political Officers.

'We are to lose our horses and our weapons are to be given up,' reported Lady Sale gloomily. 'All the servants who cannot work are to be turned out to starve, poor wretches. What have *they* done to deserve such a fate?'

Rumours of what had happened to anger the Sirdar ran wildly about all day, but by evening the truth was out and the culprit known.

A camel-driver had been waylaid and searched by Akbar's men, who discovered a tiny scroll hidden in the sole of each shoe. These revealed a secret correspondence between Major Pottinger and the Political Officer in Jellalabad, Captain Macgregor.

'Very foolish of them both,' declared Lady Sale. 'What can they hope to gain beyond enraging the Sirdar and putting all our lives in peril?'

To add to the general despondency, a spell of wet weather set in. Bedding and clothes were soaked, it was impossible to cross the courtyard without becoming plastered with mud, and the usual problems of sanitation became more pressing than ever. *As if the clouds wept for our misfortunes*, confided Lady Sale to her diary, though she would not have allowed so gloomy a sentiment to pass her lips for fear of undermining morale. As it was, it worried her to see the ladies' spirits so low, and the way poor Thea Quinn brooded over her lost children was, she thought, becoming morbid.

'Can *you* do nothing to cheer the unfortunate girl?' she asked George Mein during one of their confidential chats. 'I fear she will make herself ill. Heaven knows, this life we lead is hard enough without making matters worse by neglecting our health.'

'If only I could! I would give anything – *anything* – to see her smile again,' responded Mein so fervently that she gave him a startled glance, wondering if she was right to encourage what had plainly become an infatuation.

'She is so beautiful!' he went on dreamily. 'Like a painting by Titian, or . . . or Rubens, perhaps.'

This further astonished Lady Sale, who admitted that Mrs Quinn had a certain allure, but would not have described her as beautiful.

'Oh, you need not look at me like that!' said Mein, accurately reading her thoughts. 'I shall be discreet. She shall never know how deeply I worship her.'

'If you are discreet, Mr Mein, allow me to remark that it will be for the first time in your life,' said Lady Sale tartly, and Mein grinned.

'There is a first time for everything – even falling in love!'

She was not sure how seriously to take this declaration. George Mein might be a rattlepate, but he would not, she thought, wear his heart on his sleeve if there was any chance of it suffering real damage. Besides, he had an understanding with a young woman in England. Nevertheless, she watched with a certain anxiety as he laid siege to Thea's affections, hoping that neither would be hurt by it.

Like a good strategist, he began by using his cousin as a stalking-horse, artlessly attaching himself to the two whenever he found them together, but never approaching Thea alone. He gossiped, fetched and carried for them, and generally made himself so agreeable that Georgiana soon guessed what he was about. But for all his efforts, progress with Thea was slow. Though she smiled politely and listened with apparent interest to the cousins' chatter, any attempt to involve her in their discussion showed only too clearly that her thoughts were miles away. She had a worried, abstracted look, as if listening or waiting for something they knew nothing about.

Waiting for that bounder Quinn to send her a cheering word, thought Mein, who had made it his business to discover that of all the ladies with husbands in Sale's brigade, Thea was the only one who had received no communication from Jellalabad. Too busy chasing boys in the bazaar to worry about his wife, reflected Mein indignantly. I wonder how much she knows of what her precious husband gets up to in the *Chowk?* For all his ingenuous manner, George Mein had his share of worldliness, and the thought that James Quinn could indulge his perverted appetite and neglect his wife with no word of reproof from his superiors made him boil with righteous wrath.

He doesn't deserve such an angel, he pursued; and then: it would serve him right if I took her from him. But first he must make her notice him as a desirable man, instead of just Georgiana's cousin. He cursed his lack of inches and the round, fresh-complexioned face topped with tow-coloured curls which made him look so much younger than he was. Oh, to be tall and saturnine, with dark Byronic looks! His ears stuck out like jug handles and his big blue eyes thickly fringed with pale, upward-curling lashes made ladies smile rather than sigh.

Like many small men, he looked his best on a horse, but here in captivity he had no chance of showing off his equestrian skills. He longed to make some dramatic gesture, save her from flood or fire, knock down some brute who insulted her . . . anything that would change him from clown to hero in her eyes.

But as the prisoners' life continued its dull routine, with nothing to enliven it but rumour and speculation and the menacing rumble of guns from Jellalabad, nothing George Mein said or did roused Thea from her apathy.

She brooded over James's silence, and guessed its cause.

heavily. 'It *is* unfair! You should not have told me anything if you didn't mean to tell it all. Now I shall imagine the most terrible – *Oh! What was that?*'

She had been looking directly at her cousin's face, and now to her consternation it swayed violently from side to side as Mein struggled to retain his balance on ground that had begun to heave beneath his feet. The buildings all round them rocked, too, and the bench on which Georgiana was sitting gave a sudden lurch as if a leg had broken. The ground shivered, and was still, and shivered again.

Then the whole fortress rose and dipped like a ship in a storm. Cries of alarm burst from the others in the courtyard as the tall walls shook and bulged, and there was a loud rumbling overhead as if a heavy ball had rolled across the sky. There was a stunned silence as the earth stabilised again, but before anyone had time to voice relief, a second shock, more violent than the first, brought the crash of falling masonry. Several flat roofs collapsed like a pack of stacked cards.

'Mamma!' screamed Alexandrina, staggering up to run to the stairway up which Lady Sale had vanished, but before she had reached its foot, her mother's tall figure, smothered in dust and still clutching an armful of linen, cascaded down the last steps and nearly fell into her daughter's arms.

'Thank God you are safe!' they exclaimed in unison.

At the same moment Captain Mackenzie, who had been enjoying his morning pipe on the adjoining roof, sprang nimbly down the last flight of stairs, with Brigadier Shelton – indignant, blown and shaken – hot on his heels.

Great clouds of dust hung over the fortress, and before these had even begun to settle, a third heavy shock set the earth heaving yet again.

Georgiana slumped to the ground, half stunned by a lump of brick which struck her on the point of the shoulder and would have crushed her skull had she not ducked in time. As the rattling and crashing subsided, the screams died away and were replaced by an eerie

221

silence broken only by the whimpering of the youngest children, the mournful braying of donkeys outside the walls, and Lady Macnaghten's quavering voice calling for her cat.

'Cousin George?' Through the thick, reddish haze, Georgiana stared at several tons of rubble heaped up where Mein had been standing. Her own escape had been narrow. If Mein was under that he would have no hope of survival.

With frantic haste she began to tear at the shattered mud bricks, pulling them out and tossing them aside, oblivious of skinned fingers and broken nails, until Lieutenant Eyre, grasping the situation, ran over to help her.

'Who is it?'

'Mr Mein. He was standing just there.'

'My God!'

'Can't be Mein,' said Major Pottinger, walking over to join them in his quick, decisive way. 'I saw him run into the building, just before the second shock collapsed that wall. He went over there.' He pointed towards the largest of the captives' apartments, upon whose roof Lady Sale had been drying her linen, and in a flash Georgiana understood why Mein had gone in there.

'Mrs Quinn!' she gasped. 'She went to lie down.'

'Quick, men. Over here!' Pottinger ordered. 'We'll have to go carefully. The walls may come down any moment.'

Willing hands began to clear the rubble from the doorway leading to the inner chamber, while others formed a chain to pass the debris back along the passage they had cleared. Men and women, so grimed with dust it was hard to tell one from the other, worked, apart from the occasional murmured command, in silence, fearful of disturbing the precarious balance of the tottering building.

Splintered beams and shards of tile had collapsed in higgledy-piggledy mounds, and when a booted foot was spotted sticking out beneath a mattress, the rescuers stifled groans, fearing that their toil had been in vain.

But the boot stirred. A muffled voice called, 'We're

222

here!' As Major Pottinger and Lieutenant Eyre gingerly raised the mattress, they found Mein alive and conscious beneath it, shielding with his body the still form of Mrs Quinn.

Mein had a broken arm. 'But for that, I should have carried you to safety before the roof came down,' he assured Thea, who had suffered nothing worse than shock and bruises.

'You were so brave! When the walls started swaying I was afraid to move, and then it all came crashing down . . . '

'Don't think about it,' said Mein, well pleased by the effect of his exploit.

'I can't forget it. I think about it all the time. If you hadn't come, I should have been killed.'

At first she had thought the dizzy swaying merely an extension of her headache, and had closed her eyes to combat it. Only when she opened them to see who was shaking her mattress so annoyingly had she realised what was happening. Never having felt an earthquake before, she had lain paralysed until Mein flung both himself and the mattress of the next bed on top of her.

'Practical, if hardly *convenable*,' said Lady Sale dryly, but she had to admit that the narrow brush with death had miraculously revived Thea's interest in living. Gratitude to Mein and guilt at being the cause of his injury made her insist on nursing him herself, accepting only a little assistance from Moore, the obliging fair-haired young private of the 44th who cared for General Elphinstone. Both Elphy Bey and his *bête noire* the Brigadier had been brought to join the hostages before the final massacre of the Kabul force, and their efforts to avoid one another's company imposed uncomfortable restraints on the other captives.

As his arm began to mend, George Mein considered himself well compensated for the pain by the fuss the ladies made of him. They awarded him the sunniest bench in the courtyard, and gathered about him in an eager,

223

chattering flock as he decoded the messages their friends had begun to send from Jellalabad by the simple expedient of marking certain letters in old newspapers.

'*There will be no relief before April,*' he announced, to a collective sigh; and then, more cheerfully, '*Pollock has been named to command the Army of Retribution.* A Company man – hurrah! That will put paid to rumours of jobbery! He is on his way to Peshawar already.'

This was heartening news. General Pollock was a grand old warhorse, straight and steady as a rock – but would his relief come in time? Other forts in the Lughman Valley had been more severely damaged by the earthquake than Budeeabad. Jellalabad had been badly shaken.

'The guards say there were three hundred killed at Tighree,' announced Lieutenant Eyre, for once beating Mein with the news.

'I heard a rumour that the walls at Jellalabad have been levelled to the ground,' put in Captain Souter, a recent addition to the band of hostages. He had arrived at Budeeabad curiously attired in the regimental colours of the 44th, which he had saved by winding them round his waist during the final desperate stand at Gandamak, and he attributed his survival to this talisman.

'When the Ghilzai chief saw my strange rig, he thought I must be worth ransoming,' he explained. 'He would have sent me on to Jellalabad, too, only the Sirdar heard of it and made him give me up. But for that, I should be with Fighting Bob by now.'

'If Broadfoot's walls have been breached by the earthquake, it will be all up with Sale,' said Captain Johnson, shaking his head gloomily.

Lady Sale turned on him quite fiercely. 'Meeting trouble halfway will not improve our spirits, Captain Johnson! What has been thrown down can be built up again.'

Whatever their private opinion on this subject, no one cared to contradict her openly. They waited in painful suspense for the outcome of Akbar Khan's next assault on Jellalabad. This was delayed a few days, since his men

insisted on dispersing temporarily to assess the earthquake's damage to their own homes and livestock. Working night and day, Major Broadfoot's sappers had repaired
the walls, and by the time Akbar Khan's men
reassembled, Sale was ready for them. Once again the
hostages rejoiced when news trickled through to them that
the Sirdar's latest attack had been repulsed.

It means nothing, Thea told herself when George Mein
smiled at her and called her his ministering angel. It is
just a joke with him, she thought when he caught her
hand and kissed it passionately. He is only a boy. But
there is nothing like male admiration for raising female
spirits. As the Afghan winter melted suddenly into spring,
Thea sometimes found herself smiling for no reason. Her
steps felt light again, and once or twice she surprised
herself by humming a tune.

While he could not write, she took down letters at his
dictation. To his parents in Cheshire he described their
wild surroundings and as much of their hardships and
misadventures as he thought would pass Afghan scrutiny
and not worry his mother too much. He added cheerful
messages to his sisters and to Miss Amanda Legge, the
neighbour's daughter with whom he had an Understanding.

Thea thought that Miss Legge would have preferred a
letter of her own, rather than being lumped in with the
rest of his family, but when she said as much, George
reddened. 'Oh, she won't mind. It is not as if we were
betrothed, or any such rot. She's an heiress,' he added
disparagingly. 'Pots of money, you see.'

She thought him less than lover-like, and was not
wholly surprised when, in a burst of confidence, he
explained that their parents were the prime promoters of
the match.

'They want us to join the two properties,' he said. 'I
used to think it a good notion, but now I ain't so sure.
It's all very well for the Pater to say we'd have twice the
money and twice the land. He won't be waking up each

225

day to find her button nose on the pillow beside him! Or have to listen to her damned sermons!'

He gave her a soulful look. 'I'd rather choose a wife for myself. Someone more like you.'

She could not help laughing.

'I mean it,' he insisted.

'But I am married already.'

'I know. More's the pity,' he sighed theatrically. 'Perhaps Captain Quinn will be killed gallantly defending Jellalabad.'

'Mr Mein! I cannot allow you to speak in that way,' said Thea quite sharply.

'I was only joking.'

'I don't like that kind of joke.'

'Please don't go,' he said quickly. 'I'm sorry if I offended you. My damned tongue runs away with me, you know that! Blame it on the bullet.'

She could never be cross with him for long, and spent a good deal of time keeping him amused.

'Sit with me,' he would plead, as he watched Captain Mackenzie run races with their Afghan guards, or the Trevor boys wrestle with their children. 'It is so dull sitting still while everyone else is playing.'

She found she could talk to him with a freedom she had never known with James. He was so easy, so interested in all she felt and thought. It is because we are fellow-captives facing the same dangers, she told herself, but could not repress a treacherous, insidious longing for the same kind of comradeship from James.

Gently George led her on to speak of her husband, and almost before she knew it, Thea was pouring out her worries; how he had changed after he was wounded; his moodiness; his dependence on Hinghan Khan.

'The Afghan boy he bought in the bazaar?' said George, who knew perfectly well.

She nodded unhappily. 'He saved James's life, you know. I ought to be grateful to him, as James is, but . . . '

226

She paused, and said with a return of constraint, 'Perhaps I should not speak of it.'

'Oh, you may be easy. It will go no further. What a fellow you must think me!' he exclaimed in a hurt tone.

She said seriously, 'I am sorry. I did not really think you would betray my confidence. In a way, I find it a relief to speak of it, after remaining silent so long.' With this George was satisfied that another advance had been made in their friendship.

And so it proved. His mother, far away in England, had asked for a sketch of him, and Thea was glad to undertake the commission. It gave her the opportunity to study her admirer with more than sisterly interest. Though small, he was well made and his movements had the grace of the natural athlete. The round face with its snub nose and wide, pugnacious jaw could not be called handsome, but no one would deny its character and charm.

'Excellent! You have caught him exactly,' decided Lady Sale, appraising the sketch with her quick, sharp glance. 'That innocent look – so deceptive! Take my advice and leave it there. So many portraits are ruined by overworking.'

Thereafter it became quite the fashion among the younger officers to sit for Mrs Quinn. Though some wives were jealous at first and inclined to disparage her talent, they soon saw that Thea had no interest in ensnaring their men. Besides, Mein's increasingly proprietorial attitude discouraged thoughts of flirtation among her sitters.

So the slow, tense days of March crawled past under still-rumbling skies that produced the occasional earth tremor to alarm the hostages, though nothing on the scale of the first shocks. However hard they tried to keep busy and cheerful, there were times when a woman would begin to sob uncontrollably for no particular reason; when quarrels would flare over trivial matters of space or precedence; or when a man would lapse into silence with a look of frozen pain as past horrors returned to haunt him. Within his head he would be hearing dead friends' voices

– brother officers, stoical sepoys of his regiment, helpless camp-followers – pleading for help, or for the quick death he could not bring himself to give them. How many had lingered in torment, or been hacked apart by Afghans because his own will to survive had driven him onward, ignoring their plight? Such questions were hard to confront, but even acknowledged heroes of the retreat could remember shameful moments when they had turned blind eyes to the pain of those weaker than themselves and hurried onward. Such memories would remain with them all their lives, and with dark shadows hanging over their own futures, who could say that it would not have been better to die in the passes with a clear conscience?

Every day brought new rumours, and now the coded messages reaching them from Jellalabad had begun to sound a desperate note. Provisions were low. The native troops were on half rations. Why was General Pollock's advance so slow? Could it be true that Brigadier Wild had suffered a terrible defeat at the hands of the Khyber tribes? If Jellalabad fell, their own position would be still more precarious. With their value as hostages gone, Akbar might have them killed, or carry out his oft-repeated threat to sell them into slavery in Bokhara.

'Before that happened, I would shoot my wife and myself,' said Lieutenant Eyre with quiet resolution, and most of his fellows agreed.

'That is all very well for women with husbands,' objected the irrepressible Georgiana. 'What of us poor females with no male protector? Do you expect us to shoot ourselves? If anyone shoots me without my permission, he will have Dolly to answer to.'

But her attempt to lighten the general gloom fell flat. Emily Eyre, a pale, serious young woman, remarked coldly that she did not think it a laughing matter, and even Lady Sale turned away as if she thought such frivolity in poor taste.

'I meant it, though,' said Georgy defiantly to Thea in the corner of the bedchamber where they had arranged their mattresses to give themselves a little privacy. 'I

228

should give Mr Eyre a piece of my mind if he tried to shoot me for my own good! Where there's life there's hope, say I!'

Thea agreed. 'Men are far too ready to assume they know best in such matters. Who knows, a Khan might fall in love and make you his favourite concubine. Think of the Empress Theodora.'

'I knew you would understand.' Georgy put her arm round Thea's waist. 'We have not endured the hardships of the past year only to be shot by Mr Eyre! We will have a pact, and agree that no one is to shoot either of us without our *express* permission.'

The absurdity of the discussion struck them both at the same time, and they rolled on their mattresses giggling like a pair of schoolroom hoydens. It made them feel a great deal better, but the relief was short-lived.

That evening, the hostages were called together in the refectory by a grim-faced Major Pottinger, who told them in tones that could not conceal his own anger and apprehension that the Sirdar's father-in-law, the implacable Mahomed Shah Khan, had returned to replace the easygoing Mirza as their gaoler. All their remaining servants were to be turned out of the fort, their horses taken away, and their possessions thoroughly searched.

Lady Macnaghten turned pale and gave a little cry, for this signalled the loss of her precious cashmere shawls and all her remaining jewels.

'The Sirdar has suffered a defeat at the hands of General Sale,' Pottinger went on, but the murmur of excitement died away as he added, 'I endeavoured to propose terms for our release, but was told we must follow the fortunes of the Sirdar and prepare for a long journey.'

This was worrying news.

'How can we travel without horses?' someone called.

'Transport will be provided,' said Major Pottinger, and there was a general groan, for that meant camels and *kajavas* for the ladies and the sorriest nags in Afghanistan for the men. 'The Sirdar believes that General Pollock intends to send a strong force directly to Budeeabad to rescue us. Before it can come within striking range, we are to be hidden away in the hills.'

CHAPTER THIRTEEN

It is all Freddie's fault, thought Rohais, as she rocked back and forth, back and forth on the verandah, looking listlessly out on the dusty brown oblong that would be lawn again when the Rains came. Away to her left, behind the bungalow, a brainfever bird called maddeningly. Apart from the steady movement of the rocking-chair, nothing stirred in the parched, exhausting noon of late May in the Plains.

For as long as she could remember, she had spent the Hot Weather in Simla, and if it hadn't been for Freddie, she thought resentfully, she would still be there now, queening it over dashing, bewhiskered officers and going to balls and parties every night, instead of sweating out the summer in a dull, up-country station, with only her father for company. Freddie should have told her he was married. If she had known that, she would never have let him persuade her to hide in the shrubbery with him at Mrs Macnamara's Mystery Picnic.

That had been the start of the trouble. Or perhaps, reflected Rohais, it had started still further back, last Christmas, when her mother had died so suddenly of the blackwater fever. If she had been staying at dear Ferndale with Mamma, instead of lodging with vague, well-meaning Cousin Everilda, her godmother, she might never have accepted Mrs Macnamara's invitation. Mamma had not approved of the large Macnamara family with their free and easy ways, but Cousin Everilda was less selective about her friends. She had made no objection when Rohais said that a Mystery Picnic sounded delightful and that she meant to go. Delightful it had been, indeed, right up to the moment when Mrs Macnamara proposed the game of Hide and Seek.

At once Freddie had taken Rohais's hand. Captain the

Honourable Alfred Sherborne was the most dashing of all Lord Ellenborough's aides, tall and Grecian-profiled, with bold blue eyes and soft golden whiskers. He had gazed soulfully at Rohais from the moment she stepped out of her *palki*.

'Come with me, Miss Quinn! We'll hide together. I know the perfect place,' he had whispered, his moustache tickling her ear. 'No one will find us there.'

Flattered and intrigued, she had gone willingly into the secret green den among the rhododendrons, and there they had huddled, nearly bursting with silent laughter as the others searched in vain through the shrubbery. As the hunt moved away, she even allowed Freddie to kiss her, but when she tried to tell him that that was enough, he would not listen.

Almost before she knew it, the Unthinkable had happened, and Freddie – red-faced and flustered – was urging her to straighten her clothes and clumsily trying to pick dried leaves out of her hair, while saying over and over again that he was sorry.

Sorry! What use was that?

She had cried and declared that she was Ruined, and then waited for him to say he would marry her, but instead he had said sharply that she should have known better than to lead a fellow on and what could she expect? While she was gasping with indignation at this injustice, he had broken the news that he was already married . . .

She remembered the dreadful sinking feeling in her stomach when she had heard it, and the way her mind had begun to race in circles, trying to find a way to save her reputation.

Freddie had sworn eternal silence, so how, she wondered, had the story reached Cousin Everilda's ears? Could Mrs Macnamara herself have been to blame? Whatever the source of the information, Rohais had been startled and shocked when her godmother had told her with a firmness that brooked no argument that she could no longer hold herself responsible for Rohais's behaviour.

'You have abused my trust, child, and I have no alterna-

tive but to tell your father to come and take you home,'
she had said with most uncharacteristic vigour. 'You have
made yourself the talk of Simla, and it is far better that
you should withdraw at once and allow the scandal to
subside, rather than attempt to brazen it out.'

'But Cousin Everilda! What have I done?'

'That is between you and your own conscience,' the old
lady had said obstinately. 'I only know that there is no
smoke without fire, and your dear mother would turn in
her grave if she heard her daughter talked of as I have
heard people talk of you. No, my dear, it is useless to
cry. I shall not change my mind. You had much better
take my advice and go home quietly. I shall give out that
your father needs you.'

'Will you tell Papa?' Rohais had asked, trembling, and
Cousin Everilda had smiled rather sadly.

'No, you may rest easy on that. I am as much to blame
as you are for not keeping a better watch on you, but I
thought – I hoped – I could rely on your own good sense.
Now that I see my confidence was misplaced, I can only
hope that no harm comes of this foolish escapade.'

No harm! Rohais knew very well what kind of harm
Cousin Everilda had had in mind, and great had been her
relief when the onset of her monthly courses reassured her
on this point. But the harm her reputation had suffered in
that short interlude in the shrubbery seemed likely to be
still more insidious, and possibly even more damaging.
There were ways to get rid of unwanted babies, but freeing
herself from the burden of scandal acquired so easily had
begun to seem beyond her powers.

It did not help that most of the ladies in the station saw
Rohais as a natural enemy, spoiled, arrogant, and far too
attractive to their husbands, brothers and sons. They had
greeted the rumour of her fall from grace with ill-con-
cealed glee. Rohais's response had been characteristically
defiant. What did she care what the old cats thought of
her? If they wanted to talk, she would give them something to talk about.

Cautiously at first, and then with growing confidence,

233

she had set out to satisfy the dark cravings awakened in Mrs Macnamara's shrubbery. Freddie had shown her how easy it was to find an excuse to be alone with a gentleman, despite the conventional hedge of restrictions on an unmarried lady's conduct. Rohais cared nothing for convention. Early-morning strolls, drowsy afternoons in the summerhouse, evening promenades by the river could all, she had found, be turned into assignations, and she had revelled in her new-found power to draw men to her with a smile and a lift of the eyebrow.

In Ludhiana, as in every up-country station that year, British thoughts were concentrated on the fortunes of General Pollock as he fought his way towards Kabul, and on the fate of the hostages still held by Akbar Khan. You could not pick up a news-sheet or listen to a conversation without having the subject endlessly debated.

Rohais, however, had soon tired of hearing about the hostages. She thought her sister-in-law had brought her misfortunes on herself by rushing off to be a heroine in Kabul. If she perished, it was her own fault. Sometimes Rohais thought that if she heard the word 'Afghanistan' again, she would scream.

It had given her a guilty thrill to make some excuse to leave the company and hear through the open windows the voices of visiting officers gravely discussing such matters with her father, while she panted with passion in the arms of a good-looking corporal of Horse whom they supposed to be attending to quite other duties. She had known, deep down, that she was playing with fire, but so great was her loneliness and boredom that she even welcomed the danger.

When disaster had finally struck, it had not been unexpected and she had laid her plans, but to her surprise and consternation none of the remedies she took to rid herself of the unwanted baby had the least effect. Violent exercise and hot baths, infusions of herbs and purgatives had all proved quite unavailing.

Keep calm, she had told herself, there must be some way out of this; but with every day's passing she grew more desperate. It was the beginning of September, and she was steeling herself to confront her father with her predicament, when she heard the sound of hoofs on gravel and, looking out, saw a familiar figure dismount from his horse.

Her heart leapt joyfully. The one – the *only* – person who would help her without asking awkward questions. Before his horse had been led away, she was running down the verandah steps, eyes misty, lips a-tremble, to fling herself into his arms. As ever, they closed round her protectively. With a little sob of relief, she laid her head against his chest.

'Oh, Toby!' she murmured. 'I am in such trouble, I don't know what to do. Please, *please* say you will help me!'

Toby looked down at the large blue eyes swimming in tears, the delicate, flower-like face with its new puffiness about the jawline, and a knife seemed to twist in his heart.

'Tell me about it, my angel,' he said gently, and wiped the tears away.

'But will you help me? I'll – I'll *die* if you don't.'

He sighed. It wasn't difficult to guess what kind of trouble she was in, or what she was asking him to do.

'Don't cry, my love,' he said. 'Of course I'll help you. You can count on me.'

High on the cliffs at either end of the valley of Bamian, two gigantic figures carved into the soft pudding-stone stood guard over the ancient city of Gulguleh, which was already old when it was sacked in the thirteenth century by the slit-eyed troops of Genghis Khan. Gauzy stone draperies, cunningly worked, veiled the enormous statues. Although, in the sixteenth century, the artillery of another conqueror, the Persian Nadir Shah, had obliterated the features of the female deity in an access of religious zeal, his gunners had made a poor job of destroying the 160-foot-high male head. Across the centuries, his archaic smile still beamed benignly upon the latest inhabitants of the valley.

God and goddess? King and queen? Who were they, and whose long-dead hands had contrived so vast a memorial? Who had built the stairs and galleries by which the nimble antiquarian with a good head for heights was tempted to climb to the very crowns of the tutelary deities, to view the world from their lofty vantage point?

Such questions preoccupied Lady Sale as she sat in a small arbour of juniper branches, sketchbook on her knee, contemplating the vast, silent figures in the slanting rays of a September sunrise. Even asking questions without hope of an answer was better than rehearsing their own troubles, and she found the enigmatic grandeur of the vast guardians of Bamian strangely comforting.

The nine dragging months of their captivity were just a blink of the eye compared to the centuries these statues had spent staring sightlessly across their valley. Kingdoms and empires had risen and collapsed, generations flourished and vanished while they watched, unmoved. How trivial her troubles seemed in such a time-scale! What did it matter if any of *them* lived or loved or suffered or died?

A casual acquaintance – someone, say, who had known her in London or Calcutta – would have needed a second, perhaps even a third glance before recognising in this tall, scrawny, sunburnt gipsy the handsome wife of Major-General Sir Robert Sale, Fighting Bob of Her Majesty's 13th Light Infantry. She was dressed in an ill-fitting, off-white gown, patched in many places, and a grubby, faded turban whose fringe hung over her right shoulder. The long months of captivity, hardship and perpetual anxiety had aged her by ten years in appearance and mentally even more. So long had they lived in the constant fear of death that the hostages had forgotten how to think more than one day ahead, and the rescue that had seemed so close in April had receded like a mirage with every step they had taken since leaving Budeeabad at the Sirdar's command. Now Budeeabad seemed a lifetime away. It was hard to remember the hopes they had entertained as General Pollock approached Jellalabad, so complete was their erosion now . . .

236

Their hurried departure in the charge of their old enemy, Mahomed Shah Khan, had resulted in a succession of nightmare marches from one wretched fort to another, their clothes soaked with incessant rain, deprived of servants and all comforts as their worn-out ponies slipped and stumbled over rough mountain tracks.

With Jellalabad in Pollock's hands and his own fortunes in swift decline, Akbar Khan clung tenaciously to his hostages. Deeper and deeper into the hills he dragged them, and wherever they went, Mahomed Shah Khan delighted in adding to their misery. When Captain Lawrence appealed for the ladies and children to be allowed to rest, the fierce old brigand turned on him in a fury.

'While there is an Afghan prisoner in India or a *feringhi* in Afghanistan, so long will we keep you – men, women and children,' he snarled. 'While you can ride, you shall ride. When you cannot, you shall walk. When you cannot walk, you shall be dragged. When you cannot be dragged, *your throats will be cut.*'

It was galling for the hostages to see Dr Tobias Black riding a sure-footed pony alongside the Sirdar and exchanging jokes and courtesies while they bumped along in their excruciating camel panniers.

'How that young man has the gall to show his face before us, I cannot imagine,' complained Lady Macnaghten. 'Why is he not in Kabul, tending his patients?'

'Dr Primrose is with them. Dr Black is endeavouring to negotiate our release,' said Lady Sale patiently.

Lady Macnaghten snorted. 'So he claims! I, for one, take leave to doubt his good faith. Look at him! Thick as thieves with our captors, and no doubt well recompensed by both sides for his meddling,' she snapped, shifting her cat's basket to her other knee. 'He has always been a good deal too indulgent towards natives for my taste, and so I shall tell him if I get the chance.'

But no such chance came her way. On Akbar Khan's orders, Toby's contacts with the hostages were very carefully monitored by their guards. Friendly he might appear, but he had no intention of letting any of his

English 'guests' speak to their intermediary in private. Only when Georgiana Mainwaring suddenly fainted off her pony and lay as if dead beside the track was the Hakim-Sahib summoned to use his special skills to revive her.

'He told me he is trying to negotiate a ransom for us,' she reported, rubbing her bruises. 'Oh, I am black and blue! I should have looked for a softer place to fall.'

'You mean you did it on purpose?' asked Thea, wishing she had thought of the ruse herself.

'Of course.' Georgy laid her hand on Thea's arm and added gently, 'I asked him if he had been able to find any trace of – of Dandy, but he shook his head. I am so sorry.'

Thea's eyes filled with tears. She turned away, unable even to thank Georgy for her efforts.

'What else did he tell you?' asked Lady Macnaghten sharply. 'Why can he not agree a ransom?'

'From the little he was able to say, I understood that the Sirdar might ransom us – if the price was right – but his father-in-law is adamant that we should end our lives in captivity. He says it is the best way to ensure that no *feringhi* ever invades his country again.' Georgiana spoke sombrely, and the listening ladies gave little gasps of dismay.

In strained silence, they continued their march into the hills.

Ten days of rough travel killed off old Elphy Bey. He and Brigadier Shelton had joined them in captivity just before the army's final destruction, but his spirit was dead long before it finally left his body.

'Poor gentleman, 'e didn't want to live no more,' said kindly Private Moore, his servant, fighting back tears.

Lady Sale, who had been delirious with fever during much of the painful ride, was unable to summon much sympathy. General Elphinstone's dithering and blundering had brought them all to this pass. By dying he had evaded the ultimate disgrace of a court martial, and relieved the other hostages of the anxiety of watching his disintegration. Relief far outweighed her pity when she

238

was told of his death, and her practical spirit cried out against the Sirdar's decision to send his emaciated remains to Jellalabad for burial.

Her instinct was soon proved right. The coffin was ambushed and desecrated, the unfortunate Private Miller, his other servant, who had travelled with it disguised as an Afghan, was detected, badly beaten, and brought back to join the other hostages.

Lightning-storm rages, however, were just as typical of Akbar Khan as such quixotic gestures of chivalry. Once he ordered a miscreant flayed to death in front of him, starting at his feet, and quite recently an unfortunate henchman whose pistol had caught in the Sirdar's ornate girdle as he was assisting him to mount and discharged, wounding Akbar Khan in the arm, had been instantly ripped open and disembowelled before he could so much as mutter a verse from the Koran. You never knew where you were with such a man. Even Mahomed Shah Khan's implacable hostility was easier to deal with.

Four blistering summer months were spent near the Capital, cooped up in a fort from which they could hear the guns of the Bala Hissar and receive at second-hand every rumour that ran through the Kabul bazaar. *Chupao* was then the word on everyone's lips. *Chupao* meant a surprise attack, and as Akbar Khan's influence waned there were plenty of his former adherents who sought to secure their own futures by *chupaoing* the British hostages and claiming the ransom themselves.

Those months of close confinement and uncertainty wore down the captives' health, producing boils, a gaol-bird pallor, and shadowed eyes in prematurely lined faces. Typhus raged through their small community, laying low the ladies one after the other. Though most recovered in time, Captain John Conolly and a number of infants died.

Hopes ran high every time the Political Officers were sent to acquaint General Pollock with Akbar Khan's latest proposals for a settlement, only to be dashed when they returned from Jellalabad to report that negotiations were at a stalemate. Akbar Khan offered a free exchange of prisoners, to include his father Dost Mahomed, provided that British troops were immediately withdrawn from Afghanistan. General Pollock's inability to sign such an undertaking looked each day more likely to prove the hostages' death-warrant.

Late in August came the order they most feared: Prepare to march tomorrow. Caught in a pincer movement between Pollock's advance from Jellalabad and General Nott's deliberate swing north to pass through Kabul on his retreat from Kandahar to India, Akbar had resolved to play his last card. The British generals would arrive in the capital to find their birds flown.

Leaving behind only those ladies who were too ill to rise from their beds, the hostages were again bundled on to camels and ponies and, escorted by a strong band of armed cavalry under the command of a bombastic, flamboyant turncoat named Saleh Mahomed, who had once been a *subadar* in Hopkins's Afghan levy, they were hurried away north across the Lughur River towards the remote valley of Bamian.

'Lady S-a-a-a-le! Look – at – us!'

The armed guard who was crouching a few feet to her left with his blanket draped about his shoulders, glanced keenly in the direction of the faint cry, shading his eyes against the sunrise.

Three – no, four – manikins had appeared on the very top of the female deity's head, like individual hairs stirred by a breeze. After a moment's careful scrutiny, she identified them; Lieutenant Eyre, a keen antiquarian, Lieutenant Mein, and Mrs Quinn, with, of course, their Afghan guard.

Lady Sale put down her sketchbook and waved back vigorously.

'Wait – for – us. We're coming down!'

Twenty minutes passed before they joined her, hot and excited after their scramble down the cliff. Like the other male hostages, whose uniforms had been reduced to rags,

George Mein and Vincent Eyre had adopted the Afghan dress of striped turban with low-necked white vest under a bright cotton overshirt worn ungirded, the whole surmounted by a dark, flowing robe – and very well it suited them, thought Lady Sale, regarding the two young men with approval. Mein's fair complexion was becomingly tanned and the cloak gave him an unexpected dignity, while his turban added at least four inches to his stature, and Vincent Eyre's handsome, hawkish features might well have passed for those of an Afghan tribesman.

Thea wore a crumpled and faded yellow cotton gown which she had made herself from locally woven longcloth provided by the Sirdar. A broad white fichu on which no louse could crawl undetected was draped about her shoulders and pinned at the neck. Vermin were a constant problem for those ladies who refused to be parted from their long tresses, but Thea had solved the problem, more or less, by having the camp-barber crop her hair close to the skull. The resulting riot of short curls blazed round her head like an aureole, and her eyes were sparkling and cheeks glowing.

'Such a view!' she exclaimed. 'We could see the top of Koh-i-Baba – quite pink – and right out beyond the Haji-guk Pass.'

'I know, my dear. Well worth the climb.' Lady Sale looked at her approvingly. George Mein had done wonders for her spirits, she thought. She looked vital and attractive despite her shabby rags of clothes – very different from the depressed creature she had been at Budeeabad.

'We saw something else,' said Eyre meaningly.

Lady Sale gave him a sharp glance. 'What was that?'

'A party of cavalry coming up from Killa Topchee. Riding fast.' Eyre nodded briefly to George Mein. Don't frighten the ladies, said that nod, but warn them the crisis may be near . . .

'Do you think . . .?' began Thea.

Long months of uncertainty had taught Lady Sale not to cross her bridges before she came to them. She rose, shaking dust from her skirt.

241

'We had better go back.'

Briskly she gathered her sketching materials and handed them to the guard, who accepted them with a look of disgust.

'We shall find out who they are soon enough,' she said, and set off with long strides down the path, the others close behind.

The horsemen were already closeted with Saleh Mahomed when Thea and Lady Sale reached the little fort with its miserable collection of windowless mud huts which had been their home for the past week. With their own hands the ladies had pulled out stones to admit light and air, but they could do nothing against the tormenting bedbugs.

Eyre and Mein, who had run on ahead, shook their heads when asked for news. 'Major Pottinger has been sent for. It looks bad,' said Eyre.

This gloomy view was soon confirmed. Eldred Pottinger emerged grim-faced from his interview with their gaoler, and strode quickly to where most of the hostages were anxiously waiting.

'Bad news, I fear.'

'Oh, tell us, quickly!'

'Saleh Mahomed has been ordered to take us instantly to Kulun and sell us to the Khans there for whatever we will fetch.'

There was a moment of horrified silence, then general uproar. Men cursed, women wept, and children wailed in sympathy.

'For what we will fetch?' echoed Lady Macnaghten, her voice shrill with indignation as well as fright. 'But we are Akbar's *hostages*! He has sworn on his father's head to protect us. He has no right to treat us like – like cattle! No civilised nation treats helpless prisoners in such a way.'

No one cared to waste his breath pointing out how often Akbar had broken his promises to them, or enquiring if her ladyship really thought Afghanistan a civilised nation.

'We are in the hands of Providence,' murmured Emily

Eyre, clinging tightly to the baby she had borne in captivity.

Lady Sale said nothing. Her quick eyes followed Major Pottinger as he moved about the courtyard, observed the jerk of the chin by which he drew Captain Johnson to his side, then raised his eyebrows and nodded to Captain Lawrence, who immediately left his conversation and sauntered over to join them. Inconspicuously the three officers wandered away to sit on the low wall surrounding a mulberry tree, heads together in earnest discussion.

Presently Lawrence approached her and spoke in a low voice. 'Will you allow us to use your room for a conference, Lady Sale? It is the most private place.'

'By all means,' she answered readily. 'May I ask why?'

Lawrence glanced round, then said in a low, hurried tone, 'The Mir Akhor has ridden to visit Zulficar Khan at Bamian. This is our best chance – perhaps our only chance – to subvert Saleh Mahomed.'

The Mir and his fanatical horsemen had been sent by Akbar Khan precisely to ensure that Saleh Mahomed made no deals with his captives.

Lady Sale nodded. 'I wish you all the luck in the world, Captain Lawrence,' she said gravely, and clasped his hand. 'Would that I could add my voice to yours!'

'Pray for us, then,' he said and walked quickly away. As the small group of officers vanished into the dark little hut, Lady Sale gripped her hands together on her lap and prayed as she had never prayed before.

Resplendent in a British officer's blue frock coat with jingling epaulettes, Saleh Mahomed lounged at his ease. His flat, black Tartar eyes surveyed Major Pottinger with assumed indifference.

'I have shown you Akbar Khan's orders,' he said languidly. 'Why do you trouble me again?'

'Because it grieves us all to see one who has treated us well betrayed by the master he has served so loyally and cheated of his just reward,' said Pottinger smoothly.

243

The black eyes flickered and shifted a fraction. 'Cheated, Sahib?'

'What profit will you make from selling us in Turkestan? What will the Khans of Kulun pay for women too weak to work and children who are skin and bone?' Pottinger laughed contemptuously. 'Forty rupees a head? Twenty?'

'I am a poor man,' said Saleh Mahomed cautiously.

'A man who throws away riches deserves to be poor.'

'What riches, Sahib?'

'When you take a fistful of rupees from the Khans of Kulun, you will throw away the reward that General Pollock is offering for our safe return.'

'The ransom is offered to Akbar Khan. He would not give it to me,' said Saleh Mahomed, well aware there was one rule for the strong and quite another for the weak in his country. 'If I were to take you to General Pollock, you would go into his camp and say, "Be damned to you, Saleh Mahomed".'

'I give you my word we should not.'

'What good is your word to me? Will you give me a paper, written in Persian and in English, guaranteeing that the ransom offered to Akbar Khan will be paid to me?'

Pottinger was in a quandary. He had no authority to give such a guarantee, and Saleh Mahomed suspected it. Though he knew that Akbar's star was fading and it would be wise to secure his own future against British retribution, he was not yet ready to betray his master unless the price was right.

Captain Lawrence said in his friendly, direct way, 'Listen to me, Saleh Mahomed. We can't speak for General Pollock, nor yet for the Government, but we can speak for ourselves. I am ready to pay you five thousand rupees down, no questions asked, if you will release us now, before Akbar Khan arrives.'

'I will do the same,' agreed Johnson. 'Think, man! That is more than you would get from selling us in Turkestan.'

Pottinger nodded decisively. 'Same here. And if you

claim the ransom money as well, we will not stand in your way.'

Saleh Mahomed considered, stroking his beard. 'Akbar Khan is a vengeful man,' he muttered. 'Thirty thousand.'

'Twenty,' said Lawrence promptly.

'Twenty-five. And a pension. A thousand rupees a month for life.'

The three officers tried to hide their dismay. None of them was rich, and should the Company Directors decide they had acted improperly and refuse to sanction the payment, they would spend the rest of their lives paying off their debt.

'The anger of the British is very terrible,' warned Pottinger.

'The British are far away.'

'Far from here, but near your wives and children,' said Lawrence. 'What will become of them when it is known that you have sent us to our deaths?'

It was a question which already preoccupied Saleh Mahomed. He said uneasily, 'When Akbar Khan comes, he will ask why I have not carried out his orders.'

'Tell him your men would not go on to Turkestan without their pay. The Hazareh chiefs will back you up,' urged Lawrence. 'Well, how about it? Twenty thousand down, and a thousand rupees monthly thereafter.'

Slowly Saleh Mahomed nodded. 'The Mir Akhor must know nothing of this,' he warned.

Pottinger said firmly, 'He will hear nothing from us.' He tore a blank sheet from his notebook and swiftly penned the few lines of their undertaking in Persian and English, then signed it: *Eldred Pottinger, Major, Bombay Artillery* and handed it on for the others to add their names.

With a slightly ironic bow he presented the paper to Saleh Mahomed, who perused it carefully before hiding it away in his turban.

'I shall never speak slightingly of Political Officers again,' vowed Lady Sale, who had in the past shared her hus-

245

band's view that this branch of the Company Service was overpaid, underworked, and far too fond of sticking its nose into matters that did not concern it. Along with most of the other captives, she had readily agreed to set her signature to a guarantee that Major Pottinger and the other Politicals should not bear the cost of their freedom alone, even if the Government refused to bail them out.

Only Brigadier Shelton declined to put his name to the pledge. 'Damned if I will,' he said crustily. 'Should have asked me before, not after. How dare they take this action without consulting me? Serve 'em right if it costs 'em every rupee they've got.'

Major Pottinger's announcement that Saleh Mahomed had turned his coat once again had been greeted with cheers and not a few tears, although once they recovered from their initial relief the hostages realised they were by no means out of the wood yet. Their fate still hung in the balance and the scales were delicately poised. By this action they had forfeited their protected status as hostages, and Akbar Khan would have no compunction in killing them should he reach Bamian in pursuit of his treacherous lieutenant before General Pollock could send a rescue force to their aid.

Meantime, the best they could do was to improve their defences, turning water into the moats around the little fortress, posting pickets to give early warning of trouble, and establishing friendly relations with the Hazareh chiefs in the neighbourhood, several of whom professed themselves disillusioned with recent events and ready to support the re-establishment of British rule. Whether or not this was merely lip-service was difficult to decide.

'Can't say I trust Zulficar Khan very far,' muttered George Mein, shaking his head after the white-bearded local chieftain had despatched an envoy to tender his formal submission to Major Pottinger, as representative of the British Government. 'Says he's ready to take up arms against Akbar, even if he appears with a thousand horses to back him. I wonder! I say we should march out and meet our friends halfway, rather than wait here like rats in a trap.'

Most of the younger officers supported this view, but their seniors argued that it would be folly to leave their present defences and risk being caught in the open.

'There's nowhere we can count on shelter between here and Killa Kazee,' grumbled white-faced, skeletal Colonel Palmer of the 27th BNI. He had been tortured and then suffered months of close confinement after the fall of Ghazni, and had quite lost his fighting spirit. All he yearned for was rest, something he was unlikely to get in the present uncertainty of their fortunes.

Drums beat to arms at odd hours, often at the dead of night. Patrols galloped in with reports of spies or sightings of bands of cavalry who vanished when challenged. Conflicting rumours kept the garrison's nerves on edge, dreading the sudden appearance of an avenging Akbar Khan.

One evening during this week of stretched nerves and readiness for fight or flight, Thea and her friends were talking quietly outside in the cool air when a sudden hullabaloo by one of the watch-towers alarmed them. They heard shouts, thumps, the scurry of running feet and a child's high-pitched cries. George Mein rose abruptly and went to investigate.

'It's all right,' he reported, rejoining them. 'The guards have caught a spy. They say he has been hanging about for the past two days, so they set a trap and caught him.'

'A spy!' The ladies turned pale.

'One of Akbar's scouts, I imagine. Come to take a look at our defences.'

'It sounds more like a child,' Georgiana objected. 'Don't let the guards hurt him, poor fellow.'

'Don't worry. I told them Major Pottinger would want to question him. They won't kill him before he comes back.'

Major Pottinger and the other Politicals had ridden to a meeting with local chiefs. Despite Mein's reassurance, it was plain that the guards were giving the captured spy a severe drubbing.

247

'Oh, I can't bear it!' Georgiana exclaimed, putting her hands over her ears. 'Worse than killing pigs. Do tell them to stop, Cousin.'

Reluctantly Mein went to intervene. 'If you ask me, he deserves everything he's getting,' he reported. 'Says he isn't a spy, and only came because he's got a child for sale, but he's asking a ridiculous price. Four thousand rupees! The guards think they can beat him down.'

'Vile wretch!' said Lady Sale strongly. 'This trading in children makes my blood boil. Where is the fellow? I'll give him a piece of my mind. Four thousand rupees, indeed!'

She marched off. After a momentary hesitation Georgy and Alexandrina followed.

'Don't go,' said Mein in a low voice, delighted by this opportunity of a few minutes alone with Thea. 'Leave it to her ladyship and talk to me instead. I hardly seem to see you nowadays. There's always some damned fellow butting in, trying to claim your notice.'

'You know I don't care a fig for them,' she said, smiling.

'So you say. So you say.' He took her hand in his. 'But do you care a fig for me? That's the question.'

'What do you think?' Her smile became mischievous.

'Ah! That's what I want to talk about.' Tucking her hand through his arm, he drew her towards a less frequented spot and began to speak earnestly.

When the guards saw Lady Sale approach they stopped beating their prisoner and, at her sharp command, raised him to his feet. He drooped in their arms, a slim youth with a wisp of moustache and the hawkish Semitic looks of the mountain tribesmen. He was bruised and dishevelled, his turban unrolled, clothes torn and filthy. One side of his face was swollen, with a purplish, rapidly closing eye, and blood trickled from his split lips. Yet for all his battered appearance, there was something familiar about him. Even as she pitched into her lecture about the evils of the slave trade, Lady Sale wondered where she had seen him before.

By the wall of the watch-tower crouched the unlucky slave-dealer's stock-in-trade, a small, handsome boy, his closely shaven head topped with an embroidered skullcap, and the long cotton shirt which covered him from shoulders to heels surmounted by a short, gaily embroidered waistcoat. He cowered against the mud wall, pressing his hands against his ears. His skin was smooth and pale, and his large dark eyes shadowed with fear.

Georgiana bent over him. He darted her a terrified look, then squeezed his eyelids shut as if by doing so he could make himself invisible. She waited until he opened them again.

'Don't be frightened,' she said in halting Pushtu. 'What is your name?'

'They call me Sekunder Sahib Bahadur,' he said gravely, and she smiled. Alexander the Great – a proud name for a small boy.

'Where are your parents, Sekunder-Sahib? What are you doing here?'

He stared at her solemnly and said as if repeating a lesson, 'My mother and my father are infidels, but I am a good Mussulman.'

'*Infidels?*'

She frowned, and the child moved back, shielding his head as if to ward off a blow. She said in a more gentle tone, picking her words carefully, 'Who taught you to say that, Sekunder Sahib?'

He peeped at her between his fingers to make sure she was not angry, and said in a whisper of sound that barely reached her ears, 'Hinghan Khan . . . '

'Mr Mein!' said Thea, trying to sound severe.

'George.'

'Very well. If you insist. George!'

'Yes, Mrs Quinn?' he said innocently.

'You must not put your arm around my waist.'

'Why? Don't you like it?'

'That has nothing to do with the matter.'

249

'On the contrary, it has everything to do with it. Can you honestly tell me that you dislike it?'

'But my dress is full of holes!'

'That is the very reason why I like it.'

'Mr Mein!'

'George.'

Thea sighed. 'You are incorrigible. What if Lady Macnaghten sees us?'

'Lady M is far too busy whispering sweet nothings to her cat to bother herself about you and me.'

'You would not say that if you shared a hut with her.'

'Thank God I am spared that, at least.'

'Well, I have to, and hardly an evening passes without her making some disagreeable observation on your attentions to me,' said Thea ruefully. ' "Mrs *Quinn*" – emphasis on the surname, you note – "Mrs *Quinn*, do you think it *wise* to *encourage* that young officer? You are a married lady. People are *talking*, you know".'

'The old cat,' said Mein in disgust. He picked up her hands and kissed them fervently. 'In that case, we must give her something to talk about. It is our plain duty.'

His arm tightened around her waist, and despite Lady Macnaghten's strictures, she felt a thrill of pleasure. 'You are so beautiful!' he murmured huskily. 'It drives me crazy, never being able to see you alone without setting a dozen tongues wagging. But now – '

His face was very close to hers. The blue eyes, serious for once, gazed at her intently, as if memorising every line, every feature. With one finger he traced the feathery line of her eyebrow. 'So beautiful . . . '

He is going to kiss me, she thought, and her pulse began to race. The gentle finger moved outwards, towards her temple; it hesitated, then stopped.

'Keep very still,' he whispered.

She closed her eyes, but instead of the warm touch of his lips, she felt his hand moving in the thickly clustered curls above her ear. It fumbled, searching for something, then pounced with a painful tug.

'Got you!' he exclaimed triumphantly.

Outraged, she jerked away. 'George! What in heaven's name – ?'

'Light cavalry, my dear. Look!' He held out his hand for her inspection. Firmly pinched between finger and thumb she saw the squashed remains of a flea. 'You've got to be quick to catch the little devils,' he remarked with satisfaction. 'Shall I have a look to see if I can find any more?'

'Certainly not!' She was humiliated and furious, more at her own weak desire for his kiss than for the fact of the flea itself. 'If you dare tell anyone – *anyone*! – I swear I'll never speak to you again.'

'As if I would.'

'As if you wouldn't! I know you, George! "Blame it on the bullet", you'd say, and laugh. Look at you now!'

Indeed, George was struggling to contain his mirth. 'Oh, oh!' he gasped. 'If you could have seen the look on your face! I'm sorry, Thea darling. I'm truly sorry. I know it isn't funny, not in the least, it's just that I can't help laughing. Now let me give you a real, proper kiss.'

'Just try it and see what I give you in return,' Thea was saying vengefully, when she was startled by a cry from the watch-tower – a cry so urgent and shrill that it was almost a shriek.

'Thea! Where are you? Come here quickly! Your son is found!'

It troubled Thea that she had nothing to give Hinghan Khan.

'Why should you give him anything? He deserves no reward for returning your own child to you,' argued Mein, who had taken a strong dislike to the young Afghan as soon as he learned his identity. A plausible rogue, he thought, and found it monstrous that Thea should regard him as Dandy's saviour.

'Depend on it, he only brought him back because he wishes to curry favour with us, now that Akbar's star is fading. As for the story that he paid four thousand rupees for him – pooh! I don't believe a word of it. Very likely

Master Hinghan was the fellow who abducted him in the first place.'

'Oh, no! He would not do such a thing.'

'You think not?' said George cynically. 'Selling stolen property back to its owner is a favourite Afghan trick. Look at our camels and horses! Look at Lady Macnaghten's cat! Take my advice and send that young rascal packing before he causes any more mischief.'

In her heart, Thea knew this was sound advice, yet she could not bring herself to repulse someone who had rendered her so signal a service. Even now, she woke every morning unable to believe that Dandy had returned from the dead until she had kissed him and felt his warm smooth hand in hers. In the past she had wronged Hinghan Khan, mistaking his devotion to James for viciousness and resenting the way he had tried to stand between her and his master. She was determined to make amends now and reward him for the courage and loyalty with which he had protected James's son. George was wrong, too, when he claimed that Hinghan Khan should have returned Dandy sooner. Even now he was risking Akbar's anger by attaching himself to the hostages.

'Oh, he knows what he's doing,' said George scornfully. 'Weathercocks turn where the wind blows strongest. I should say that Master Hinghan's decision to come to us is a very fair indication that Pollock will triumph in the end.'

Thea sighed. George was in a strange mood these days. He did not seem to understand how she felt about having Dandy restored to her, or the extent of her gratitude to Hinghan Khan. Of course he was worried – they all were – lest Akbar arrived here before any relieving force did. A still grimmer possibility was that General Pollock might not send a relieving force at all. They had broken the terms governing the treatment of hostages, and might be left to shift for themselves.

'I hope you are right,' she said. 'But whether we live or die, I trust James will see Hinghan Khan properly recompensed.'

'I don't doubt he will. Properly or improperly,' Mein snapped, and turned on his heel. She stared after him in dismay, wondering what she had said to offend him.

It was time – high time – to leave Bamian, the narrow valley in which they could so easily be trapped. General Nott had marched from Kandahar and recaptured the great fortress at Ghazni and Pollock was fast approaching Kabul, but no one knew where Akbar Khan was lurking. Some said he had fled to the Kohistan; others whispered that he had sworn to avenge himself on Saleh Mahomed before retreating to the wastes of Turkestan.

The former hostages dared delay no longer, and at sunrise on 16 September their cavalcade streamed out of the ramshackle fort that had sheltered them, and headed south down the valley. Old, young, sick and wounded were packed into *kajavas* carried by camels supplied by Zulficar Khan. Saleh Mahomed, nervous and bombastic by turns, headed the armed escort. He was by no means the only one to ride with his heart in his mouth, eyes straining into the heat-shimmering distances where any movement might signal the approach of Akbar's horsemen.

As they rested at Killa Topchee after riding all morning, a despatch from General Pollock's military secretary, Sir Richmond Shakespear, set their spirits soaring. *I have a strong body of horse, and will ride to your relief with all speed*, he wrote from his camp at Sir-i-Chusm. But the few officers who knew the country counted the many rough miles that still lay between them and their rescuer, and wondered anxiously whether friend or foe would reach them first.

After crossing the Kaloo mountain the next day, they rested again at its foot, intending to renew the march in the cool of twilight, and meantime negotiating with some villagers for a few fowl and an elderly goat to provide their supper.

Thea and Georgiana walked down to the river and bathed their feet in the shallow, sparkling water, while

Dandy threw stones into a pool to amuse little Jung-i-Bahadur, who crawled about the bank, crowing with delight at the splashes.

'How peaceful it is!' said Georgy, wading back to the shingle and picking up her shoes. 'Do you think – ' But what she was about to ask was never known, for at that moment a bugle blared and a drum began to beat to arms.

'Someone's coming! Horsemen . . . '

White to the lips, both girls scrambled out of the water and struggled to force their wet feet into stockings and shoes. Georgiana scooped up the Jung-i-Bahadur, but Dandy had already run back to where the men were snatching up weapons and untying their horses.

He climbed on a rock and gazed across the valley. 'Horses coming, Mamma!' he called excitedly. 'Lots of horses!'

Above the moving dust-cloud on the slope opposite, tall slivers of steel glittered, and below it myriad legs hammered over the hard-packed ochre ground.

'I can't bear to watch,' murmured Georgiana, clutching the wriggling baby to her breast. 'After this taste of freedom, we cannot – must not – allow ourselves to be taken captive again.'

Other ladies joined them at their vantage point. Lady Sale held a brace of fowl she had just bought; Alexandrina carried her baby; Mrs Boyd and Mrs Eyre stood on tiptoe, straining their eyes into the distance.

Then keen-sighted Dandy spotted a familiar emblem.

'Kuzzilbashis, Mamma!' he shrilled, pointing to the long silken banner streaming over the horsemen's heads, and the shout was taken up by the rest of the hostages.

A solitary horseman detached himself from the rest and galloped towards the ladies. Though he wore Afghan dress and his strong, good-humoured face was caked in dust, they recognised him at once.

'Lady Sale!' he exclaimed, dismounting and sweeping off his turban, and the anxiety that had furrowed her weather-beaten face smoothed magically away to leave her looking ten years younger.

'Sir Richmond!' she said, with a laugh that sounded suspiciously like a sob. 'You cannot know how glad – how *very* glad – we are to see you!'

CHAPTER FOURTEEN

James tossed Dandy in the air and caught him, then perched him on his shoulder, where he clung, chattering gaily, as James returned his attention to his wife.

'Your hair!' had been his first startled exclamation after greeting her, for the red-gold curls clustered on her head were barely two inches long. Of late she had paid her own looks so little heed that at first she could not think what he meant.

'Oh!' she said, putting up a hand to it. 'It will soon grow again. The lice! You cannot imagine.'

James laughed, his eyes warm and teasing. 'I can imagine only too well. My poor love! How you have suffered. Everything will be very different now.'

His glance caressed her; his admiring tone lent deeper meaning to his words. He had not looked at her with such love and pride since the first days of their marriage and her heart felt ready to burst with happiness.

The hostages' ordeal had been too long and their relief too intense for them to indulge in extravagant jubilation upon the arrival of Sir Richmond Shakespear and his Kuzzilbashi guard. Brigadier Shelton had even chosen to be offended because their rescuer had greeted the ladies first, and poor Captain Mackenzie, sick of a fever since leaving Bamian, could hardly summon the strength to lift his head from the pillow on hearing that they were saved.

Two days later, when General Sale and his brigade met them at Sir-i-chusm, the scene was very different. The fact of freedom had now sunk in, and the former hostages were in a mood to rejoice. The reunion with so many of their friends at the pass near Kote Ashrufee was an emotional one, and the men of the 13th Light Infantry pressed forward to greet each captive individually, congratulating them on their survival with such deep feeling that few could restrain their tears. Captain Backhouse's mountain train fired a royal salute, and the children went wild with excitement, running here and there with their mouths crammed with sweetmeats and hands full of souvenirs as friendly arms reached out to hug them and present them with cap badges, sticks of sugar cane, silver trinkets or any other thing that caught their fancy.

Dandy quite failed to recognise his father among the many smiling faces bending down to pet him. This was hardly surprising, but when James held him in his arms the resemblance between them was so strong as to be almost absurd: two close-cropped dark heads with the same eyes, nose and mouth, but in different scale.

James was lean and hard and sun-bronzed, the white stripe at his temple now the only reminder of his near-fatal wound. He had distinguished himself during Akbar's siege of Jellalabad.

'Without your godson, my dear, we might have starved before Pollock came up,' Fighting Bob confided to his wife. 'He *chupaoed* a herd of cattle that grazed too near the walls and drove them inside before the herdsmen realised what was happening.'

'Bravo, James! We could have done with you to supplement *our* diet,' smiled Lady Sale. 'All we got was tough goat and tougher mutton, week in, week out, and when the Trevor boys won wrestling bouts against the young Afghans, their reward was a great lump of mutton-fat! I shall never look with favour on a roast gigot again – the very smell fills me with revulsion.'

Thea had felt sick with apprehension as she watched Hinghan Khan make his salaam, but James greeted him with casual friendliness, and seemed to find nothing remarkable in his care of Dandy.

'Quid pro quo. Did I not rescue *him* from slavery? Of course he would feel it his duty to do the same for my son.'

'Should you not reward him?' she asked diffidently, and James laughed.

'For discharging his obligation to me? Allow him some

257

pride, my dear. The very suggestion of a reward would offend him mortally. All he asks is to go on serving my family, since he has lost his own.' He caught the look on her face, and added in a lower tone, 'You need not fear he will be more than a servant, my dear. During these grim months of separation I have had plenty of opportunity to regret the wrong I did you, and now God has brought us together again, I mean to do everything in my power to make you happy.'

'Nothing could make me happier than I am to be back with you,' she said, feeling a warm rush of thankfulness. Whatever madness had possessed him in Kabul, whatever passion he had felt for Hinghan Khan, it was over. Standing in the circle of his arms, listening to his halting words of love and remorse, she knew that the doubts which had tortured her throughout her captivity had been phantoms of her own devising. James had kept his promise. With the help of time and his own good nature he had cut Hinghan Khan out of his heart. Even his long silence was easily explained. His right wrist had been broken by an Afghan sword before he even reached Jellalabad.

'I didn't wish to add to your worries, my love, by dwelling on my own injury, but for months I could hardly put pen to paper.' He smiled down at her with warm affection. 'You don't know how proud I am of my wife! Lady Sale has been singing your praises to me. That terrible retreat!'

'I still dream of it,' she admitted. 'We all do. When I woke to find little Vicky frozen in my arms . . . That was the worst moment of all.'

James's own eyes had filled with tears. 'She is safe with God,' he said quietly. 'If only I could have seen her, just for a moment!'

The sharing of memories, even sad memories, brought them closer than they had ever been. For Thea, the only sour note in the whole ecstatic reunion was the sight of George Mein's despondent face, and when she tried to cheer him by saying he would soon see Miss Legge again,

he turned on her with a suppressed bitterness quite foreign
to his sunny, easygoing nature.

'Miss Legge! What do I care for her?'

'Did you not tell me there was an understanding
between you?'

'Between our parents, more like,' he said morosely.
'Oh, Thea, are you blind? It is you I care for – you alone!
How do you think I feel, seeing you smile at your husband
when you should be mine, body and soul!'

'George! You must not say such things. You know very
well they are not true, and even if they were – '

'They are! They are! I love you – there, I've said it
now. I thought – I was almost sure – you loved me, and
the thought of you in the arms of that – that *monster* makes
me desperate.'

'What are you saying? Are you out of your mind? James
is no monster.'

'He is. You, of all people, must know it.'

'What are you trying to tell me?' she asked in alarm.
Her heart had begun to pound unevenly. George looked
so strange and wild-eyed, his face no longer cheerful but
set and drawn. She hardly recognised the happy-go-lucky,
irresponsible subaltern who used to turn every hardship
into a joke.

'You know what I mean,' he said in a hard, tight voice.
'Everyone knows what goes on between him and that
catamite.'

'*Catamite?*' Thea caught her breath. *Did* he know, or
was he only guessing? George spread rumours as the wind
spread thistledown; if he could say such things to her,
who else might not repeat them?

She stared at him with wide, frightened eyes. Her marriage, her children, her husband's whole career could
depend on convincing George he was wrong.

'It's not true!' she said fiercely. 'How dare you say such
a wicked, malicious thing to me?'

'You can't deny it. Forget your loyalty, Thea. You
know as well as I do that their relationship is an open

259

scandal. I can't bear to see you married to such a man. If he were not Lady Sale's godson – '

'Stop it, George!' By now her anger was genuine, driving out fear. 'I will not listen to your lies. James is my husband and I forbid you to slander him. Or Hinghan Khan.'

'They're sending me home, Thea,' he said as if he had not listened to a word she had spoken. 'Putting me out to grass at the age of twenty-five.' He laughed bitterly. 'That bullet put an end to my dreams of military glory, but I won't regret it if you will come with me to England. I can make you happy. Truly happy. I'll give you everything you dreamed of, and more.'

His vehemence frightened her. 'Hush, George. You don't know what you're saying.'

'Oh, yes, I do! I love you, Thea. I want you beside me for the rest of our lives.'

'How could I leave my husband and child? What sort of woman do you think I am? Do you expect me to destroy my marriage on a whim?'

His face twisted bitterly. 'That is all I am to you, isn't it? A whim. A passing fancy, "Good old George",' he mimicked savagely, ' "our Mein of Information. Such an amusing little fellow, but of course one can't take him seriously". Well, for once in my life, I am serious. I love you. I want you for my wife.'

Touched by his misery, she put her hand on his arm. 'You're dreaming,' she said softly. 'You know it's impossible. But you must know, as well, how much I value our friendship. All through these terrible months it has meant so much to me. I honestly believe I could not have survived without you.'

'Friendship!' he exclaimed disgustedly. 'You offer me friendship as you might toss a bone to a dog. No, thank you, my dear. I am no hungry dog, and *friendship* is not enough for me. I am ready to do anything in the world for you, but I will not – *not* – content myself with being your friend.'

'But, George, can't you understand – ?'

He cut her short. 'Oh, I understand all right. Too well. You've got your husband back, and you mean to save your marriage, whatever the cost. That's right, isn't it? Deny it if you can. You know just what James is, but you prefer to close your eyes to it.'

'Don't say such things.' She took a deep, steadying breath, and went on as calmly as she could. 'You tell me you love me, George, yet you are trying to destroy any chance of happiness I have left. Can't you see that? Whatever you may have heard about James – whatever he may have done in the past – it is over now. Finished. I have his promise.'

'And you believe him?'

'Of course,' she said simply.

'I never thought you such a fool.'

'Then why must you interfere?' she flared at him. 'What I believe is no affair of yours.' She saw his wounded look and added more gently, 'Please, George, don't make things harder for me. These last years have been so full of pain and hardship that we must put them behind us and make a fresh start.'

'Make it with me!'

She smiled at his perseverance, but said steadily, 'You know I can't. The best thing you can do, for yourself as well as for me, is to go back to your Amanda and forget all about me. Will you do that?'

'I'll try,' he said in a strange, strangled voice that sounded quite unlike his own. 'On one condition.'

'What is that?'

Before she guessed his intention, he pulled her into his arms and put his lips to hers. For a moment she resisted, angry at his temerity, and angrier still with her own involuntary response to his kisses.

'I want you,' he murmured in her ear. 'You'll never know how much I want you for my own.'

Recovering herself, she pushed him away and he let her go, a strange half-smile on his face. 'At least I'll have that to remember! No, Thea – ' as she drew in her breath '– you don't have to tell me I'm a cad and a bounder. I'm going now, and won't bother you any more, but if you'll accept one last word of advice from someone who loves you, little though you care . . . '

'Well?' she said, as he paused. 'What is it?'

'Get rid of Hinghan Khan,' said George, and walked quickly away.

Get rid of Hinghan Khan. She couldn't, of course. Not after he had saved Dandy. Not when James had promised to put the past behind him. Even to suggest it might easily destroy the fragile seedling of trust which they were both trying to nurture. James had made his position clear. By siding with the *feringhis*, Hinghan Khan had burned his boats with his own people, and James felt responsible for him. In years to come, she might be able to suggest that Hinghan Khan left their employment, but not yet; not while the scars of the Afghan adventure were still unhealed.

George had already left camp when she looked for him the next morning, riding ahead of the main column with the other wounded officers bound for Home leave. Two days later the rest of General Sale's relief party marched back to Kabul, where the silent, empty streets and blackened shell of the Great Bazaar showed how thoroughly the Army of Retribution had carried out its work.

They were going home. All the simple pleasures of good food, clean clothes, and servants to attend their needs began to dull the memory of the filthy, vermin-ridden hovels in which they had passed their long months of captivity; the cold and hunger; the constant worry at what the next day might bring.

'Yet, by his own lights, Akbar Khan treated us well,' said Lady Sale judiciously, as she and her group of friends sat round a cheerfully blazing fire awaiting the call to supper on their last night in Afghanistan. Over their heads loomed the mighty ramparts of the Khyber Pass, through which they would file on the morrow, and faintly in the distance came the crackle of musket-fire as their pickets exchanged compliments with the unrepentant Ghilzai tribesmen, who had sniped at the columns all the way down from Kabul.

'How can you say that?' objected Captain Mainwaring, sitting on the edge of the circle with his arm about his wife's waist. 'Starved, threatened, dragged about the hills in the vilest weather, robbed of all you possessed?'

'Our captors were certainly light-fingered gentlemen,' she conceded, and Captain Lawrence laughed.

'When Sultan Jan made me give up my father's watch to him, I took good care to give the spring one turn too many before handing it over!'

'But as for the other hardships, Captain Mainwaring, you must remember that the Sirdar's own family fared no better than we did.'

'The sensibilities of Afghan women can hardly compare with those of delicately bred English females, Lady Sale!'

'Certainly they set less store on washing their persons or their clothes,' she agreed, 'and if they open their plaits once a week it is remarkable, yet living among them as we did, I came to see that human beings are infinitely adaptable and our ways, though different, are not necessarily *better* than theirs. In certain circumstances, indeed, they may have the advantage over us.'

This was going too far for her audience, however, and a chorus of disagreement broke out, with each of the former captives citing some instance of Afghan filth or treachery. The thought that they might have ended their lives as slaves to the barbaric Khans of Central Asia still made them shudder, and none of Lady Sale's expressions of tolerance could alter the fact that Akbar had intended this to be their fate.

As the 'Do-you-remembers?' settled into a steady hum, Thea leaned back against her cushions, content merely to watch and listen. The past week had been like a second honeymoon, despite the gruesome reminders of last year's retreat in all the skeletons clad in rags of uniform, and the broken trunks and vehicles that still littered the road through the passes.

Whenever his duty permitted, James rode at her side,

263

and every night they shared a bed. With sorrow she had learned of her mother-in-law's death after a week of delirium, and its devastating effect on General Quinn.

'He relied on her more than you would think,' said James. 'He hardly speaks now, and he has changed. Nothing interests him – not even the antics of our new Governor-General, Lord Ellenborough. It may cheer him to see you again, and young Dandy.'

On the subject of his sister, James was reticent. There had been a scandal, she gathered, in Simla. The young man had been abruptly recalled to Calcutta; it seemed he was already married.

'It would never have happened if Mamma had been there to head him off,' said James. 'Fellow should be horsewhipped, of course, but by all accounts Rohais made most of the running. No good crying over spilt milk! She's back at home now, and I daresay it will all blow over in time.'

He was more interested in Thea's own experiences of the past year, and questioned her closely about her months in captivity. As she spoke of them, their horror began to fade. It would never leave her completely, but events that had been terrible at the time became dulled by repetition until it seemed almost as if they had happened to someone else.

Certain incidents were classified as 'amusing' – anecdotes worth trotting out before any new audience. Over and over again, stories of George Mein's April Fool pranks on their guards were retold, and Captain Mackenzie's account of the earthquake was another favourite, repeated until each of the hostages knew it by heart.

'Old Shelton and I were smoking our hookahs, minding our own business, when damn me if the roof didn't begin to shake us about like peas in a drum. I scrambled down the steps double-quick, I promise you. When it was over, Shelton calls me across to him, looking like thunder. "Mackenzie!" he says very solemnly. "You went downstairs *first* today." For all the world as if I should have asked his permission! "So I did," says I. "I'm sorry: it's the fashion in earthquakes, Brigadier." '

That reminiscence always raised a laugh. Like the slow draining of a septic wound, memories trickled forth and were discussed until they lost their terror.

By degrees the captives pieced together a picture of what had happened in the world while they had been out of it. 'For all the world like a lot of Rip Van Winkles,' as Georgiana put it. As they prepared to leave Afghanistan their thoughts turned forward rather than back, knowing that, finally, their ordeal was firmly behind them.

That last night James retired early, for he was to go with the Advance guard at 2 a.m. Thea hesitated at the entrance to his sleeping quarters, but decided not to disturb him before going to her own.

Through her dreams she was aware of the Advance's departure while the night was still brilliant with stars. Drums beat, horses whinnied, harnesses jingled and camels groaned. These were familiar sounds from every camp, and when they faded down the pass, she turned over and settled back to sleep.

It must have been three hours later, as a faint, pearly light began to filter into the gorge, that she woke again with a start, knowing something was wrong.

Georgiana was bending over the charpoy, shaking her by the shoulder. Her dark hair, still tousled, streamed over the ribboned collar of her nightgown. Evidently she had risen in haste.

'Thea, wake up!' she whispered urgently. 'Something has happened. Something terrible.'

'Is it Dandy?' Shaking off the mists of sleep, Thea swung her legs to the floor, heart hammering. 'Is he ill?'

'No, no . . . Oh, Thea! They sent me to tell you but I don't know how to.'

'James?'

Georgiana's throat moved convulsively. She gripped Thea's hand. 'Yes. He has been shot. Wounded. Badly, I fear. He has lost a lot of blood.'

'*Wounded*? Was the Advance in a skirmish?'

'No.' Georgiana hesitated, then said without quite meeting Thea's eyes, 'Captain Quinn did not ride with the Advance guard. This morning they found him, wounded, in the Pass.'

Thea shook her head dizzily. It made no sense to her. If James had not ridden with the Advance, how could they have found him already in the Pass?

'He had been there . . . some hours. Perhaps all night.'

'Alone?'

Georgiana hesitated and seemed to brace herself. 'No,' she said, as if the word was being dragged from her. 'His bearer was with him.'

'*Which bearer?*'

She knew, of course. She felt sick and hollow, smothered by a black cloud of despair. George Mein had been right to call her a fool. Ever since their reunion at Sir-i-chusm she had hoped and believed that things had changed, but she had been deceiving herself. Between James and Hinghan Khan, nothing would ever change.

'He was wounded too,' said Georgy, still not meeting her eyes, 'but he did what he could for Captain Quinn. He crawled to a stream and fetched water for him to drink. They are carrying them back now. Oh, Thea, I am so sorry! For it to happen now, just when we are all safe again! You must be very brave.'

She showed a brave face during the long, agonising week it took James to die, but the truth was that she felt nothing. Tears would come later, friends said, as they pressed her hand, gazed at her white, set features, and assured her of God's unfailing grace. She hoped they were right. Even tears would be better than this numbness, this frozen sense of futility. After surviving so many dangers, how could James throw away his life uselessly, senselessly, almost within sight of home? What was the use of struggling against Fate when one spin of the wheel upset all your painful efforts?

Since it was too dangerous to linger in the Khyber Pass, they carried the wounded men as far as Peshawar, and there Thea remained as the army continued its march. General Avitabile's personal physician attended James, although the case was hopeless from the start. He had been shot through the stomach and was delirious most of the time, eased only by ever-increasing doses of opium.

Towards the end, when he was sinking visibly, his mind cleared and he looked at Thea with a ghost of his old, teasing smile. 'Rotten luck, eh? A damned Ghilzai sniper. Who'd have thought he'd have been there at that hour? After all we've been through . . . ' For a time he was silent, gathering his strength, then he said very urgently, 'Promise me you'll look after Hinghan Khan? For my sake?'

Her heart sank. She said, 'I can't, James! You know I can't.'

'You . . . must,' he said painfully. 'Promise me you will! I shan't die in peace unless you promise.'

'Don't talk like that. You're not going to die.'

'Oh, yes, I am. Don't lie to me, Thea. I haven't much time. Tell me you'll keep Hinghan Khan, and look after him.'

'He'll be all right. I'll give him a pension and send him home. You mustn't worry about him. Not now.'

She could not bear to see his distress. He moved rest-lessly on the string cot, his face twisted with pain, muttering, 'Promise! You must promise. Can't send him back. Burned his boats. Life not worth a straw.'

'Lie still, darling,' she pleaded, but he threw himself from side to side until reluctantly she said, 'All right, I promise. I'll look after him, if that's really what you want.'

The anxious lines smoothed from his face. 'Good,' he sighed, and his eyelids drooped. 'Good . . . girl. Knew you wouldn't . . . let me down.'

An hour later, he roused again and asked, 'Where's the boy?'

'Hinghan Khan?'

'No, no. Dandy. Want to see him. Bring him in.'

Dandy was brought in, wide-eyed and ill at ease. On seeing him, James revived a little.

'Come here, my boy.'

Nervously Dandy approached the bed, and James took his small hand. 'I am going away and shall not see you again,' he said quietly.

'Where are you going, Papa?'

'I can't tell you that, for I don't know myself. I want you to promise to look after Mamma when I'm gone. Will you do that?'

'Yes, Papa,' said Dandy, with a doubtful look at his mother. 'If she will let me, that is.'

'Oh, she'll let you, all right. You will be the man of the family. Promise you will look after Hinghan Khan, too?'

'Oh, yes, Papa.' Dandy looked more cheerful. 'He is better today, you know. The doctor told Ayah he won't die.'

'I am very glad to hear it,' said James, and his head fell back against his pillow. 'Off you go then, my boy, and never forget what you have promised.'

Imagining their homecoming had been a favourite pastime among the hostages, whose fancy dwelt – according to temperament – on food, wine, or elegant clothes, or the deep, luxurious baths in which they would wallow as soon as they were free again, but this homecoming was more melancholy than anything Thea had visualised.

Word of James's death had gone ahead of her, and soon after leaving Lahore on the last stage of her journey across the Punjab, a *cossid* brought her the welcome news that her father-in-law was riding to meet her. Next day, however, came a further message. General Quinn was not well enough to travel, and Dr Black would come in his place.

Thea hoped he would hurry, and bring armed guards as well. Since leaving Lahore, the caravan she was travelling with had been threatened several times by marauding bands of Sikhs bent on mischief. They would not have dared to harass travellers while old Ranjit Singh's iron hand had ruled the Punjab, but since his death the whole territory had been in turmoil, and two of his heirs had already suffered violent deaths.

It was therefore with a sense of relief that Thea heard that Toby and his party were encamped at the village of Secunderpore, two days' march from the Sutlej. Leaving the slow-moving caravan as soon as the village was sighted, she cantered ahead to meet him.

A cluster of tents was pitched by the stream, a little beyond the huts. She rode towards them, the pony's hoofs drowned by the gurgle of water.

Toby Black was sitting outside the nearest tent, absorbed in the manufacture of trout-flies. His table was littered with miniature tools: tweezers, hooks, a tiny vice, pots of glue and spools of thread, scissors, knife and gaily coloured feathers. His hands moved patiently, deftly, teasing out a wisp of hackle, manipulating pliers in an invisible knot.

At his feet lay a small, stout terrier, eyes closed, panting gently. Now and then its paws twitched. She waited for them to become aware of her presence, but a minute or two passed and neither looked up.

Waist-deep in the stream, another man was fishing, a burly, red-bearded giant who was casting a long line across the current to the dark shelf under the farther bank where the fish would lie, and the sight took her back in memory to the days when she used to watch her father's big hands working his light fly-rod with the same delicate precision.

'A fine watch you keep, Dr Black!'

At the sound of her voice, the peaceful tableau fractured. Toby jumped up so quickly that the table rocked and its contents cascaded to the ground. Making amends for its neglect of duty, the terrier set up a furious yapping. The fisherman turned, shouted something she could not catch, and began to wade ashore.

'My dear Thea!' exclaimed Toby, lifting her off the pony and kissing her warmly. 'How very glad I am to see you! You have stolen a march on us. We did not think we would meet you so soon.' He raised his voice. 'Hal! Look who's here!'

Hal?

Thea's head snapped round. She stared at the fisherman with a sudden leap of the heart. Next moment he, too, was enfolding her in a bear-hug, oblivious of the water from his clothes which streamed impartially over them both.

'My dearest sister, is it really you? Little Thea?'

Tears choked her voice. She smiled at him mistily, hardly able to believe he was the same beloved brother she had last seen leaving for Home at the age of eight. A thousand questions clamoured at her mind, but for the moment it was enough to feel his arms round her, and know she was no longer alone.

The terrier was jumping up at them, barking hysterically.

'Down, Foxy, down!' said Hal, laughing. 'We're all one happy family here.'

Something in the way he said it caught her attention.

'All?'

She raised her eyebrows at Toby, who said, 'Trust your brother to let the cat out of the bag before I had a chance to tell you myself.'

'To tell me what?' A strange premonition came over her. She guessed what he was about to say before he opened his mouth.

'Rohais and I were married last month. Won't you wish us happy?'

Late into the starry night they talked, while the camp-fire subsided into glowing caverns of ash and night-birds called from bank to bank of the murmuring stream. So much had happened since she had last seen her brother, but any fear they would be strangers was quickly laid to rest. As if a curtain had been drawn aside, they resumed the old easy comradeship they had known in nursery days. Hour after hour they chatted, with Toby smoking in companionable silence, his back against a tree, and before the first streaks of dawn touched the sky, they had filled in the gaps in each other's lives and begun to look towards the future.

Hal was on his way to Lahore. 'Appointed aide to the Resident!' he said jubilantly. 'I'm the envy of every Political Officer in Calcutta.'

'Why, Hal! Congratulations! How did you manage it?'

Hal grinned. 'Ask him!' He nodded at Toby. 'It ain't *what* you know but *who* you know that counts. Influence, jobbery, call it what you like, the fact is that Toby there put in a good word for me, and the Lat-Sahib was pleased to accept his recommendation.' He leaned across to say in a stage whisper, 'He's the man of the moment, you know. His lordship hangs on his lightest word – '

'What rot your brother talks!' said Toby equably. 'He was the best man for the job. Top in every examination – law, administration, Punjabi, Persian. None of the other candidates came within hailing distance.'

She looked from one to the other, uncertain which to believe, and they both laughed.

'If only dear old James were here, too,' said Hal, sobering suddenly. 'I fagged for him my first term, did he tell you that? I used to worship the ground he trod on. I remember he found me snivelling by his study fire one afternoon because I was homesick for India and I couldn't get the damned thing to draw properly, so he gave me his own handkerchief and fed me buttered crumpets to cheer me up. I've never forgotten it.'

Thea's eyes filled with tears, remembering the side of James she, too, had loved, and Hal took her hand and held it tightly.

'I didn't mean to upset you,' he said gruffly. 'I just wanted you to know.'

'I'm glad you told me. He could never bear to see children unhappy. I shall always remember that, too,' she said, and turned away for fear of catching Toby Black's cynical glance.

CHAPTER FIFTEEN

The home-coming of his daughter-in-law and grandson seemed to give General Quinn a new lease of life. Rohais watched with jealous eyes as he installed her former governess in the rooms which had been her mother's, and the small bright-eyed boy firmly took posssession of the corner of the General's heart which she had always considered her own exclusive domain.

It was not that Thea had any intention of driving Rohais from her home. On the contrary, she would have liked her friendship and company, but Rohais's resentment of what she saw as the erosion of her own position in the household soon became so acute that it was a relief to everyone when Toby announced that he, too, had been posted to the Punjab, where worsening relations between the Sikh Army – the Khalsa – and its British neighbours threatened to flare into open warfare.

'You must come and visit us, and see your brother,' he told Thea, as the bullock carts laden with household goods prepared to leave for Lahore. 'As soon as Rohais is properly installed, I will get her to invite you.'

Oh, no, you won't, thought Rohais, offering her cheek for a parting kiss. Beneath the brim of her shady hat her eyes were as cold and hard as aquamarines. Thea has pushed her nose into my affairs too often for my taste, and the further apart we are, the better pleased I shall be.

Even the excitement of her wedding had been spoilt by the news that Sir Richmond Shakespear's daring dash to save the hostages had succeeded. Who wanted to talk about the bride and her beautiful dress after that? And instead of a honeymoon, she had had to watch Toby ride off to Simla to consult with the Governor-General on the terms for Dost Mahomed's release, leaving her feeling ill-used and neglected, an object of pity to the station's whole community.

She watched her husband now, kissing Thea's hand, and a sense of injustice burned like a choking lump in her throat. She was barely nineteen and trapped. What a fool she had been to let him persuade her – *trick* her – into marriage! She should never have sought his help or trusted him with her secret. Once it was out, there had been no taking back the shameful admission that she was pregnant, and though she had begged him to arrange an abortion that would rid her of the child and leave her free, he had refused. All he would offer her was marriage, and reluctantly she had accepted because she had had no other choice.

Well, he would live to regret that refusal just as much as she did. One day, she vowed, he would be glad to let her go, and she was determined that day should not be long delayed.

Looking round the assembled servants, her eye fell on Hinghan Khan and brightened a little. That was the best thing to come out of the whole sorry Afghan business, she thought. Trust James to pick up a jewel on a dunghill! It seemed a waste to leave him here with Thea, who showed no sign of appreciating his charms.

She sighed, and Toby followed the direction of her gaze and frowned, guessing at her thoughts. Firmly he took her arm.

'Come, my love, there is a long journey ahead of us,' he said, and handed her into the carriage.

When Rohais had gone, the rest of the servants and their master settled to the agreeable task of making the Chota-Sahib feel at home, and very soon the sedate routine of General Quinn's well-ordered household had been turned upside down.

Greybeards full of years and dignity could be seen hitching up their robes to scurry in pursuit of rubber balls, or pouncing upon beetles and grasshoppers to supplement the diet of Dandy's favourite pet, a young demon-bat with

273

a face of engaging ugliness and trumpet-shaped nostrils constantly aquiver. Its mother had been murdered by a mob of crows, and Dandy had found the infant clinging beneath her wing.

It was the first of many unfortunate small animals brought to him by natives who knew they could be sure of earning an anna or two from the General-Sahib by this means. He and Dandy referred to this collection of oddities as 'The Menagerie', but Thea called it Dandy's hospital.

Every week, it seemed, another of the bungalow's big airy rooms lost its proper function and became devoted to some interest of Dandy's. The dining-table became a battlefield for lead soldiers, where great engagements from Blenheim to Waterloo, Agincourt to Assaye, were fought and refought. Ponies stood in the stables next to the General's tall chargers, and there was even talk of a baby elephant for Dandy to ride until Thea firmly vetoed the idea. She wanted Dandy to grow up an ordinary English boy, not an imitation raja, but all the same she was touched by the General's delight in his grandson.

'The young monkey's James all over again,' he told her with pride, watching Dandy jump his pony over a set of small hurdles. 'Doesn't know what fear is. We'll make a soldier of him, you mark my words.'

She did not contradict him. In his eyes, soldiering was the only career worthy of a man in India, and planning Dandy's future was some small compensation for the loss of James. In the quiet years that followed, her own pain at losing him gradually diminished, though she would often dream he lay beside her and wake weeping to find him gone.

She grew fond of the General, despite his taciturn nature, and for his part he was glad to hand the reins of the household into her control, since the relentless build-up of men and munitions between Ludhiana and Ferozepore kept him very busy, bringing the likelihood of war against the Sikhs ever closer as Lord Hardinge replaced Lord Ellenborough as Governor-General, and 1843 gave way to 1844. The horrors of the Afghan campaign faded from British minds, and the covetous eyes of the Honourable East India Company fastened on the rich lands beyond the Sutlej River, where anarchy ruled in Ranjit Singh's former domains.

'Ripe for the plucking,' muttered bellicose young officers thirsting for military glory. 'Time we taught the Khalsa a lesson and macadamised the Punjab.'

Keeping the armies from one another's throats grew ever more difficult. 'We Politicals have no more power than King Canute to hold back the waves,' said Toby ruefully, visiting them on his way to Simla. 'There'll be fighting soon if Lord Hardinge does not pull back his troops. Call it provocation or self-defence, it makes no odds.'

Thea thought he looked tired, thinner than she had ever seen him, with deep new lines about his mouth. She asked after Rohais and little Lucy, now eighteen months old.

'Fair as an angel and the image of her mother,' he said, and his face relaxed in a smile. 'I am sending them to the hills in a few months to escape the heat, so you will be able to see her for yourself.'

That was in late November, but before the first week in December had passed the long-threatened war had erupted. The Sikh Army crossed the Sutlej and as soon as he received the news, the Governor-General issued a formal declaration of war from his camp near Ludhiana. There could be no question of women and children travelling until the end of hostilities.

By common consent, Thea and her father-in-law pushed the question of sending Dandy to school in England to the very back of their minds. Instead, a venerable *munshi* of great charm and sagacity called every day to instruct him, Thea herself undertook his religious and historical education, and Hinghan Khan taught him to ride, climb trees, and swim.

Her fear that the young Afghan would prove a disrup-

275

tive element among General Quinn's elderly servants had proved unfounded. The shock of James's death had left him sad and subdued, and when he was well enough to work again it was plain that he was making great efforts to turn over a new leaf. Two years later, he had made himself so indispensable that she doubted if the household could function without him. Though she gave the orders, it was Hinghan Khan who made sure they were carried out, and the way he achieved this without antagonising old Golab Singh, the butler, or any of his minions, was a feat of diplomacy that earned General Quinn's approval.

'Officer material, that boy of yours,' he grunted. 'If you can get an Afghan to go straight, you're on to a winner. But most of 'em are too damn sharp for their own good, more's the pity. Can't trust 'em.'

'I used to think Hinghan Khan was too sharp,' she agreed, 'but he has changed since we came here.'

'Bound to. Off his home ground, so he has to watch his step. No bad thing. You know the rhyme about the nettle?'

She shook her head, and he quoted:

'If you gently touch the nettle,
He will sting you for your pains.
Grasp him like a man of metal,
He from hurting you refrains.

'So it is with human nature;
Treat them gently – they rebel.
Be as harsh as nutmeg grater,
And the knaves will serve you well!'

She laughed. 'I must remember that!'

'It's good advice. My old father taught me that. James wouldn't believe that you have to be cruel to be kind. Natives used to take advantage of him. '"Be as harsh as nutmeg grater . . ." Better in the long run.'

She thanked him for the advice, though she hardly needed it. She was not likely to turn soft when dealing

276

with Hinghan Khan; her main difficulty was not to be too hard on him. Try as she might, she could not like him, and while recognising his good qualities, still heartily wished that James had never taken him under his wing.

He was clever, efficient and hard-working, full of initiative and no shirker of responsibility. Dandy adored him, the other servants worked willingly for him, and he had a genius for getting the best out of difficult horses . . . So why can't I sing his praises as everyone else does? she wondered. Why do I feel it is all an act, and that one day he will revert to type: cruel, treacherous and deceitful? Why can't I put the past behind me, and forgive and forget?

Such questions only intensified her longing to send him packing. The one ray of light in the otherwise gloomy prospect of seeing Dandy depart for school in England was that it would provide her with a valid excuse to dispense with Hinghan Khan's services.

As if he knew that his mistress would seize on any chance to get rid of him, the young Afghan did everything in his power to please her, but still – unfair, unreasonable as she knew it was – she did not trust him.

Neither Sikhs nor British emerged with much credit from the short and bloody conflict that was later known as the First Sikh War, least of all the Rani Jindan, widow of old Ranjit Singh and mother of seven-year-old Dulip, his youngest acknowledged son.

The Rani had preferred life with her lovers to dutiful immolation on her husband's funeral pyre, and in the years following his death, her extravagance and promiscuity had earned her the nickname among British officers of 'The Messalina of the Punjab'. By the last month of 1844, however, she found herself in the difficult position of a woman who has bought a fierce dog for her protection, only to find she cannot control it. The well-armed, well-drilled Khalsa, which had been Ranjit Singh's pride, was straining at the leash. She feared that unless it tasted blood soon, it would turn on her. A sound thrashing from the

277

hated British would, she reasoned, bring the Khalsa to heel. If, on the other hand, the Khalsa triumphed, it would make her son head of the most powerful state in India. Half hoping, half fearing it would be defeated, she let slip the dog of war, and when, after four ferocious battles, it slunk back beaten, its treacherous mistress besought the conquerors to chain and muzzle the beast that had escaped from her control.

Nothing loath, Lord Hardinge decided to reduce the Khalsa's strength to a mere twenty-five battalions, with twelve thousand cavalry, and demanded that all thirty-six remaining guns which had seen action against the British should be handed over. Leaving Dulip Singh as titular head of state, he then set up a Council of Regency to govern on his behalf and appointed Henry, eldest and gravest of the fighting Lawrence brothers, as British Agent in Lahore, with plenipotentiary powers. Lawrence, in his turn, at once set about recruiting like-minded officers who had served with him before and whom he could trust to help him settle the country, among them his brother John, young Herbert Edwardes, who had opposed the Mission to Afghanistan and foreseen the disaster that would follow; and Dr Toby Black, whose wide acquaintance among the Sikhs and understanding of their ways made him a natural choice as head of Political Intelligence.

The war cost Thea many old friends. Reckless to the last, Fighting Bob Sale was shot dead at the Battle of Mukri, and red-haired George Broadfoot, whose brother had been killed with Sir Alexander Burnes at the Residency, fell at Ferozeshah, the third of his family to die in India in five years.

With a sense of melancholy, Thea heard news of former fellow-hostages, and knew that the close bonds that had united them were fraying, one by one. Major Pottinger had died of typhus fever before his ship reached England. Captain Mackenzie had married on his Home leave, but was expected to return to India; Lady Macnaghten and her cats had already retired to Brighton; and Brigadier

278

Shelton, having survived a Company court martial, had been killed by a fall from his horse.

'I hear the 44th turned out on the parade-ground and gave three cheers when they heard he was dead,' reported General Quinn sardonically. 'Cantankerous fellow. Impossible to work with. Still, he didn't deserve that! He had the heart of a lion, despite his bitter tongue.'

Georgiana Mainwaring, at least, seemed quite unaltered when she visited Ludhiana soon after the treaty put an end to war with the Sikhs. Two small sisters had now joined the Jung-i-Bahadur in the Mainwaring nursery, and Georgy herself was as merry, plain-speaking and generous-hearted as ever. She stayed a month, and brought news of many other friends. During her visit, quite half their sentences seemed to begin 'Do you remember . . . ?' as they relived their days in Afghanistan.

'Do you remember when Cousin George dressed up as an Afridi,' said Georgy, 'and made Lady Macnaghten give all her hoarded sugar to him for the children? How furious she was when she found she'd been tricked!'

They laughed, then Georgy said, 'Poor Cousin George! By all accounts it is hard to make him smile nowadays, let alone indulge in practical jokes. My sister says he has changed out of recognition.'

'Did he marry his heiress?' asked Thea, bending over her work to hide her face.

Georgiana gave her a curious look. 'Oh, no. I never believed he would. She wasn't his style. He's a magistrate now, you know, and they say he'll stand for Parliament. Very serious and grand.'

'I can't imagine it.' Thea suddenly felt an intense longing to see Mein's impish face as she remembered it, and hear his laughing excuse for every misdemeanour: 'Blame it on the bullet, my dear girl. Blame it on the bullet.'

'Dear George!' she said, rather shakily. 'What would we have done without him? I hope – I truly hope – he finds happiness.'

'So do I.' Glancing at her averted face, Georgiana forebore to mention her sister's opinion that Cousin George's head had mended better than his heart, and that he had looked a lost soul ever since he had returned from India.

Georgiana's lively nature soon made her a favourite with General Quinn. As the Hot Weather approached, they took to rising early to ride together soon after dawn, trotting past the Civil lines and the bandstand before turning on to the racecourse, dusty and pockmarked with rat holes, but still the best place for a gallop.

Georgiana cantered her pony in circles, the plumes in her hat streaming behind her.

'That's what I call a goer,' muttered General Quinn, eyeing her appreciatively.

Georgy threw him a sparkling glance. 'Race you to the post, General?'

'Done!'

They were off in a flurry of dust and tossing manes, grey and chestnut striding neck and neck, while Thea followed more soberly on her steady countrybred.

Afterwards it was impossible to say just what happened. Both horses swerved. Georgiana hung on to the horn of her saddle and kept her seat, but the General was catapulted over the shoulder of his galloping horse. He rolled in the dust and then lay still.

He died that night, without regaining consciousness. The hand that had clasped Thea's through the long, hot day slowly slackened its grip, and with an overpowering sense of regret, she knew he was gone.

His will was simple. After bequests to servants and provisions for herself and Rohais, his estate was left in trust for his grandson, Daniel Alexander Quinn, with 'my dear daughter-in-law Dorothea, and my son-in-law Dr Toby Black' appointed co-trustees. This did not surprise Thea, but what fairly took her breath away was the discovery of how much the old General was worth. His frugal habits and lack of ostentation had blinded her to the fact that he was very rich, and he had made Dandy heir to a substantial fortune.

'Most of it acquired during the Maratha Wars, I should

guess,' said Toby Black, who had ridden over for the funeral. 'He began his career as a soldier of fortune, you know. Military adviser to Holkar Rao, the last of the Maratha Confederacy to submit to British rule.' He laughed. 'He was a thorn in the Company's flesh in those days – strange to think of it now! For years there was a price on his head. It was only after his marriage that the Company contrived to draw him back into the fold.'

Much of that evening's talk was of General Quinn's flamboyant youth. Senior officers who had known him in those far-off days rode in from neighbouring stations to honour him. More than one expressed surprise at Rohais's absence, and there was a certain constraint in Toby's manner as he explained that his wife had not been well enough to accompany him.

'Looked all right when I saw her a week ago,' snorted Brigadier Urquhart of the Bombay Europeans, who had been in Lahore to witness the signing of the treaty. This ceremony had been followed by the usual round of assemblies, balls, and military parades. 'My guess is she was enjoying the *bundobust* too much to bother with her father's funeral. That gal never saw any reason to please anyone but herself.'

Thea saw Toby's lips tighten and knew he had overheard. She thought he looked tired and strained, and hoped that now the treaty was signed he would not have to ride about the country so much.

Next morning, however, he had recovered his spirits, and before he left went out of his way to compliment her on Dandy. 'A fine boy,' he said. 'You must be proud of him.'

'I hate the thought of losing him,' she admitted. 'Everyone tells me I should send him Home without delay. How I wish I knew what James would have wanted!'

'Did you never discuss it?' he asked, and she sighed.

'There wasn't time. It seemed – you know – so far in the future. And now the decision is upon me and I don't know what to do for the best. James told me he hated being sent away. "Exiled", he called it. Would he want

281

me to put his son through the same unhappiness? Surely not. Yet everyone tells me I have already left it very late, and that his *munshi* is spoiling him.'

'Could you engage an English tutor?'

'That is what I would prefer,' she said eagerly, 'but would it answer? I am sure every lady of my acquaintance would still lecture me on my selfishness in depriving my son of the happiest days of his life.'

'Don't listen to such nonsense,' he said bracingly. 'I thought you had more sense.'

'You don't agree with them?'

'Of course not! Happiest days, indeed! In my opinion, this unnatural habit of separating small children from their home and parents is as crippling to their spirits as binding the feet of Chinese girls is to their bodies.'

His vehemence surprised her. 'What should I do, then? He must be educated.'

'Then do as you think best.'

'But I don't *know* what I think!' She ran her hand distractedly over her hair, which gave, as usual, the impression of wanting to escape from its pins. 'If I keep him here, he won't learn all he should, and if I send him away he may be unhappy and lonely, and I shall not know until it is too late.'

'Well, don't expect me to make up your mind for you,' he said rather sharply, wishing she would not look so beautiful and helpless. He knew very well she was by no means helpless, and felt irritated that she should adopt the old feminine tactic of appealing to male strength in order to evade responsibility.

'I wasn't asking you to.' She was surprised and hurt by his brusqueness.

'That's what it sounded like to me.'

'I thought I could trust your advice,' she said defensively, and again he felt exasperated by her lack of self-confidence.

'Because I'm a man? Or because you want someone to blame if you make the wrong decision? What has happened to you, Thea? Don't you trust your own judgement any longer? You never used to be afraid of making up your own mind.'

'Much good it did me!' she muttered, thinking how Toby had warned her against rushing into marriage with a man she hardly knew, and her immediate impulse to do exactly the opposite. How much unhappiness she might have saved herself by listening to his advice then! But whatever the cost, she could never wholly regret marrying James. Without the temptations placed in his path by the Afghan campaign, he might never have shown her the dark side of his nature. If they had not been separated so long . . . If Hinghan Khan had been pockmarked and ugly . . . If, if, if!

'Very well,' she said coolly, 'since neither you nor Hal seem disposed to help with my problems, I will find my own solution. A fine pair of uncles you are to my poor orphaned boy!' she could not resist adding. '*You* scold me for asking your advice, though how *I* can be expected to know how an eight-year-old boy feels is more than I can tell, and as for Hal – he is impossible! Never a letter or a visit in three years. I know he claims to be busy, but now the war is over he has no excuse for neglecting me.'

Toby laughed, by no means displeased to see her restored to combative mood. 'Don't be too hard on him! A better or more conscientious Commissioner I have never met! Henry Lawrence has a great opinion of him. His work in reconciling sworn enemies among the Sikhs has been beyond praise, and now he has been put in charge of the young Maharaja, whom he treats with just the same impartiality – much to the little chap's astonishment!'

'Why should that astonish him?'

'Only because he is used to being fawned on by his attendants and accorded such exaggerated devotion that it might turn any child's head. Yet he seems to welcome Hal's brisk ways, and enjoy obeying orders instead of giving them.'

He paused, as if struck by some idea, then shook her hand, saying, 'Goodbye, Thea. Do not be too hasty in sending Dandy away. I think – I am almost sure – that I can see a better plan.'

More he would not vouchsafe, but when, after another month of fending off enquiries about when she meant to send Dandy home, she received a letter from her brother, she began to see what Toby had had in mind.

My dearest sister,

I write to acquaint you with our latest news, to wit, the discovery of a dangerous plot to poison Henry Lawrence. If this had proved successful, it would have removed the strong hand now guiding the Punjab towards a fair and settled peace. The culprit made a full confession, which leaves no doubt of the guilt of the Rani Jindan and her lover Lal Singh in promoting this conspiracy. She is to be banished to Sheikapoora, where it is hoped she will have less opportunity to indulge in such mischief. The young Maharaja remains here in my charge until a more suitable guardian can be appointed.

The little fellow has taken the news bravely, though distressed by the prospect of separation from his mother. This brings me to the purpose of my letter. In my view, the blow would be much softened if we were able to provide the boy with a companion of his own age, since his nephew the Shahzadah – who alone matches him in rank – is too young to be a suitable playmate.

From Toby Black and others I hear excellent reports of your son, and write to propose that you bring him here with a view to his sharing the Maharaja's studies and giving a degree of boyish companionship to a life which has hitherto been sadly solitary.

I enclose a recent portrait of His Highness . . .

The sketch showed an attractive child with soft features as yet barely defined and large, melancholy eyes. Poor little fellow, she thought, deprived of his kingdom and his mother as well. So this is what Hal and Toby have hatched together!

She considered the matter all that day and most of the night, and by morning her mind was made up. Calling for her writing case, she sat down to tell her brother that she and Dandy would be very pleased to join him in Lahore.

The boys' first meeting was painfully stiff. After their formal greeting, Dulip Singh and Dandy stood tongue-tied, covertly eyeing one another, while their elders waited anxiously.

Nothing happened until Hal, losing patience, ordered them off to play, and they wandered away, still in silence, showing little enthusiasm for one another's company.

'I hope they will hit it off,' said Hal doubtfully. 'His Highness is not used to playing with other children.'

'No more is Dandy,' said Thea. 'But we can hardly force them to like one another.'

To their relief, it soon became clear that no coercion would be necessary. Twenty minutes after the boys had disappeared, they heard laughter and splashing from the pleasure garden, and going in that direction they found Dandy, knee-deep in the pool surrounding the fountain, trying to catch goldfish in his bare hands, while the young Maharaja, convulsed with mirth, pelted him with dripping bundles of water lilies.

He looked so different, with his big black eyes sparkling and the droop of his soft mouth transformed by giggles, that both Thea and Hal knew at once that henceforward their main worry would be how to stop Dandy leading his royal playmate into mischief.

'Well, we're over the first hurdle, at least,' observed Hal with satisfaction, as he prepared to return with his charge to the Maharaja's splendid apartments in the Citadel.

'Sir! Sir! Dandy-Sahib must ride with me tomorrow,' announced Dulip Singh imperiously. 'He can have the bay pony my uncle gave me.'

Dandy gave him a measuring look. 'I will ride my own pony, thank you.'

'No, no! This one is better.'

'Either I ride my own, or I don't come.'

285

'I am the Maharaja!' Dulip Singh stamped angrily. 'You must obey me.'

'You needn't think you can order me about,' said Dandy coolly. 'I'm not one of your servants.'

'Mind your manners, my boy,' whispered Thea, but to her surprise Dulip Singh made a swift, assenting gesture and laid his small hand on Dandy's arm.

'I did not mean to offend you, Dandee-Sahib.'

'All right. I don't mind coming,' said Dandy graciously and the grown-ups looked at one another with relief. That was the second hurdle behind them.

The morning rides became a routine, and it was a charming sight to see the two boys chattering away as they rode by on their lively, long-tailed ponies, apparently oblivious to the tall Sikhs of the mounted bodyguard surrounding them. The Maharaja's English guardians maintained constant vigilance over him, being well aware that many of the boy's subjects would like to snatch him away from their control. Everywhere he went he was accompanied by guards as well as by his courtiers, and only the most trusted servants were allowed into his apartments.

Quiet though the Punjab now appeared on the surface, the former warriors of the Khalsa were seething with resentment at having their wings clipped. The strong British presence in the country had put an end to their power to name their own price for their support and loyalty, and their long-established practice of plundering villages for food and forage now brought heavy penalties.

As she sat by her window watching the gorgeous cavalcade that made up the royal *sowaree* – all tossing manes and rainbow silks, glittering lances and tall turbans – Thea would sometimes wonder what the future held for the two boys at its centre. This could only be a temporary solution to the problem of Dandy's education. By keeping him with her now, was she laying up trouble for the future?

And what would be the fate of the little Maharaja, now so trusting, friendly and eager to please? Would he end up a depraved, deprived, dispossessed prince on a pension? How long could the British maintain the pretence of protecting him from his own army, his own people? This isolation from his subjects might be expedient, but it would hardly help him when the time came for him to rule over the nation created by the great Ranjit Singh.

Two years later, peace in the Punjab was still a fragile plant, and prosperity only a hope for the future, when Henry Lawrence was ordered by his doctors to take Home leave in order to avoid a complete collapse of his health. Conscientious to a fault, he had worn himself into a state of exhaustion, and his friends were thankful when he sailed for England and a well-deserved knighthood in November 1847.

Deprived of his presence, it was not long before unrest in different parts of the Punjab gave rise to suspicion that the Rani Jindan was up to her old tricks, fomenting trouble from her retreat at Sheikapoora. In February her agents were seen in Multan, where they had no business to be, and when Mulraj, governor of that province, refused to pay his taxes, it was not hard to guess whose hand was behind his defiance.

Between plot and counterplot, rumour and intrigue, Toby was busier than ever.

'Too busy to keep an eye on his own wife,' sneered the gossips who resented his influence with the Resident. During her husband's long absences from home, Rohais scarcely troubled to conceal her flirtations, and these provided the Lahore garrison with a welcome source of scandal.

Whisper as they might among themselves, though, the gossips soon learned better than to discuss Mrs Black's indiscretions in her sister-in-law's hearing. Lonely years in the Orphanage had taught Thea to value family ties, and she would fly to Rohais's defence at the first hint of malicious criticism. She was fond of Rohais, and sorry to see the pretty, wilful girl lose the sparkle that had made her so attractive. Neither husband nor child seemed to give her pleasure, and her dreams of travel and social

287

success were as remote now as they had been in the school-room.

'Why does everything go wrong for me?' Rohais complained peevishly. 'Mamma promised to take me to England, but she died, and then Toby said that if I married him, he would take Home leave, but he forgot all about it when Sir Henry called him here. It's not fair! I would never have accepted him if I'd known it meant living in this dreary place. It's all right for *you*, Thea. You live in the Citadel and see all the fun. I should have known better than to marry a Political Officer! Even the thought of spending his pension can't compensate for the boredom I suffer here.'

'Rohais!'

'You needn't look so shocked,' said Rohais scornfully. 'What else have I got to look forward to? And don't tell me the thought of James's pension never crossed your mind when you married him!'

'Of course it didn't.'

'Some people have all the luck.' Rohais sighed with exasperation. 'Look at you! Free as air – no husband to bother you, and all the money you'll ever need. Why couldn't Papa have left me more than that miserable pittance? I can hardly scrape up enough to buy a new bonnet on what Toby gives me – not that he'd notice if I wore nothing but sackcloth and ashes.'

Since the elaborate confection she was wearing must have cost more than a subaltern's monthly pay, Thea took this complaint with a grain of salt, but when she attempted to turn the conversation by praising it, Rohais shrugged and the corners of her mouth drooped still more.

'Last season's, can't you see? These brims have gone quite out of fashion. Toby said I would have to make do with my old clothes as he couldn't afford to buy me more – I should have known he'd be a wretched husband.'

'Then why did you marry him?' asked Thea, tired of this litany of complaint.

'My dear, what else could I do? Anything to get away from home! You can't imagine how horribly dreary it was.

288

No one but old men to dance with, and everyone droning on and on about Afghanistan. It was all right for you. You were one of the heroes – the Afghan hostages. You've never known what it was to be bored to death.'

'No,' said Thea, looking at the pretty, discontented face with detached curiosity. They had been frozen, starved, exhausted, terrified – but never bored to death. She laughed suddenly. 'You're right,' she said. 'I suppose I *have* been lucky, if you look at it that way.'

'What other way is there to look at it? Everything goes right for you and wrong for me. Look at us now! You've a son who plays with the Maharaja, and I've nothing but a miserable daughter. If only Lucy had been a boy! Then she could have made friends with the Shahzadah, and I would have been invited to call on the Ranis and see their jewels . . . '

'I can take you to call on the Ranis, if that would please you,' said Thea on impulse.

'Would you really? Oh, Thea!'

'It isn't very exciting,' said Thea apologetically, 'but they are very sweet and their jewels are magnificent. They like nothing better than showing them to visitors. Why not come and stay with me in the Citadel while Toby is away?' she went on, pleased to see Rohais in better spirits. Once roused from her self-pitying lethargy, she looked animated and attractive.

Rohais turned the matter over in her mind for so long that Thea thought she would refuse, but at last she nodded.

'Yes,' she said, 'that would make a change. I will bring Lucy with me. It is time she and Dandy got to know one another.'

Somewhat to Thea's surprise, neither Dandy nor Hal were pleased to learn of the proposed visit. Dandy's chauvinistic grumbles about Lucy's age and sex were easily silenced, but Hal's complaints were more difficult to dismiss. It was, after all, his house to which she had invited Rohais, and Hal had a strong sense of territory.

'You might have asked me first! Oh, you may smile,

but it is no laughing matter for me. Mrs Black thinks any bachelor is fair game. I tell you, I would rather have a tigress at my table than your sister-in-law.'

'Leave her to me, dear brother,' said Thea soothingly. 'I will undertake to protect you from the tigress at all times.'

'I've no quarrel with Toby,' said Hal, still ruffled, 'dammit, I like him – always have – whatever Papa thought of him! All the same, I wish he would take a stronger line with his wife.'

'Oh, poor Rohais! It's not her fault that he is never at home and she has to make her own amusements.'

'Call them amusements? I call them a public scandal,' said Hal vigorously. 'She has no business flirting with every junior officer and getting us a bad reputation. If the Black Hawk don't know what she gets up to while he's winging his way about the country, it's high time someone told him.'

'Why do you call him that?'

'The Black Hawk? Oh, it's the name the Sikhs give him. They say he hovers over the land and no one knows where he will swoop down next. Nonsense, of course, but it does no harm. Keeps 'em guessing.'

'The Black Hawk.' Wild and free, dark and fierce – yes, it suited him, she thought. Who could pinion such a bird? Poor Rohais! She would have been happier married to a lap-dog than a black hawk.

She smiled at Hal, but said quite firmly, 'Well, I've invited her now. I'm sorry I didn't ask you first, but I can hardly tell her she's not welcome. She wants to meet the Ranis and see their famous jewels.'

'Oh, let her come, let her come,' said Hal impatiently. 'I shall be far too busy to bother with her, and I daresay you can keep her from bothering me. Only, if you love me, dearest Thea, make sure she does not stay too long.'

How long was too long? Thea wondered uneasily a month later, when Rohais showed no inclination to leave her comfortable set of rooms in the old *zenana* of Hal's house

290

in the Palace gardens. While it was gratifying to know the visit had been a success in the matter of improving Rohais's spirits and, consequently, her looks, Thea was well aware that her continued presence was an imposition on Hal. He did not complain but simply absented himself from the house at dawn and returned after nightfall, and Thea felt very guilty that by bringing Rohais in she had effectively banished him from his own home.

For her part, Rohais had no intention of returning to her own dull quarters in the Civil lines a moment before she must. They will have to throw me out, she thought, and Thea would never permit that.

She much preferred living at the centre of affairs, in the Citadel surrounding the Palace. She revelled in the pageantry of court life, the gorgeous clothes of the courtiers, the constant comings and goings, and embroiled herself joyfully in the small intrigues by which Ranjit Singh's many widows, the Ranis, enlivened their existence. Twenty-two of these former wives still lived in the Citadel, jealously maintaining the best state they could and constantly wheedling to have their pensions increased above those of their rivals. Drinking tea with these languid, melancholy beauties, sighing with envy over their jewels, passing small titbits of gossip from one to another occupied Rohais very happily.

And then there was Hinghan Khan.

Five years after his master's death, the young Afghan's looks had fulfilled their early promise. With his long, flashing eyes, high cheekbones and fine features, smooth skin and slim, athletic body, he was well aware of his own attractions. Rohais discovered a new interest in horses and sought his opinion on their care and schooling. She visited local shrines and monuments with him in attendance. Within a week she was leaving open the *zenana* window and sending her ayah to sleep in the baby's room as she welcomed the lithe, oiled shadow that was Hinghan Khan to her bed.

Like two halves of a magnet, they were drawn together irresistibly, but being skilled dissemblers neither betrayed

291

by the smallest look or gesture that they were lovers. In private they laughed at the ease with which Thea and Hal were deceived, while in public Rohais pretended to dislike him, deriving malicious pleasure from putting her sister-in-law on the defensive.

'Look at that insolent jackanapes,' she said, watching the small boys playing an impromptu game of cricket in the evening sunlight. While the Maharaja panted to and fro, Hinghan Khan directed the game with loud, peremptory shouts, just as he used to in Afghanistan when playing with the Trevor children. 'He's hardly my idea of a servant! I can't understand why you put up with him, Thea.'

'James made me promise to look after him.'

Rohais heard the constraint in her tone and gave her a sharp, assessing look. 'But that was years ago!'

'Only five.'

'All the same! Do you mean you have to keep him for ever? I call that rotten luck. James should never have asked for such a promise.'

'He was very fond of Hinghan Khan.'

I bet he was, thought Rohais. Just his type. And mine. She smiled inwardly, watching from the corner of her eye as the slim, agile figure bent and arched like a bow, reaching for a high ball. She hoped the rebels in Multan would keep Toby busy for a nice long time. The longer the better.

CHAPTER SIXTEEN

Around the polished table in the Residency, the council of advisers to the Acting Resident, Sir Frederick Currie, sat and sweltered as the lazily flapping *punkah* wafted hot air from one end of the room to the other.

The officers in their tight uniforms envied Toby Black in his light linen coat, while he, in turn, yearned for the *punkah-wallah*'s loose robes, but they were all united in wishing that 'Caution' Currie would make up his mind. The meeting had already lasted two hours, yet the Acting Resident showed no sign of coming to a decision.

A ditherer, diagnosed Toby, watching Sir Frederick mop repeatedly at the moisture pearling his broad, ruddy face. Another Elphy Bey. Too old, and too frightened of making a mistake. Why the devil aren't these old men put out to grass before they make the blunder that ruins an honourable career? Why, oh why, did this trouble have to blow up in Henry Lawrence's absence?

The double murder of Captain Patrick Vans Agnew and Lieutenant Anderson soon after they and the new Governor appointed to replace the recalcitrant Mulraj had arrived in Multan had sent waves of shock and indignation through British India.

The Governor-General had ordered that the culprit should be punished at once, but Lord Dalhousie was new to the country and did not appreciate the practical difficulties. Not only had Mulraj taken refuge in his fortified citadel, whose walls could defy all but the heaviest siege guns, but the Hot Weather was at hand, and no one in his senses would embark on a summer campaign in the terrible heat of the southern Punjab.

Before succumbing to his wounds, Vans Agnew had managed to send an appeal for help to Lieutenant Edwardes in neighbouring Dejerat, and he had responded by ferrying a small force of Pathans across the Indus into Multan. It was a gallant attempt to call Mulraj's bluff, but it had failed. Until his little party was reinforced, poor Edwardes was – as he put it – in the position of a terrier barking at a tiger.

When he first heard of the murders, Sir Frederick Currie had warned all available troops to be ready to march to Multan. Now he was having second thoughts.

At the far end of the table, Hal leaned forward. 'We must strike while the iron is hot, sir,' he urged. 'If we do not suppress this trouble at once, there may be further outbreaks. You said yourself – '

'I am asking your opinion, Mr Dundas, not your free interpretation of my own,' snapped Currie, harassed and tetchy. 'Am I to understand, then, that you are in favour of military intervention?'

Hal looked chagrined. 'Yes, sir.'

'Without a siege train? It would be doomed to failure before a shot was fired. Since Mulraj has gone to ground in that rabbit warren of a citadel, we need heavy artillery to blow him out of it, not popguns. How long would it take to bring down a siege train, General?'

'A month. Five weeks.' General Whish tugged at his walrus moustache. 'Better concentrate your strength here in Lahore, Sir Frederick, and let the Durbar deal with Mulraj. It is the Maharaja's government he has rebelled against, not ours.'

This was hair-splitting, and everyone knew it. The Durbar no longer had either the will or the power to chastise rebels. 'British officers have been murdered,' pointed out Hal, who had been a particular friend of Pat Vans Agnew.

Currie turned a cold eye on him. 'General Whish is right, Mr Dundas. We must not allow emotion to sway our judgement. No doubt that is what Mulraj expects, and while he laughs at us from behind his thick walls, the rest of the Punjab may rise to stab us in the back.'

His gaze roamed round the table and rested on Toby, who had been summoned in haste from Ferozepore. 'I am

294

obliged to you for joining us, Dr Black. I am told you know Mulraj well.'

'As well as any doctor knows his patient, I suppose.' Which is not to say very well in this case, thought Toby wryly, remembering his own shock of disgust on learning of Mulraj's deviant sexual appetite. He who had believed himself unshockable! Every man – and woman for that matter – had weaknesses. Why was it so peculiarly disconcerting to discover the cloven hoof in a quiet, diffident little fellow like Mulraj?

The table waited expectantly.

'Pray enlighten us, sir,' said Currie impatiently. 'What sort of man is he?'

'Weak, I should say, sir. Weak but obstinate. Reclusive. Certainly no hothead, but if forced into a corner he might well defend it to the death. I find it difficult to believe him guilty of instigating this outrage unless some stronger hand pushed him into it.'

'Hmm . . . ' Sir Frederick considered, tapping his teeth.

Toby said quickly, 'With your permission, sir, I would like to ride to Multan to negotiate with Mulraj. The matter will be better settled that way, without recourse to siege trains and substantial movement of troops.'

'Negotiate with a murderer? You are asking rather a lot, Dr Black,' said Currie stiffly.

'I believe it is worth a try. There is more in this rebellion than meets the eye, sir. Mulraj is only the scapegoat.'

'A willing scapegoat,' muttered Major Tomlinson, who longed for glory. Sir Frederick ignored the interruption.

'Who is behind it, then?'

'Who has been behind every plot since the war ended?'

'The Rani Jindan? Impossible.'

'She has been corresponding with Mulraj – that we know. Even from Sheikapoora she is capable of exerting pressure on those who are susceptible.'

'Blackmail, eh?' Hal cocked an eye at Toby.

'This is getting us nowhere,' broke in General Whish, whose quivering nostrils had caught the rich aroma of curry and sent an urgent message to his stomach that the sacred hour of *tiffin* was slipping past. Like most of the military hierarchy, he resented the influence wielded by Political Officers such as Dr Black, and disagreed with them on principle.

'One moment, General, if you please,' interposed John Lawrence. Brother to Sir Henry, with a taller, more robust version of the Lawrence good looks, he was known to be of the 'macadamising persuasion' and in favour of annexing the whole Punjab – a policy resolutely opposed by his elder brother. He had sat silently through most of the discussion, with only his quick dark eyes moving from one face to the next.

'In what way is Mulraj susceptible to blackmail, Dr Black?' he asked now. 'Politically, or by reason of his private life?'

'The latter.'

In Toby's mind's eye rose an image of Mulraj as he had last seen him, with a naked, squirming brown child on either knee. His gorge rose at the memory.

Mulraj had said quite seriously, 'All your medicine, Hakim-Sahib, cannot give me the strength I gain from the bodies of these little ones.'

The Rani would know of Mulraj's weakness, and might well have threatened to expose him to the strait-laced new masters of his country unless he joined in her conspiracy to overthrow them. When he had resigned his governorship in an attempt to escape her demands, she would have struck back by arranging the British officers' murders and throwing the blame on him. Poor wretch! thought Toby. Trapped between Scylla and Charybdis, what could he do?

'If I could spend an hour or two with him, I am sure I could discover the truth behind Mulraj's revolt,' he said, hoping John Lawrence would throw his weight into the balance, but after only a moment's hesitation, Lawrence shook his head.

'That would be tantamount to condoning the murders, in my view,' he said decisively. 'Well, Sir Frederick? Shall we send support to Lieutenant Edwardes, or hold our hand? If we allow the Durbar to undertake the chastisement of Mulraj, what guarantee have we that the Sikh regiments will not go over to him?'

This was a possibility at the back of every mind. The loyalty of the newly raised Sikh regiments was as yet untried. Asking them to fight their fellow-countrymen might well prove too harsh a test of their allegiance.

The Acting Resident sucked his teeth and consulted his watch. He, too, was hungry. 'Caution' Currie had been his nickname throughout his career, and now he lived up to it.

'I am indebted to you gentlemen for your counsel,' he said, rising, 'but everything you say strengthens my conviction that this is a matter for the Commander-in-Chief.'

In other words, I won't take the responsibility, thought Toby disgustedly. Better shift the burden on to other shoulders, even if it means leaving poor Edwardes high and dry in Multan, and increases the chance that a small, local uprising will lead to a full-scale war. An excuse for war was what the Governor-General wanted, and John Lawrence too. In Sir Henry's absence they had a better chance of building this Mulraj molehill into the required mountain, and poor old Currie was trapped into playing his part in the charade.

As if to confirm this guess, Currie caught his eye, saying with a hint of apology, 'The situation is delicate, as you know. I must keep the Commander-in-Chief fully informed. I am hardly my own master.'

And by the time Sir Henry returns, war will be inevitable, thought Toby. What a damnable business! Well, he would go down to Multan with Currie's permission or without, and see what he could do to mend fences. Mulraj was no fool. If he could be persuaded to surrender voluntarily before the whole paraphernalia of troops, siege train and heavy artillery arrived to smoke him out, there was still a chance of containing this rebellion.

Hal did his best to keep the young Maharaja in ignorance of the trouble in Multan, but of course he knew. Dandy saw to that. In any case, Dulip Singh was far too intelligent not to guess why Sikh guards had been withdrawn from the Palace and replaced by men of the Shropshire Regiment, and why a number of his personal attendants had been removed without explanation.

'The Sirdars wish to capture me, but I shall not trust myself to them again,' he told Thea with the solemnity that sat strangely on a ten-year-old. It worried her to hear him refer to his subjects as if they were his enemies. How would he ever be able to rule over men he had been taught to distrust?

Yet apart from the moments when politics forced themselves on his attention, or when he attended the Durbar, sitting patiently for hours of long-winded debate before putting his name to whatever papers were presented for his signature, he was as lively, affectionate and mischievous as any boy of his age. Thea was very fond of him, and encouraged Hal to make his life as normal and informal as he could.

'Poor little chap! I feel sorry for him in his heavy robes and jewels, listening to old men talking. He's only a child. Why can't they let him behave like one?'

'He certainly behaves like one when he is with Dandy,' observed Hal rather dryly. It was true that Dandy frequently led Dulip Singh into mischief, most of it harmless enough, though now and again Thea felt obliged to remonstrate with her son.

'Really, Dandy, you must not encourage His Highness to be so naughty,' she scolded, after hearing how the boys had made the dignified, white-bearded Vizier and other court officials play Follow My Leader through the Palace gardens, flapping their venerable arms and crowing like barnyard fowl.

'Dippy thought it was funny. You told me to make him laugh,' said Dandy with a look of injured innocence.

'I did not mean he should make his courtiers look

ridiculous. And I forbid you to call His Highness by that absurd nickname.'

'He likes it, Mamma! He told me so.'

'Nevertheless, you will oblige me by giving him his proper title,' said Thea. She knew that if Sikhs saw their Maharaja treated with too much familiarity it would damage his standing and give ammunition to the supporters of the Rani Duknoo and her son, the six-year-old Shahzadah.

'Oh, Mamma! You fuss too much!' Dandy's mouth set in a sulky line. Aunt Rohais had thought it funny, too, and laughed like anything, but he knew better than to say so to his mother. There were a good many things on which Mamma and Aunt Rohais did not see eye to eye, which was a pity, because Aunt Rohais let him do all sorts of jolly things which would have made Mamma cross had she known of them. She was always interested in hearing what he and Dulip Singh had been doing, and when he told her how they had stood on the wall above the Palace gate sprinkling water on the people passing below, she had laughed so much that tears came into her eyes.

Thea sighed. She knew she should be firm with him, but she hated to see his lips droop in a way that brought less than happy memories of James. No one else had Dandy's power to amuse the Maharaja. For the pleasure of hearing his delighted peals of laughter, she allowed Dandy a great deal of latitude. Sometimes the fear that he would grow into another Rohais made her try to curb his high spirits, but with little success. Hal was too busy to be strict with his nephew, and what with the deference of the Palace servants, the Maharaja's adulation, and Rohais's encouragement, Dandy was becoming so filled with the idea of his own invulnerability that he believed he could laugh his way out of anything.

It was true that he accorded a degree of respect to Dr Black, but that, thought Thea, was because he depended on Toby's help in doctoring the ever-growing menagerie he kept in the Palace grounds. Most of them had been rescued from dire circumstances and needed expert medical attention.

'Not another, my love!' Thea would exclaim in despair as Dandy presented her with his latest treasure: a snake whose tail had been crushed by a waggon wheel; a puppy with a twisted leg; an orphan monkey; a flying squirrel which had fallen from its nest. But somehow room was found for them all, even the deer which soon became so tame that she followed Dandy about the house and lay under the hammock while he rested.

Toby's peripatetic affairs kept him away for weeks on end, but no sooner was his horse back in the stable than Dandy would be badgering him for advice about his pets' various ailments and disabilities.

'You must not let him annoy you,' said Thea, meeting Toby in the garden early one morning and realising by the instrument case he carried that he had been ministering to some four-legged patient. 'You have enough to do without looking after Dandy's pets as well.'

'Didn't your father call me a horse-doctor?' he said with a grin. 'Perhaps he understood my true vocation after all.'

'It is too bad of Dandy to give you so much trouble,' she exclaimed, deliberately ignoring the reference to her father and the memories it evoked.

'Why should you think I find it troublesome?'

'Oh! You know how children imagine their own concerns are more important than anyone else's.'

'Don't worry,' he said seriously. 'If Dandy bothers me, I'll soon send him to the rightabout.' He paused, then added, 'He's a good boy. I enjoy working with him.'

In the way of mothers, she hurriedly rejected the compliment. 'Those pets! I think he cares more for them than he does for any human being.'

'Does that surprise you? I was just the same at his age.' For a moment they strolled between the flowerbeds in companionable silence, then he said, 'I have been meaning to ask you – I have some leave due, and wondered if you would give permission for Dandy to join me on a week's *shikar?* Captain Ellis is bringing young William, and the boys would be company for one another.'

She accepted the offer with pleasure. 'Whenever you like,' she said. 'The sooner the better.' A hunting trip would be Dandy's idea of heaven, and if war broke out again, as seemed likely, all leave would be cancelled.

Negotiations with Mulraj had not prospered. As Toby had predicted, he reacted to pressure by digging in his toes, and by the time Sir Henry Lawrence returned to duty in early August, after cutting short his Home leave, the fortress of Multan was under siege by both Company troops and the young Maharaja's Sikh Army. For the moment, however, the trouble appeared localised. The rest of the country was quiet and most Punjabi villagers seemed happy enough with their change of rulers.

'Settle the country, make the people contented, and take care there are no rows,' Sir Henry advised his Commissioners, and they did their best to carry out this programme.

The Maharaja's birthday fell in the first week in September, and when the pundits and astrologers had agreed on the most auspicious day, festivities were planned.

Despite heavy rain, seventeen of the Ranis, dressed in their best, appeared at the Palace that morning to present their compliments to the boy as he sat with his feet tucked up on Ranjit Singh's throne. He received their *nuzzurs* with grave dignity, resplendent in his gold-threaded surcoat and embroidered sash, his five ropes of large matched pearls, diamond aigret, pearl earrings, and the broad gold armlet in which was set the historic Koh-i-Noor diamond – the Mountain of Light – flanked by two lesser gems.

Later that day, Hal gave a party more suited to the age and inclination of the birthday boy, to which he invited a dozen children, sons and daughters of officers stationed in Lahore. For a time even the Resident forgot the siege of Multan and his other cares in the pleasure of watching the young guests romp about the gardens before settling

301

down to consume vast quantities of ices and jellies and delicious tiny cakes.

Thea had never quite overcome her dislike of children's parties. Even now the squeals of delight as the magician drew coloured doves from a silk scarf made her head ache, but for the sake of the children she tried to push such thoughts aside and enter into the party spirit.

After tea there were games, and any remaining shyness among the young guests was soon dispelled by Oranges and Lemons, followed by Ring-a-Roses. The Resident was cajoled into taking the name part in Blind Man's Buff, and even Thea could not help laughing to see the grave, ascetic figure of the most powerful man in the Punjab blundering about the dusty lawn, arms outstretched and a scarf tied over his eyes, while the giggling children skipped about, eluding him like minnows swimming past a pike.

'Tee-hee-hee! Can't catch me!' taunted Tommy Scott, dancing to within inches of those clutching hands.

'Behind you, Sir Henry!' called Dandy, and gave the great man's coat-tail a daring tug.

'Oh, I give up! I am too old for this lark!' gasped the Resident, whirling round to catch at thin air.

'Catch me, then, Sahib,' whispered a voice at his elbow, and gratefully his fingers closed on the plump shoulder of the Maharaja. Dulip Singh made no attempt to evade him, and the other children groaned in disappointment.

'You have to guess who you've caught,' called Dandy. 'Three guesses, sir.'

One touch of the stiff, gold-embroidered surcoat had already removed any doubt, but Sir Henry knew the conventions. He shook his head in pretended bafflement. Carefully he felt his captive up and down, while Dulip Singh vibrated with suppressed giggles.

'Is it Master Tommy Scott?'

'No! Guess again.'

'Hmm . . . Let me see. Can it be Miss Emily Soames?'

'Wrong again!' The children squealed delightedly.

'Only one more, Sir Henry,' Dandy warned. He put a

finger to his lips to prevent the captive giving the game away.

'Last guess, eh? I must get it right this time.' The Resident screwed up his face in ferocious concentration while his audience waited on tenterhooks. 'I *think* – I am almost *sure* – it is none other than His Highness the Maharaja Bahadur Dulip Singh!' he announced sonorously, and the children cheered and clapped wildly.

'Ab-so-lutely correct! Very clever guess!' said the Maharaja with shining eyes as Sir Henry thankfully pulled off his blindfold. 'Now it is my turn to choose what to play.'

'Don't you want another Blind Man's Buff?' asked Hal, while Thea gestured to a bearer to offer Sir Henry some iced lemonade.

No, Dulip Singh wanted Hunt the Slipper. He became very busy placing his guests in a circle, sitting with their knees drawn up to form a tunnel, and when this proved too small for his liking, he ordered some of the hovering court officials to join the ring. They looked agonised at first, then, remembering how the Lat-Sahib had just played a foolish game, they took their places without protest.

Only Missar Makraj, Hereditary Guardian of the Jewel House, whose fierce dark eyes never left the Koh-i-Noor diamond on the Maharaja's arm, stroked his luxuriant beard and maintained his vigil.

A pair of beautiful gold-embroidered slippers with curly toes, specially made for the occasion, was presented to Dulip Singh. He took one and began to walk round outside the circle, tapping the children's shoulders and intoning, 'Cobbler, cobbler, mend my shoe. Get it done by half-past two.'

'Half-past two is much too late.

'Get it done by half-past eight!' chorused the guests.

How many generations had chanted those couplets? Thea wondered, watching the age-old ritual. Every Anglo-Indian ayah knew them as well as she knew her own traditional rigmaroles.

'Better make this the last game,' said Hal, returning

quietly from seeing the Resident to his carriage. 'It will be dark enough for the fireworks soon.'

Thea nodded, relieved that the party was nearly over and had gone well. No tears, no tantrums, no obvious breaches of etiquette. No one had been sick . . .

Hal put a hand on her shoulder. 'I'll go and speak to Hinghan Khan. Make sure everything is ready. Come on, children,' he called. 'Keep the slipper moving. No sitting on it, Emily. Play the game.'

Dulip Singh had tossed his slipper into the circle and begun to count, hands over his eyes.

'Forty-eight, forty-nine, fifty!' he announced. 'Now where is my shoe?'

For a long moment he scanned the upturned faces while the children froze, hiding their smiles. Then a small movement between Emily and her brother Jonathan caught his attention.

'Jonathan! You've got it.'

Sheepishly, Jonathan surrendered the slipper. 'You should have kept it!' he hissed at his sister as Dulip Singh, smiling delightedly, squeezed into the circle, looking like a brilliant little bantam cock among the demurely dressed European children. The game began again.

It seemed to Thea that there was a lot of unnecessary scuffling and jostling during the next few rounds. The swift tropical dusk was falling, but she hesitated to stop the game until Hal told her the fireworks were ready.

She could see that Dandy and Dulip Singh were getting overexcited, pulling at one another's clothes and laughing too loudly. She wondered if she should call them to order. Although it was nice to see the Maharaja enjoying himself and it *was* his birthday, she wished he was more suitably dressed for playing games.

What if one of his priceless strings of pearls broke in the scuffle? Not to mention the danger to his sparkling diamond aigret. She was glad to see that he was no longer wearing the armlet with the Koh-i-Noor in it, and blessed the good sense of Missar Makraj in divesting his small master of so dangerous a liability. Any damage to *that* would do much harm to the already strained relationship between British and Sikhs, she thought, wishing Hal would hurry back and wondering why the Guardian of the Jewels was moving forward until he stood within a few feet of the romping children. He looked, she thought, like a tall, fierce mastiff watching an unruly litter of puppies.

She had just made up her mind to stop the game, whether or not the fireworks were ready, when the old Sikh's deep, gruff voice cut through the shrill babble like a watchdog's bark.

'Maharaj! Where is the Koh-i-Noor?'

Thea's heart skipped a beat, and then began to race. *Hadn't* he taken it off? For a startled moment the children were silent, staring up at the fierce old man with his beetling brows and badger-striped beard. Then Dulip Singh lifted his elbow and stared at his sleeve.

'Gone!' he whispered.

A collective sigh that was half a groan burst from all who heard him. Thea could hardly bear to look at Missar Makraj, whose face was a mask of outrage and shame. Instead she stared at Dandy who, to her horror, was quite openly laughing.

Missar Makraj saw him too, and drew the same conclusion. Like a striking snake, one gnarled brown hand darted down to seize the boy by the collar of his best velvet jacket, while the other drew out his sword with a harsh metallic rasp.

'Devil spawn!' he growled. 'Where is it, before I kill you?'

Though frightened, Dandy stood his ground. 'I haven't got it. Not now.'

Before the horror-struck watchers could intervene, the glittering arc swept down with lightning speed a hair's breadth from the boy's neck. Once, twice, three times – and Thea feared his last moment had come. Three feints, and then the fatal blow . . .

'Where is it, *shaitan*!'

Dandy was white as death. 'In the slipper,' he muttered.

For a moment it looked as if Missar Makraj was going to resume his sword practice, but a sharp command from Dulip Singh arrested the swinging blade. Picking up the embroidered slipper from the floor, he felt inside it, and to Thea's unbounded relief, withdrew first the tapes of the armlet, then the large diamond with its flanking satellites in their setting of solid gold.

Fire flashed from the stone as he turned it this way and that, examining it minutely. He rolled it in a scrap of cloth and stowed it away in his robes; then, bending his fierce head close to Dandy's ear, he growled the single word, '*Remember!*'

Silent, mouths agape, the children stared at Dandy, who stood as if turned to ice, his usual swagger quite vanished.

'Oh, Dandee!' said Dulip Singh, laying a gentle hand on his arm. 'That was a veree, veree foolish trick to play.'

Dandy swallowed with difficulty. His mouth was dry. 'It was only a joke,' he muttered.

Into the silence, Hal's cheerful voice came as a relief. 'Finished the game, children? That's right. You're very quiet all of a sudden – what's up? Doesn't anyone want to see the fireworks?'

CHAPTER SEVENTEEN

Rohais dreamed of treasure.

Gleaming, glinting, twinkling, winking heaps of gold. Milky mounds of pearls. Cool emeralds and rubies like drops of blood. Sapphires and opals, topazes, amethysts and tourmalines; bowls and goblets of beaten silver; rings and earrings, necklaces, bracelets, armlets; the jewelled hilts of swords and pommels ablaze with gems. They were all there in the Toshkhana, the Jewel House, not a quarter of a mile away. Just a handful would settle her debts and make her rich for ever more . . .

Her debts! They had grown and spread like some foul fungus, invading every corner of her life. She was drowning in her debts and no one cared. No one lifted a hand to pull her out.

One more chance – that was all she asked. One last chance to pay off the moneylenders with their accursed interest. After that she would live on her allowance and never gamble again. Why did no one believe her? Why did people move away when she spoke of her troubles, for all the world as if she had some contaminating disease?

She had begged Toby to pay her debts one last time. His response had been to ask Thea to take charge of Rohais's money and dole it out to her when she needed it. That was the most humiliating thing of all.

He treats me like a child, she thought resentfully. An ignorant child who can't be trusted with her own money. It would serve him right if I left him, and ran away with Captain Hardcastle, or Mr Eames, or . . . or . . . She couldn't think of anyone else. The list of her admirers had mysteriously shrunk, even though there were now more British officers than ever in Lahore. Last summer, while Mulraj's revolt simmered in the south of the Punjab, Company forces had been built up in expectation of

307

further conflicts, and at the outbreak of the Second Sikh War in November 1848, Sir Hugh Gough had been ready. Bravely though the Khalsa fought, they had been betrayed by their leaders and finally defeated at the battle of Gujerat in February 1849.

Now the Khalsa was crushed and disbanded, Mulraj and his allies were state prisoners, and the Punjab formally annexed by Britain. It remained only to remove the deposed Maharaja to lifelong exile, and present his famous diamond, the Koh-i-Noor, to Queen Victoria, and the macadamising process would be complete.

Of course, everyone wanted to salvage what he or she could from the wreck of old Ranjit Singh's proud kingdom. There were loose ends to be tidied, a new constitution to be agreed, pensions fixed for the Ranis and other redundant members of Dulip Singh's huge household, and a full catalogue of his possessions to be compiled.

All those jewels in the Treasure House, those rooms full of cashmere shawls, tents with poles of silver and gold, plates and goblets, daggers and swords, even a silver summerhouse. No one – not even Missar Makraj – knew exactly what was there. Heaps of gems lay uncounted and unrecorded. What a bitter irony, thought Rohais, that the man who could most easily help himself from that fabulous hoard was one who would never even dream of doing so.

The new Governor of the Citadel, Dr John Login, was an old friend of Sir Henry Lawrence and, from what she had seen of him, in Lawrence's own mould – a high-minded, Bible-thumping Scot who would swoon at the offer of a bribe and die at the stake before he could be persuaded to slip a handful of those uncounted jewels into his own pocket.

Whereas she . . . ! Rohais felt faint with envy just to think of the opportunities available to Dr Login and denied to her.

Available to Thea, too, she reflected, though she was probably too stupid to realise it. It made Rohais wild with jealousy to see her former governess playing the part of hostess when Dr Login entertained. He had assumed day-to-day responsibility for Dulip Singh while Hal worked on assessing pensions, but Dr Login had wished to keep familiar faces around his young charge and this, of course, included Dandy and his mother.

It was beastly unfair! thought Rohais. While Thea was consulted on all matters concerning the Maharaja's health and happiness, she herself merely *existed* on the fringes of court life – a nonentity, the disregarded wife of a Political Officer, living in constant dread of her creditors, unable to afford the clothes she craved, lonely, out of looks, bored, bored, bored!

How long was it since Toby had even come to her bed? Six months at least, thought Rohais, who in fact remembered the last occasion all too well. When he slid his arms round her she had called him a rough, unfeeling brute, and said she would rather sleep alone.

He had pulled himself up on one elbow and looked at her thoughtfully for so long that she had begun to wish she had not spoken. Then he had pulled on a dressing-robe, said that if that was what she wished, he would be happy to oblige her, and had called for his bearer to remove his belongings to another room.

That had been the worst of it. He had as good as told that interfering old fool Ram Dass that he was tired of his wife. Since that night they had slept in different apartments.

All this made the present irregularity in her health somewhat embarrassing. Hinghan Khan had sworn that nothing of the kind could happen, but he was a liar like all Afghans, and was probably planning to blackmail her out of the few miserable rupees she could still call her own.

Well, he was wrong. He would not get another anna out of her, ungrateful wretch that he was. Nowadays he spent most of his time hanging about the barracks, haggling with the European artillerymen who guarded the Citadel. She was well rid of him. Never trust a native, she thought bitterly. In the end they always let you down.

Self-pity brought a lump to her throat. She reached for the glass in its usual place at her elbow and found it empty. *That* was how well she was served!

'*Koi hai?* Brandy-pawnee – *juldi!*' she called, clapping her hands.

When Mustafa shuffled on to the verandah, he carried on the tray along with the bottle and the soda water a letter. 'Chit coming from Palace, Memsahib.' Curiosity glistened in his eyes.

Recognising Thea's handwriting, Rohais opened it languidly. Her sister-in-law wrote to say that Dr Login had expressed a wish to make Mrs Black's acquaintance. He would be pleased if she would honour him with the pleasure of her company at dinner the following week.

So now Thea took it upon herself to send invitations on behalf of the Governor! Was there no end to her officiousness? Rohais's first instinct was to refuse, but that would be cutting off her nose to spite her face, as Miss Peabody used to say. The truth was, she was dying to meet the new Governor, and could not think why he had not asked her to dine before.

'Memsahib going to Palace?' said sly Mustafa, who of course knew what was in the letter.

'None of your business,' snapped Rohais, and Mustafa withdrew, offended.

She would go – oh, yes! Curiosity demanded it. Every morning for the past three weeks she had watched the tall, spare, upright figure of Dr Login canter past her window on his chestnut Kabuli horse, accompanying the Maharaja on his daily ride. She had hoped to attract his attention and now, apparently, she had succeeded. Rohais's instinct told her that even a high-minded Bible-thumping Scotsman need not necessarily be impervious to feminine charm. This was her chance to put it to the test.

'A delightful woman, your sister-in-law,' said Dr Login, smiling at Thea after she had brought Dandy across the garden to join the Maharaja's lessons. She was a bonny lass, he thought. Strange she had stayed single so long after her husband's death. In India most women remarried within the year, but Mrs Quinn seemed content to keep house for her brother and he had not heard her name linked with anyone in particular, though she did not lack for admirers.

'We found we had many friends in common,' he added, 'but I must confess she surprised me when she said you had once been her governess. You must have been very young at the time?'

'It was my first post after leaving the Orphanage,' Thea admitted. 'Sometimes I wonder what would have become of me had Mrs Quinn not chosen me to teach Rohais. I owe her so much.'

'A sad loss to us all,' he agreed. 'I was glad to make her daughter's acquaintance. She was so interested in my work here – I only hope I did not tire her with all my prosing.'

'I am sure you did not,' she said warmly. One of Dr Login's most engaging characteristics was his modesty. He was utterly without conceit and seemed genuinely surprised to find himself in a position of such influence.

Rohais must have behaved well, and Thea was conscious of relief. Of late her sister-in-law had been inclined to bolster her spirits with brandy-pawnee before social engagements, sometimes with embarrassing results. From the faint questioning note in the Governor's voice, she guessed he had heard of this weakness and been pleased to find her reputation exaggerated.

'I have engaged myself to show her round the Toshkhana when I make my next visit,' he said diffidently. 'She was eager to see for herself the "Aladdin's Cave", as she put it! I wonder if you would care to accompany us, Mrs Quinn?'

Was he regretting the invitation and asking her to chaperone him? The thought provoked a smile.

'Do come!' Dr Login continued persuasively. 'I have a particular reason for asking you. I am authorised to choose certain valuables from the Jewel House to form part of

311

the Maharaja's personal property before he surrenders the rest to the Government. Since you know His Highness's tastes as well as anyone, I should be glad of your advice when making my selection.'

It was a request she could hardly refuse; nor did she wish to. Poor little Maharaja! Not only had he lost his mother and his throne in the past year through no fault of his own, and been condemned to perpetual exile, but now his fabulous treasure was to be plundered as well.

Evidently Dr Login shared this view, for he said with a conspiratorial air, 'Between ourselves, Mrs Quinn, I mean to see the little man gets a fair share of the valuables, no matter how much the Government may grumble. He is obliged under the treaty to give up the Koh-i-Noor, but Lord Dalhousie has left it to *my* discretion to choose jewels for His Highness's personal use, and I mean to exercise that power to the full. Do help me!'

'I shall be glad to,' she said. 'He has lost so much. The least we can do is see him well provided for.'

It was agreed that she should compile a list of items which she thought would appeal to the boy, and add it to Dr Login's selection. They would then confer with Missar Makraj and other experts to put together a representative collection of the best in the Treasury.

Thea walked back across the gardens with the comforting certainty that Dr Login, at least, had the interests of his charge uppermost in his mind, and would resist all attempts to pluck this most defenceless pigeon.

On the appointed day, Rohais made her tour of the Toshkhana in an ecstasy of covetousness. Even her dreams had not envisaged such riches. Under Dr Login's supervision, the jewels were being catalogued, assessed and marked for the first time in their history, but it was a long job, and still there remained whole chambers full of jumbled gold and silverware, cashmere shawls and priceless ceremonial trappings for horses and elephants, all heaped in such confusion that even Missar Makraj had no very precise idea of what was there.

In the flickering light of many lamps, diamonds glittered and rubies glowed. Her dazzled eyes ranged over aigrets, armlets, bracelets, rings, earrings, nose-rings, girdles, necklaces, swords, ankuses and jewelled scabbards. There were silken tents, a summerhouse of filigree silver, and ceremonial chariots with golden shafts and ivory wheels.

With a showman's instinct, Dr Login led the little party from room to room, saving the best till last. As they entered the innermost chamber, he murmured an instruction to Missar Makraj, who drew forth from his voluminous robes the armlet the Maharaja had worn for his last birthday.

'The Koh-i-Noor!' breathed Rohais, her eyes like stars.

Silently Missar Makraj displayed it to each lady in turn, though he took care to keep the armlet's strings in his own grasp.

Thea murmured admiringly, but in truth she was a little disappointed. Close examination showed that despite its astonishing size, the great gem had little depth or brilliance. Even her untrained eye could detect the flaw in it, and the colour was more yellowish than blue-white. The setting was heavy, clumsy even, and the flat Indian style of cutting had robbed the stone of much of its potential beauty. Yet despite these imperfections, the legendary diamond still had the power to silence beholders. When Rohais at last spoke, it was in an awed voice very different from her habitual languid drawl.

'Oh, Dr Login, I never saw anything so beautiful! Can I – may I – hold it myself? Just for a tiny moment?'

'Let the Memsahib hold it.'

Slowly the old Guardian unwound the strings from his fingers, reluctant to let the armlet out of his grasp for even an instant. While Rohais examined it he hovered so close that the garlic on his breath overpowered her and she would have waved him away if she dared. No conjurer, however skilled, could have caused it to vanish beneath that vigilant scrutiny, thought Rohais, turning it this way and that while her fingers itched to thrust it in her pocket.

When she sighed and handed it back, it was with the doleful certainty that while the fierce old Guardian had its keeping, the Koh-i-Noor was safer than it would be in the Tower of London.

'The setting is loose,' she told Hinghan Khan, lying with his dark head pillowed on her breast in the green gloom of the creeper-covered summerhouse. 'If that old scarecrow had taken his eye off me for a single minute I could have wrenched it out.' The great diamond obsessed her. She had thought of nothing else since her tour of the Toshkhana.

'There are many other jewels in the Maharaja's Treasury,' said Hinghan Khan, stretching like a lazy cat. 'As many, they say, as stars in the sky. When Missar Makraj waits upon His Highness, anyone can take them.'

'Foolish talk! They are guarded night and day.'

Hinghan Khan said thoughtfully, 'There are those among the soldiers who owe me money.'

'Who does not owe thee money, usurer that thou art?' she taunted in his own tongue, tweaking his ear. 'Half the servants are in thy debt, and I myself can hardly satisfy thy demands.'

He raised his head, staring with his heavy-lidded, unfathomable eyes at her pale nakedness until she twitched irritably at the sheet.

'Well?' she snapped. 'What of thy debtors? Why should they concern me?'

'Because some are men of the artillery, whose duty it is to guard the Toshkhana.'

Despite herself, interest flickered. 'So?'

'The walls are not so thick that a man might not break through – if the sentries looked the other way.'

Rohais caught her breath sharply, and Hinghan Khan abandoned his indolent pose. He rolled over on his stomach, eyes keen, fine-boned face intent.

'Could it be done?' she said doubtfully.

'To breach the wall is simple, if it is done in the right place, but such a fortress has as many cells as a beehive.'

'I have seen where the jewels are kept. I could draw a plan,' said Rohais, catching his excitement.

'Was it not for this that I arranged our meeting?'

Rohais had supposed it was for a different reason. Her affair with Hinghan Khan had followed the usual pattern of clandestine relationships. While she resisted and kept him at arm's length he had been all eagerness, but as soon as she lowered her defences his interest began to wane. Familiarity bred contempt and then boredom. This was the first time for several months that they had disturbed the dust in their secret trysting place.

'Why should I help thee? Thou wilt steal all thou canst carry and run away, leaving me with nothing,' she said bleakly.

'Would *I* do such a thing?'

'Most assuredly, if retribution did not follow.'

'Is not my word surety enough?' He reached for a lock of her long blonde hair, twisting its flaxen silk round his fingers and caressing her neck in the way she loved. But even as she sighed with pleasure, her mind was busy with the question of how far she could trust him.

'When the Maharaja goes into exile, the treasure will be dispersed,' he murmured in her ear. 'Before that day comes, the Lat-Sahib himself will visit Lahore to do him honour, and *that* is when we must strike.'

'During the Governor-General's visit? Are you mad?' She twisted her head round to stare at him.

'It is the best time. Only think! While the guards are running hither and thither with parades and durbars, who will have time to keep watch on the Toshkhana? Missar Makraj will attend the Maharaja, and while he shows the Mountain of Light to all the great sahibs and memsahibs, the other jewels will be mine for the taking! Now listen well, and thou shalt hear my plan.'

Dandy's small, happy universe had begun to crumble. Before long it would vanish altogether and he would be sent alone to a dark, cold, foggy land far from all he knew and loved. With drooping mouth and eyes like dark pools

315

of gloom, he sat cross-legged on his mother's bedroom floor, watching her dress for the grand dinner Dr Login was giving in honour of the Governor-General's visit, and brooded on the sad truth that troubles never come singly.

He was clear-sighted enough to recognise that most of these present troubles sprang from a single cause: the moment when some evil djinn had prompted him to untie the armlet from the Maharaja's sleeve during last year's ill-starred birthday celebrations. Uncle Hal had been very angry and the whipping that had followed was something Dandy would not easily forget. Worse even than the whipping was the change in his uncle's attitude to him. Almost overnight, extreme indulgence had been replaced by excessive strictness. From then on hardly a day had gone by without some reference to the benefit he would derive from an English public school.

'You must not let him grow into a spoilt little nabob. It is no kindness to him or yourself,' he heard Uncle Hal tell his mother. 'Look at him! Petted and pampered like a native prince. A few cold baths and a fagmaster who stands no nonsense would do him no end of good. Make a man of him.'

Cold baths! A *fagmaster*! How horrible it sounded. Dandy resolved to be very good and see if he could not avoid this fate for as long as possible.

But, when the war ended and the proclamation deposing the Maharaja was read and signed, still more British officers and their families took up residence in Lahore. Dozens of voices repeated Uncle Hal's refrain.

'My dear Thea, you'll ruin the boy if you keep him here.'

'Spare the rod and spoil the child.'

'Tying him to your apron-strings does nothing but harm in the long run.'

'Missing the happiest days of his life . . . '

Poor Mamma, bombarded with advice on all sides! But whereas a year ago she would have tossed her red head and said she would bring up her son as she chose, now Dandy saw with dismay that she had begun to listen to the advisers. She asked about schools and fees. She was wavering . . .

Just a fortnight ago, the blow had fallen. She had decided to send him Home, she announced. Her old friend Lady Sale, now a widow, was sailing for England and had agreed to take her godson's child under her wing. During the school holidays, his father's uncle and his wife had been persuaded to provide young Daniel Alexander with a roof over his head.

'I won't go, Mamma. I'll run away!'

Mamma had tightened her mouth until she looked quite grim and had said she did not intend to discuss the matter any further. It was time he went to a proper school. She had made up her mind and completed the arrangements, and that was *that*.

'She won't listen to me, Uncle Toby,' he had complained later. 'Can't you do anything?'

With his mother and Uncle Hal united against him, Hinghan Khan busy with his own mysterious projects, and the Maharaja's mood swinging between excitement and apprehension as preparations for his move to India were put in hand, Uncle Toby was the only person from whom Dandy could expect a fair hearing. Brusque, perhaps, but fair.

'You can hardly blame her, old fellow.' Toby looked up from the gun he was cleaning. 'I am sure she believes she is acting in your best interest.'

'Do you think she is?'

'Does that matter?' A glance at the boy's quivering lips told him it did. He put a firm hand on Dandy's shoulder and said quite angrily, 'No, I don't, and so I have told your mother, but she won't listen to me any more than to you. But then, I am eccentric. I don't believe in separating children from the civilising influence of their families and herding them together in boarding schools. Never mind! You'll survive the experience, just as the rest of them do, and you can comfort yourself with the reflection that you have already escaped a couple of years of school life. That's not bad going, I'd say. Most of the poor little devils

317

are sent away at the age of eight, so you have cause to be thankful. There you are! You asked my opinion and you've got it, for what it is worth.' He smiled suddenly. 'Cheer up, Dandy! It won't seem so long, after all. When you come back we'll celebrate with a month's *shikar* in the Kerali Hills. Just you and me.'

'And Hinghan Khan?'

'Of course. If he is still here, that is.'

'Oh, he'll be here.' Dandy was confident. 'Papa made me promise to look after him, you know. Sometimes he talks of going back to Afghanistan, but only when he's angry with me.'

'Is he often angry with you?'

Dandy looked uncomfortable. It was another of his worries that Hinghan Khan spent so much time hanging about the barracks where the European soldiers were billeted. His mother would be displeased if she knew, but when he said so to Hinghan Khan, he had laughed disagreeably and said he was no longer a boy to be ordered about by a woman.

'N-not often,' he said constrainedly.

'I am glad to hear it,' said Toby.

That conversation had improved Dandy's spirits a little. It was good to know that Uncle Toby agreed with him, even if his mother would not listen to either of them . . .

'How do I look?' asked Thea, turning from the dressing-table with a smile. Dandy studied her attentively. For a mother, he thought, she did not look at all bad.

She wore a flounced gown of pale lavender silk, cut low enough to display her white shoulders and neck to advantage. It was tightly fitted in the waist and very full in the skirt. At her throat was the triple row of pearls he knew Papa had given her as a wedding present, which matched the earrings and bracelet he had given her before leaving for Afghanistan. Her flaming hair was drawn back from her brow, piled high and twined with fresh flowers and more pearls, with just a few frivolous curls allowed to escape about her temples and ears. She carried a fan of painted silk, and the flowers in her corsage were secured with a brooch of milkily opalescent moonstones given her recently by Uncle Hal.

'Well, darling?'

'You look beautiful,' said Dandy, adding gloomily, 'I wish I could come with you. Dippy won't enjoy the dinner half as much as I should.'

Her mind was already elsewhere. She did not even appear to notice his use of the forbidden nickname. She and Narwan, her ayah, began fussing over which shawl she should wear, and Dandy relapsed into his own thoughts.

All week the Citadel had echoed to the tramp of marching men and elephants, camels and horses, to shrill bugle calls and jingling harnesses. The Maharaja had ridden out to meet the Governor-General and welcome him to his capital, and in his turn Lord Dalhousie had ridden forth to escort the Maharaja to his tented city outside the walls. Each had held a magnificent durbar. There had been parades and reviews, presentations and interminable meals, at all of which Dulip Singh had had a leading ceremonial role.

A lot of silly fuss, thought Dandy, deprived of his friend's admiring company and feeling left out. He was so used to being treated as a person of consequence that it came as an unpleasant shock to discover that in Lord Dalhousie's eyes he was quite unimportant, existing only as an English playfellow for the Maharaja.

Tonight's great durbar dinner would be the final ceremony of the state visit, and when the Governor-General had departed the next day along with all the panoply and splendour of his tented city, it would be time for the last Maharaja of the Sikhs to assemble his own convoy for the journey into exile.

Time, too, for Dandy to sail to England.

'What will I do without you?' Dulip Singh had asked mournfully. 'Who will ride with me and fly my falcon when you are gone? Who will make me laugh?'

'It's all very well for you,' said Dandy pettishly. 'I don't know why you are complaining. *You* don't have to go to a beastly school with cold baths and beatings. You can go on doing just as you please, you lucky devil. The Proclamation says so. You won't even have to sit through all those silly durbars now you've been deposed.'

Dulip Singh's eyes flashed. He had always enjoyed sitting on the *guddee* with his feet tucked under him, dispensing justice and listening to the long, repetitive petitions that would have driven an English boy mad with boredom.

'You must not speak so disrespectfully of the customs of my country,' he said stiffly.

'It won't be your country much longer,' pointed out Dandy with a lamentable lack of tact. 'Not unless the Sikhs attack your convoy. I say! Perhaps they'll kill Dr Login and carry you off. What a lark that would be!'

Dulip Singh did not think it would be a lark at all. He had become very attached to Dr Login, whom he called his Ma-Bap, or foster father, and had no wish to be captured and used as a figurehead by his turbulent, intriguing fellow-countrymen. Dr Login had promised to take him to London one day and present him to the young Queen. He longed to see England almost as much as Dandy yearned to stay in India.

'We ought to change places,' said Dandy moodily. 'You could go to my horrible school and I would live in your new palace and go hawking every day.'

Hawking was Dandy's latest passion. When Mamma had finished dressing and left the house, he thought he would go down to the mews and talk to Mustafa Kemal, the Maharaja's head falconer. He might find Hinghan Khan there too, taking bets on tomorrow's races and gossiping with the syces. The barracks would be deserted tonight, since every soldier who could be spared from guard was already lining the route to the Citadel in readiness for the arrival of the Governor-General.

Darkness had fallen when Dandy slipped out of the gate and threaded his way through narrow streets he knew as well as a rabbit knows its warren. He loved the city at night, though it was strange to find all the alleys empty at an hour when normally every merchant and stallholder, craftsman and man of business would be about his affairs. Tonight the little booths were shuttered. Everyone had gone to watch the procession, but Dandy had had enough of parades and proclamations, pomp and ceremony. He wanted to forget it all in comforting, familiar talk of hawks and horses and hounds.

His luck was out. In the moonlit mews the hawks sat hooded and motionless on their perches. Mustafa Kemal had not been able to resist the lure of the procession.

Dandy walked on. In the royal stables, at least, he could be sure of company. There would be bustle and shouting, horses being walked and washed down, harnesses polished, manes combed to floating perfection.

Mamma would be horrified, he thought, if she knew how often he came here when she believed him tucked up in bed. For the first time in all his nocturnal prowls, he felt a little guilty at deceiving her. Aunt Rohais knew, of course, for Hinghan Khan had told her. She thought it very funny that Mamma believed the lies Dandy told her. But lately he had begun to realise that anything which discomfited his mother amused Aunt Rohais. Poor Mamma! She tried so hard to be both father and mother to him. Dulip Singh thought it wonderful that she would play games and run about in a way that even the youngest Ranis would not dream of doing. All the same, there were some things she simply could not manage: throwing a cricket ball, for instance, or impaling a wriggling maggot on a hook. It was when he came up against one of these disabilities that Dandy felt the burden his father had laid on him when he said he must be the man of the family.

What was that? Dandy stopped suddenly, his attention focused on a muffled tapping which seemed to come from within the Toshkhana's encircling wall. Nimbly as a cat he scrambled up the rough-hewn sandstone blocks which formed the outer fortification and peered down into the courtyard.

Immediately below him, twin pinpricks of glowing ash marked the positions of two sentries, lounging against the wall, snatching their chance of a gossip and a smoke while their officers were otherwise engaged. Dandy grinned. He wondered how close he could get before they became aware of his presence, and began to look for the best place to drop down from the wall.

Tap-tap-tap. Thud-thud-thud.

Two other dark shapes detached themselves from the shadows and joined the smokers. From the way they moved he could tell they were Europeans, not native sentries. He tried to remember which regiment was on guard duty this week. Wiltshires? Cornwalls? He could hear heavy breathing, as of men unused to physical labour in a hot climate.

Then one spoke and Dandy's scalp prickled, for the low, furtive tone was instantly recognisable as that of a man up to no good.

'Nearly through. Couple more good swings and she'll go easy.'

'I'll finish 'er off.' The speaker flung away his glowing stub.

'No. Wait till 'e comes. Should be 'ere soon.'

Silence. Then the first speaker said irritably, 'Where the devil's the black bastard got to? Can't 'ang about 'ere much longer. Abdul will wonder where I am.'

Silence again. As the moon sailed out from behind a cloud, he saw them more clearly. Four heads turning this way and that, waiting . . . For whom? For what? He sensed their tension and lay still as a lizard on his wall, knowing they would deal roughly with an eavesdropper.

' 'Ere 'e is!'

A fifth shadow had materialised from the surrounding darkness. Voices dropped as they huddled together, arguing. Dandy caught the odd phrase.

' . . . at the end 'ouse. Under the bleedin' wall.'

' . . . dare double-cross us . . . '

' 'Urry! 'Urry! Abdul's on 'is way back!'

Dandy was quivering with excitement and alarm. Should he run and alert the sentries? But these *were* the sentries. Everyone else was watching the procession. Better wait and see . . .

The dark shapes had returned to where they had been working. Twice the pickaxe thudded dully against the wall. The third blow produced a different sound, a kind of hollow crunch, and the pick-wielder dropped his tool.

'Whew! That's done it. 'E can get through there. Big enough for a little 'un.'

' 'Urry up now. In you go, and don't forget . . . '

' 'Ere, 'Ardyman, run and keep Abdul 'appy while we patch it up arter 'im.'

For a few moments there was intense activity round the wall. Then an urgent voice hissed: ' 'Op it! Quick!' and they scattered. Dandy was left looking down into an empty courtyard with only the soft shuffle of retreating footsteps to prove he had not imagined it all.

Carefully he lowered himself to the full extent of his arms and dropped on to the hard-packed earth. At a casual glance the wall looked normal enough, but the breach – cunningly placed where a buttress overshadowed it – was easy enough to spot if you knew where to look.

Two big sandstone blocks had been levered out and loosely replaced, leaving a narrow gap that a slim body could slide through.

Curiosity battled with caution – supposing the sentries came back? But Dandy knew there was really no question. He must see for himself what was happening and, if possible, take a look at the thief. The eel-like way he had slithered through the gap proved clearly enough that the soldiers were making use of a native thief. Without dwelling too much on thoughts of what might happen if he was armed, Dandy wriggled through the breached wall and padded forward.

Moonlight filtered through marble latticework high above. He was, he soon realised, in one of the outer storerooms where carriages and harnesses and elephants' ceremonial trappings were jumbled in chaotic heaps – an area of the Treasury to which Dr Login's catalogue compilers had not yet brought order. The silvery light shed a faint radiance upon gilded furniture and gleaming ivory. The thick, warm, musty smell tickled Dandy's nose.

He strained his senses for some indication of the direction his quarry had taken, and was rewarded by a faint chink of metal. Past rooms full of shawls in bales, of armour and gold and silver vessels, he padded silently, keeping close to the wall. In one of the chambers, the thief was scooping jewels into a sack with frantic haste, hardly even looking at what he was taking. He plunged his hands into bowls full of precious stones, swept ropes of pearls and rings threaded on strings into his sack, then picked up the clinking burden and carried it into the passage, so close that Dandy smelt the rank scent of fear on him.

The thief returned to the jewel-chamber and a moment later Dandy heard the scrape of a lucifer. A dark lantern was lit, spreading a subdued glow over the cluttered shelves as the thief moved to and fro, searching systematically now, picking up items and scrutinising them before discarding them or tucking them in his sash. These must be the spoils he meant to keep for himself, smaller – more valuable – than the hastily snatched loot he would give the soldiers. Dandy began to edge closer, hoping for a glimpse of his face.

Dust swirled up from the floor, irritating his eyes and making his nose itch unbearably. Suddenly, with awful certainty, he felt a sneeze coming and clapped his hands over his face to smother it.

In vain. Once, twice, three times he sneezed explosively, and after an instant's shocked silence, the thief panicked. Whirling round and knocking over his lantern, he bolted for the passage, grabbing up the heavy sack he had filled. As he scurried away down the passage, tongues of flame licked at the spilt oil and quickly spread to dry wood and silken rugs. Smoke began to billow towards the door.

Dandy ran after the robber. By the time he reached the harness storeroom, the fugitive had wriggled through the gap between the stones and was about to pull the sack after him when Dandy, coming up behind, grabbed it.

They grappled silently, tugging from either side. Dandy was strong for his age and determined. Nevertheless, he felt himself being dragged forward until both he and the sack were halfway through the aperture.

Still he clung desperately, fingers locked in a bulldog's grip. His head and shoulders slid into the open. He braced his legs against the crumbling wall, trying to get a purchase, and looked up into the fierce, concentrated face of Hinghan Khan.

'*You!*' he breathed.

For a fatal second surprise relaxed his grip and the sack was twitched out of his grasp. Then a heavy blow on the back of the head plunged him into blackness.

CHAPTER EIGHTEEN

From his seat at the end of the table, Dr Login looked down the long expanse of polished mahogany with a rare glow of satisfaction. Not that much of the wood could be seen beneath the silver and glass, cutlery and candles, flowers, place cards, finger-bowls with floating lotus blossoms, and all the other impedimenta of a grand dinner. The *burra-khana* was nearing its end, and even the host's hyperanxious eye had found nothing to criticise in the setting or service of the long, elaborate meal.

The Governor-General had been effusively gracious, the company convivial and well behaved. No one – except possibly young Mrs Black – had drunk too much; there had been none of the culinary disasters common to Anglo-Indian entertaining. The ladies had withdrawn some time ago, and now port and brandy were making their final rounds of the flushed and jovial gentlemen.

Dr Login turned to address a remark to the judge who was sitting on his left side, and found between them a slim brown hand offering him a silver salver with a folded chit on it. Frowning, Login scanned it. Then with a hasty word of apology, he hurried from the room.

In the book-lined chamber opening on to the gardens which served as his study, the officer on guard duty awaited him. Captain Connell of the Queen's 53rd was a thin, lugubrious young man whose manner always suggested he had bad news to tell. On this occasion his looks did not belie him.

Login greeted him briskly. 'A fire? At the Treasury? That's bad. You have it under control? Good. Good. Is there much damage?'

In doom-laden tones Captain Connell made his report. The native sentry had smelt smoke and raised the alarm soon after eleven. The State Treasurer and his assistant had been summoned to unlock the gates, but the fire had proved to be quite a small affair. A few buckets of water were enough to extinguish it and there was little damage.

'Hm. How did it start?'

'An overturned lantern, sir.'

'A *lantern*! Robbers?'

'I fear so, sir.'

'Go on,' said Login grimly. 'Let me hear the worst.'

All the warmth and satisfaction of dinner had vanished. He felt cold, sickened by the persistence of human greed. All his care, all the meticulous arrangements he had devised to protect the precious contents of the Toshkhana set at naught, and – as a special blow to his pride – during the State Visit.

Captain Connell continued his recital. Believing the thieves might still be in the building, he had instituted an immediate search. A breach had been discovered in the outer wall.

'Under the noses of the sentries?'

'Yes, sir.'

This put a still worse complexion on the matter. It meant the breach must have been made with the connivance of the guards, if not their active assistance.

'Who was on guard duty?'

'First Bombay Fusiliers, sir.'

One of the Company's European regiments – worse and worse! Dr Login said quickly, 'Had any attempt been made to conceal the breach?'

'No, sir. It looks as if the thieves left in a hurry. We found several lucifers at the scene, and . . . ' He hesitated fractionally. ' . . . and a boy.'

'A native?'

'No, sir. It is young Daniel Quinn.'

'What the devil was he doing there?'

'I don't know, sir.'

'Didn't you ask him?'

'He's injured, sir. Unconscious. I had him carried to the civil hospital. Dr Talbot is attending him.'

'This is terrible!' Login sprang up and paced the floor,

327

thinking hard. He said, 'Order all the Citadel gates to be closed immediately.'

'I have already done so, sir.'

'Good. Not a soul must pass out without a written permission from me. Put all sentries on full alert and make a strict search round the Treasury in case the thieves are still in hiding.'

'Sir.'

'Summon the Kotwal to attend me, and instruct the Assistant Magistrates to offer a reward of – of a thousand rupees, diminishing by one hundred daily, for information leading to the discovery of the thieves and recovery of any stolen property.'

'Sir.'

'The barracks must be searched at once.'

'But, sir, Colonel Money – '

'The barracks will be searched whether Colonel Money likes it or not,' said Login crisply. 'You will also impose a curfew on all persons in the Citadel. They must not leave their quarters or communicate with one another until further notice. Is that clear?'

'But sir,' said Captain Connell a little hesitantly, 'your guests – '

'Ah, yes. My guests,' said Login heavily. 'These orders cannot, of course, apply to them. Have you anything to add?'

'Young Quinn, sir. He may have seen something.'

'Leave that to me. Time enough to question the poor lad when he recovers his senses. Report back to me when you have carried out my instructions. Oh, and ask Dr Black if he would spare me a moment. He may be able to throw light on this affair.'

Connell saluted and withdrew. For a few minutes Dr Login stared at the miniature of his wife, propped on the corner of his desk. He wondered how best to break the news that her son was injured to Mrs Quinn. She had been in such looks and spirits tonight. This would be a sad shock to her. He sighed. Lord Dalhousie must be informed, too, but that could wait. First he would consult with Toby Black, then call in old Missar Makraj and try to establish just what had been stolen. What a shocking business! Just when he had been fool enough to congratulate himself on the way his arrangements were working. Well, they said pride went before a fall. *Quis custodiet ipsos custodes?* he thought ruefully. If the British sentries could not be trusted, all his care was useless. His first task must be to catch and punish them and recover all they had taken.

By degrees the calm gaze of his wife restored his serenity, as it always had the power to. All was not lost. With God's help he would get to the bottom of this trouble before it damaged Anglo-Sikh relations.

Login said a brief prayer and composed his features into their usual expression of calm cheerfulness. Then he went to bid his guests farewell.

'Memsahib, wake up! You must hide me. Wake up!'

An insistent pressure on her instep roused Rohais from her brandy-hazed sleep. She had hardly been able to sit still through the long ceremonial dinner or make polite responses to the pompous old bores to the right and left of her, so intently was her mind fixed on what Hinghan Khan might be doing. Would his nerve fail at the eleventh hour? Afghans were braggarts, always making wild plans which came to nothing. She had done all in her power to bolster his resolution, taunting him with faint-heartedness when he spoke of the dangers, playing on his love of money, repeating what he already knew: they would never get so good a chance again.

The Bombay Fusiliers on guard duty were in debt to Hinghan Khan. They would cover his tracks and hold their tongues in return for a share of the loot. It might be months before the loss was discovered, and by then she and Hinghan Khan would have long disposed of their booty.

Too nervous to eat, she had drunk too much, but she and the other ladies had already withdrawn from the table before Dr Login was summoned out of the dining-room, and nothing in his demeanour when he took leave of his guests had warned her that the theft had been discovered.

They had agreed to preserve an appearance of complete normality and wait several days before meeting to share out the stolen gems. It was therefore with a sense of actue annoyance that she opened her eyes now to see Hinghan Khan standing at the foot of her bed, turban awry, face and clothes streaked with dust and cobwebs, eyes white-ringed with alarm.

'What is the matter?' she hissed, for her ayah slept across the doorway. 'I told you not to come here.'

'Hush, do not make a noise.' He glanced nervously over his shoulder.

'Why not? What's the matter?'

As he bent towards her, she saw his face was glistening with sweat. Her own heart contracted suddenly. Something had gone wrong – badly wrong. Nothing remained of Hinghan Khan's cool, arrogant composure. He had gone to pieces.

'Hide me, hide me!' he babbled. 'The soldiers are hunting me. Login-Sahib, Keeper of the Citadel, has closed the gates. They will hang me, shoot me, blow me from a gun!'

His panic and the threat of discovery cleared Rohais's mind as nothing else could have done. A surge of anger overwhelmed her. How typical of a native she thought. He bungles the robbery and comes blundering to me, leaving a trail like a rogue elephant!

'Where are the jewels?' she demanded.

He stared at her stupidly, eyes rolling back. 'I – I gave them to the soldiers.'

'All of them, fool? All of them?'

At last he seemed to grasp what she was saying, and fumbled at his girdle, drawing out a pouch and tipping it on to the bed as if he could hardly bear to touch it.

'Take them! Take them! They are accursed.'

He covered his face with his hands.

The sparkling cascade poured on to the sheet, glinting in the moonlight. Precious stones – more, far more than she had dreamed he could steal. Rohais caught her breath. Up to that moment she had never quite believed he would get inside the Toshkhana, for all his boasting. It had been a fantasy, an enthralling game of Let's Pretend. Suddenly it was real, and excitement bubbled up within her. Here under her hands was a fortune. A king's ransom! Her passage to England!

'Hide me,' whined Hinghan Khan, plucking at the sheet. 'They will catch me and kill me. What shall I do?'

The blood of generations of officers rose to meet the emergency. 'Pull yourself together,' she snapped. 'Now! Tell me what happened.'

As he blurted out his story, her mind darted here and there, seeking a way of escape. The jewels were hers! No one should take them from her. By the time he stopped speaking, she was ready with her plan.

She asked, 'Can the soldiers betray you? Do they know who you are?'

He was recovering from his panic now, and replied with a touch of his old sang-froid, 'No, Memsahib. They call me "black bastard" and " 'Ere, you!" I have not told them my name.'

'Good.' She considered a moment, then said, 'Listen carefully, for we must not speak together again. Leave the jewels with me and go at once to your quarters. Stay there, pretending illness, until the hunt dies down. I shall leave tomorrow, to visit a friend in Ferozepore. She knew my mother, and has often asked me to stay with her. I will take the jewels with me, and later, when all is quiet, you shall join me there.'

'How will you carry them out of the Citadel? No one may pass the gates without a paper signed by Login-Sahib.'

She laughed, exhilarated by the danger. 'Fool that thou art,' she scoffed in her old, affectionate tone. 'If I ride forth in the Lat-Sahib's train, who will dare to search my baggage?'

His face cleared. He salaamed gracefully, touching his

fingers to his brow. 'It is well,' he murmured. 'Thus can they be carried past the guards. And I? What shall I do?'

'Just as I said. Go to bed and feign fever if any question thee. When it is safe, I will send word.'

He melted into the moonlit shadows, and she let out her breath slowly, scarcely daring to believe that the coup had succeeded; that the jewels were in her hands. She played with them, trickling them through her fingers, enjoying their cool smoothness with a miser's delight.

Further sleep was out of the question. She lay on one elbow, her arm curled protectively round her treasure, while outside the sky grew pearly grey and the crows struck up their harsh salute to the dawn.

Dandy lay on a cot in his mother's boudoir, his face nearly as pale as the bandages enveloping his head, his lashes dark half-moons beneath his shadowed eyes. Above the bed he listened to the grown-ups talking softly, afraid of disturbing him.

'Keep him as quiet as you can.' That was Uncle Toby's voice. Dandy heard the snap of his medical case. 'I know that's easier said than done,' he added, as through the windows came the muffled roar of the crowd watching the departure of the Governor-General.

Since the Citadel was still under curfew, none of the population were allowed on the streets, which had been blocked off by armed guards while the procession made its slow way to the city gate. All the same, enough people had achieved vantage points on balconies and rooftops to satisfy Lord Dalhousie's expressed desire to see and be seen by Queen Victoria's newest subjects, and their dutiful cheers mingled with the rattle of firecrackers and the furious squealing of elephants jostling for position.

'Give me strength!' exclaimed Toby in exasperation. 'The sooner His Excellency takes his travelling circus back to Calcutta, the better I shall be pleased. How can I investigate a robbery with half my men snatched away for ceremonial duties and the other half drunk?'

He looked tired and distracted, his hair rumpled and his linen coat as badly creased as if he had slept in it.

'Has Rohais gone with them? I didn't see her this morning,' said Thea. 'My ayah told me she has gone to stay with Mrs Marshall in Ferozepore.'

'God knows what pleasure she'll get from travelling with such a crew,' he said contemptuously. 'Well, there's no accounting for tastes. So long as Mrs Marshall looks after her.'

'Oh, I'm sure she will,' said Thea, correctly translating this as a hope that Mrs Marshall could keep Rohais out of mischief. But Ferozepore was only a small, dull station, offering little chance to even the most determined trouble-maker, and Major Marshall, a dyspeptic antiquarian in his sixties, was hardly the type to attract Rohais's roving fancy.

Toby was looking at her questioningly, and she wondered how much he guessed of what she was thinking. Sometimes Thea sensed a weariness in his manner as he made excuses for Rohais.

'Will you be all right now?' he asked. 'I must be off and see what they've dug up at the barracks. I'll leave you a sleeping-draught. Mind you take it! You look in need of a good sleep.'

'Allow me to offer you the same advice, my dear doctor!'

Years ago, her compulsion to challenge his male superiority used to irritate him. Now he recognised it as one of the mainsprings of her resilience.

'An admirable notion, Mrs Quinn, but if I accept it, I will be neglecting my duty to Dr Login. Poor chap, it will look bad for him if we don't lay these robbers by the heels. Missar Makraj puts the loss above six lakhs.'

'So much! Sixty thousand pounds?'

'That's only a rough estimate, of course, and the stolen goods must still be within the Citadel. Captain Connell had the good sense to close the gates as soon as the alarm was raised. If the thieves had had time to repair the breached wall at their leisure – as, no doubt, they meant to – the loss might not have been discovered for days. Weeks, even. We have Dandy to thank for that.'

'Do you think he will remember what happened?' she asked as they moved towards the door.

'I can't say. He has had a bad crack on the head, and memory plays strange tricks. We shall have to wait and see.'

He laid a hand on her shoulder, and to his surprise her own fingers rose to clasp his.

'Thank you,' she murmured.

Her vulnerability touched him; more than that, some long-suppressed emotion he had never allowed himself to examine surfaced so suddenly that he was taken by surprise. Drawn by an irresistible compulsion he bent his head to seek her lips.

'*Toby!*'

Abruptly he drew back, his mind in turmoil. 'I'm sorry. I – I don't know what came over me.'

Didn't he? Eleanor's daughter. Eleanor's smile . . . Good God, what was the matter with him? Shaken and puzzled, he took himself off, and only remembered as he cantered away toward the barracks that he had never given her a sleeping-draught after all.

The long leather boots which James had given him were Hinghan Khan's special pride. Their appearance provided an accurate barometer to his state of mind. When happy, he neglected them, but if ever he was worried or uneasy he lavished care on them, boning out each tiny scratch and buffing them to a glassy shine.

In the days following the Governor-General's departure, Thea noticed the unusually high polish on Hinghan Khan's boots, and wondered what was preying on his mind. It must be Dandy's accident, she decided, seeing the way he hung about the sickroom. She tried to reassure him by repeating Dr Black's opinion that the Chota-Sahib would soon remember the events of that night.

'One day, his memory will return,' she said. 'It is only a matter of time.'

That was just what Hinghan Khan feared. He watched Dandy carefully, but in the week following the robbery the boy gave no sign of recalling what he had seen. Sometimes he would mutter in his sleep, but as the days passed the young Afghan grew more confident that the moment of startled recognition had been obliterated.

Yet even as that worry faded, another rose to plague him. Though the curfew had been lifted and the people of the Citadel were again free to come and go as they pleased, no word had come from Rohais to summon him to Ferozepore. Hinghan Khan's ready suspicions flared: *she meant to cheat him*. He knew – none better – her capacity for deceit; the way she ignored debts and broke promises with a smile. He should never have given the jewels to her. How could he now reclaim them?

When a messenger eventually delivered a letter from her, it was addressed to Thea. She was, she wrote, enjoying herself very much; she had met a great many interesting people and attended a number of balls in honour of the Governor-General. Towards the end she added with elaborate casualness that Lady Anstruther was pressing her to accept an invitation to spend the Cold Weather with her. Would dearest Thea be so kind as to care for little Lucy until she returned?

'Depend on it, she means to take ship for England if she gets half a chance,' said Hal shrewdly, when shown this epistle. 'This is the thin end of the wedge, no doubt. Poor Black! Now she has slipped her leash, he will have his work cut out to entice her back. Well, my dear sister, you might as well face up to the fact that you've gained yourself a daughter.'

'How nice that would be!' For a moment she allowed her thoughts to dwell on that bitter morning when she woke to find her own daughter stiff in her arms. Vicky would be much the same age . . .

'My sympathy is for poor Black,' said Hal, not without a touch of complacency. 'God knows how he has put up with her megrims so long! I never knew such a feather-headed female. Sometimes I wonder if she is really as silly as she likes us to believe.'

'Why on earth should she pretend?' asked Thea, laughing.

'That's what puzzles me. She's thick as thieves with Hinghan Khan, and you know what I think of *him*.'

'You must admit he is useful with the horses.'

'And who does that benefit?' asked Hal dryly. 'He spends twice as much time with Rohais's nags as he does with yours or mine.'

'Dear Hal, you *are* in a critical mood this morning! Ayah would say you got out of bed the wrong side.'

'I don't like seeing them take advantage of your good nature,' said Hal doggedly. 'If I were you, I should send Master Hinghan Khan packing. He has battened on you quite long enough. As for your sister-in-law, I should tell Toby Black quite plainly that now the war is over there is no need for his wife and child to live here with us.'

'I can't do that, Hal!'

'I don't see why not. She's no friend of yours, my dear. I've seen her watching you when she thought no one was looking, and if ever there was jealousy in a woman's eyes, it was in hers.'

'Oh, Hal, that's absurd! Why should she be jealous of me?'

'Use your head, my love. For one thing, I have no doubt she begrudges Dandy the size of his inheritance, and feels ill-used that her father did not leave more of his fortune to her.'

Thea looked worried. 'She is always hard up, it's true, but I know she'll spend anything I give her – '

'The old General knew that too, you can depend on it,' said Hal firmly. 'He was a shrewd old bird. What puzzles me most is why Black lets her carry on the way she does. Can't he see she's making herself a laughing-stock, besides getting us a bad reputation among the natives?'

'Love is blind,' said Thea sadly.

'Love!' Hal snorted. 'Well, *chacun à son goût*.' His own taste was for a rich, well-born female who would bring solid advantage to his career. The Governor of Bombay's second daughter, Evangeline, embodied all the qualities he sought, and he hoped to announce their betrothal soon.

'Of course,' he added thoughtfully, 'Black was head over ears in love with our mother once – do you remember? It used to make Papa wild with rage, not that she cared! *De mortuis* and all that, but there's no denying that Mamma had a good deal in common with Rohais. You were probably too young to see how she enjoyed playing the deuce with all the young men in the station. Poor Papa! What a dance she led him! She was always complaining how deadly dull it was living in the *mofussil*, and urging him to apply for a transfer. I suppose it *was* dull for her . . . '

They were silent, lost in the past. Then Hal said briskly, 'Here are the horses. I must be off. Shahpur tonight, then on to Nawabganj and over the Bejar Hills. I'll be back next Thursday, God willing and old Hotspur's legs permitting. If he goes lame on me I'll have to make do with Ram Gopal's nag. Goodbye, my dear. Look after yourself.'

'Godspeed, dear brother!'

He kissed her cheek, and she watched him run down the steps and speak to the syce holding Hotspur, then feel the old horse's legs and grimace a little before swinging into the saddle.

Hotspur looked sound enough now, she thought as the small cavalcade trotted away, but this must be his last tour of the district. It was Hal's birthday on Friday, and her present to him would be a tough, good-looking Herati stallion which she had bought at Captain Shadwell's dispersal sale without Hal's knowledge.

She smiled, enjoying her secret. Hotspur had earned his retirement. When Hal had been gone an hour, she sent for Hinghan Khan and told him to ride over and fetch the new horse while the Commissioner-Sahib was on tour. She wanted him well fed and looking his best for his new owner's return.

'I will fetch him today, Memsahib.'

Hinghan Khan's face looked drawn, and his eyes burned feverishly. His boots gleamed as if he had spent all night polishing them.

'Tell me,' she said on impulse, 'is there something troubling you, Hinghan Khan?'

'What should trouble me, Memsahib?'

'I am asking you. Is there anything you wish to discuss with me? You know I will help if I can.'

'Nothing is wrong, Memsahib.'

'You have quite recovered from your fever?'

He assented, adding after a fractional pause, 'When does the Hakim's Mem return? I have no orders for the horses.'

'Oh dear. I can't help you there. You must speak to Dr Black when he comes home.' It was typical of Rohais to have gone off without leaving instructions, but she was glad to have discovered what was troubling Hinghan Khan.

'When will she return?' he repeated.

'I don't know yet.'

'Did she not write it in her letter, Memsahib?'

She was surprised at his persistence, and said firmly, 'I tell you I do not know when she will return.'

He went off, muttering to himself, and she wondered what she had said to upset him. He was becoming very moody. She wished she could take Hal's advice and send him back to Afghanistan. Surely James would not have expected her to keep him beside her for the rest of her life?

Brooding over the news, Hinghan Khan went to the kennels and collected Dandy's dogs, then chirruped to the pet myna, which fluttered down and perched on his shoulder. At once the young lemur which Dandy had reared on the bottle loped across the enclosure and ran up to his other shoulder, chattering jealously.

Thus loaded, he crossed the courtyard and entered the boudoir adjoining Thea's own bedroom, where the invalid was holding court.

The Maharaja and his retinue had arrived for their daily visit. Hinghan Khan put down the monkey and myna and slipped unobtrusively into the embrasure of a window, where he began to search the dogs' ears for thorns.

Dulip Singh had made up his mind to view his change of circumstances in as rosy a light as he could. The beastly war was over and he could look forward to a new life. He was determined not to regret the old one. Those troublesome, quarrelsome Sikhs, always fighting for one reason or another! He was glad to be leaving them behind for the British to knock some sense into. Of course he was sorry to lose his great Koh-i-Noor, but dear Dr Login and Mrs Quinn had chosen plenty of fine jewels for him to take to Futtehpore, and above all things, he wanted to live like an English boy.

Under Dr Login's influence, the Maharaja had embraced British ways with enthusiasm. Sometimes, when he passed a foraging Brahmin bull, he even wondered secretly what beef tasted like.

'I say, old boy, good news!' he exclaimed now, perching on the end of Dandy's bed. 'Two of the rotters who raided the Toshkhana have confessed their crimes to Dr Login.'

'Have you got back your jewels, then?'

'Alas, not all. Some are missing still, but chin up! We shall soon lay hands on them.' He tucked his small feet under him and looked closely at his friend. 'By Jove, old fellow, you look very seedy still! Has your memory come back to you?'

'Not really. My head aches, you know.'

'Did you not see the faces of the miscreants?'

Dandy frowned. The question was hard to answer. He made an effort to explain. 'I feel as if there's a door in my mind which begins to swing open, but before I can see behind it, it slams shut again.'

'Aha! Most illuminating. And what does Dr Black say about this swinging door? Will it open to reveal the thieves?'

'He says I must be patient.'

The Maharaja wrinkled his nose disapprovingly. 'If you

are seedy, you should not keep your bedchamber full of wild beasts. It is not good for your health.'

It was true that a fair proportion of Dandy's menagerie had infiltrated the sickroom with their own distinctive smells. A young cheetah was lying in a heraldic pose on a low couch, the lemur groomed her fur on the crown of the mosquito-netting, and the myna had taken up her usual station on the *punkah*, now hanging idle because the Cold Weather had begun. Grip and Fang, Dandy's fox-terriers, bustled importantly to and fro, sniffing ankles.

'I like having them here,' said Dandy. 'They don't talk, you know, and bother me.'

'You mean I bother you?' The Maharaja was offended.

'Don't be an ass! I like people who tell me what they've been doing. It's only when they ask questions that my head aches.'

'Oho, then you shall hear what I have been doing!' This was just the opening Dulip Singh wanted. He launched into a spirited account of yesterday's races.

'Some wag had entered his horse in the name of *Doctor Login*!' he chortled. 'How we all shouted, "Come on, Doctor Login! Gallop faster, Doctor Login!" It was a good joke.'

Dandy smiled dutifully, but his attention was wandering. The door in his mind had begun to swing open again, just a crack at first, then inch by tantalising inch the gap widened. He was drifting, running through dark, cluttered chambers thick with dust, tripping and stumbling after a will-o'-the-wisp flitting ahead. Behind them roared flames, muffling the Maharaja's animated chatter. If only the fugitive would turn and show his face . . .

With a startled gasp, he woke. The features he had glimpsed in his dream were still imprinted on his mind's eye. Across the room they stared at him, but now he was no longer asleep.

'Dandee! You are not listening to me!' reproached Dulip Singh. 'Shall I waste my breath talking when you respond only with snores?'

'I – I'm sorry. I didn't think I was asleep,' muttered

Dandy, confused. He took a sip of water from the glass beside the bed. He could hardly bear to look at Hinghan Khan, sitting there so calmly, pulling the dogs' soft ears through his fingers as he searched for thorns.

Old loyalty struggled with new. Hinghan Khan was his brother. He owed him his life. How could he denounce him? All through the terrible winter following the retreat from Kabul, Hinghan Khan had looked after him, fed and sheltered him, hiding him from the Afghan fanatics who would have killed him. Other Khans had kept British children as hostages, but Hinghan Khan had asked nothing when he restored Dandy to his mother.

That was why Mamma kept him on, though Dandy suspected she did not like him. His own memories of those far-off days were hazy now, but he had long accepted that his debt to Hinghan Khan could never be discharged. He could not betray him.

Yet how could he remain silent, knowing what he did? The jewels belonged to Dulip Singh, and it was unfair that kind, worried Dr Login, whom the Governor-General held responsible for the security of all the Maharaja's property, should have to shoulder the blame for Hinghan Khan's crime.

In Afghan eyes it was no crime to plunder a foe, and Sikhs had helped themselves freely to Afghan treasures in the past. That was why Missar Makraj had never allowed Hinghan Khan to accompany him to the Treasury. The British artillerymen who had been his accomplices were fools and would pay for their greed and folly, but unless *he* spoke out, Hinghan Khan would escape with his booty.

Where could he have hidden it? Not in his own quarters, that was certain. Within hours of the robbery, the Citadel had been scoured from top to bottom and every person who lived there had been accounted for. Not one native had entered or left it. Even Aunt Rohais had been obliged to travel attended only by an ayah who lived outside in the city itself.

How I wish I could ask Mamma what to do! thought Dandy distractedly. But she would guess at once whom I

341

mean and make me tell her everything. It's no use. I shall have to decide myself.

His head ached as if tom-toms were beating inside it. He wished ungratefully that old Dippy would stop his confounded jawing and go away.

When they were alone at last, he called Hinghan Khan to his bedside. 'Listen, my brother. I have had a strange dream,' he said, watching him closely.

'Tell me your dream, brother.' Hinghan Khan's tone expressed no more than polite interest, but his black eyes were wary.

'Behold, I stood in a dark chamber, with vessels of gold and silver and chests of precious stones around me,' said Dandy, pitching his voice in the professional storyteller's singsong. 'And lo, there came a robber with a sack and a lantern, to carry the treasure away.'

He paused. There was a long silence while Hinghan Khan's expression changed from wariness to alarm and then fear.

'Is there more?' he asked at last.

'When he had filled his sack, he went away, and I followed him through many dark chambers until he came to a hole in the wall. And there were flames behind me, and I was afraid. I caught at his sack to stop him and would not let go, and then a great stone struck my head and I fell into darkness.'

Again he paused. Hinghan Khan watched him intently and said nothing.

'But before the darkness covered me, the robber turned, and lo, he had my brother's face.'

There was a long silence, broken only by the monkey's soft chittering. Thea, sewing quietly in the next room, raised startled eyes from her work. The boys were speaking in Pushtu, which any listening servants would not understand, but *she* could follow what they said, and her heart began to beat very fast as she strained to catch every word.

Then Hinghan Khan laughed softly. 'Truly, thy wits are still addled! Why tell me such foolishness?'

'How much did the soldiers pay thee for that night's work?' asked Dandy coldly.

'I was sick of a fever. I know nothing of this matter.'

'Liar! How much?'

Hinghan Khan said sulkily, 'If those dogs had put back the stones as they swore to, none would have known of it. I should have left thee to the flames, meddling little fool that thou art. Am I to suffer thy threats because I saved thy life?'

'Only tell me where thou hast hidden the jewels, and I will say nothing of thy part in the affair,' said Dandy persuasively. 'Come, brother, is not that a fair offer? What profit can they bring thee? The Toshkhana mark is known to every merchant in the land.'

'Mark?' said Hinghan Khan sharply. 'What foolishness is this? *I* saw no mark.'

'Only with a jewel-glass can it be seen, yet its power is so great that no merchant would dare to buy stones so marked, for fear of the wrath of the Guardian. This the Maharaja himself has told me.'

Was he bluffing? Thea wondered. She had never heard that the Maharaja's jewels were identified in this way, but it was quite possible that Dr Login himself had instituted such a precaution against losing them.

Dandy said urgently, 'Tell me where they are hidden, brother!'

'I cannot tell.'

'Do not play games with me, blockhead! Where are they? The Hakim-Sahib and his men have searched the Citadel not once but a dozen times. They have looked in thy quarters – '

'The Hakim-Sahib would have done better to search his own,' sneered Hinghan Khan, and Thea's mouth opened in shocked surprise. *Thick as thieves*, Hal had said, that very morning. Even the keenest-eyed man has his blind spot. In Toby Black's case, Hinghan Khan had known just where to find it.

How Rohais must have been laughing as she rode away in Lord Dalhousie's train, leaving her husband to hunt

343

for something which was no longer there. Who would dream of searching her baggage?

'You let Aunt Rohais take them? Oh, you *prize chump*!' exclaimed Dandy in deep disgust. 'She has gone to Bombay, didn't you know? She will take them to England, and even Missar Makraj cannot reach her there.'

CHAPTER NINETEEN

Most mornings, Doctor Black worked at the hospital, but when Thea drove there in search of him, she found his assistant, Amos Engineer, in sole charge of the patients. He hurried out to welcome the visitor.

'Pray be seated and repose yourself until the doctor returns,' he cried hospitably, ushering her into a bare but pleasantly cool antechamber and pulling forward the single rattan chair.

'When do you expect him back, Mr Engineer?'

'Oh, very soon, I have no doubt.' He bustled about, proud to show the new hospital's amenities. 'See, here are periodicals donated by the Ladies of the Gymkhana Club to distract you. Here are also in this glass case some interesting artefacts collected by Major Sampson in his travels.'

'Thank you, Mr Engineer.' Thea sank into the chair, but she could not relax. Why were men always away when you needed them most? 'Are you sure he will come back soon?'

'Oh, indubitably, I assure you.'

He skipped away, and at intervals in the next two hours popped back to offer tea or lemonade, and reassure her ever more fervently that Dr Black would soon return.

It was only when her patience finally expired at noon that Mr Engineer reluctantly divulged the information that Dr Black's destination had been a village some twenty miles away in the hills. Even if he grew wings he could hardly arrive back before nightfall.

She said despairingly, 'Why did you not tell me this before? I have wasted two whole hours waiting for him.'

Mr Engineer looked pained. 'How could I reveal to you that your hopes were in vain?'

Thea left abruptly, angrier with herself for being duped than with the well-meaning young Eurasian.

Hurrying home, she sent at once for Hinghan Khan, resolved to have it out with him and learn the truth, but after a prolonged absence, the *chuprassi* returned to say he was nowhere to be found. A dreadful suspicion seized her.

'Are his clothes in his room?'

'Yes, Memsahib.'

'Go to the stables and see if he has brought back the new horse.'

She hurried to Dandy's room and found him lying face down, muffling sobs in the pillow.

'My darling boy! What is the matter?'

He sat up, scrubbing furiously at his eyes. 'Hinghan Khan has gone, Mamma. He gave me his boots. He said he would not need them again.'

Gleaming and reproachful, the boots stood as if on parade, the clearest of indications that Hinghan Khan was cutting all ties with the Sahib-log. Thea felt a profound relief to be rid of him. She put her hand on Dandy's shoulder. 'I am sorry, my love, but it had to happen some time. He will be happier in his own country.'

'But I – I drove him away!' said Dandy miserably. 'If I hadn't called him a thief – '

'It would have made no difference,' she said. 'I was sewing in my room. I heard what you said to him.'

'Oh!' Dandy flushed. 'I wanted him to tell me where he had hidden them. I wouldn't have given him away. But then he said Aunt Rohais had taken them . . . Oh, Mamma! What if Missar Makraj finds out?'

'Or Hinghan Khan tries to get them back.'

They were silent, assessing the risks. At last Dandy said tentatively, 'Do you think if we told Uncle Toby, he could make her give them back?'

'I thought of that. I have been trying to find him,' said Thea distractedly. 'We can't just wait and do nothing – it may be days before he comes back. What time did Hinghan Khan give you his boots?'

346

'Before *tiffin*.'

Three hours ago. By now, he might be halfway to Ferozepore. With all her heart, Thea cursed Mr Engineer's well-meant prevarications. Even if Toby started at once and rode all night he could hardly overtake Hinghan Khan. Even if *she* rode all night . . .

She tried to dismiss the idea of taking matters into her own hands, but it had been growing on her all through those wasted hours at the hospital. Rohais must be warned of her danger, and who else could do it in time?

She said: 'Was it true, what you said about the jewels being marked?'

'Oh yes. Dippy showed me how to look for it with a jewel-glass.'

As Thea's thoughts raced here and there, searching for the best plan, her messenger returned from the stables. With a smugness that reflected his dislike of the young Afghan, he reported that Hinghan Khan's own pony had just been brought back by one of Captain Shadwell's syces.

'Where is the Herati stallion, then?'

Already she guessed the answer. Instead of leading home her present for Hal as he had been told to, Hinghan Khan had transferred his saddle to the new horse and ridden away on him, calmly instructing Shadwell's groom to take his discarded pony back to the Commissioner-Sahib's stables.

'This is too much!' Thea exclaimed. She turned to Dandy. 'Darling, I shall go to Ferozepore, to get Uncle Hal's new horse back and bring Aunt Rohais home as well. If I start now, I may be able to catch Hinghan Khan. If your Uncle Toby comes back tonight, tell him what has happened and ask him to follow me without delay.'

'Let me come with you, Mamma!' Dandy sat up in bed, his soul in his eyes.

'I wish you could . . . ' She smoothed his hair. ' . . . but no, it would be madness. Besides, I need you here to tell your uncle where I have gone.'

Dandy's lips were quivering, but he forced a smile.

347

'Take Grip and Fang, Mamma. They're good dogs. They will look after you.'

To please him she agreed, and whistled to the terriers as she left the room. They hesitated, looking back at their master.

'Go on, boys. Go with Mamma. *Walk-time!*'

They knew the phrase, and scampered away with excited yaps. Dandy maintained his smile as his mother's footsteps receded down the passage, and he heard her calling for Ali Bux Khan, the *jemadar*. The lemur looked carefully round the room to make sure the dogs had really gone before dropping down to curl in the angle of his neck and shoulder. She chattered softly, telling him her worries. Dandy nuzzled his face against her soft fur, and tears began to slide slowly down his cheeks.

Rohais's first attempt to raise money from the jewels had been wholly successful. Mr Chaudhury the jewel-merchant had paid what she asked so readily that she immediately wished she had doubled the price.

Despite its ease – or perhaps because of it – the transaction left her in an unsettled frame of mind. Mr Chaudhury had paid a trifle *too* readily. She had not quite liked the quick, assessing glance he gave her after examining the little ruby ring she had chosen from her hoard, or his haste to conclude the deal. It was hardly natural for a merchant not to haggle. Could he have sensed something amiss? Could he – by any horrid chance – have known the ring was stolen?

Alone in her room after *tiffin* on the afternoon of little Alicia Marshall's christening, in the hour before her ayah came to dress her, Rohais shook the rest of the Toshkhana jewels from their wash-leather pouch and looked carefully at each one, but the examination told her nothing. Ranjit Singh had collected precious stones as avidly as, and scarcely more discriminatingly than, a magpie. Hers was a typically mixed bag: jewels of great beauty and value mingled with inferior gems.

There were magnificent emeralds flanked by flawed,

yellowish diamonds; lustrous great pearls surrounded by washy amethysts; some in tarnished antique settings, others bright as if fresh from the goldsmith's hammer. Rings, earrings, pendants, bracelets . . . Hinghan Khan had piled them together pell-mell, but considering the circumstances he had made an impressive haul.

She wished she could examine them through a jeweller's loupe, such as Mr Chaudhury had used, and at once she remembered the powerful magnifying glass her host used for deciphering inscriptions – Charles Marshall's passion for old Persian tablets and manuscripts had ruined his eyesight. She would borrow the magnifying glass from his study and return it before it was missed.

The big bungalow was quiet as she opened the door of her room and tiptoed into the cool, shadowed hall. Everyone was resting before the christening, though the scrunch of hoofs on gravel indicated the arrival of an early guest.

She eased open the study door carefully, ready with an excuse of looking for a book if by any mischance Charlie should be working there, but the room was empty. So far, so good. Hurrying over to the desk, she looked for the glass which had lain beside the blotter, but it was no longer there.

With guilty haste she riffled through the drawers, wondering how she would explain herself if anyone came in, conscious that precious minutes were passing and she had left the jewels lying in plain view on her bed. What if that prying fool of an ayah came early to dress her? She must go back – it was too risky. Ah! there was the glass.

Footsteps crossed the hall and she froze, dreading the opening of the study door. They passed, going on down the passage towards the bedrooms, and behind them came the patter and click of dogs' claws on the marble floor.

Now she was in a fix, cut off from her own room by whoever was roaming the bungalow at this most inconvenient moment. In her loose peignoir, with hair streaming down her back, she could not risk being seen emerging from Major Marshall's study.

As soon as the sounds of movement ceased, she took a

349

quick look round the door. The hall was empty. Silently she pattered across the cool floor and down the passage, holding her breath until the door of her own room swung shut behind her.

She leaned against it, gasping, hands clasped to her breast to quiet the pounding of her heart. Now for the magnifying glass, she thought; but before she had even taken a step towards the bed, she was startled to see first one, then two fox-terriers trot from behind the screen that protected it. Barking a rapturous welcome they rushed towards her, and with dismay she recognised her nephew Dandy's horrid little dogs.

'Get away, you brutes,' she scolded, pushing them back. 'Get down! How did you get here?'

Then the magnifying glass slipped from her fingers and her voice faltered into silence as the still less welcome figure of her sister-in-law followed the dogs round the screen. She was holding the wash-leather pouch, and Rohais's dreams shattered like the magnifying glass as she spoke.

'Missar Makraj is looking for these. I have come to take them back to him.'

They told Mrs Marshall that Rohais's daughter was unwell, and she, generous soul, insisted on providing them with tents, servants and all they needed for the homeward journey.

'You cannot travel through a second night, my dear,' she said, looking at Thea's pale face and dusty clothes. 'You will be quite done up. I wish you would rest here a little before you start back. A few hours cannot make much difference.'

'You are very kind, but I think we should go at once,' said Thea, and Mrs Marshall sighed.

'Of course. I quite understand your anxiety. Poor little Lucy. You will wish to nurse her yourself,' she pursued, looking at Rohais with a hint of enquiry. 'I know when my own precious lambs were seedy, I could not bear to let anyone else care for them.'

Her precious lambs were now strapping young officers with families of their own, but the worry their childish ailments had caused her was still fresh in her memory. She found it remarkable that during the whole of her visit, Rohais had barely mentioned her daughter. Nurse the child? She would be astonished to hear that Rohais knew one end of a thermometer from the other.

That young woman looked sulky and aggrieved at being dragged home, thought Mrs Marshall, observing her shrewdly. Her friend Kate had certainly been luckier in her daughter-in-law than in her daughter. Yet Dorothea's own mother had been a flighty piece, she remembered . . . It just went to show how often the nicest parents had the nastiest children, and vice versa. In future she would be rather more careful, she resolved, about issuing open invitations to the offspring of old friends.

She hurried away to make arrangements for their journey.

After crossing the Sutlej River, Thea insisted on pressing on several miles before allowing the servants to make camp by a great mud-walled water-tank on the outskirts of a village.

'Why did you do it?' she asked, as soon as she and Rohais were alone.

Since leaving Ferozepore, Rohais had ridden in sullen silence, but now she turned on Thea with a look of utter misery and despair.

'Why do you think? Because I needed money, of course.'

All the reproaches that had burned on Thea's lips through the long, hot, anxious ride suddenly seemed as futile and cruel as scolding a cat for torturing mice. Any suffering her actions caused was quite immaterial to her, and no amount of moral argument would persuade her she had done wrong.

Nevertheless, Thea tried. 'But it was stealing!'

'*I* didn't steal them,' said Rohais disdainfully. 'It was Hinghan Khan's idea.'

351

'Didn't you try to stop him?'

'Why should I? The Maharaja has more jewels than he knows what to do with, and now they are going to be taken over by the Company, in any case. Just think of it – all those rooms and rooms full of money and jewels, and they are all going to disappear into Company coffers where no one will ever see them again. It's such a terrible, terrible waste! Jewels should be worn and admired – not locked away in some dark vault. Why shouldn't I take just a few?'

'But don't you see it's wrong? If you are caught, Toby will be disgraced. He might lose his job.'

'Much I care for that!' said Rohais defiantly. 'It would serve him right for not giving me enough to buy what I need. Why should I be the laughing-stock of the station in my dowdy old dresses? You don't know what it's like to be in debt, with moneylenders dunning you wherever you go.' She laid her hand on Thea's arm and her voice turned to a cajoling, little-girl whine. 'Oh, please, Thea! Dear, kind Thea! Let me have them back. No one will ever know. If Hinghan Khan has run away, we can put the blame on him and no one need know I had anything to do with it.'

'I can't,' said Thea unhappily. 'You know that.'

'You hate me, don't you?' said Rohais, turning her face away. 'You've always hated me and tried to make me unhappy. You like seeing me poor and miserable and lonely when just one simple gesture from you could make all the difference to my life. Just a handful of jewels!' She laughed bitterly. 'That's all I'm begging you for. You don't need them, nor does Dulip Singh. The Company needs them least of all. *I* need them, but of course you won't give them to me because you want to ruin my life. I should have known better than to ask you.'

'Stop it, Rohais,' said Thea fiercely. 'You know that's quite untrue. All I am trying to do is find some way to save you from the consequences of your foolishness. I don't want your name dragged through the mud, as it would be if you had tried to sell even one of those Tosh-khana jewels.'

'What consequences? What do you mean?'

'Those jewels bear the Toshkhana mark. Any merchant who saw it would send word to the Guardian, Missar Makraj – What *is* the matter?'

Rohais had gone very pale, and now her hand clutched Thea's arm not in cajolery but fear. She said in a small, scared voice, 'But I did sell one little ring. I needed money so badly.'

'Oh, Rohais!'

There was no mistaking the alarm in Thea's voice.

Wild-eyed, Rohais sprang to her feet. That terrible old Guardian! She babbled, 'Let me go! I – I can't stay here. I'll get a passage on a riverboat and go to Bombay. He won't follow me there. Oh, Thea, you must let me go. He'll kill me if he finds me.'

'Sit down.' Thea was trying to master her own fear as she remembered the flashing blade that had sliced down so close to Dandy's neck. Recovering the Maharaja's property was a sacred duty to the Hereditary Guardian, and he would not hesitate to kill anyone who stood in his path. How long would it take for him to discover where they were?

She said, 'It's no use running away. We must return the jewels to Dr Login just as soon as we possibly can. He will deal with Missar Makraj and get him to call off his hounds. How long ago did you sell the ring?'

'Only y-yesterday. Oh, Thea! What if he is already looking for me?'

It was useless to tell her she should have thought of that before. The old instinct to protect Rohais reasserted itself and Thea said wearily, 'Don't worry, you're safe enough for tonight. He can't possibly get to Ferozepore and back here before morning. Go to bed! Tomorrow we'll make an early start and push on as fast as we can.'

'I'm frightened. I shan't sleep a wink.'

'Don't be silly, you'll be all right. I'll tell Ali Bux to

353

set a double guard, and if you need me you've only to call out.'

The tent Mrs Marshall had lent them was a grand affair, twenty foot square, with double walls to the living quarters and well-appointed sleeping apartments lined with shawls.

After she had seen Rohais comfortably installed, Thea told Ali Bux to feed the dogs, then settled the tired Grip on a blanket under her own cot. Fang was restless, pacing the walls and whining, so she looped her leash through the handle of her dressing-case, tethering her firmly. After a few whines and tugs, Fang accepted the restraint, and curled up.

On the far side of the partition, Thea heard Rohais's voice grumbling at her ayah. Presently even this ceased, and Thea closed her eyes.

The scream that ripped through her dreams, jerking her from the depths of slumber, came from behind the canvas partition. Even before she was fully, shudderingly awake, Thea had flung back the sheet and was fighting her way out of the billows of the mosquito-net. She ran across the tent, pulling aside the flap of curtain that served for a door, and stumbled over the swaddled figure of Ayah, sleeping in her usual place across the threshold of her mistress's room.

'What's happened, Rohais? Are you all right?'

Rohais was sitting bolt upright in bed, hands clutched to her throat, lungs filling for another scream. On seeing Thea, she let the breath escape on a long sigh.

'Save me, save me!' she babbled. 'He's here. He tried to kill me.'

Clearly she had had a nightmare. The room was undisturbed, with no sign of any intruder. Thea sat down on the edge of the bed and put her arm round Rohais's trembling shoulders.

'It's all right,' she said soothingly. 'You must have had a bad dream.'

'I didn't! He was really here. He tried to kill me.'

Rohais's eyes were dark with fright and her teeth chattered.

'Who did?'

'Hinghan Khan! I opened my eyes and saw him standing there. Just where you are now. He had a dagger in his hand, and he was *shining*. He asked me where the jewels were, and when I said I didn't know he put the dagger against my throat, and – and – '

'You woke up?'

'No! I was awake, I tell you.' Rohais gulped. A pulse in her throat fluttered rapidly like the heart of a frightened bird. 'I know I was,' she added rather less certainly.

'Where did he go?' Thea looked round the orderly room. As far as she could see, nothing was out of place, nothing missing. From the doorway came Ayah's regular snores. Thea stifled a yawn.

'Go back to sleep. You're quite safe, and so are the jewels. I've locked them in my dressing-case. There's nothing to worry about.'

'I did see him. Stay with me tonight, Thea. I hate being alone,' said Rohais plaintively.

'You're not alone. Ayah's just over there. You're quite safe.'

'She's a fat lot of good! It would take an earthquake to wake her.' Nevertheless, she lay down as if exhausted by emotion, pulling the sheet up to her chin. 'He won't come back, will he?' she murmured drowsily. 'Not if you're here.'

'He won't come back. I promise.'

Rohais closed her eyes. Thea stayed beside her bed until she was sure she was asleep, then tiptoed over to the sleeping ayah and shook her shoulder.

'Wake up!'

But the woman simply rolled herself more tightly in her layers of shawl, hunching her back and muffling her head. Fearing that more strenuous efforts to rouse her would disturb Rohais, Thea left her to sleep and returned, shivering, to her own bed.

355

Wild confused dreams haunted her sleep. She was cold and tired, heavily burdened, wading through deep snow and searching, always searching . . . Horsemen rode past, but when she cried to them for help they looked at her with dead, blank eyes and would not stop. Hounds bayed behind her. She was galloping over a great plain dotted with boulders and deep, narrow gullies choked with piles of corpses. The hounds were gaining on her, wanting her blood. Their furious yelping was almost at her heels. Her horse was failing, the blood-cry resounded in her ears. A shot rang out . . .

She woke with a pounding heart, knowing the shot was real, and still hearing the wild yelping close at hand. There were confused shouts outside the tent, a scuffle, the patter of fleeing feet.

Instinctively she put out a hand: the dressing-case was gone.

'*Robbers! Dacoits! Stop, thief*!'

The stentorian bellow of Ali Bux Khan convinced her this was no dream. She heard a volley of shots close outside the tent, and a long, agonised yell. The canvas walls shook violently as someone fell over a guy rope. There were grunts and groans and the brutal thud of a rifle butt against bone.

A fight was in progress, that much was plain, but she could not make sense of what was happening within. Both Dandy's dogs were barking hysterically, but she could only see one of them. Grip was jumping up and down and scrabbling at the canvas wall, flinging his compact, muscular body against it in an agony of frustration, but Fang had vanished, apparently between the two skins of wall, which shook and bulged like a sack full of mongooses.

'Quiet, dogs! Quiet!' She could hardly think through the din.

Pulling on a wrap, she unhooked a section of the canvas and Grip darted through. In the dim, narrow passage thus exposed, Thea could see the white blur of Fang, apparently pinned against the outer wall and wheezing as if she were choking.

'All right. I'm coming.' She edged through the gap. 'Here, Fang! Good dog. Leave it!'

Fang's whole body trembled with the strain, her short legs braced back, neck unnaturally stretched, muzzle jammed against the outer wall. Only when Thea tried to move her did she realise that the lead to which her collar was attached had disappeared under the canvas.

With hasty, clumsy fingers, she unbuckled the collar, and Fang shot backwards, gasping and wheezing. Whining, she crept back to lick at Thea's face as she tugged hard, trying to free the leash, but it would not budge. The thief must have snatched up her dressing-case without noticing the small dog attached to it, and it had been Fang's furious protests that had alarmed the guards. But where was the case now?

'Ali Bux? Did you catch him?' she called.

'Alas, the miscreant has escaped,' replied the old *jemadar* heavily. 'He slipped through our fingers before we could close our hands on him.'

'He has stolen my dressing-case, Ali Bux.'

'No, no, Memsahib. It is here, quite safe.'

Thank God for Fang, she thought. She called, 'Wait there, Ali Bux, and don't lose sight of it. I am coming out.'

To reach the tent's door, she had to pass through Rohais's sleeping-quarters.

'It's all right, Ro. It's only me,' she said softly, and drawing aside the separating curtain she picked up her skirts to step over Ayah's recumbent form. The untidy bundle of blankets and shawls lay just where she had last seen them, but they were empty. Ayah had vanished.

Where had she gone? Thea stared into the dark corners of the tent. The outer door was still securely laced and the oil-lamp burning low. Thea moved across to turn up the wick.

'Rohais?'

After the commotion outside, the tent seemed very still

357

and quiet, an oasis of peace to which the cries of beasts and men penetrated only faintly, like echoes from another world.

All the same, it was strange that Rohais should be sleeping undisturbed . . .

With sudden dread, Thea walked swiftly across to bend over the bed. Rohais lay on her back, one hand upflung, the fingers curled inward against her cheek in a childish, defenceless gesture. Her long golden hair fanned out across the pillow; her wide eyes were the untroubled blue of a summer sky. Around her white throat she wore a broad scarlet ribbon whose ends stretched down to the floor, then trickled away into two dark pools. Ants were scurrying about, dabbling antennae in the sticky flood, then running home to spread the news and call others to the feast.

Thea swayed dizzily, her gorge rising as she smelt the blood. She turned away, fighting nausea, and stumbled towards the door.

Outside, Ali Bux Khan was calling, his voice high and agitated.

'Memsahib! Memsahib! There is dirty work afoot.'

'What is it, Ali Bux?' she called faintly.

'Ayah has been foully murdered, Memsahib. She is here, behind the tent, naked and quite dead.'

'*Dead*?'

'She has been stabbed. Here in her back is a dagger I know well. This is the work of that dirty Afghan, Hinghan Khan.'

CHAPTER TWENTY

Dandy moped about the Citadel, missing Hinghan Khan. 'I never thought he really would go back to Afghanistan,' he said disconsolately, perching on Thea's bed one morning.

She thought with a shock how fast he was growing. Since his accident he looked taller, the rounded childish contours of his face fining into sharper planes; legs longer, shoulders wide and angular. One day he would look very like James.

'Uncle Toby thinks you ought to come to England with me,' he said offhandedly, but his eyes were anxious.

'Oh, he does, does he?'

'He says that now Mrs Login is coming to take care of Dippy – '

'His Highness, if you please.'

'Oh, all right. Of His Highness the Maharajadiraja Dulip Singh – '

'Don't be cheeky, my boy,' she warned, and he shrugged impatiently. She knew she ought to scold him, but decided instead to ignore the insolence. 'Go on. You were saying that when Mrs Login arrives from England, my presence will no longer be required.'

'Yes. Well, it won't, will it? So you can come with me.'

'But, my darling boy, you won't need me either, if you are at school. What would I do with myself in England?'

'Oh, Mamma! Think of the holidays.'

'You are going to spend them with Aunt Dora and Uncle Frederick. It is all arranged.'

'But I don't know them, Mamma, and neither do you!' he wailed in a babyish, unmanly way which would have horrified his Uncle Hal. Words tumbled out in a torrent, the pent-up fears of many weeks. 'Uncle Toby hated school, Mamma. He says it was the most miserable time

359

of his life. He had to stay with horrid old cousins who took boarders and didn't give him enough to eat. Mamma, do Uncle Frederick and Aunt Dora take boarders?'

'Of course they don't,' she said, exasperated.

Dandy looked unconvinced. 'Uncle Toby says he would never leave a child of his with people he doesn't know,' he muttered.

'Then I am thankful he has no say in the matter,' said Thea crisply.

'I wish he had! He ought to have, because he is my Trustee! I wish I was his son, not yours,' cried Dandy, his face very red.

'Hold your tongue! I forbid you to mention the subject again.'

For a time he was silent, playing with the tassel on the curtain round her bed, pulling strands of silk from it until her fingers itched to slap him. At length he said in a calm, rational tone, 'If I work very hard at my lessons and do everything you tell me without arguing, will you let me stay here, Mamma?'

She caught her breath. They were almost the same words she had used to Mrs Tomlinson all those years ago, when the threat of the Orphanage loomed. *'If I work very hard . . . If I'm good – very, very good . . . '*

Had it been the same anguish she was feeling now that had made Mrs Tomlinson's mouth tighten and twist as if she were sucking a lemon? Disturbed by the memory, she said more sharply than she meant to, 'No, Dandy! It's no use thinking you can get round me with promises. You are going to school in England, and that is the end of the matter.'

He stood his ground, although she could see he was close to tears. 'What will happen to all my animals?' he asked in agonised tones, and her patience snapped.

'As to that, I neither know nor care! Perhaps you should ask your precious Uncle Toby to take charge of them.'

As soon as the words were uttered, she wanted to take them back, but it was too late.

'I hate you, Mamma,' said Dandy very distinctly. 'I wish I was dead.'

He turned and ran out of the room, slamming the door.

Thea cursed Toby Black roundly for stirring up these fears. What business was it of his? She did not see Dandy again that day, but when Hal paid his usual visit to her boudoir she could not help saying casually, 'Was it very bad, having to go Home to school? Can you remember?'

'How could I ever forget?' Hal shuddered. 'It was *terrible*.'

'Then don't you think . . . ?'

He gave her a curious glance. 'My dear sister, you are not contemplating a change of plan, I hope? Terrible it may be, but we all have to go through with it. Boys must be educated, and Dandy has run wild quite long enough. Too long, if you want my honest opinion. Believe me, it's all for the best.'

Before quitting his capital, the Maharaja held a durbar at which to take leave of the British officials and administrators to whose care he was committing his country, as well as those who were leaving to serve elsewhere.

Dandy was among the last to be called. Scrubbed and uncomfortable in his Norfolk suit and stiff collar, he advanced to make his bow.

Dulip Singh sat motionless between the horns of the *guddee*, his right foot tucked under him and the left in its little pointed slipper hanging straight down. From head to toe his small person glittered with jewels. Over one shoulder was draped a striped, embroidered shawl with deep fringes, and two handsome armlets set with large emeralds clasped the silk sleeves of his upper arms above his neatly folded brown hands. Pearl necklaces encircled his plump throat and twined in the folds of his snowy turban with its splash of vivid crimson under-turban and glittering diamond aigret. From his ears hung more pearls. But amid all this splendour his chubby face looked melancholy and remote, the great brown eyes hooded under heavy lids, the soft mouth drooping. There was nothing

361

English about him now. Dandy knew that he could sit for hours without moving or altering his expression, even when his courtiers barked out their ritual salutation of 'Maharaj!' with the explosive suddenness of a pistol shot. He was a different being from the giggling companion of the schoolroom, and Dandy's smile evoked no flicker of response.

He doesn't care that I am going away, thought Dandy, and a hard lump formed in his throat.

A servant glided forward, holding out a miniature of the Maharaja in an oval frame set with brilliants and carefully signed by the sitter in both Persian and English. As etiquette demanded, Dandy put it aside without a glance, bowed again, and prepared to withdraw.

A small, languid hand beckoned him nearer.

'So this is the parting of the ways, you lucky dog!' said Dulip Singh with horribly forced joviality. 'My word, I would give my ears to come with you.'

'I'd give mine to stay here.'

'Oho, yes. What a joke!' The heavy-lidded, mournful eyes implored him to laugh, but Dandy's expression remained stony.

'I wished to give you a hawk, but Dr Login said it would die when you were at school. I will keep it here until you return, Dandy-Sahib.'

Dandy gulped and said nothing.

'When the Queen gives me permission, I will come to England. Won't that be top-hole?'

Dandy's reply was uttered so fast and low that neither the impassive courtiers nor the British officials caught his words. But Dulip Singh heard. For an instant the heavy lids lifted in a flash of comprehension. A gleeful, entirely mischievous look flickered across his dark face and was gone.

'You mean to give them the slip? Oh, what a lark!' he whispered in English, and then formally, in his own tongue, 'May good fortune attend thee, my brother.'

At his sign of dismissal, Dandy bowed low and retired.

362

Though his closed face gave nothing away, inside he was smiling.

The citizens of Lahore and their new rulers turned out in force to watch Dulip Singh's departure on the morning of 21 December 1849. A number of last-minute hitches had delayed the cavalcade by two hours, and it was nine o'clock, with the sun already high, before Major Burn, Deputy Secretary to the Board of Administration of the Punjab, saw the long procession clear the city gate and set off across the dusty grey-brown plain.

Tall and lean, with a brow perpetually creased in worry, Burn was a fusser by nature and could not feel certain that he had sufficiently impressed upon the Maharaja's guardian the need for vigilance on this journey. He considered Dr Login altogether too easygoing in the matter of security surrounding his young charge. Imagine what might happen if a gang of desperadoes made a sudden attack, prepared to risk their lives for the chance of abducting the boy! What use would horse artillery and Light Cavalry be if one of the Maharaja's bodyservants proved treacherous?

Login might claim to have weeded out all doubtful characters from the boy's retinue, but the question – as always – was whom could you trust? The four artillerymen who had broken into the State Treasury last month had proved all too conclusively that British soldiers were every bit as susceptible to bribery, coercion, or plain greed as natives were.

That had been a shameful business. The missing jewels had been recovered, but that was neither here nor there. Burn was a military man who knew little and cared less about the machinations of Dr Tobias Black and his Intelligence wallahs. Once the Maharaja and his small nephew the Shahzadah were safely out of the Punjab, most of these tiresome Palace intrigues should evaporate – providing, of course, that neither of the children was abducted and used as a figurehead round which to rally Sikh warriors to arms once more.

In the usual way of worriers, Burn's thoughts had returned to their starting-point. Had Login taken enough precautions to ensure the safety of his charges? He ran his eye over the men and horses as they passed: gunners, cavalry, Skinner's Horse in their flamboyant yellow tunics, beefy-faced men of the 18th European Infantry swinging along in step, and the softer shuffle of the 50th Native Infantry.

There was the Maharaja, on his white Arabian pony, with Login riding the big chestnut gelding which Dulip Singh had given him for his birthday. With them was young Dandy Quinn on his fiery little racing pony; Burn knew he had obtained permission to accompany the first two marches. A little way behind rumbled the carriage carrying the six-year-old Shahzadah and his beautiful mother, widow of the former Raja Shere Singh, and around the whole royal party rode the splendidly accoutred bodyguard.

Burn counted them, frowning. Only twenty, when he had particularly ordered double that number, and where was the European officer commanding them? This would not do at all. He reached for his pocketbook.

As the long glittering procession vanished in the usual dust-cloud, the Deputy Secretary began with pursed lips and frowning brow to draft a reproving note to Dr Login.

Thea had been glad enough to give Dandy leave to ride with Dulip Singh on the first two stages of his journey into exile. Anything was better than having her son underfoot, sulky and morose, while she tried to organise the packing up of her household. For the past few days his behaviour had been intolerable. His reproachful eyes and mutinous expression had haunted her as he mooched about the dismantled rooms of the Citadel, and his interference with the disposition of his own clothes and possessions had reminded her all too vividly of his father's departure for Afghanistan.

'Very well, you may ride with them for two days, if Dr Login has no objection,' she had agreed, hoping to see him smile, but he looked at the ground and shuffled his feet before thanking her with bare civility.

'You don't sound very pleased, I must say!' she could not help exclaiming. 'Don't I get a kiss for sending you off to enjoy yourself while I struggle with your packing?'

He kissed her cheek in a perfunctory way, but said in the same offhand tone, 'There would be no need to pack if you let me stay here.'

'None of that, now,' she warned, and he slouched away with hands in pockets, kicking a pebble in front of him.

Her own shoulders drooped. She knew she ought to call him back, insist that he spoke more respectfully and walked briskly like a sahib, head up and shoulders back, but she could not face another confrontation. Hal was right. He was getting too much for her. It was time he went to school and learned manly English games instead of giggling and dreaming with natives and playing tricks on Dulip Singh's patient courtiers. She hated, too, the way he had begun to treat her as an enemy, to be defied and disobeyed if he thought he could get away with it. He couldn't realise that it was harder for her to see him go than it was for him to leave.

Since she could not spare Ali Bux Khan, she had sent a sturdy, stolid young Sikh named Jowahir Singh to look after Dandy and keep him out of mischief, giving them both strict instructions that they were to return by the end of the week.

With her sulky son out of the way, and Hal once again travelling in his district, her packing made better progress, but it was dismal work dispersing all Dandy's possessions, some going with him to school, some to the servants' children, and it seemed to signal the end of his childhood – certainly the end of her maternal role. When she next saw him he would be sixteen or more; the boy who depended on her for his every need would have vanished for ever.

The arrival of a packet of mail from England came as a welcome interruption to her labours. Among the many letters and papers for Hal, there were also three addressed to her, and she retired with them to the summerhouse to enjoy them in private. One was from Georgiana Mainwaring; on the second she recognised Emily Eyre's neat hand; and the third she turned over and over for some minutes before summoning the courage to slit it open.

She was still scanning the closely written sheets, crossing and recrossing the thin paper, when she became aware of the snowy beard and stately tread of Ali Bux Khan approaching across the paved courtyard.

'Chitty for Memsahib,' he said quietly.

'Another?'

Absently she took it, her mind still on the letter she had been reading, but as she recognised her son's scrawling fist, her heart began to pound.

My dear Mamma, he wrote.

I have gone to find Hinghan Khan. You must not be angry with Jowahir Singh. It is not his fault but yours that I have run away. I did not want to go to England, but you would not listen. Do not try to find me, for you never will.
Your affec and dutiful son,
Daniel Alexander Quinn.
P.S. I have asked Uncle Toby to care for my animals, so you will not be troubled.

She read it through twice, then put it aside with a shaking hand. The curt, unforgiving words seemed to burn her eyes. Not his fault but yours . . .

Feeling Ali Bux's anxious gaze on her, she brushed away the threatening tears.

'Did Jowahir Singh bring this? Send him to me.'

'At once, Memsahib.' He hurried away.

When the young bearer approached nervously, she had her feelings under control.

'Don't be frightened,' she said, knowing it had taken courage for him to return with such news. 'Tell me plainly what happened.'

With many hesitations and sidelong glances, he recounted how he and Dandy had left the Maharaja's

366

second encampment at Sundighur, and retraced their route as far as the river-crossing at Bore-Gola. There had been a party of Afghan horse-dealers camped with their animals on the farther bank, and after speaking with their Sirdar, the Chota-Sahib had announced that they would camp there, too, although it was still early in the day.

While he was busy setting up the tent, the Chota-Sahib had contrived to spill all the milk they had bought that morning, and had insisted that Jowahir Singh should go back to the village for more, though he knew quite well that the buffaloes had already gone out to the fields and would not be milked again until evening.

' "Fetch me fresh milk to drink," he commanded, and stamped his foot,' reported Jowahir Singh. ' "Do not return until thou hast filled this *lota* to the brim." '

Reluctantly, Jowahir Singh had recrossed the river on the ferry boat, and waited for the women to drive in the buffaloes and milk them. By the time he had returned across the river, it was nearly dark, and when he reached the camping-ground he was horrified to find it deserted. The horse-dealers had gone, taking the Chota-Sahib with them.

'All night I followed them, but when the moon set and I could no longer see their trail, I turned again and came back to tell you what had happened.'

'You have done the best you could, Jowahir Singh,' she reassured him, though the time wasted in futile pursuit made her want to scream. Now Dandy and his Afghans had a commanding start. Could anyone catch them before they disappeared into the mountain fastnesses beyond the Khyber Pass? How easily a boy could be hidden among a caravan of pack animals and their drivers! Dandy was as fluent in Pushtu as he was in English. He could pass as an Afghan with no difficulty – indeed, he had already done so. How was she to get him back?

Her mind flew to and fro, seizing on ideas and rejecting them.

'The Hakim-Sahib comes,' said Jowahir Singh with undisguised relief, and Thea turned quickly to see Toby striding towards them. Never had she been more glad to see him.

'What's this I hear?' he said quickly. 'Dandy missing?'

Wordlessly she handed him the letter. He read it with a deepening frown.

'Well, I'm damned. I should have guessed he was planning something! He asked me to take care of his menagerie when he was away. I thought he meant while he was in England. So he's gone to look for Hinghan Khan, has he?'

'Oh, that horrible, treacherous creature! Will I never be rid of him?' she exclaimed, trembling with fear and fury. 'I have never regretted anything so much as the promise I made to James to keep that vile, murdering wretch with me.'

'Steady, Thea,' he said, seeing hysteria threaten. It won't help to lose our heads. We must tackle this calmly.'

'How can you say that?' she stormed. 'Hasn't he injured *you* enough? When I think of poor Rohais, lying – '

'Let's leave Rohais out of this,' he said with a grimness that invited no argument. 'Pull yourself together, and try to concentrate on matters that can be mended. It is clear from this note that it was Dandy's own idea to abscond.'

'Yes! Because you scared him half to death with your stories of bullying and beatings!' she exclaimed, rounding on him as the nearest target for her anger. 'But for you, he would have gone Home quite happily.'

'And his shock would have been all the greater when he found himself stuck there.'

'Don't tell me how to manage my own affairs!'

'I wouldn't dream of doing so if you did not involve me in them.'

'*I* involve *you*?' she said in amazement. 'My dear man, all I have ever asked is to be allowed to order my life without interference from you or any other well-meaning busybody.'

His jaw tightened but he said quite calmly, 'Even at the risk of offending you, I cannot watch you ruin your son's happiness without registering my protest. As his uncle, I feel an obligation to protect him as best I can.'

'Protect him? What rubbish you talk!' she said scornfully. 'I suppose you think I am sending him away for my own pleasure?'

'Your own convenience, certainly.'

'Convenience! When I dread the passing of each day because it brings his departure nearer?'

'Then why in the world are you sending him?' he asked in exasperation. 'After your own experience, I should have thought you would be the last person to condemn your son to the same misery.'

Remembering Hal's admission, she bit her lip. 'We must get him back. We must!'

'We will, never fear.' He was silent for a moment, deep in thought. 'Where is Jowahir Singh?' he asked at last. 'I will need him to identify those ruffians. They have a long start. We must leave at once.'

She stared at him. 'You can't go alone. Even if you found them, what would you do against a dozen of them? Can we not ask Sir Henry to call out Lumsden's Guides, and have them search every caravan bound for the Khyber?'

'And set the whole country in an uproar? Don't be a fool,' he said brusquely. 'You know as well as I do that the roads are alive with horse-dealers from Kabul at this season. Even the Guides could not search them all.'

'Then what can we do?' she asked despairingly.

'Leave it to me.' He put an arm round her and for a moment she clung to him, then gently he put her aside.

'Listen carefully, now. You must stay here as if nothing has happened, and warn your servants to tell no one that Dandy is missing. News travels fast and we don't want to alarm our quarry. They are probably heading for one of the big horse fairs. It should be easy enough to pick up their trail so long as they don't make a bolt for home. And when we find him . . . ' He paused.

'What then?'

'We shall see what we shall see. Don't worry, Thea.

369

Waiting is the worst part, I know, but you may be sure I shall do my damnedest to get Dandy back safe and sound.'

'Oh, Black Doctor! What should I do without you?'

The words were out before she could censor them, and she stopped aghast, the echo of her mother's voice in her ears.

Toby looked at her curiously. 'It's a long time since anyone called me that,' he said, and shook his head as if to clear it of memories.

'Try not to worry,' he repeated. 'I'll find him, and then . . . '

Again he paused, eyebrows asking a question. She knew what he wanted her to say, but refused to bow to such pressure.

'Just bring him home safe,' she said, and watched him turn and stride back towards the stables, shouting for Jowahir Singh to bring fresh horses.

Thea stood as if turned to stone, her eyes burning with unshed tears. She looked down at the letter she had been reading earlier, and her blurred gaze focused on a single phrase towards the end, black and heavily underlined. *I am coming back.*

Dandy stirred in his sleep, and the hand that had been gently stroking his neck stilled for a moment, then resumed its slow, caressing movements, gradually easing beneath layers of material to gain access to the smooth warm skin beneath the blanket's protective cocoon.

'Light of my eyes, awake!' breathed a husky voice close to his ear, and a heavy waft of garlic-laden breath mingled with the smells of woodsmoke, dung and greasy clothing. Dandy half-raised his eyelashes, caught a glimpse of Nasrullah Khan's wolfish, bearded features not six inches from his face, and hurriedly shut them again. He lay still and silent, wondering what to do.

Round the embers of the fire lay the humped bodies of his travelling companions, but Nasrullah Khan was their leader, and he knew they would not interfere with his

370

amusements. What those amusements might be, Dandy sensed only dimly, but he knew very well that he did not care for being stroked.

'Come to me, O white gazelle, my heart's desire!'

As he felt himself pulled towards that avid, hot-eyed face, revulsion overcame Dandy's fear. He tried to wriggle away, but the sinewy arms held him fast, and as his struggles loosened the blanket round him, the exploring hand delved lower, sliding down his back to caress his buttocks.

So this was what Nasrullah's sly smirks and accidental-on-purpose contacts had been leading up to. Dandy shuddered, suddenly aware of vulnerability. Secure in his sahib's status, it had not until now occurred to him that by giving Jowahir Singh the slip he had placed himself in this shifty-eyed, none too clean horse-dealer's power.

Half-heard, half-comprehended tales of boys stolen and sold into slavery invaded his mind. It had happened to Hinghan Khan; it might very well happen to him, too, and it would be all his own fault. Dandy began to tremble violently, and the groping hand, emboldened, reached for his private parts.

This was too much. Careless of the consequences, Dandy brought up his knees in a jackknife and uttered a loud roar. Some of the sleeping humps raised their heads to stare at him.

'What ails thee, heart of my heart?' asked Nasrullah irritably, withdrawing his hand.

'Aiee! My stomach is bad – very bad.'

He sat up, hugging his knees and rocking to and fro. The horse-dealer recoiled.

Still moaning, Dandy shook free of his blanket and staggered upright, but at once the sinewy hand shot out to grip his arm.

'Whither goest thou?'

'I must be alone. Very necessary. Very quick. Aiee!'

The sinewy grip slackened. Before he could change his mind, Dandy stumbled rapidly away towards the stream, the horses tethered among the trees snorting and stamping as he passed through them.

Still groaning at intervals to allay suspicion, he squatted beside the water, wrestling with the problem of where to go. Less than a mile back they had passed through a village; could he reach it and hide before Nasrullah Khan came after him?

Clear in the moonlight he could see his own chestnut racing-pony, Sherif, given him by the Maharaja on his eleventh birthday. Though it broke his heart to leave Sherif with the horse-dealers, he dared not untie him for fear of rousing the drivers sleeping close by. He must escape at once, alone, on foot. It was his only chance.

Hardly had he come to this decision than he was slipping silently between the clumps of willow that fringed the stream, making a detour that would keep him clear of the road until he was close to the houses. With dry mouth and hammering heart he ran as fast as he dared along the bank of the stream, ears straining back to catch the first sounds of pursuit.

A low mud wall loomed before him. He had reached the strips of cultivation surrounding the village and plunged into a tall stand of feathery rye, which closed over his head with a rustle. Dropping to hands and knees, he crawled forward a few yards, then turned and lay still, trying to quieten his breathing.

Not a moment too soon had he found refuge. In the grove where the Afghans were camped lights were moving, and presently he heard hoofs thudding fast on the baked track that led to the village. He thanked his stars he had not chosen to go that way. Here in the rustling rye he would be safe enough until daybreak, provided no sleepy tiger or wild pig had chosen to spend the night in the same patch of cover.

He crawled deeper into the rows of feathery stems until he could no longer see the lights. Soothed by the murmur of wind through his gently swaying refuge, he fell asleep.

The season of horse fairs was nearly over, and the roads

around Peshawar were thronged with buyers taking their purchases home and sellers still hopeful of making a deal with the last of the horses brought down from Kabul. By the time Toby's small party encountered Nasrullah Khan's straggling cavalcade some ten miles short of the city, he and Jowahir Singh had scanned dozens of Afghan faces in the hope of recognising Dandy's abductors. The young bearer was becoming increasingly doubtful that he would know them again. He had been occupied with making camp while the Chota-Sahib spoke with them. Among the strangers there had been no mark or characteristic he could recall, though he had noticed a showy dapple-grey stallion with a dyed tail.

'Well done, my son! That is something to look out for,' said Toby to cheer him, but Jowahir Singh remained gloomy. Asked if the Afghans were Hazaras or Pathans, Parsiwas or Kuzzilbashis, he replied simply that all dirty Afghans were alike to him.

Toby suppressed his irritation at such defeatism, and tried not to consider how many dapple-grey stallions with dyed tails were brought down through the passes every year. Riding hard, they pressed on towards Peshawar, though their hopes of finding Dandy were fast fading. If he did not want to be found, the chances of tracing one boy among so many travellers were very slender.

As they passed along beside the slow-moving caravan of men and animals, Toby glanced into each swarthy face and back at Jowahir Singh, waiting for some sign of recognition, but the young bearer's pockmarked features remained impassive. The caravan's pack-animals were all heavily laden, which suggested that the dealers had sold their horses and converted the proceeds into merchandise for the Kabul bazaars. Yet again he looked in vain for dapple-grey stallions with dyed tails.

Headcloths drawn across their mouths to keep out the dust, the men trudged silently beside their animals, squeezing to one side of the narrow track to let the faster party overtake them. When a pony flung up his head to whinny he was silenced by a savage chuck at the lead-rope.

'*Manda nabashi*! May you never be tired!' called Toby courteously, drawing level with the leader.

'*Zenda bashi*! May you flourish!' The Afghan turned his face briefly, his eyes guarded above his hennaed beard.

Toby glanced enquiringly at Jowahir Singh, but he was peering abstractedly down the line of animals, his brow furrowed.

He's no damned use, thought Toby with irritation. Blind as a bat. Wouldn't recognise his own brother at forty paces. He spurred ahead. Time was running out. Another day's ride would bring them to the Khyber Pass and the end of British jurisdiction. He dreaded the thought of Thea's distress if he returned to report failure. How could he face her?

'Hakim-Sahib! Wait for me!'

His horse had outpaced Jowahir Singh's countrybred. As he waited for them to catch up, Toby saw the boy's stolid face transformed by excitement.

'Wait, Sahib, wait!' he gasped. 'Those dirty Afghans have stolen the Chota-Sahib's horse.'

'The deuce they have! Are you sure?'

'I swear it on my father's head. Did you not hear him call to us? They have taken him to sell in Kabul.' He paused, then added with rising anguish, 'But where is the Chota-Sahib? What have they done with him?'

'That, my son,' said Toby grimly, wheeling his horse, 'is what we are going to find out.'

CHAPTER TWENTY-ONE

'He promised us gold to let him ride with us to Kabul,' said Nasrullah Khan bitterly, and spat. 'Devil's spawn! Though I treated him as tenderly as a son, he ran away from us last night, at the village of Kandikotwa.'

'Leaving his horse with you, O father of liars?'

'By the beard of the Prophet, I am no liar,' said Nasrullah Khan with dignity. 'Was I not havildar to Broadfoot-Sahib at the siege of Jellalabad, and laboured night and day to raise the walls after the great earthquake threw them down?'

Toby looked at him with new interest, not unmixed with respect. If this was one of George Broadfoot's redoubtable *jezailchis* – ruffians and marksmen all – who had served their British master most faithfully in Afghanistan, it was quite possible that he was telling the truth. Toby's eye roved thoughtfully along the line of laden camels. A boy might hide among the bundles and panniers, but he had no authority to institute a search. His instinct was to trust the word of the former havildar, but if he was wrong and they carried Dandy out of the country, he would be gone for good.

'Where is the boy?' he asked quietly, and Nasrullah Khan shrugged.

'I cannot tell. I am a poor trader, Sahib, whose fighting days are long past. Must I delay my business for the sake of an infidel brat? Take the horse – he is yours. But allow me to go on my way, for winter is coming and we must clear the passes before the first snowfall.'

'Inshallah! Go in peace, Havildar-Sahib.'

Nasrullah Khan shouted an order and Dandy's pony was brought forward, the pack-saddle removed, and the load distributed among his companions.

Then the caravan moved on, and with Jowahir Singh

leading the chestnut pony, Toby turned back towards the village of Kandikotwa, half a day's march to the southeast.

When they had made camp in the grove, which still smelled of the horse-dealers' occupation, Toby sent for the village headman and offered a reward for information on the missing boy.

'I shall stay here until he is found, dead or alive,' he told him, and the headman nodded gravely, stroking his beard and promising to make a search the next day.

The moon rose, shedding its soft radiance in the clearing, and Toby sat by the fire, smoking his pipe and praying that Broadfoot's havildar had not deceived him. No one could lie as convincingly as an Afghan, who often did so for sheer devilment, with no prospect of gain beyond the satisfaction of outwitting an infidel.

Rustling shadows outside the circle of firelight told of night creatures setting off to hunt or forage. An owl swooped low over the clearing, its silent wings almost brushing the rolled hump of blanket that was Jowahir Singh. In the crops by the stream he heard the warning bark of a deer and, a little later, a pig's indignant squeal and noisy departure.

Some large animal was moving along the bank of the stream, disturbing the night-hunters and foragers. There are only three jungle-dwellers for whom the wild pig makes way, and this was neither elephant nor tiger. Toby listened to the small sounds of its passage and was satisfied. Presently he knocked out his pipe, heaped up the fire, and rolled himself in his cloak. Soon his snores were reverberating across the clearing in competition with Jowahir Singh's.

The moon rose higher, small and cold in the indigo night. The horses stamped uneasily at their pickets. Toby unrolled himself silently and moved to stand between the horse-line and the trees. A shadow was moving among the animals, trying the knots, but Toby had taken care to fasten the chestnut pony with extra heel-ropes, which would bring him up short before he had moved four paces.

'It's no good, Dandy,' he said to the dark figure tugging at Sherif's headstall. 'You won't get him that way.'

There was a gasp in the gloom, a moment of startled silence, then the swift scurry of feet. Toby launched himself in pursuit. He reached out a long arm and caught the boy's shoulder as he bolted for the shelter of the trees, holding the biting, kicking, scratching fury until his struggles ceased abruptly.

'Come over here.'

Dandy offered no further resistance as Toby pushed him down beside the fire and kicked the embers to a blaze.

'I shan't go back!' he muttered, shivering but defiant.

'We'll discuss that later. I expect you could do with some food.'

Dandy was very hungry. He had braved the dogs at a farmstead outside the village, begged a little food, and eaten enough fallen mulberries to sicken him, but although he knew he could not subsist for long on such fare, the thought of returning home filled him with dread.

Jowahir Singh produced cold chupatties and dhal, which Dandy devoured wolfishly. When he had finished, he began to yawn, propping his elbow on his knee and his chin on his hand.

'Feeling better?' asked Toby. 'Good. Now sit up and pay attention. Before I let you drop off to sleep, you and I are going to have a talk.'

Dandy gave him a bleak, unchildlike stare. 'Jaw all you like,' he said ungraciously. 'You won't get me to come back. Not unless Mamma drops the idea of sending me Home.'

'If that's what you want, young man, you're going the wrong way about getting it,' said Toby coldly. 'Running away like a coward, leaving your bearer to take the blame. What kind of behaviour is that?'

'I'm not a coward!' Dandy was scarlet with indignation. 'I told Mamma it wasn't Jowahir Singh's fault.'

'How do you suppose she felt when she heard you'd

gone off with such a crew? After her experiences of the Afghans, I'd have thought you would have spared her that.'

'What else could I do?'

'You've caused your mother a great deal of worry and distress,' said Toby remorselessly. 'If I thought it would do the least bit of good I should give you the thrashing you deserve.'

'Go on, then.' Dandy hunched his shoulders. 'I don't care. You can beat me as much as you like. I'll still run away again when I get the chance, and next time you shan't catch me, so there!'

'That's what I mean. If beating won't change your mind, we'll have to think of something that will.' He paused, and Dandy propped his chin on his fists and his elbows on his knees, and stared into the fire with an expressionless face, though he was listening with all ears. Had Uncle Toby thought of some way to change Mamma's mind? Would he escape a beating?

Toby said thoughtfully, 'Quite apart from worrying your mother, you've given *me* no end of bother, one way and another. I've spent the best part of a week chasing after you and quite frankly, my boy, I've no wish to repeat the performance.'

'You didn't have to come after me.'

'If you believe that,' said Toby with a half-laugh, 'you don't know your mother!'

'Oh, but I do,' said Dandy wearily. 'When she says, "Would you like to do this or that for me?" she isn't really asking. She means you've got to do it, whether you like it or not.'

'Don't I just know it, old fellow,' said Toby with rather more sympathy. 'I've been caught by that often enough. It's one of the ways women get us men to do what they want.'

'*Women!*' Dandy sat up straighter, pleased by 'us men', but he could not help adding rather anxiously, 'If only my father was alive! He made me promise to look after

378

Mamma, you know, but how can I, if she sends me away to England?'

'Difficult,' agreed Toby, and silence fell between them as the logs smouldered into red-hot caverns and beside the stream the frogs set up a chorus.

After a time, Toby said casually, 'Would it help if *I* looked after her for you?'

'As well as the animals, you mean? Isn't that rather a lot? Mamma is always telling me not to bother you because you are a busy man.'

'Busy people can usually find time for things they want to do,' said Toby, smiling. 'I expect I could manage.'

'But you are away from home so much.'

'If I married your mother, I might not go away so often. Or she could come with me.'

'If you *married* her?' exclaimed Dandy, startled. 'Do you want to?'

'Well, yes. That was the general idea. Very much, in fact. How would you feel about that? Would you like it?'

Dandy turned the matter over in his mind, started to say something, thought better of it, and eventually nodded. 'I – I think so. Yes. *I* would – but what about Mamma? What will she say?'

Toby laughed and ruffled his hair. 'That is the question, isn't it? We won't know that until we ask her.'

Thea was seated at her little satinwood bureau, absorbed in the monthly ritual of examining the household account books, when Toby returned from his mission. A snowstorm of papers covered with the flowing, elegant copperplate hand she had learned long ago from Miss Oldershaw showed that she had been engaged in answering letters before the arrival of her major-domo, but the accounts were a serious matter for which all other occupations must be put aside.

A pace behind the desk stood Ali Bux Khan, erect and dignified in his snowy robes and turban, ready with a justification for every item in the long list of payments he had made on her behalf and for which he now expected reimbursement.

Thea's back was towards the door. Toby was able to watch unobserved as she traced a slow, careful path through the labyrinthine complexities of her household's petty expenditure. For form's sake, a memsahib was expected to challenge a proper proportion of the meticulously noted but curiously spelled entries, but everyone knew that the scene would end as it always did, with her paying all her major-domo claimed, plus his personal commission.

'You have been very extravagant this month,' he heard her say, with just the right combination of surprise and reproof. 'You must not allow yourself to overspend because the Sahib has been promoted.'

Ali Bux Khan gave her a compassionate look. They both knew perfectly well that every increase in his master's salary would be faithfully mirrored in the household expenditure, and precisely the same proportion of Hal's earnings would end up each month in Ali Bux's savings. Like every Anglo-Indian householder, Hal complained that the harder he worked, the stouter grew Ali Bux, but neither complaints nor careful scrutiny of accounts would ever change the system.

'All, all is necessary expense, Memsahib,' he said gently. 'See, it is written here, every small thing.'

'Let me look . . . ' She ran her pencil down the closely written columns. 'What is this? *To making white for Master's hat: five pice.* That hat was new, Ali Bux. There was no need to use pipeclay on it.'

'Sahib liking hat more white,' insisted the old man with fervour.

'What about this, then? *Grain to crow: one anna, five pice.* Surely you have not taken to encouraging those dreadful crows? You know how the Sahib dislikes them!'

'Chota-Sahib's crow eating much grain,' said Ali Bux, armoured in righteousness.

'Dandy's myna? Oh, really!' She set a tick against birdseed and flicked over the pages, searching for discrepancies, but Ali Bux was too old a hand at this game to fall into the trap of overpricing any one item. He stood by with hands folded, grave and courteous, ready to rebut every query.

Toby waited patiently, admiring the graceful curve of her slender neck above the severely cut dark morning gown. He thought how much he would like to see her dressed in pale, frivolous shades – cornflower blue or leafy green – with matching ribbons in that glorious russet hair.

The hovering pencil stabbed triumphantly. 'What is this? *Butones for Master's kameez: one anna.* I remember quite clearly that I gave you two dozen shirt-buttons only last week. You can't have used them all.'

Ali Bux shook his venerable head. 'That *dhobi* breaking all button on kameez and pantlon. Making Master very angry.'

'That *dhobi*!' For a moment they were united in indignation at the ruthless martyrdom of Hal's undergarments at the hands of the careless washerman, his shredding of cuffs and smashing of buttons.

'Very well,' she conceded. 'You shall have some more buttons and I will speak to the *dhobi* myself.'

'Thea?' said Toby, from the doorway.

She turned and rose in one swift, flowing movement. 'Did you find him?' She caught his hands, holding them tight, and his strong fingers closed on hers.

'I did.'

'Thank God! Oh, thank God! I have been so worried. Where was he? Is he all right?'

'He's fine. I caught up with him at a village just short of Peshawar. Another day and we would have been too late. The dealers he was with were making for Kabul.'

'Another day . . . ! Oh, Toby, how can I ever thank you?' She pressed his hands, her eyes sparkling with unshed tears, and he thought she had never looked so beautiful. She said, 'If I had lost him – through my own foolishness – I don't think I could have gone on living. Where is he now?'

381

'Where do you think? In the garden, making sure none of his pets have escaped or fallen ill during his absence.'

'That boy! He cares far more for his wretched menagerie than he does for his mother.'

'Don't blame him,' said Toby quickly. 'I told him to run off and look at them so that I'd have a chance to speak to you alone.'

'About Dandy?'

'No.' He took a turn about the room, then planted himself squarely before her. 'There is something I must ask you.'

'Me?' His earnest tone puzzled her. What could he have to say that Dandy must not hear? She thought he seemed less at ease than usual, with a certain rigidity in the set of his jaw, and hands that moved restlessly among the objects on her table, picking up a paper-knife, an ivory fan, a small soapstone image of the Buddha, fiddling with them, putting them down in a way that reminded her of Dandy with some misdemeanour to confess.

'Well? Aren't you going to tell me what it is?' Although she tried to speak lightly, she was very much aware of his tension. He stared at her with an intensity she found disturbing.

'Can't you guess?'

The answer that flashed into her mind was so preposterous that she refused to entertain it. Yet what else would explain his expression, at once eager and apprehensive?

'No,' she said quietly.

She thought he braced himself still further, as native boys diving from the temple roof to the river would fill their lungs and stand poised a moment before launching their bodies into space. He took her hand, and holding it tightly as if to give himself courage, said simply, 'Will you marry me, Thea?'

A moment earlier instinct had warned her, yet the words came as so profound a shock that she could not at first believe she had really heard them. For a moment she found herself speechless; then she stammered, 'But Toby

– *Rohais*! We are still in mourning. How can you ask me – how can you say such a thing when – '

As if he had anticipated this reaction, he cut her short. 'Oh, it is too soon, I know. I should not ask you yet; but I am going away. I dare wait no longer. These months since Rohais died have been a torment to me, forced to remain silent, always afraid that another would steal your heart.'

She said in a low, shaken tone, 'You cannot mean it.'

'I do! Come, Thea, you are not blind. You must have seen that Rohais and I were not suited, that our marriage was unhappy.'

Of course she had known. Rohais had never troubled to hide her dissatisfaction, but it had not occurred to Thea that Toby might feel the same.

'You gave no sign of it.'

A shadow crossed his face. 'How could I? I was bound to her. I had made my bed and must lie on it. Poor Rohais! I failed her, and God forgive me, when she died my first thought was that I was free at last. That shocks you, but it is the truth. How could I hate Hinghan Khan when he had given me my freedom to court the woman who meant everything in the world to me? Oh, Thea! We have wasted so long. Say you will marry me, and make me the happiest man alive.'

'I – I cannot.'

'Why not? I swear you will never regret it. We have known each other so long . . . '

Too long, she thought. He was offering her all the things she needed: love, security, respect, companionship. Why could she not accept them? Before him lay a brilliant career: a governorship at least, perhaps a knighthood. They would be happy ever after. Why couldn't she settle for that and forget the treacherous quicksands of love, with their vague, impractical yearnings and impossible dreams?

She sought for words that would not wound him, but there were none.

'I'm sorry, Toby,' she said painfully. 'I cannot marry

383

you, nor can I give you a reason, but one day I hope you will understand.'

She tried not to weaken before the hurt in his eyes, the gradual realisation that this rejection was final. Animation and hope left his face, replaced by grim disillusionment. Suddenly he looked old.

'Then I am too late,' he said heavily. It was a statement, not a question. 'That is what I feared most. There is someone else.'

Tears stung her eyes. She turned away, catching her breath on a sob.

'I don't know,' she said bleakly. 'I just don't know.'

Cursing himself for a bungling fool, Toby rode away. She was overwrought. He should have had more sense than to spring a proposal on her at such a moment. The sudden wave of desire that had overwhelmed him when he saw her in that domestic setting, gently teasing old Ali Bux, had awakened a yearning for permanence and security that he believed himself proof against, and had quite upset his judgement.

She would be the kind of wife he needed. Not a feckless, captivating kitten like Rohais, but a strong, serene presence who could make a home merely by being in it, who could bring up children and welcome him with loving arms when he returned from his wanderings.

I should have held my tongue, he thought. I have waited so long, it would not have hurt to wait a little longer, until Dandy was at school and loneliness made her turn to me. Nobody could be better suited than we are – she knows that as well as I do. Surely she will come round?

But the shadow of a rival skulked at the edge of his mind. He could not banish the suspicion that his chance was gone for ever.

A shabby, drooping figure in a gaily striped robe that had seen better days squatted patiently by the gate, the tail of his turban drawn across his mouth to keep out the dust of passing bullock carts. He joined his palms in grave salute as Toby trotted out of the courtyard.

Some poor devil of an Afghan, waiting to pitch his hard-luck story to the Commissioner-Sahib, thought Toby, returning the greeting. Like all British officers who had served in Afghanistan, he felt guilty and deeply sorry for the plight of the many Afghans who had valiantly supported the British invaders both in victory and defeat, only to find themselves abandoned to the tender mercies of their fellow-countrymen once their allies had withdrawn. Many had been forced to abandon their property and flee into exile, and it was a sad sight to find Kabuli noblemen reduced to begging for pensions which the Directors of the Honourable East India Company were all too reluctant to grant.

At any other time, Toby would have stopped to listen to the supplicant's story, and done his best to interest Hal in his case, but smarting as he was from Thea's rejection, he thought the slow recital of wrongs he could not right and demands for compensation he had no power to dispense would be more than he could endure, so he continued on his way, while the man who had risen eagerly at his approach once more sank back on his heels against the wall, and drew his turban tail closer about his mouth.

He was still there when Dandy, reassured that all his pets were present and had suffered no harm in his absence, wandered out to the gate with time on his hands. He was longing to go to his mother and tell her he was sorry for running away and causing her so much worry, but Uncle Toby had said he wanted to speak to her alone, and had told Dandy to give him an hour's grace.

A whole hour! What could he possibly say that could take so long? Restless and fidgety, Dandy crossed the courtyard, and when he spotted the distinctive striped turban, flattened and rolled in the Afghan style, his heart leapt with hopes of a message from Hinghan Khan. Defying the frown of the Sikh guards, who were determined that no dirty Afghan was going to penetrate their courtyard unless they received express orders to admit him, Dandy sauntered closer and squatted in the dust beside the stranger, saying politely, 'May you live!'

'May you never be tired,' responded the stranger hoarsely, in an accent unfamiliar to Dandy.

'Whence come you, brother?'

'From the hills of the Kohistan, Chota-Sahib. Once I was a great chief with ten thousand lances at my command, but now I have been betrayed by my friends and am poor and old and in distress.'

'And what seek you here?' Dandy settled himself comfortably on his heels, prepared for the usual rigmarole of sorrow and destitution.

'I am come here to claim the great reward promised me by the Memsahib.'

'Reward?' Dandy was startled. 'Why should the Memsahib reward you?'

'Did I not shield her from harm when the earth shook and trembled? For many moons, did I not serve the hostages of Akbar Khan in their captivity? Did they not promise me *lakhs* of rupees for bringing them food when they hungered and for clothing their nakedness? Did I not carry their messages to Sale-Sahib, hidden in the soles of my shoes, though if the Sirdar had discovered it I would have died. Now I am old and poor and cast out of my own land, and the memsahibs have forgotten their promises. Aiee! Woe to those who trust the word of the *feringhi*!'

He is laughing at me, thought Dandy, catching a twinkle in the man's eyes that was utterly at variance with the professional beggar's whine. I don't believe he is nearly as old and poor as he pretends, and that horse of his is a fine animal under its dusty coat and ragged mane. He is a rogue, and I ought to tell the guards to send him packing.

But rogue or not, he could not help liking the man's jaunty effrontery. Every Afghan beggar who came to petition Uncle Hal claimed that he had befriended Akbar Khan's hostages, but he wondered in this case if it might not be true.

'Chota-Sahib, will you ask the Mem to come down and

speak with me? These dogs will not let me through the gate.'

'That is for her to decide,' said Dandy cautiously.

'Tell her I have proofs written in English with her name upon them,' urged the beggar.

'Show me your proofs.'

The man gave him a sly, sidelong glance. 'I will show them to no one but her. Will you ask her to come, Chota-Sahib?'

'Oh, all right. Peace be with you, brother.' He rose and salaamed briefly, then glanced at his watch, wondering if he should make the beggar at the gate an excuse to interrupt the grown-ups' conversation. But Uncle Toby's hour was by no means up yet and Dandy had no wish to court any more trouble. The fellow could wait. He wandered off through the archway leading to the heart of the Citadel.

At the entrance to the Royal apartments where Dulip Singh used to live, a young guard was squatting on his haunches, musket across his knees. He sketched a languid wave, very different from the ramrod-stiff salute he once used to acknowledge the Maharaja's approach. With mounting nostalgia, Dandy recalled the shouts that echoed from wall to wall when he and Dulip clattered in after the daily *sowaree*, surrounded by the bodyguard in their fluttering silks and winking jewels. The big, swaggering Sikhs in their snowy turbans with crimson linings would loom over the boys like a forest of tall trees as they dismounted amid all the colour and gaiety, before the ponies were led away.

Then the Maharaja's plump fingers would pluck his sleeve. 'Come, Dandee! Show me a new game. A game that English boys play.'

All that fun was over; the glamour and glory fled. Now the abandoned courtyards and colonnades, the deserted temples and pavilions looked unkempt and neglected. Nothing was left but squalor, dirt, and poverty. Dandy gazed with new eyes at the maimed beggars exhibiting their sores in hope of alms, the mangy dogs among the garbage, the bone-thin horses with battered legs and galled

387

shoulders drooping in the shadow of the great walls. Had they always been there, behind the splendid façade?

Aimlessly he wandered through the empty Royal apartments, stripped of their beautiful rugs and furnishings. The old order he had loved was dead, replaced by a drab, efficient, modern bureaucracy administered by well-meaning civilians like his Uncle Hal, who would hardly recognise a bribe if it was dangled under his nose.

No doubt the Punjab would know a new age of peace and prosperity under their care. No longer would peasants hide their cattle from marauding Khalsa warriors, or watch helplessly as their granaries were plundered. British justice would protect the weak and reform the age-old tangle of taxation. Life in the Maharaja's former domain would be free and fair and decent and dull. Dandy wanted no part of it.

Head bent, hands deep in pockets, he moved like an unquiet spirit through deserted pleasure gardens, stopping to pick a flower and crush it in his fingers, or stare morosely into tanks of brightly coloured fish. It was odd to think how often he had wished to be alone here, without old Dippy tagging along, nagging for new amusements. Now he had his wish he felt bored and lonely. No courtiers to tease, no hawks to fly or cheetahs to take hunting on the wide plains outside the walls. The royal cages stood empty, for the best of the Maharaja's menagerie had already left for their new home.

What am I to do? thought Dandy, pressing his forehead against the bars of a cage which had housed a black panther with a ruby-studded collar. They've all gone away and left me. Self-pity settled on him like a black cloak.

For a few minutes he amused himself by throwing a ball against a wall and counting how many times he could catch it, but without an admiring audience the game soon palled. When he missed, he did not bother to chase the ball, but let it roll away into the bushes. There was no pleasure in playing alone. He felt an insidious, half-ashamed yearning for companions of his own age and race; English boys who understood cricket and boxing and the

other sports which Dippy considered rough and barbarous.

Perhaps, he admitted to himself, standing on one leg
to consider this new idea, perhaps school would not be so
bad after all. His gloom lightened a little. Mamma would
be pleased. He might even persuade her into certain concessions. He would talk to her at once, tell her he had
changed his mind.

Fired with enthusiasm, he retraced his steps more pur-
posefully, forgetting his melancholy enough to creep up
behind the dozing sentry with a shout of '*Koi hai!*' which
nearly made him choke on his betel-nut.

'Aiee, Chota-Sahib!' he protested, grinning as he spat
out a scarlet stream. He made a feint at Dandy's head
with the butt of his musket, and the boy danced out of
reach and ran off chanting,

'Jimmy Kelly good for belly.
Taste and try before you buy!'

in imitation of the camp sweetmeat seller.

He saw his mother through the window of her boudoir,
which opened on to the lawn, sitting at her desk with her
head propped on one hand, looking so lonely and sad that
it wrenched his heart.

'Mamma!'

He put his arms round her shoulders and laid his cheek
against hers. With a sob, she clasped him to her, and for
a moment or two neither spoke.

'Oh, my darling boy,' she said at last, 'don't ever leave
me like that again. I have been so unhappy. I thought I
had lost you.'

He had expected her to be angry, and finding her sor-
rowful instead quite undermined his spirits.

'I *am* sorry, Mamma. Very, very sorry,' he said penitently. 'I would have come back – really I would. I'll
always come back to you, no matter how far away I go.'

'But now you won't have to go.' She smiled at him
mistily. 'You see, I've changed my mind. I never really

389

wanted to send you but I thought it was best for you. Now I see that Uncle Toby was right and I was wrong. It *is* barbaric to send boys away to school. I shall find you a tutor instead, and you can stay here – what's the matter, darling?' she asked, feeling him stiffen and try to move away. 'Isn't that what you want?'

Dandy said awkwardly, 'The trouble is, Mamma, that I've changed my mind, too. I *want* to go to school. I – I've been thinking about it so much, and now Dippy has gone away, there isn't much to do here, and – '

'Oh dear!'

They looked blankly at one another and then, to his relief, she began to laugh.

'Well,' she exclaimed, 'we are a fine pair! I decide I can't do without you just as *you* decide to leave me. What are we going to do?'

Dandy said diffidently, 'You won't need me – not so much, I mean – when you marry Uncle Toby. He will look after you.'

'I am not going to marry Uncle Toby.'

Her tone did not invite argument, and strangely he felt relieved. Relationships were difficult enough to untangle without your uncle becoming your stepfather overnight. Besides, he could hardly imagine Uncle Toby settling into any kind of domestic routine. It would be nearly as bad, thought Dandy, as putting a wolf in a cage. He was always restless, here today and gone tomorrow. Dandy had seldom known him stay in the same place two days in a row, and felt instinctively that no matter how well a nomadic existence might suit a man, it would not do for his mother.

Searching for a topic to steer the conversation from such uncharted waters, he remembered his promise to the Afghan at the gate.

'It must be Uncle Hal he wants to see,' said Thea, listening with half an ear as she sorted heaps of papers, her face averted. The memory of her conversation with Toby was painful. What is wrong with me? she thought. Why couldn't I accept his love? He looked so hurt . . .

so *old*. I have hurt my best friend, and all for nothing. She wished Dandy would go away and leave her to weep alone.

'No, Mamma. He asked for you.' Dandy was surprised by his own eagerness to promote the beggar's cause. 'He says he saved your life, in Afghanistan.'

'Oh, darling, they all say that,' said Thea wearily. 'You know what they're like.'

'This one is different. Please, Mamma! I told him you'd speak to him.'

'Oh, all right, but he'll have to wait. I'm busy this morning.' She picked a letter from one pile and put it in another. 'So much to sort out! Now, my love, run and find Ali Bux and tell him to come back with his accounts. We must finish them before your Uncle Hal returns.'

'But, Mamma!'

'Go on. It's all right, darling, I'll go down later. Truly.'

The noon heat bounced off the courtyard's massive enclosing walls and a shimmering mirage enveloped the gateway where Dandy's beggar squatted motionless in the dust, a lonely, dejected figure, his mouth muffled against the flies, hands hanging limply.

The guards had prudently withdrawn to the cool of the watch-tower, but they still kept an eye open to see the dirty Afghan did not slip in while they dozed.

Thea's head ached and the skin round her eyes felt tight and dry with the salt of recent tears. Ali Bux had looked at her with curiosity and perhaps a little sympathy as they concluded the household accounts, and she guessed he had eavesdropped on her interview with Toby, and that soon the story that she had rejected the Hakim-Sahib would be all over the station.

Toby would not stay to hear it. No doubt he would be off before daybreak, putting the past behind him with the steady rhythm of his horse's hoofs, whilst she must remain to face the whispers and sidelong looks of all those who knew what she ought to do so much better than she did herself.

391

Dazzled by the glare, she could not at first see the huddled form at the gate. Gone, she thought, with a spasm of irritation against Dandy, who had stopped to chat with the guards.

Then Grip and Fang, who had followed her, bustled ahead to sniff and whine at the darker patch of shadow, and her irritation turned to guilt for having made the poor fellow wait for her in the midday sun.

'Here, boys! Heel!'

Natives in general and Afghans in particular had a well-founded fear of the teeth of sahibs' dogs, and their dislike was usually reciprocated. On this occasion, however, Dandy's usually obedient terriers ignored the command and continued to sniff at the beggar's clothes.

Hastily he rose, pushing them away, then staggered and lurched sideways. A moment later he lay sprawling in the dust at her feet.

'*Pani*! Water! For the love of Allah!' he groaned.

Guilt turned abruptly to alarm.

'Quick, Dandy! Call the guards!'

They ran up together, and she ordered them to carry the unconscious man indoors. Brawny, black-bearded Abdullah hesitated, poking contemptuously with his toe at the once splendid robe.

'Dirty Afghan! It is a trick, Memsahib. A trick to get within the walls.'

'What nonsense!' She turned on him angrily. 'Have you no pity for a sick man? Do as I say – *juldi jao*!'

Grumbling, they lifted the limp form and carried it into the blessed cool of the marble colonnade, where they dumped their burden none too gently on the paving.

'Go and fetch water, Abdullah Khan.' She surveyed the unmoving heap anxiously, hoping it was not too late to save him. 'And you, Sher Singh, run and ask the Hakim-Sahib to come here.'

'I'll go, Mamma,' offered Dandy eagerly, and ran off with the terriers bounding beside him, while Sher Singh followed as slowly as he dared.

392

'What bundobust over a dog of an Afghan,' he complained. 'He would be better left to die.'

Thea pretended she had not heard. When they had gone, she tried to make the comatose figure more comfortable by propping him against the wall, but he resisted her attempt to free his mouth from the muffling folds of cloth.

At least he is not dead, she thought, but as if to prove her optimism misplaced, he began muttering and moaning in Pushtu, a meaningless jumble of sounds in which she caught only the words, 'Dying . . . I am dying . . . '

'What ails you, brother?' she asked gently, bending close.

'Aiee, aiee! Woe is me! I am far from home and dying for love,' he gasped, choking for breath.

She wondered if she had misheard.

'For . . . *love?*'

'O, Moon of the North, the beauty of your eyes has pierced my heart!' he wailed.

She drew back sharply, sitting on her heels, eyes narrowed in sudden suspicion. With a quick snatch that took him by surprise, she ripped the turban from the beggar's head, exposing a well-known face contorted with mirth – a face she had given up hope of seeing again.

'Mr Mein!'

'George,' he gasped, pushing himself upright and wiping away tears of laughter. 'Oh, oh, oh! I nearly died. I thought you would *never* guess! Thea, dear love, don't cry – I can't bear you to cry. I shouldn't have done it, I know, but I couldn't resist surprising you. Didn't you believe me when I said that I was coming back?'

'It's been so long!' She struggled to master her emotions. 'Oh, George! I'm not crying, not really. I'm just so glad to see you. I thought something had gone wrong and you would never come.'

She put out a tentative hand, and he grasped it strongly.

'I can't believe you are real,' she said with a kind of wonder.

'Real enough!' His laughter filled her with delight. His shock of fair curls had been oddly flattened by the turban, emphasising the jug-handle ears; his tanned face was unshaven and grimed with dust; and the deep groove where the bullet had passed through his scalp was now a broad, shiny track across his head. But his candid eyes, with their light, upcurling lashes still sparkled with the same old mischief, inviting her to share the joke, and his voice held the same teasing, provoking note that had haunted her dreams for so long.

'You're more beautiful than ever,' he sighed, and laughter bubbled up in her throat like a spring from which the silt of years had been unexpectedly cleared.

'At least you will find no light cavalry in my hair today!'

'You remember that?'

'How could I forget it? I was so angry . . . '

'You would not believe how often I have regretted that I did not quell my hunting instinct on that occasion!'

'Rubbish! I have no doubt you would do exactly the same today, Mr Mein.'

'George.'

'George. So do not think you will get anywhere by flattering me, for I am proof against your wiles . . . '

'Are you sure?' He moved closer, gazing at her with the same half-earnest, half-quizzical expression she remembered so clearly. 'How I wish I could say the same! But I have been your devoted slave ever since that terrible march. I remember so well how I watched you struggle through the snow with no one to help you, and the awful frustration of knowing I could do nothing – *nothing* to relieve your sufferings.'

'Why, George!' she said, not a little moved by this declaration. 'Nobody did more than you. Bringing us brandy for breakfast – making us laugh – keeping up our spirits! Without you, I believe we should all have given in to despair.' Despite the heat, she shivered, reliving her own terror and hopelessness in that bleak dawn when she had woken to find Vicky stiff in her arms. She had gazed round at the stark, unearthly beauty of the frozen landscape as the rising sun tinted the jagged peaks blood-red, knowing it would never bring a ray of life-giving warmth

394

to the tiny bundle she held in her arms, or the huddled humps of bodies, animal and human, all about her in the snow. Black on white. Shadows on the snow.

'Don't think of it,' said George, following her memories with his own. 'Just remember that as long as we live, nothing can ever be so bad again. Cold, hunger, dirt, exhaustion, sickness, *vermin* . . . None of them mattered so long as you were with me. *My* worst moment came when you sent me away. The rest I could stand, but that nearly did for me. Time and again, these past years, I've been tempted to finish off the bullet's work.'

'Don't say anything so dreadful!'

'It's true. I tried to forget you, tried to hate you, even. Hopeless! I saw you wherever I went. London, Rome, Paris, even Australia. I tried my luck in the Colonies – started a newspaper in Sacramento – joined the California Gold Rush. What a country! I found enough gold to make a wedding ring, but no one to put it on. I couldn't escape your spell. You followed wherever I went, and if I managed to banish you from my thoughts, you haunted my dreams. So in the end – '

'In the end?'

'I came back,' he said simply. 'I can't live without you – that's the plain truth. Don't send me away again, my love. I don't think I could bear it.'

She smiled, though her eyes were full of tears. 'I'll never send you away again,' she promised, and raised her lips for his kiss.

So it was that Dandy, returning with the panting terriers to report that Dr Black was nowhere to be found, was confronted by the unexpected spectacle of his mother clasped in the arms of a fair, tousle-headed gentleman in shabby Afghan robes, whose lively, haphazard features had long been as familiar to him as those of the other hostages whose portraits Mamma had drawn during their captivity.

Lieutenant George Mein of Her Majesty's 13th Light Infantry, he thought, surveying him with interest and attention. He knew quite a lot about Mr Mein, the man whose head had proved harder than a bullet. He was a *Hero*. He had struggled back into the horror of the Khoord-kabul Pass to bring out poor Captain Sturt. He had rescued Mamma from the great earthquake at Budeea-bad. He had carried messages disguised as a camel-driver and tricked information out of their Afghan guards.

'All sahibs are mad, and Mein-Sahib is maddest of them all,' Hinghan Khan used to say in his soft, sneering voice. Hinghan Khan had not liked Mr Mein, but Mamma had always had a very special smile when she spoke of him. Dandy had long wished to meet him, especially since his fondness for practical jokes sounded remarkably similar to Dandy's own.

So few grown-ups thought them funny. Uncle Toby, he remembered, had been quite angry when the *chatti* of water which Dandy had painstakingly suspended over the doorway had emptied itself on his head.

Smiling at the memory, he had begun to walk towards them when a hitherto quite unrecognised instinct warned him this might not be an appropriate moment to introduce himself. Though his mother's face was hidden in Mr Mein's shoulder, he could hear her making little longing, mewing sounds, not unlike a hungry kitten, and while he could not distinguish much of what Mr Mein was whispering so urgently in her ear, the word *Love* recurred so often there was no mistaking it.

Later, thought Dandy, with rare tact. They're busy now. I had better not disturb them. After all, they haven't seen one another for a very long time.

Unnoticed, he slipped away, still smiling.